The Raggedy Man

This is for Shirley,
Who keeps me from falling apart in both the best
and stressful of times.
I love you

A special thanks to artist Dustybroth for the cover. Working with him as been a blast, and that *face*! Grotesque and frightening and I love every single thing about it. Check out his other works @dustybroth and tell him hi for me.

TABLE OF CONTENTS

I'm rotting inside
My flesh turns to dust
Whisper, are you dying in my ear?
I'm so sick to death
Tumors in my head
Whisper, are you dying in my ear?

-Green Day

One

Clayton Couch sat uncomfortably in the chair in Mr. Maisel's office, feeling the almost-insane urge to scratch himself as he thought, *This goddamn fucking itch.*

He supposed that every man had that thought at least once maybe twice a day. Maybe it's on his back while wearing a prickly jacket his wife or girlfriend got him for his birthday, or he didn't wipe good enough, or the kind of a hidden bug bite applied during the night that could drive him insane. Sometimes there is that type of itch that is never there until he is physically in a position that he is *unable* to scratch it when it decides to just rear it's dry and scaly head and say "Howdy!" Sometimes the itch is in his mouth because the piece of steak he had was crispy and brushed the roof of his mouth in just the right spot, or he happened to be allergic to a certain plant or chemical he happened to touch. In any case-

Why the FUCK am I thinking about steak?

"Clay?"

"Hmm?" Clay said returning to the real world and staring at his boss with eyes that would have belonged to a deer in headlights. If that deer happened to have a menacing itch that just refused to go away as just an icing on the wreck of a cake. He felt his back prickle, he refused to scratch the itch.

Mr. Maisel rolled his baggy eyes and stared down at the paper on his desk. His office was stuffy and hot, and there was a thick stain of sweat on the front of his blue-collared shirt. On the walls behind him were awards and plaques concerning achievements for the store that read stuff like, "Overall COMP 90%" and "30 Years and Counting!" (that sounded just fucking depressing) and finally, "Best HR Score: 2015 Top 3!" All that was missing was the one with a large nose on the plaque with the engravement, "Biggest fucking brown-noser!"

Clay figured that many employee's and Maisel's peers had read those awards countless times as they hung on the wall among the few pictures of Mr. Maisel and his first and second wife like mounted trophies a hunter might display in such a way that anyone and everyone *had* to see. The pictures hung side by side the awards like two sides of a sick coin, almost like a joke. The rest of the pictures were mostly consisting of his daughter or pictures that she herself drew, which Clay wasn't too heartless to say were terrible even though they *were*. There was a picture of her holding up a poster from graduating Kindergarten and her and her dad at Disneyland in-between Mickey Mouse and Winnie the Pooh, which Clay didn't give two shits about anymore than he gave a shit about Mr. Maisel's daughter or his fucking awards for being an absolute brown-noser and helicopter-boss. Clay and his peers often joked about how chapped Mr. Maisel's lips were, given how much he kisses corporate's asses.

Mr. Maisel said something, and Clay returned his eyes back to his boss. "Yeah, I... I understand."

It was the right answer to give, and he really *did* understand. That was not him bullshitting to get out of another earful. He knew exactly why he was in here and why Mr. Maisel was so impatient. He had been late to work three times this week alone. That wasn't the only problem though. He felt like he was *dragging* this past week and apparently Mr. Maisel thought the same. He just didn't have the motivation to zone the fucking aisles or push out the abandoned shit that customers decided they didn't want anymore. Twice he called some middle-aged woman lazy for not putting something away, or some kid an asshole for throwing a toy on a random endcap. Maisel had heard about those incidents as well, and Clay still didn't care enough to listen.

He had come to work every day he was scheduled for the past four years and he wasn't getting anywhere. He would get his raise and the fucking state would raise minimum wage so that the random kid Maisel would hire would be paid the same amount as he would. Or his bonus would be so pitifully small it would be insignificant even as his rent got higher, or his court payments didn't go through and he got charged another fine. He just didn't have the motivation anymore. Every time he went home, he would eat his TV dinner, drink an entire six pack (sometimes twelve or eighteen) or a bottle of cheap whiskey just so that he could numb the painful thought that he would be doing the same thing the very next day, among other things that often plagued his mind like an itch that wouldn't go away, no pun intended of course.

"You just aren't keeping up, Clay," Mr. Maisel said in a tone that sounded almost bored, exasperated as if he was all out of trying to break it to him gently and just giving him the cold-hard truth. "Look, I don't know if something has just come up all of a sudden, but this has been going on the past four days. Everyone is worried about you. It's affecting the team."

Yeah, right. What, did they say? 'Clay looks like he's having a rough day?' Or are they saying 'The guy sucks at his job?'

"Is it..." Mr. Maisel cleared his throat before asking, "Is it about what happened-"

"No," Clay said cutting his boss off. He didn't want to talk about that, not now, not ever. Add that to the list of things he would like to numb or completely erase. "Sir, I'm sorry, I just..." Clay shrugged. "I don't know what to tell you."

Mr. Maisel sat back in his office chair, causing the poor thing to creak. How damp was his seat cushion, under that heavyset ass no doubt drenched in sweat? It was probably made worse by whatever flatulence Maisel releases when no one else was in his office.

"Well, you know we have expectations," he finally said. "We have a schedule to keep and scores to keep. You slacking off is a struggle for the entire team; You're creating an unnecessary anchor someone else has to hoist."

Please don't do anymore boat metaphors, Clay pleaded telepathically, as if Maisel could actually hear him. *If I hear one more from you today, I'm gonna scream like a wild banshee and go crazy. Just go crazy and let the men in white take care of me as I eat crayons in a padded cell. Wheeeee!*

Maisel continued, "What you don't finish, someone else has to."

Yeah, just like the morning team who can't push truck, who leaves it for the day crew who has their own stuff to do, who in turn dumps it on us the closing team, who gets shit for not finishing everyone's stuff.

"I understand," Clay said instead. He understood and hopefully Mr. Maisel understood that he wanted this conversation to end. Give him the slap on the wrist if he needed it, just end the fucking conversation and jot it down in Workday; another thing checked off the list. He didn't want to hear his boss's voice, see his kid, or the goddamn paper that had a list of all the employee's names on it with his highlighted in red. Red, the color that meant 'stop,' 'anger,' and more importantly and in this current situation, 'bad.'

"This is your… second coaching this month," Mr. Maisel said having to snap his fingers to bring his memory back like a magician. *Now you see it, now you don't Clayton.* "You know what your third means?"

"Three strikes and you're out?"

Mr. Maisel looked at Clay more seriously. "Look, we don't call it that. It's called a Disciplinary Action."

Yeah, you can call a shit a piece of work, it's still a piece of shit. Sometimes they look like men in sweaty blue shirts and have pictures of their two wives on the wall with their awards and their daughter; their pride and joy.

Mr. Maisel sighed and folded his hands together on his pudgy gut. "But in a way, yes. Three strikes. Not three strikes and you're *out*. Three strikes and we need to do something about it. It is not necessarily just a way to make sure you understand your obligations here. It's to make sure others get the message too. What if other people look at you and think 'he is always late I'm gonna be late too?' Or 'he doesn't do his job, why should I?'"

Rather than point out that Clay was more than likely not the only person who slacks off around here, he replied in saying, "That would be bad for business."

Maisel smiled the way a teacher would to a boy who said he had done wrong. Yes Mr. teacher, I did give Roger a wet-willy. Yes, Mr. teacher, you caught me looking at Jennifer's panties when she bent over. Yes, Mr. teacher, I cheated on my math test, and I'll do it again! That fucking "Good boy" look that always angered Clay. He wanted to slap that smirk of a smile right off the man's face.

The itch was coming back. He reached up and scratched it behind his ear. This one had gotten worse during this conversation and as he did so, Clay felt something give way underneath his fingernail. Thinking it was a scab or some sort of dry skin, he thought nothing of it and when he brought his bands back behind the desk and out of Maisel's line of sight, he flicked whatever it was away. Down into the depths beneath Maisel's desk, where god knows what else was there.

But hadn't the itch been on the back of his neck the last time? He was sure it was, he remembered the feeling of the skin beneath his hairline like it was alive and wriggling. The thought made him subconsciously scratch his head. Now *that* began to itch. *God what was with this itch?* He thought it had to be the laundry sheets he had purchased yesterday. They had been out of Downy and he had to get a Great Value brand. He was probably allergic to the ingredients in that. That had to be it.

"So, you understand?" Mr. Maisel asked, the disciplinary teacher's smile unchanged on his pudgy and red face.

"I understand," Clay answered.

"I'm only looking out for you, Clay."

Yeah, I bet that's what you tell everyone you have this sort of chat with. "I know."

"Good." The man then dismissed Clay to go back to work. Clay did so with a smile up until he shut the door to his boss's office behind him.

"You fucking prick."

And fuck this fucking *itch!*

He went down the hall to head back out onto the salesfloor, now scratching his right shoulder where the neck met it. It was 3:56 in the afternoon.

Two

Clay got off work around seven o'clock. The day had only gotten more aggravating after his talk with Mr. Maisel and by the time he finally clocked out of his mid-day shift, his patience had been strained like a frayed guitar string about to snap and protrude in a dangerous coil. Between dumbass coworkers and dumbass customers all under the watchful eye of an equally dumbass boss, Clay just had enough and was glad to jump into his beat-up 2002 Saturn that was more rust than the golden paint it used to have and head home.

The car was in need of an oil change and new tires that were now practically bald. The interior smelled of cigarette smoke which was fine because that was where he preferred to have his smoke breaks. Clay knew of the smoking area a hundred feet to the right of the store or even in the back alley, but he preferred to sit in his car. He didn't have the patience to deal with his other smoking coworkers when all he wanted was to sit and listen to music. On the CD/Radio that was sticky with old soda and covered in a film of dust, Clay was listening to Marilyn Manson's Get Your Gunn. He hummed along to the pasty singer as he smoked and decided he would stop by the gas station for a cheap and extremely greasy pizza with a pack of Rolling Rock. He deserved it after all, given the three strikes *he* gave to the entire store. Stick that up your pipe and smoke it, Mr. Maisel, I am out. Tell both wives and kid the same.

The first strike given was when some bitch started to argue with him about a clearance tag. In the store, clearance was marked by a green sticker with the original price on top and the new price on the bottom in large bold numerals. Someone had ditched some KitchenAid mixer on a clearance endcap and the woman who was wearing a purple arm cast and had her long gray hair in a ponytail happened to stumble upon it. Her reasoning was that she found it under clearance so it should be clearance. When Clay explained that if it was clearance it would have a sticker on it, she went from being all nice like she had been when she asked him to scan it and check the price, to Karen, Retail's Worst Nightmare.

"Then why is it in the *clearance* department?" she demanded scornfully, the tragedy too much for her to handle reasonably and without a nasty sneer.

"Someone must have ditched it. Happens; people find something then find something cheaper here than rather than put it back on the shelf they just ditch it here."

"I found it *here* though."

"I understand that but-"

"It should be on clearance."

"I'm sorry but it isn't."

"Then I'd like to speak to a manager."

Clay had shrugged. "Fine."

He had radioed Mr. Maisel who asked him to switch channels and when he explained the situation, Mr. Maisel said he was busy and to just tell the customer that the clearance would have a sticker. When he relayed the message, the woman went berserk.

"That's false advertisement!" she declared dropping the mixer into her cart with a loud jangly sound. Her face had gone a deep shade of red, almost purple, and her eyes were sharp and menacing. "I found it there, so you should honor the price!"

"Sorry ma'am, but I can't. Besides, there is no clearance price on the-"

She cut him off with a dramatic wave of her hand. "Do you know how much money I spend here?"

"What does that have to do with-"

"I will *never* come back here again! I will make sure none of my friends give you business either!"

Clay couldn't help it. "You promise?"

"Oh, *fuck* you," the woman said turning her cart hard enough to smack the shelving and send some of the *actual* clearance product spilling onto the floor. Clay went to pick it up, thinking that would be the last he heard from her.

But then the front end called, asking why he said a woman in a gray jacket and purple arm cast could get a mixer for clearance price. He said he hadn't that the woman was lying but even that wasn't the end. Mr. Maisel got a call from Corporate and met with Clay on the salesfloor asking about the situation. Apparently, the woman had called and gave his name and said Clay was very rude and unwilling to be helpful. When Clay told what happened, Mr. Maisel said he would overlook it.

"We'll just tell Corporate that we had a discussion," he said with a wink. "I got your back." Clay didn't think it was funny, nor did he believe his boss.

The second strike was for an employee from the clothing department. He had complained to the sorting area where everyone brought in their abandoned merchandise they find and sort it out for those who own specific areas in the store could push them back out onto the salesfloor. Clay owned the grocery, kitchen, and household paper department. The employee from clothing, Rebecca Bowen, had brought up a bunch of random abandons from the fitting room and just dumped it all into his sorting basket. There were toys, sporting goods, some infant clothes that didn't belong in clothing, and finally some essentials from the check lanes that were used for convenience purchases. Clay had sorted it out (took a solid fifteen minutes there was so much crap) so it wasn't a *huge* deal. He just made sure to inform Rebecca next time he saw her to please sort her stuff whenever she was up front and save him and the others time or an additional trip back. She said she would.

She did not.

She did the exact same thing and this time Clay had called her on the walkie, and asked her why she didn't do it right again. But he didn't use those exact words. His wording, was, "Are you dumb, or do you not give a shit?"

That got him in trouble. Rebecca told Mr. Maisel he called her dumb, he explained the situation, and Mr. Maisel told him to not call her dumb again. He did not discipline Rebecca for her uncaringness to the front, and the entirety of the shift she just continued to dump her load without a care in the world, and Mr. Maisel would demand why Clay took so long getting his abandons from the front. This time-consuming issue only made what came next a real pain in the ass and ground Clay's gears almost to dust.

The third and final strike happened between him and Austin Strickland, the salesfloor manager who overlooked the truck process and push. He had left early today leaving his workers to finish the truck. But as they all say, "The cat's away so the mice will play!" They hadn't finished the truck and no one during the backroom hours had mentioned it. So, it sat there until five and Mr. Maisel found it and told Clay to finish it and then to wrap up his workload. Already behind, Clay had said he wouldn't have time, but Mr. Maisel had the absolute perfect solution: "Make time, then."

In the end, he finished the truck but couldn't finish clearing some abandoned merchandise or the labeling in grocery, and as he was clocking out, he had to tell Mr. Maisel that he didn't finish. His boss only gave him a disappointed look. Because of Strickland, Clay got that look even though he had his own stuff to do. It was bullshit that what one person couldn't do, and others didn't want to, since he was there, *he* had to take the fall. The same would go for whatever poor closer had to deal with Clay's own abandons, which was all he was truly sorry for.

All the while, during this whole ordeal, Clayton's body was itching like crazy.

What started as a minor annoyance had escalated into an epidemic. His neck and entire upper body had begun to itch, and he was scratching it nonstop the last hour of his shift. When he had gone to the bathroom to look at it, the skin where he itched the most was red as if he had been sunburned. When he ran his long and probably dirty fingernails across the areas, he pulled up no skin but he felt the occasional bumps or dryness one might expect from a bite or a rash. The skin was hot at the touch, but other than that he couldn't really tell what was wrong other than the itch would not go away. He would pick up some ointment from the gas station as well as his dinner and beer. It would be more expensive than what would be sold at the store, but Clayton was already halfway there and would rather castrate himself with a pair of blunt rocks than go back to that hellhole just to shop.

He resisted the urge to scratch the entire time he was in the gas station, but it was the driving factor for him to make the decision whether to get a 12-pack or a 24-pack. The anti-itch ointment, which in the store would have cost him $3.99 (minus ten percent as part of his employee discount), had cost him $8.99; the final nail in the coffin known as today's shitshow, toilet paper not included.

Three

He arrived at his apartment around 7:30 that evening. He walked up the two stories and unlocked apartment 302. It was a studio apartment, costing him about $650 to live in, not including the electricity or garbage. At the very least water and sewage came with the monthly rent.

His apartment was simply-decorated with a bed in the far corner of the living room and a closet just across from the bathroom down the hall to the right. The kitchen which you could see to your left upon entry, was even tinier with limited counterspace but it had enough room to eat at as if you were in a bar. The low sink was full of dirty dishes and there was a tower of trash sticking out of the garbage can that looked to be on the verge of collapsing. Bags of McDonalds and Taco Bell were scattered across the counter with their own garbage inside. In the fridge there was milk and some yogurt as well as a few Hungry Man dinners in the freezer sitting right next to the ice machine. The TV Clayton had in his apartment was a 40-incher sitting on a toppled over bookcase that he had refurbished to hold his gaming system and a DVD player. On the walls either hung up or stacked on the floor, were Clayton's hobbies that he called 'Windows.'

Clay used to paint in his free time. It was a hobby and talent he had picked up in high school. A majority of his extracurricular classes his senior year consisted of art, whether that be Art 101 or Art Appreciation. He also took a few photography classes, and he had a few cameras still lying around somewhere in the boxes he had never seemed to get time to unpack. A majority of his paintings were of landscapes; photocopies really from pictures he took with his camera or what he could find in magazines.

Occasionally he would paint something different, and he had offered some of his painting services on Fiverr in order to make a little spending money. He had a few clients who needed paintings for book covers and magazines, and one person only wanted a painting of his cat which he had provided a picture for. Some clients wanted naked portraits of women, or bastardized paintings from Van Gogh or Da Vinci, things that were normally easy for Clay to produce. The painting in question had a copy of it printed out and Clay kept it in a little black book to look at among a few others that he considered his best works.

He was by no means a professional, he was neither prideful enough nor crazy enough to think that. But he knew he had potential. His old girlfriend thought so too. He wanted to catch the attention of other people or even corporations and just paint for a living. He knew that there were people out there who painted advertisements for chips and even for logos of rising brands. Although he wouldn't do it for the money per se, but he would do it if it meant doing what he loved for the rest of his life rather than being a dead-end blue-collar worker at some store. Whenever he wanted to escape the world, he would paint his way, his 'Window,' to another, and that alone was satisfactory. Of course, he hadn't drawn so much as a stick figure, let alone the Virgin Mary, in weeks which to Clay felt like months borderline *years* since the accident.

On his way to the bathroom, he passed by one he had hung up in the hallway of a woman in a red dress dancing around a rose, careful not to prick herself upon the many thorns. She was a redhead, that hair seeming to wave around her like a fire. It wasn't his first painting, but it was among the few he did without having to refer to any other source to do so. This was one completely out of his own mind and he cherished it almost as much as 'Bikes in the Yukon' or 'Fairy Dance' or even 'Owls in the Night' just to name a few. Seeing it made him sad, but that was the point of him keeping it. So that every day he awoke he could pass by and look into her pale gray eyes which once gave him the motivation to paint again and again.

Not anymore.

The bathroom was lit by a desk lamp since the overhead light was broken. He had tried to replace the bulb, but it appeared to be more of an internal problem and the landlord said someone would come by to look at it next time he had time to spare. He had brought a beer with him to the bathroom, and after cracking it open and setting it on the counter, he took off his shirt to survey the area where he was itchy. It was still all red, and the expensive white paste he smeared on his shoulders and neck felt cold. But it numbed the itching and so he gratefully rubbed it in some more, vigorously and as deeply as he could. When he was finished, he took a dump and then went into the living room after washing his hands. The first beer had been gone before he wiped.

There was no couch in his apartment, just his bed. This he collapsed on using one of his pillows to prop him up into a sitting position. His pack of beer on the floor next to him, he cracked another and guzzled it down as he turned on the TV and searched the channels for something to watch. When he had found something, he had finished his beer, tossing the empty can into a corner where he had his easels and boxes of acrylic paints. He cracked open a third. This would be his down time. He would use this time to relax and put the day and everything else behind him. In an hour or two, he would eat, and he even went as far as to tell himself that he would try and work on a painting. Or at least he told himself that, knowing well that he wouldn't.

He had new canvases and even purchased a new easel and brush set to start anew after he had broken up with Rachel

(HA HA you mean Rachel broke up with you)

but he just couldn't do it. He just didn't have the motivation nor the capability to even pick up a brush. He once stood in front of an empty canvas one morning with black paint already drying on his new brush and he just couldn't think where to begin. He felt like an author suffering from writer's block, unable to write and unable to even think. He just never felt creative since his girlfriend had left to be with some fucking schmuck who owned a nightclub back in town. In the end, he had just placed the brush into a cup of water and there it sat this whole time, with mold having grown in the blackened water untouched and *sometimes* unnoticed. He had just reached a point in his life, where he wasn't climbing or falling. He felt as though he was just suspended, waiting for someone or something to let him go and instead of bracing for impact, he probably would just embrace the asphalt beneath him with a hug and kiss.

He watched an episode of Family Guy and an episode of Game of Thrones. After that, he ate his shitty pizza and a small bag of Doritos. After looking at the canvas that still stood in the corner across from his bed, looking depressing and at the same time accusatory, he went back into bed and watched another show. There he stayed until he fell asleep, about ten beers in and four trips to the bathroom later drunk as a skunk. In his drunken stupor he would fail to notice that the third time he had gotten up to pee, he had peed blood, and even chuckled at the pink/orange whirlpool as he flushed. He fell asleep at some point unaware that he had passed out at all and not caring in the slightest. There he had watery dreams that were hazy and incomprehensible. Muddied by the alcohol, and thankfully keeping the nightmares at a safe and manageable distance.

The next morning, around nine o'clock, he awoke with his arms feeling like thousands of fire ants were crawling all over them.

It started off as just a feeling one often has in their dreams. A sense that your body really is experiencing what your subconscious shows you. In this one, he was dreaming he was swimming in black water which he soon realized to actually be a sea of beetles. Then he realized it was only his arms feeling it and he started to wake up thinking he just fell asleep on them and they had no blood circulation. By then he woke up, and saw that it was just his arms being all itchy like his back was yesterday. With a groan he got up naked from his bed and hurried to the bathroom where he had his ointment. It was in the lamplight where he saw that his skin looked very dry, with some areas peeling as if he had been sunburnt or had athlete's foot on his forearms. Squeezing a good spread out, he lathered his arms up until they were as pasty as someone applying plaster for a lifelike model for some art gallery. It was only until the ointment covered his arms about a quarter of a centimeter thick like a second layer of skin when he felt the itching pass. He stood there relieved and staring at his reflection. It looked like he was wearing only a pair of sleeves and nothing else. The idea made him chuckle, sending a spurt of hangover pains throughout his skull.

He decided he would buy another box of laundry sheets, regardless of whether or not that was in his budget.

Four

After work that day Clay agreed to meet his friend José at a bar on Clemington Rd just three blocks from the complex. It was a small joint, but the drinks were cheap and the food cheaper. He decided that he would eat there tonight and just eat cheaper the next few days until he got paid Friday. Besides, it was Taco Tuesday, and the Incubus sold the cheapest and most unhealthy tacos in all of Idaho (according to José of course).

He had gotten off at eight that night and met with José a half hour later. He had changed in his car and took out forty dollars out of the nearest ATM to pay for his drinks and the food. There was a possibility that José would pay just the same amount as well, so they both had eighty between the two of them. Which may or may not turn to significantly more if they became dumb enough or drunk enough to cash out more from an ATM. Which was a possibility that Clay could admit to if one were to ask him. They started off with Spider Shots which consisted of cheap tequila and orange juice for $1 and it only escalated from there both in drinks and in budget.

At some point in the evening about ten dollars past his budget, Clay had turned to find that the large Hispanic with a buzz-cut and a Virgin Mary tattoo on his right bicep known as José, had been replaced with some woman wearing a black dress way too tight for her and showing off more cleavage than an old cartoon. She was blonde and wearing high heels and hoop earrings, just like Rachel used to wear. About three drinks into her (paid by Clay of course) they were in the bathroom stall. It was good to feel another woman again, and this one *loved* to talk. She spoke many sweet nothings into his ear, sometimes in a language he didn't understand. But after their little lovemaking in the filthy bathroom that smelled of stale piss and vomit, she disappeared. Whether that was because she actually left after getting her own itch scratched or Clay was just too drunk to find her among the many shifting faces of the patrons at the Incubus, he didn't know or particularly cared. His vision had doubled and tripled to the point of untrustworthiness. More and more people began to appear the same with ghostly-pale faces and he could have sworn that at some point everyone here had blazing red hair.

That was all right. It was a good night so far and it was just getting started.

He later found José playing pool in the back room drinking a Trash Can with two biker guys. Clay joined in and the group played a good game and bought each other more rounds. Then they went to darts and that was when tempers flared. All Clay would remember was smashing a bottle into a biker's face and dousing his handlebar mustache with beer, and getting into a fistfight with the other. He would then remember getting thrown out and the fight continuing in the parking lot. They all scattered as soon as they heard that the cops had been called. Both he and José walked to his apartment with the intention of getting their cars the next day. At the apartment, the two drank more of Clay's Rolling Rock and debated going to Wal-Mart for cheap whiskey. By then they were completely and utterly sloshed, the concept of time, money, and life in general a million miles away and Clay would find himself waking up on his bed with José drunk on the floor. There were beer cans everywhere and the smell of piss was sharp like a knife cutting through the air. Feeling his stomach bloated and pushing something up, Clay hurried to his bathroom where he threw up almost two-hundred dollars worth of semi-digested booze, cheap wings, and mozzarella sticks.

As he made out with his toilet, he felt an itch on the side of his neck and went to scratch it. It hurt but he was more focused on the chunks spilling out of his guts. His nose was clogged by bits of acidy food and his eyes were watery and by the time he had finished puking, he was still sitting there hugging the bowl and coughing and blowing his nose. He didn't get up to flush until a half hour later, realizing he had passed out there. By then it was six-thirty in the morning. He crawled back into bed, still scratching the itch on his neck that was a persistent little fucker that wouldn't go away.

By the time morning came along (or at least morning according to Clay), José had gone. Probably back to the Incubus where he got his car and drove straight to the construction site where he worked, no doubt hungover and carrying a bitch of a headache. Clay stretched and heard his back and elbows make a ripple of popping sounds and more joined in as he stretched out his legs. He was shirtless and wearing only his filthy work jeans. He got up and padded barefoot into the kitchen where he poured himself a glass of water. He drank like a dehydrated man who had been stuck in Death Valley for two days because his car broke down. He felt a tickle behind his ear, and he scratched it with fingernails that reeked of vomit.

It was 10:32AM and he went to shower before work. It was another 12-8 today and he wanted to completely eliminate the scent of alcohol and vomit. He wanted to take the time to brush his teeth and hair, maybe splash on some cologne. Might as well fake it to Mr. Maisel that he was *trying* for his job.

In the shower he had turned the hot water on to almost the maximum that the dial could go. He let the scalding water punish his neck and he splashed his face countless times to wake himself up. As he was scrubbing, he found that he was using his loofah a little rougher than usual. He felt like the water today was saltier and it made his skin feel itchy. He scrubbed harder until he looked like a lobster. The worst was on his back, which felt like there wasn't water coming out of the showerhead but millions of spiders. He scrubbed and even then, the tickling sensation didn't go away. In fact, it spread to his shoulders and biceps as he started to use shampoo and conditioner. He took up the loofah again, infuriated at how easily his body itched. His back, his shoulders, his arms, his forearms and hands even! The aggravating, itching sensation just wouldn't stop and he felt himself going crazy until he got out of the shower to dry himself and hopefully satisfy that itch.

He decided he would do a new load of laundry with the dryer sheets he had purchased yesterday. He would not wear anything until it was ready. He had an hour and a half. If he could just do his work clothes, he should have time to get to work.

Even as he was loading up his washer, naked and feeling the rush of air coming from the air conditioner in his one and only window, he felt the crawling under his skin again. At some point he was looking down at his forearms that had become the most itchy. For a brief moment, he imagined a worm or some sort of alien creature burrowing under his skin, causing it to itch. But the red skin remained still with no sign that anything was living under there. Even with his coarse arm hair, Clay couldn't see anything even if he believed it.

He wondered if this was how meth-heads felt. He had heard from countless documentaries and people who dealt and use the stuff that they always felt like something was living in their skin. That was why their faces and lips were all peeled up and scarred, their arms often scabbed over from countless furrows. They would pick and scratch at the places where they thought insects or something else was living until they bled. They would scratch at their hair until it fell out just to get the bees out of their head, or their lips to get the worms out or their arms to get the ants. Whatever their long-gone minds made them imagine was living inside them; a drug-induced parasite only they could truly see and feel.

The thought made Clay shudder and he resisted the urge to scratch. He finished loading his laundry and went back to the bathroom to put on more ointment. He brushed his teeth, feeling the itch grow on his arms like a warming hand that didn't let go. In the end, he ended up hoping into the shower, determining that his towel was filthy too because of those damned laundry sheets. He would wash again, and this time just air-dry so that he didn't have to use it. It was a long and miserable morning being wet and cold in his apartment, but he was relieved when he put on his warmed and dry clothes and felt relief wash over his skin. It was like the heat was the cure all along, making his itchy back go away. There was still a slight tickle in his fingers and toes, but he put on more ointment and took the bottle with him on his way to work. He would make it only five minutes late; an improvement.

Five

During work, Clay couldn't help but feel constantly watched and/or scrutinized.

While clocking on he had passed by Rebecca in the employee offices (or as Mr. Maisel would put it, Team Member Center). As he passed by, she gave him a look of disgust as she often did, going as far as to scrunching up her nose as if a cartful of cow manure had passed by rather than Clay himself. But the coworker who was walking alongside her was eyeballing him too. Clay didn't think much of it and simply got a walkie and went to work. He had spent the first two hours what they called zoning the grocery department, pulling everything forward and scanning what would need to be restocked the following day. The entire time whenever he looked up, he would see customers or employees eyeballing him only to revert their gaze once they had registered that he noticed them. Many gave him a wide berth, which he was not particularly concerned about. He'd rather not help any customers if he could help it so he could stay on his work, and keep to his own thoughts.

As the day went on however, and more and more people gawked and stayed clear of him for no apparent reason, he began to feel annoyed, especially when Austin Strickland and the Front Registers manager, Carol Dawson were caught looking and pointing at him.

As he passed by, Clay demanded what was wrong. "Do I have something on my face or something?"

"No," Austin answered before hurrying away. Carol, who was about four months pregnant and wearing a red bow in her blonde hair, only smiled uncomfortably. She then brought a hand over her mouth and burped into it, and made a sort of gagging reflex.

Clay only eyed her suspiciously. On one occasion last week, he had found out that Carol and Austin and even the backroom manager, Angel Rodriguez, were asked by Mr. Maisel to keep an eye on him and report any unethical behavior or sayings. He had found this out after saying a crude joke to his closest coworker, Sami Kelly who thought the joke was hilarious. Carol happened to pass by, and despite never having a problem with Clay or his jokes before, the joke came up in a 'conversation' with Mr. Maisel the following day. Ever since then whatever bridge that was between Clay and Carol had been burned as far as he was concerned.

That was all this was. Mr. Maisel asked them to watch him again. Alpha-helicopter asking the drones for additional surveillance. Nodding to reassure the pregnant leader that there were no hard feelings (which there were), he walked away with his cart of outdated perishables that he planned to toss away. This was his favorite part of the job, and he wasn't going to let the way others were acting around him stop him from enjoying it.

The compactor which was used to crush and cube all garbage in the store was located in the back left corner of the backroom right next to the baler, a large machine used to flatten and cube cardboard. When the baler became full, one would tie the cube with metallic wires and the baler would spit it out onto a wood pallet to be taken out back. It was always satisfying to throw in a box and watch it crushed, and occasionally imagine it being someone's head.

The compactor was something different. It was literally just a machine in the wall leading to a large container outside. You could throw garbage and everything that could be taken to the dump into it, and it would crush it over a period of months before needing to be emptied. There had been times the past year that the people who came to collect had to come earlier, because some bum or dumpster diver decided it was a good idea to break the lock on the door of the tank and have the pressurized garbage spill out into the alley, causing an avalanche of rotting trash. On one occasion, the pressure had been so much that the garbage literally blew the door open, injuring the crooked old meth-head who decided to try and seek some discarded electronics.

Upon opening the door leading to the hatch that you could throw your garbage in, a strong smell came rushing out. A funky *warm* smell, the kind produced by the sun punishing the outer container and literally cooking the garbage within. Rotten eggs, moldy clothes and fabric, mixtures of emptied juice, milk, and cheese, as well as no doubt the decaying carcass of a rat who got trapped in the compactor once the pressure became too great. Parking his cart alongside the entrance, Clay looked inside. The first chamber had some garbage in it, but not too much. The wall of compressed trash separated the secondary chamber where everything was pressed down like a giant mouth force-fed the mountain of shit. The backwall was stained by whoever threw stuff in last time. More was going to be on that wall anyway, Clay would make sure of that. He returned to his cart and grabbing a package of Kraft shredded cheddar cheese which had been outdated for two weeks now and had splotches of black and green mold to prove it, he hurled it at the back wall and with a hollow *thump*, watched it fall down the hatch into the compactor with a loud smacking sound.

This was why he loved this part of the job. He had been introduced to this by his previous lead, Matthew Lewis who had been let go just a month ago. It was a good way to relieve stress; just to throw the food with all your might and watch it crumble or splatter against the back wall and spill into the compacter. The cleaning crew would throw a fit because they would have to spray the back of the compacter's throat down to get the stains out, but no one cared, especially not Clay. He needed this. This was the therapy he needed from his day-to-day life here. What made it even better, was that sometimes he would imagine the container of yogurt he was throwing was actually Mr. Maisel; the strawberry spread splattering everywhere as his fat gut erupted against the wall. Sometimes that package of bacon was that slob, Austin, who always talked about country music and would rather do that rather than his actual fucking job. Sometimes that package of crackers was Carol who couldn't keep her nose out of other people's business. Sometimes that bag of frozen hash browns was Rebecca, the snotty and lazy bitch that she was.

Gregory from the front lanes. *Splat!*
That whore from the Incubus last night. *Splat!*
Mr. Duncan the landlord. *Splat!*
Dad. *Splat!*
Chloe from high school. *Splat!*
Rachel, who dumped him during the trial. *Splat!*
Splat! Splat! Splat!

Food everywhere, taking the place of all the people Clay despised and wished were just gone. A majority of his problems would be gone if not all of them. Especially the last one, who he imagined splattering cottage cheese over the wall and an arc almost reaching the ceiling of the compacter. But that person in particular brought with it a painful memory that almost made the violent throw not satisfying. What had happened that day on Route 199 in Grants Pass, and when the tub of Darigold cottage cheese struck the back of the compactor, his mind pictured the accident, and what had happened to that poor girl. Now the smell had finally gotten to him, and Clay with his hands on the bars of the compactor, hung over it, breathing slowly while trying hard not to vomit and *shove* that violent image out of his mind like a mother mutt shoving the runt of the litter away from her teats.

This had been when he and Rachel were first having their problems. They were coming back home from Crescent City where they had taken a trip. When Clay thought about it, it was more of a last-ditch effort to rekindle whatever romance there was between him and Rachel. They were passing through Redwood and then Grants Pass where the highway stretched for what felt like forever through miles of trees before finally making it to the city. Route 199 had a bad reputation for being one of the deadliest highways in the United States. There were crashes almost every other day, and many of them were *indeed* deadly. They were passing through that very infamous highway, having what was the fifth argument in the car that day on the way home to Boise. Something had come out onto the road and Clay's first thought was that it was a deer, and it was coming out too soon and it would be too late to miss it.

It hadn't been a deer.

A hand on his shoulder startled him and Clay started, realizing he had been standing there just staring at the mess of cottage cheese on the back wall slowly sliding down and out of sight down the compacter's gullet. He turned and saw that it was the new guy, Richard (Dick) Bishop who had come up on the job just a week ago. He was still getting used to how to use a walkie talkie and it infuriated Clay whenever the kid couldn't hold down the button or complete his sentence. He knew that wasn't right, the kid was just learning. But whenever his nasally voice came up on the walkie and started crackling with static or cuts off completely mid-sentence, Clay would picture Dick's acne-scarred face and think about how much pus would come out should he punch it with all his might.

Again, not the right thing to think about, but he couldn't help it.

"You okay?" he asked Clay, concern just barely visible through his acne.

"Yeah, just... What's up?" he asked shaking his head clear.

Dick looked nervous, in fact he appeared sick. "S-Someone is here looking for you. A José or something."

That made Clay smile. "Where at?" Dick told him and he went out the doors leading to the sporting goods department, where he found José looking at a foosball table.

José was in his work uniform, a pair of overalls and a reflective green shirt. He was wearing a Green Bay baseball cap and his sleeves were rolled up to reveal his massive arms emblazoned in tattoos. He turned at the sound of Clay but his smile vanished.

"You okay?" he asked Clay.

That made Clay stop in his tracks. "Yes? Why? What is it?"

"You... You smell, dude."

"Like garbage?" Clay sniffed himself. He didn't remember any food splattering him as he was throwing stuff. Sometimes he never noticed so it didn't hurt to ask.

"No, like... I dunno, you smell like oranges left out for too long. Whenever my sister brings me some from California, I never finish them all and some go bad. You have *that* kind of smell on you."

Clay sniffed under his armpit. The gesture was meant more for laughs but even if it wasn't, he couldn't smell anything and he told José so. "Explains why everyone has been looking at me funny." He was irritated that no one told him sooner.

"Did you shower at all since we got to your apartment?"

"Yeah, twice. Even washed my clothes before I left to get my car back from the Incubus."

"Twice?" José shook his head in disbelief. "No offence, *hermano*, but I don't think you did a good job."

At least I don't itch...

That was when Mr. Maisel came around the corner and entered the aisle. He regarded José with a look of curious 'Can I help you sir?' eyes, but then realized the man was with Clay. He looked over at Clay, and asked him to come talk in the backroom.

Inside, Mr. Maisel inquired about Clay showering at all today, his breathing through the nose minimal as he asked but even then he couldn't help himself from wriggling his nose as he told Clay about him smelling bad.

"Everyone is complaining about it, even customers."

"What do you mean though? I showered today and I don't smell anything other than bodywash." *And your cheap cologne,* he thought.

"I don't smell bodywash," Maisel said anxiously, most likely because he didn't want to linger around Clay any longer than he absolutely had to. "I smell something like moldy cheese."

Rotted oranges and moldy cheese. What a combination. "I really don't smell anything, sir," Clay answered. He wanted to point out that he wasn't the only one who smelled. There were plenty of people on the truck team and early morning crew who had terrible B.O. with some probably having never showered in the past month or longer, the Neanderthals. But he decided that would sound like griping, or just an excuse for smelling as bad as he supposedly did. The last thing he wanted was to get into a discussion with Mr. Maisel about excuses.

'Excuses are like farts,' his boss would say. 'We all got 'em, and they all stink.'

Just like me! Clay thought distastefully.

"Well, I'll try to keep my distance for now. Should I just work on clearing the backroom? Trade with Nancy or Greg?"

Mr. Maisel shook his head. "No. Go home and take care of that."

"What do you mean?"

"I mean, go take a shower," Maisel said patiently past his teeth which he was now breathing through. Clay wondered if he was now tasting whatever he smelled like. "And don't come back until you do."

"But sir," Clay said. "I only have three more hours, it can't be *that* bad."

"Oh, it's bad. You don't smell it because you're used to it. Now go on. Clock out."

"If I'm clean I can come back?" As much as he hated it here, a guy's gotta eat.

"If there's time. Maybe. Now go." At this point, Mr. Maisel himself looked ready to puke.

Livid that he was being sent away, Clay marched back to the Team Member Center with bitter resentment. Telling José they'd catch up later, he marched on. Maybe he wouldn't come back at all today. Maisel gonna send him home when others who were still working stunk like an old gym locker? Fuck him.

His left knee began to itch and he scratched it the entire way back.

Six

He did himself a favor and washed his work clothes again. He then hopped into the shower and using the loofah, he scrubbed just as hard as he had earlier that day.

By the time he was finished, Clay had been in the shower for almost forty-five minutes. He even went as far as to brush his teeth and used AXE body spray, making sure he stunk of that rather than whatever he had smelt like. By then his clothes were ready he decided he *did* need to work considering how much he had spent the night before, and drove back to the store around five o'clock.

Where he was immediately sent away. After smelling him, Mr. Maisel looked at Clay angrily. "Do you think I'm stupid? You don't smell any different. Did you even shower at all?"

"Sir, look at my hair." Clay pointed at the brown mop on his head. "It's *damp*. I used shampoo, body wash, everything. My skin is *burning* that's how bad I was scrubbing. I used half a can of AXE for godssake. Can't you smell that?"

He had also put on some ointment to stop the itching. It had sprouted again, this time on his thighs and legs but even as he was talking to Maisel, his ears felt ticklish as well. He imagined his earwax coming to life and crawling out that was how much it bothered him. He scratched it while Maisel continued his little eviction notice.

"You know what?" Maisel said covering his nose. "Go home. You're done for the day."

Clay couldn't believe his ears which were now *excruciatingly* itchy, as if also reacting to Maisel's decision. "Sir, I need to work!"

"Not when you're gonna make my employees or customers sick. Get lost, Clay. If you really can't get rid of the smell, go see a doctor but for chrissakes, don't come back until you're better."

"But what about my shifts?"

"We'll cover them."

"What about my paycheck?"

"You can pick it up then."

"It's not going to be enough!"

"Not my problem. Now go! Before I call the police."

Clay was dumbstruck. He was being kicked out of his job until this smell, whatever it was, was gone. Furious, he stormed out of the building thinking what Mr. Maisel would say if he found himself hogtied to Clay's piece of shit Saturn and the car was going at least forty down the nearest highway. To make matters worse, the goddamn itching returned with a vengeance, this time from his left big toe as he marched across the parking lot.

When he had reached his car, something caught Clay's eye to his left and he turned towards the main road. There were more parking spots with streetlamps standing guard on the border of the lot owned by the store. There were some cars there but a majority of them were trucks and RVs. There was a Winnebago and a teardrop camper on the far side. Where these vehicles sat idly, Clay thought he saw a familiar figure standing by a 1999 Fat Boy motorcycle with more rust than paint smoking a cigarette. The man was staring at him, wearing ripped jeans and a dirty leather jacket with the shoulders cracked from years under the sun. He was wearing cowboy boots and a black bandana over his head. His skin was almost as dark and leathery as the jacket, and his intense brown eyes were staring directly at Clay. Not at the store or just idly glancing around. They were on *Clay*, and Clay knew it.

He stepped away from his vehicle with the intention of meeting the man if it was who he thought he was. A horn honked to his left and he looked away for a moment to look. When he turned back, the man was on his Harley and without a helmet on, turned and sputtered away leaving only a plume of black smoke and a smoldering cigarette butt on the asphalt.

At first, Clay was willing to consider that he didn't *really* recognize the man. The man he had seen too many times to count didn't wear a leather jacket or cowboy boots. But he did wear a bandana. Besides, the man as well whom he was associated with all had restraining orders against them. The biker in question was not to approach Clay or his work. Hell, he wasn't even supposed to be out of jail because he broke that order about three weeks ago when he was caught stalking Clay outside his apartments. So that couldn't have been him.

No, but it could have been one of them.

The thought made his foot itch terribly, and deciding to just go home before he got himself riled up again, Clay got into his car and started it up. He had pumped the accelerator too much and flooded it. He waited for a bit and started the car up again. He started forward, stalled, said some things that would have made a sailor blush before punching at his steering wheel. He had caught the attention of some woman loading groceries into her car. She was giving him a dirty look, and Clay flipped her the bird as he started the car again. This time it didn't hiccup on his way out of the parking lot, and he drove home with about the same recklessness as a drunk or a rageful teenager on the road.

He had gone home without bothering to figure out what had gone wrong and why he couldn't notice it. To go to a doctor was a stupid idea. He had no insurance and definitely didn't have enough money for a walk-in. Maisel and the goddamn store would never give benefits to part-time and even full-time managers were given forty or less so they wouldn't have any either. He knew the fine for not having insurance would almost kill him at the end of the year, but that was a while away. This was now.

On the phone, after telling him about the incident, José sympathized and said he was wondering if they should hang out that night. Clay said sure. Hell, come earlier if he wanted to. And to bring beer if you're generous. Thank you José you're a true friend.

When he got home, Clay in his anger, swiped his hand across the kitchen counter, sending his garbage sailing onto the floor. He would clean it up later. He was angry and wanted to punch something.

He set his eyes on his empty canvas that was still standing where it was. The blank face seemed to mock him upon entry, and he rushed over and put his fist right through the cotton sheet. The moldy cup of water with the paintbrush in it spilled to the floor and all over his sneakers. He swore viciously. He knocked the whole thing over, spilling the paint jars and brushes across the floor as well. He then stomped over to the bathroom, scratching his back and then screaming thinking he was losing his mind.

In the bathroom he splashed some cold water on his face to calm down. He stood there staring angrily at his reflection. His eyes looked sunken from the night before, and his cheeks were tight in fury. His left ear started to itch and he went to scratch it.

Only this time, when he pulled away his hand, underneath his fingernails was blood.

Feeling the spot where he scratched, he felt something mushy and warm. When he pulled his hand back again, he saw yellow flakes of skin sticking to the blood. Ducking down and reaching into the cabinet beneath the sink, Clay fished around until he found a shaving mirror he had gotten when he was eighteen. He had used it to shave off the little hairs that grew on the back of his neck beneath his hairline. He hadn't used it in forever, he didn't see the point anymore. He took it and looking into the mirror he positioned the little six-inch disk behind him. He saw his hair still damp and he angled it to look at his right ear and then his left. He brought it closer, and saw what was wrong. Behind his ear, right next to where his lobe met the disk symmetrical to the pinna, was a sore. The spot was bloody and covered in dried yellow skin. Upon touching it, Clay pulled back a thick sheet of yellow that was speckled with more blood. He flicked his fingers to get it off, resisting the urge to scratch the spot which had started to become more itchy.

Instead, he wetted a washcloth and cleaned the wound. He then patted it dry with the corner he hadn't gotten wet and proceeded to take a first aid kit out from the same cabinet he got the mirror from. Then he bandaged the wound, a corner of the 4X2 Band-Aid sticking into his lobe. The band-aid was annoying and caused his earlobe to itch too, but he could handle that. The itch accumulating beneath the band-aid would be a pain in the ass, but at least it would help prevent him from scratching it.

By the time he finished his little medical treatment, José had arrived. He had knocked on the door and when Clay answered, the man had a big smile on his face and a pack of Coronas. Not Clay's favorite, but any beer would do for the shitty day he had. Beer seemed to fix everything these days.

José's smile immediately vanished and he scrunched up his nose. "My god, Clay," he said.

"That bad? Seriously?"

"Worse in here it seems. Lemme in a spell."

Clay did so and José began to sniff around the apartment like a bloodhound. A Mexican Bear in the Big Blue House, sniffing about until he found the source which was *always* the watcher. Clay felt uncomfortable- actually *insulted* by the action, but he knew José was only trying to help locate the source. He went through the kitchen, then the living room, passing by Clay in the process and pausing once he was a few steps away.

"The smell is definitely coming from you," his friend announced. He lingered to the bed, and then towards the bathroom. "Smells worse near your bed."

"That right?" Clay asked using a towel to open up a bottle of beer. He remembered the mess he made and got on his knees to pick up his garbage. He took the trash out of the can as well and then replaced the liner so he could dispose of the McDonald's and Taco Bell. He then used the same towel he used for the beer and went to clean up the moldy water on the floor. The canvas and stand he pushed into the corner, the brushes he scooped up and placed on the windowsill right where his alarm clock sat. The time read 6:42 now.

José emerged from the bathroom and looked at Clay. Then he walked over to the kitchen where the beer was and cracked a bottle open with his hand. He took a long swig and then joined Clay in the living room, taking a seat on the floor opposite of the bed.

"Dude," he said. "I'm sorry, but, you *really* do stink."

"No shit," Clay said sarcastically. "So Mr. Maisel said. But I don't smell *anything*, dude. Like to me, my apartment smells no different than any other day. Save for the beer cans all over the floor..." He went to pick those up as well. José watched him probably not wanting to get too close but at the same time conflicted about appearing rude.

"What happened to your head?" he eventually asked.

Clay almost touched his new bandage and restrained his hand. God the itch was unbearable now. "Not sure. Was bleeding when I got here. It's fine though."

"Okay..." José appeared unsure, but he didn't pester Clay about it. He probably figured it was from last night, during that brawl with the dipshit biker gang. He finished his beer and got another. He downed it in four gulps then grabbed another one. He really needed it to withstand the odor.

"What does it smell like?" Clay asked. "Me, I mean."

José thought about it for a second. "Like rotting fruit. Like I said before. It's only stronger because this is your apartment, I think. Other than that, about the same as earlier."

"I don't get it," Clay said.

"Maybe you're just used to it," José offered. "Like a high schooler not thinking his room smells like a locker room."

"Even if that was the case," Clay said dumping the last of the empty beer cans from last night into the trash. It was already halfway full. "If it's as bad as everyone says, I think I would have noticed it. Or even when I came home the last two times."

"True," José murmured. But he appeared doubtful even at that. "You didn't stink last night."

"Hmm…" Clay took a seat against his bed across from José after grabbing another beer.

"You knocked over your canvas too."

"It pissed me off," Clay said with a slight chuckle.

José was staring at him now. The look on his face sparked newfound anger in Clay, and he demanded what he was looking at.

"*Hombre*," José said. "You got some flies buzzing around you."

"Huh?" That was when Clay heard the short whine of a pair of wings buzzing near his left ear. He swatted aimlessly and turning his body he looked to see a gnat buzzing around. Standing up and walking briskly away, he managed to see two more flying around, as well as a legitimate housefly. That one was crawling over his pillow, and looking down he saw another on his arm that had been reddened from the constant showering.

Marching over to the kitchen, he scoured through the cabinets until he found some fly tape. He remembered having to use some when he first moved here, the place was so trashed by the last owner. He stuck the tape on the ceiling and two more near his bed. The flies near his bed rose up at the scent of the tape and got stuck, but those who had found him continued to buzz. Clay even swatted at one, crushing it against his arm. Red and clear liquid was smeared over the crumpled black body.

"How the fuck did they get in here?" Clay asked himself not expecting José to have an answer for it. Thankfully, he didn't have one at all.

Seven

In the end, Clay was talked into going to a Kadlec Urgent Care. He had showered again and when his friend smelled no distinct difference, José offered to drive him and pay for whatever his own insurance wouldn't cover. Clay expressed his concern saying that it was probably illegal, but José insisted.

"If you can't smell it, and you can't wash whatever it is off, it's something else. Besides, if they can't do anything, then at least they can write you a note to go back to work. Maisel can't prevent you from working when it's nothing you can control. That's discriminatory. Illegal, you know?"

"I don't think that's how that works."

In the end, he begrudgingly allowed himself to be taken in. They took José 's car and on the way there, they smoked cigarettes upon José's suggestion. At first, Clay thought it was simply to calm himself down or get his own mind off the smell. But then he realized the cigarette smoke was used to *mask* the smell. It made sense, given José was in the same confined space as Clay. At first Clay felt offended but, in the end, the cigarette calmed him down as originally considered, and he reasoned that José made the right call. After all, his friend was helping him with this problem that seemed to just sprout like a weed in a garden, ruining the tranquility and blissful control.

Upon their arrival at Urgent Care, they told the receptionist what was going on, and she took Clay's information and the insurance he was providing. When they were of course denied that, they were informed of the fee for check in and the possible wait time. At this point, it would be an hour-long wait with a fee of at least $300. Clay almost walked out right then and there, but José said he would pitch in.

"After all," he said as they took a seat among many other sick patients who were now covering their noses and giving the two dirty looks. One mother in particular looked like she was about to say something, her small child who was holding a bloody rag against his nose unaware of the smell beyond his blood, but in the end the woman kept her mouth shut.

"After all," José said again once they were settled in. "You paid for most of the drinks last night."

"Did I?" Clay asked not really caring. He just wished the bloody-nosed brat staring at him with large eyes would look away. He wished he could just tell the little shit to fuck off but that would be considered inappropriate, not to mention might very well give all his new fans a reason to give *him* another reason for going into urgent care.

He wished all the patients waiting, well, *patiently* in the waiting room would look at a magazine or their phone or something *other* than him. The more he looked around and saw another pair of eyes glaring at him with a hand or mask covering the mouth and nose, the angrier he got, and he felt a familiar itch on the back of his head. The itch had trailed from the base of his hairline down his neck and between his shoulder blades, as if he had a tapeworm that had decided the back of his eyes were not worth eating and was slithering back down to his stomach. Careful not to accidently peel off his band-aid, he scratched it.

"You smell funny," the bloody-nosed brat said appearing seemingly out of nowhere right in front of Clay. He looked to be about no older than five, with strawberry-blonde hair and bright intelligent green eyes. He had removed his rag, and flakes of dried blood were drifting off his lips like autumn leaves. He coughed in his little fist. The sight and sound of it sparked newfound irritation in Clay, and he snarled at the child whose mother was watching them intensively. Just what the fuck was the woman thinking letting her bleeding kid roam about?

"Get lost," he snapped, managing to reel in his temper at the last minute.

The kid turned tail and hurried to his mother, who accepted him without so much as looking at her son. She hugged him close, protectively as she stared daggers at the man who scared him.

"Are you insane?" she demanded, the stupid bitch.

"Well, tell him to mind his own business," Clay said. "Damn kid is practically bleeding everywhere and making rude comments."

"Bro, *chill*," José said sternly.

"That fucking little shit-" Clay stopped himself. People were staring. He apologized and settled into his seat with his arms crossed. This was quickly becoming the worst day of his life.

After an *eternity*, the nurse called his name and Clay left the waiting room to go in. Since he hadn't been to a doctor since he was eighteen, he had to do a quick checkup before the doctor could come in. The nurse who introduced herself as Lola, was a pretty thing with short black hair, and a sweet smile. A cutie who Clay couldn't help but steal glances every time she turned around. She was trying hard to suppress her discomfort because of the smell, Clay could tell. Her eyes were watery as they walked the disinfectant halls to a scale and he followed his instructions as the nurse named Lola checked his height and weight.

The scale was a Global Industrial with a height rod that stretched up to catch the five-foot-nine man standing on it. As it did so, Lola shifted the weights to measure him, and Clay was surprised to see that he was coming up as a hundred and twenty-two pounds.

"I think your scale is broken," Clay said. He was barefoot and he was looking down at his feet. They had started to itch again, but they looked no different. Long, lanky, and probably smelly, but nothing stuck out to him as being *wrong*.

"Nope, that's your weight," Lola said. She asked if he would like her to reset the scale, and he spared her the effort.

"Nah, we'll keep it. I don't want you smelling me anymore than you have to."

Lola insisted that it was no trouble, but she was only trying to be nice. Clay felt bad for her, and without realizing it apologized about it. She told him to get his shoes back on and they would go to the examination room.

"I should be one-sixty though," Clay told her. "I mean, I don't eat the healthiest in the world."

"Might be good metabolism," Lola said. She coughed. She was trying *really* hard not to react to the smell, trying to be professional. But it only pissed Clay off more, his apology quickly forgotten in the midst of his discomfort and embarrassment. Which was not fair, he would tell himself, but at the moment he didn't give a rat's ass.

In the examination room, Clay took a seat next to a blood pressure monitor and while the machine checked his pressure, Lola began to check his eyes, ears, and heartbeat. She looked disgusted when she examined his ear, and taking her stethoscope, lifted up his shirt and asked him to take deep breaths. She looked nervous at this, and then checked his heart. The entire time she did this, Clay breathed deep and slowly, looking around at the posters on the wall that showed skeletons, muscle diagrams for a human being, and what to do should a patient have suspicion that they may have the Flu. The place smelled of disinfectant and illness, like most doctor places did.

"Hmm," Lola said stepping away to write something on her notepad. "You sound like you have bronchitis, but we'll have Dr. Goldman take a look at you."

Great, a fucking Jew, Clay thought. He never liked them, always thought of them as stuck-up, especially where he had used to live back in Spokane Washington. He supposed that was terribly prejudice, but he believed that everyone had something against a particular group, regardless of race, sex, or religion. At the very least, he never wished any of the Jewish community near his home harm, only to leave him and his siblings alone and keep their big noses to the sky and out of their family business. A few rotten apples had unfortunately spoiled that bunch for him.

He supposed that might have also been a major problem for his father, who sadly was the cause of a lot of problems at the Couch residence.

"Why do you say bronchitis?" he finally asked Lola.

"Your lungs sound like they are full of liquid and your heart is slow. Like I said, Goldman will take a look just to be sure." Lola removed the strap which had been crushing Clay's right arm and she frowned at the blood pressure monitor as well.

"What?" Clay asked.

Whether she had enough or just didn't hear him, Lola approached him with the same clipboard and handed it to him.

"Answer everything as honestly as you can, and the doctor will be in shortly."

Clay thanked her and looked the paperwork over as she left quickly, and looking relieved while doing so. The paperwork was more or less the usual questions one would be asked in a clinic.

Where does it hurt?
How long?
When was the last time you did this?
Are you on any medication?
Are you sexually active?
Do you use alcohol or partake in any hallucinogens?
Etcetera, et-fucking-cetera.

Clay finished filling out the paperwork as well as filling out what information he could about medical history when Dr. Goldman walked in. The man, surprisingly to Clay, was not Jewish or did not look like one. He was a black man with thinning gray hair on his head and huge glasses that made his eyes look bug-eyed. He was skinny as a pencil and had a spiderweb tattoo on the right side of his neck which looked nearly blue compared to the skin pigment. He introduced himself kindly and shook Clay's hand. His nose twitched but he was holding in his displeasure better than Lola had. Clay decided he liked this man who was now looking over his own clipboard.

"Clayton Couch, haven't had you in here since you were a kid. Walking pneumonia, according to your file."

"I've never been to this Kadlec," Clay told him. "I used to live in Spokane."

"Ahh, a Washingtonian."

"Lived here for seven years," Clay added for no particular reason.

"You need to be here a decade to be considered Idahoan, but that's just me." Goldman gave Clay a wink of good faith. Yup, that sealed the deal. "So, what seems to be the problem?" He asked this as if the problem wasn't obvious.

He took the clipboard from Clay and read what he had written, keeping an ear open as Clay told him of the problem everyone said he had. He explained his daily routine, how he had showered more times today than ever in his life, and how his boss practically kicked him out of the store. Rehashing the story made Clay feel bitter, but he kept a close eye on his temper and told the story as calmly and as rationally as he could muster.

"Yeah, I can smell it," Goldman said. "No surprise there. But you can't tell why, and you say you washed already?"

"Couple of times today. Any dead skin I have is probably gone."

"Well, I think your problem is a little bigger than just a stink," Goldman said somberly. "Your blood pressure is eighty millimeters."

Not being a doctor, Clay asked, "Meaning?"

"That's *low*, is what it means. That's the blood pressure of someone who is on their death bed."

"But I feel as healthy as a horse..." *Plus I'm stressed, shouldn't that account for blood pressure?*

"With clogged ears to match one," Goldman commented. "By the way, Lola suggests you use Q-tips to clean those out."

Clay chuckled. It was a reaction more than anything else, especially towards something that wasn't particularly funny. "Okay, so low blood pressure and filthy ears..."

"*Clogged* ears," Goldman corrected him. "Lots of buildup of wax and gunk. Lungs sound rough too. I want to check on some things, but I am pretty sure you have a minor case of bronchitis. You don't have any coughing at all though? No mucus buildup?"

"No, none at all."

"You a smoker?"

"Yes."

Goldman nodded. "But even if any of this came into play with why you are here, I don't see it. Because you aren't here because of your lungs. You're here because of the smell. However, I am pretty sure that you have minor bronchitis. I suggest we put you on a prescription to see if it will help your lungs any. As for the smell, I don't know yet." He sat the clipboard down, and asked Clay if he could examine him a little more.

It was no more different than what a physician might do. Turn and cough while I hold your balls, let's look at your fat-to-muscle ratio, please lay back and let's look down your throat, etcetera. As he was pulling on Clay's skin, some yellow residue had stained his white gloves. He looked closely and Goldman saw that it was dead skin. Oily, but definitely dead. It had come from Clay's abdomen, which had started to itch after Goldman stopped prodding him. At the sight of it, Clay felt revulsion and told Goldman so.

"But no pain?" Goldman asked. "No pressure where I pressed down?"

"Not at all," Clay answered.

Goldman looked disturbed. He took off his gloves carefully and placed them in a bio-hazard bag. He sat the bag aside and sat down in the chair next to the counter, looking over the notes.

"The yellow patches on your skin are minor, almost hidden they are so light," Goldman said. "Most of it probably soaked up into your clothes."

Clay felt his stomach roll. It was true that human beings shed a ton of dead skin and release gallons of oils and sweats, but ideally, they wouldn't be yellow or looking like encrusted pieces of fungi.

Goldman added, "But most cases where we see yellowed skin is the cause of bilirubin."

Clay asked what that was.

"It is a yellow pigment that is created by the breakdown of dead red blood cells in the liver. You are a drinker, right?"

Clay answered yes, slightly annoyed since the answer was on that clipboard Goldman was reading.

"Then it might be a minor case of jaundice too. Do you have trouble peeing at all? I can't believe I forgot to ask that too."

"None whatsoever," Clay answered, although he remembered this morning when he had gone to pee, a sharp pain had sprouted in his lower tummy. Only for a brief moment though, and that reason alone made him keep his mouth shut. There was something else too, but Clay couldn't remember, and likewise said nothing.

"Hmmm..." Goldman thought this over, his medical mind rereading all the books he had read and all the things he had seen while on the job. He looked at Clay a little more thoroughly. "Well, this is just an Urgent Care center, and I don't have the best answer for all of this. The smell *could* be jaundice on top of bronchitis too. But I don't know for certain. You have some symptoms of these but not all or at least severe enough.

Also, your blood pressure. I think *no* prescription as of yet. I think you need to go in to see a professional at St. Luke's before we do anything else."

"Sir, can I be straight with you?" Clay asked.

"I hope you would be," Goldman said with good humor.

"I don't have the money to go to a hospital," Clay told him. "I don't even have insurance. The only reason I came in today is because my buddy is helping me out."

"That won't matter," Goldman said. "Hospitals are bound to save and secure. In the state of emergencies, they are bound by law to make sure you get the treatment you need. If what you have is severe or life-threatening, a bodily functions or organs are seriously impaired, or you are pregnant and will give birth at any minute, you have the right to seek treatment. Everything else gets taken care of later down the road via monthly payments."

Clay thought, *Great. Another goddamned bill.* "But is what I have life-threatening?" Clay asked. "Will they see me?"

"Son, lemme tell ya," Goldman said bemusedly. "I've seen some things here in this clinic. I've seen infectious diseases, broken bones, all of the above and I have always sent what looks bad to St. Luke's. They will find out if what you have is life-threatening or not, but I can guarantee you that the many symptoms you have are indeed linked to life-threatening situations."

"Really?" Clay asked now worried. He felt his stomach churn, and he almost jumped when he felt it actually react to his sensation. "Even the smell?"

"It could be linked to something else," Goldman said. "But yes, I believe so. That's why I say screw the medicine and go to someone who can give us a straight answer. That sample on my gloves is going to the center where we test for viruses and diseases. One way or another, we can figure it out. They will do some blood samples and also check to see if what you have is linked to anything in the past."

To this, Clay felt relieved. "Okay..."

Goldman took to his own clipboard and went to write on something. "Go today. Tell them I sent you and they'll set you up with a dermatologist to look at your skin, and a pulmonologist."

"Sir, one more thing..."

"Yes?"

"I need to return to work. Can you...?"

Goldman shook his head. "That's for St. Luke to decide. If they send you home, they'll give you a note. Sometimes you just need time to get results."

"Okay..." Clay was somewhat disappointed, but it wasn't like he would be returning to work today anyway.

Goldman finished his paperwork, and giving Clay the note, told him to head up front for payment.

Clay and José both ended up paying only a hundred and fifty dollars. The receptionist explained that Goldman gave them a discount since it was a special situation. Clay decided he *loved* the man rather than liked him, and saying this and making his friend laugh, the two of them left for St. Luke's Regional Medical Center.

Eight

St. Luke's was located across the Boise River close to the Idaho State Capital Building. There was a cemetery and two parks surrounding the massive building and was just a short drive from the local college. When Clay and José first arrived they gave their information to the front desk as well as the note Dr. Goldman gave Clay. The receptionist (covering her nose in the process) told them both to follow her assistant through a set of doors and down a somber hallway before eventually being directed into an examination room marked for dermatology. The smell of disinfectant and something along the lines of cherry syrup struck Clay's nose, and when he asked José if he smelled cherries, his friend said he didn't.

A few minutes later, an old Dr. Lewis who had been at the hospital as an executive dermatologist for almost twenty years, proceeded to check Clay's skin where Dr. Goldman noticed the yellow residue. She took swabs with Q-tips and placed them in sealed plastic jars and even used a tool that looked like a miniature grater to collect some of the drier bits of skin that were on Clay's shoulders, knee-pits, and even some on his earlobes. During the whole process, Clay's body itched like a motherfucker, but he clenched the sides of his chair while the doctor worked, trying hard to think of something else if anything else could keep his mind off the itching. He didn't have to think of much though, the sight of his skin coming back in dry and yet oily clumps made him sick to his stomach. How Lewis was able to hold onto her lunch was nothing short of a miracle.

Lewis had a buzz cut, what hair she had being almost platinum it was so shiny. She studied Clay's skin in petri dishes with huge glasses that were bigger than Goldman's. She was terribly thin, but she carried herself with a no-nonsense attitude. If Clay gave her any lip or made her job difficult, he knew she was the type of person who would just as quickly say 'There's the door' as well as 'How are we feeling today, honey?'

When she was done a nurse escorted the two men to another room. This was a much longer walk, taking them to the Eastern Ward. Here Clay was instructed to strip and put on a smock before being placed in a room with a bed on it. It was here where a few doctors came in and took blood samples. The sampling made Clay woozy, but the nurses gave him orange juice and some cookies to regain some energy. The cookies were dry and brittle, but the orange juice tasted amazing. After that another doctor came in and performed a full examination of Clay from asshole to earholes. He took samples of Clay's urine, saliva, and even a swab of the yellow oil that had accumulated on Clay's knee-pit. Clay wondered if this how rabbits felt in a makeup factory.

By then the dermatologist, Lewis came in and asked to have a word with the doctor. By then some nurses had collected the samples and hurried away. The whole time José sat patiently in the nearby chair, watching Clay with light support and enthusiasm. His smile alone told Clay that things would be just fine.

The doctor eventually returned without Lewis. He was a short man, possibly Irish, Clay was willing to bet because of the man's copper hair and strong jawline. He sat down on the chair across from the hospital bed and spoke in a serious no-bullshit matter.

"Well, Mr. Couch, you'll be happy to know you don't have Jaundice. Your urine is clean, although your lungs sound flooded. That oily substance on your skin is nothing more than sebum, an oily substance that actually helps keeps your skin moisturized. You just happen to be developing more than the average person, and it just happens to be a different color."

"So it's just gross-looking sweat?" Clay inquired.

"A harsh way of putting it, but yes. The only real danger to this would be acne, because it makes your skin more absorbent of dirt and dead skin cells, which you happen to have around the spots where the sebum is being produced, hence some of the dryer clusters we scrape off. As for the oil itself, that is what is producing that foul odor that you have been smelling."

"You sure?" Clay asked. He wanted to be absolutely positive that it wasn't anything harmful.

"I am," the doctor said with a smile. The smile irritated Clay. It was as if the doctor was mocking him, demeaning him as if he were a child asking if the needle will hurt or not.

Doctor Frederick McFinnigan, as his name badge proclaimed him as added, "The mixture is made of a similar product of earwax as well as other oils, causing a bitter sometimes sickly sweet smell like sweet and sour pork. It is simply a matter of overactive glands. You made the right choice of coming here, though a regular dermatologist would have been sufficient in finding out what you have. However, Victor is a good friend of mine and never sends anyone here without reason, and I can see why. As mentioned before, your lungs are flooded with liquid mucus."

"How can you tell?"

"When you breathe, there is a *sloshing* sound in your lungs, also your breathing is slightly labored, nothing you can hear with the naked ear, but with a stethoscope, yes. Since you are not showing other symptoms that usually come with this phenomenon-"

"Like bronchitis?"

McFinnigan looked perplexed at being interrupted by his patient. Still, he kept his composure and answered. "Yes, that, among other things. Bronchitis, pneumonia, trauma to your chest, that sort of thing. You have a record of being in a car crash. Hospitalized for broken ribs and whiplash in your neck."

Clay felt incredibly uncomfortable at the mention of the accident. He felt his hands grow sweaty, including the areas that had been itching. Momentarily, he had forgotten all about them as he felt his stomach churn. Seeing all the blood beyond McFinnigan, somewhere far away.

He finally answered, "Yes, that's right. A couple months ago I was released back from Oregon."

McFinnigan nodded. "I am sure your organs have not yet healed since the accident, and that is why you are producing liquid in your lungs. It isn't dangerous mind you, but it can build up to the point where you can drown."

The mentioning of drowning brought a memory of something his father once said. While hunting for wild turkey together his father had said they might find some drowned turkeys in the woods, and sure enough they did, laying around a meadow that was vacant of a river or pond. When young Clayton asked how the twenty-pound male drowned, his father answered with a wry and whiskey-induced smile.

"Birds are dumb as chickens, maybe stupider. When it rains, dumb shits look up and water strikes their face. They are curious as to what it is, and just keep looking up until their beaks fill with water and they collapse. They fucking drown while standing up! Ain't that retarded?"

Whether this was true or not, the idea of drowning without water brought up the memory, and made Clay miss his alcoholic father for a moment. He felt like a little kid again, and a childlike fear of being in a hospital alone came over him. That fear was quickly discarded however, as most adults do when they experience such sensations. Like being afraid that something was with them in the dark or in the pool they swam in, they simply waved their hand and worked some adult magic called rationality and reason, and it all went away. There was no reason to be afraid of what would be discovered at this hospital, and he was not going to drown like a turkey in the rain, whether that was factual or not.

McFinnigan had continued talking as Clay was thinking about his father. "Therefore, I suggest we do a procedure called a thoracentesis. That way we can get rid of the liquid building up in you and make it easier to breathe."

"A thora-what?"

"*Thoracentesis.* Essentially, we are going to make a small hole in your side and drain the liquid out of your lungs. You'll be as clean as a whistle in a matter of hours with no physical side effects. It's really quite fascinating."

Clay who never understood that term and believed whistles were the dirtiest things a human being could compare cleanliness to, stated, "But I don't have trouble breathing."

"Maybe not, but you are also a smoker. Besides, the more clean air we can get into those lungs, the better they will heal. That will mean no smoking for at *least* a month after the procedure, depending on how much we drain."

That sounded absolutely horrible, and Clay was already dreading it. He *needed* his cigarettes. He needed one now, and considered asking McFinnigan if he could have one before he made up his mind, but decided against it. It was the only thing that could calm him down at work other than the compacter. But if the doctor was suggesting something that would save his life one day, he supposed he better listen.

"Give it to me straight, doc," Clay said to the Irish. "How much is this gonna cost me?"

The procedure happened about an hour later. Clay was asked if he was allergic to any medications or had a history of cancer or bleeding heavily, and then they got started. After being given something to sedate him, Clay was instructed to lay on his side on the bed and an ultrasound was performed in order to find the pleural space. Once an area was found between two of his ribs, the doctor cleaned and injected a numbing agent into the area just as Clay started to doze off. As he slept his dreams were a muddled mess within a red haze, as if he were standing under a heat lamp or his vision was tinged with blood. He saw unpleasant faces there to greet him, one of which was a large man with burning eyes, one of which being the third eye, burning the brightest in the man's forehead which seemed to beckon Clay like a lighthouse does ships and boats in the midst of a terrible storm.

Dr. Frederick McFinnigan had been with St. Luke's for almost five years now. He had performed many reportorial procedures in his time here, but he was mostly a diagnostic and an assistant. He was wearing a mask during this time, he had told Clay because he had to protect his face. When in reality, he wanted to try and mask the smell. It was awful, worse than any case he had ever smelled before, and he had smelled people who were dying in their own shit or had cooked themselves from the inside from tanning too long. Hell, there was one time a kid had to have a tumor removed from his head and his brain was producing some sort of bacteria that had a noxious odor that nearly filled the entire watch room where Frederick was studying.

Dr. McFinnigan then inserted the needle connected to a tube that would be used to drain the fluid in Clay's lungs. With his assistants helping him, Frederick managed to stick the needle into the left lung of the patient and using a pump, released the pressure inside the tank that would eventually collect the mucus in Clay's lungs.

But what came through the tubes when it finally came, did not look like mucus at all.

Slogging through the tube and eventually dropping into the plastic container, was a dark green slime; almost black and chunky like half-digested food. These chunky parts were fuzzy like mold, and Frederick's assistant nurse had to sprint to the nearest trash can to vomit. Isabel Kane who was present during the light procedure as a witness and Frederick's student on duty, looked appalled.

"Doc," she said gaping at the gunk spilling into the container. It reminded the young girl of oil that had been mixed with garbage from the junkyard that was just down the street from where she lived. "What the fuck is that?" She was usually a well-mannered girl with no vulgar language to speak of, and yet her question did not strike her mentor as shocking or offensive under the circumstance.

"I... I don't know..." Frederick was astounded. He had never in his years have seen anything like this. "Holy shit..."

Once the container was filled, he had his assistant quickly swap it out for a bigger one. He had turned the stopcock on the catheter device in order to give enough time for the draining process. The sample container saw set aside for testing later, and still everyone watched in revolted awe at the gunk still flowing out of Clayton Couch's lungs. What was worse, was the smell. The smell of putrid fruit, and something bitter. Something that Frederick remembered as a child living with a father who lived in his own filth, as microorganisms began to live with him on the walls of his bedroom and all over his own bathroom. A lazy man Matthew McFinnigan was, one who didn't care if he was sleeping in his own urine or feces, or that ants were crawling all over his bed because of paper plates of moldy food and stains of spilled juice and soda. The smell was *moldy*, and it brought back those memories to Frederick McFinnigan like a flood.

Thinking slowly Frederick began to calm down. He had heard of this before. The realization of what it was sunk in, and he let out a light chuckle of relief which even to him felt unsettling and unreal. "This is just... black phlegm."

"What does it mean?" Frederick's other assistant asked. He looked better, eyes still watery but otherwise didn't look eager to spill his guts again.

"This is merely a connection to our friend's bad habit. In some cases, smokers or those who live in a highly dirty or smokey environment, have their mucus turned black from the soot and filth. In other more serious cases, it would mean lung cancer, but we would have seen something in the X-rays or the ultrasound. That's all this is. It is just a mixture of fluids and years of smoking. At such a young age too, no doubt. I've never seen it before though... it's remarkable."

"So, it's nothing serious?" Ms. Kane asked nervously. She had her clipboard in hand so she could take notes. Her pencil, while in position to write, had not moved since the procedure began, and therefore was almost completely blank.

"Not at all," Frederick assured her and his assistant. "Just a bunch of gunk that had to get out."

"But what's with the smell?" his assistant asked. "Smells like something died and *liquified* in him."

"I don't know," Frederick said honestly. In this line of work, honesty was the best policy. Because the wrong diagnosis could get people killed. He had worked in the hospital long enough to know that, and had even made the dreadful mistake himself on two occasions.

"In any case," he said. "It is starting to slow. We will give it an hour and then check again. Blake, can we make sure we have a place for him to stay overnight? I want to do another X-ray tomorrow morning to make sure that what we got out will *stay* out. We'll have to inform his friend that he can go home for the day."

His assistant said he would. By then the container was almost full, but little by little, only droplets came out of the tube and then nothing came out at all. His left lung had been emptied. In about an hour's time, they would flip Clay over, and start again to do the other. It was just like the left, full of black tar-like gunk, but not nearly as much. By the time they were done, Clay was in a new hospital bed with a disinfected bandage on his back. He would sleep for a few more hours as the drugs wore off, and then Frederick would visit him upon hearing that his patient was awake. In the meantime, his friend, José Rodriguez, was given the choice to wait in the waiting room or leave until Clay woke up. He waited and came up when it was time to discuss what they had found.

Clay, still groggy, listened as much as he could as Frederick explained what they had seen. He was not happy at all when Frederick said he should not smoke at all for the next three months. He didn't look too disappointed about staying in the hospital overnight. José, who was relieved that his friend was really okay, that it all had just been a mixture of different but small things, was delighted about the news.

"When can I come pick him up tomorrow?" he asked.

"I'd say around eleven or noon," Frederick answered. When José said he would be working until three, Clay said that that would be okay. He would wait.

"Give you plenty of time for whatever final things you need to check," Clay said to Fredrick.

Dr. McFinnigan smiled. He hadn't liked Clay in the beginning, but now the man kind of grew on him. Like an unruly chicken who liked to squawk and peck it's owner, but in the end it was still your chicken, and you felt a sense of duty to care for it and make sure it grew up fat and healthy and more importantly, able to lay more than a few eggs.

"I'm sure it will be fine. It's just procedure, you understand."

Clay did, and that night, he slept in the hospital. He slept, but he did not sleep soundly. In fact, sleep took it's sweet time to come, and he was left alone with his own thoughts that plagued him nearly as bad as his dreams from earlier had.

Nine

Nights spent in hospitals were often somber and brooding. The thought of people sick all around you, that someone in some room probably on the far side of the building was going to sleep and would never wake up again, it sobered up even the most medicated of minds.

For Clay, it was the loneliness. José had to go home to see his girlfriend and sleep for work in the morning, so Clay was all alone. He had his phone nearby but didn't have anyone to talk to. He had burned a lot of bridges over the course of his life, and all he really had as of late were José and Rachel. He thought of texting Rachel, to let her know that he was in the hospital, but thought better of it. There was nothing wrong with him, so he would only be bothering her.

Not that she would probably care anyway, he told himself.

But that was just bitterness speaking for him.

He knew that she had made her decision for her own good. For his own good too. They had become stale, as one might say. There had been too many arguments, too much blame to give and share, and unfortunately, too much under the surface which would break it and rear their ugly heads. It had gotten to the point where neither of them was truly happy. And though he missed her greatly, he knew in his heart he loved her enough to wish her the best, no matter how bitter his anger and hatred of being alone; of being *left* alone, burrowed into his brain like a tapeworm hellbent on eating the backs of his eyes. When you had enough time on your hands just to lay and think, without the distraction of beer or television (nothing was on that he could stand on the hospital flatscreen) and to really mull over the feelings and thoughts he had since the split.

He was still thinking it over, when he fell fast asleep, alone, and in the dark, where eventually the dark would remain, but his loneliness would not.

In his dream, he was on a desolate two-lane road that seemed to stretch on forevermore. On either side of him, pine trees some tall enough to pierce the blood-red sky with their spires, lined up like soldiers, blackening the world within. In the darkness between the trunks, he saw red eyes watching him. Thousands of them. Terrified, he remained on the yellow division line, where the passing dashes were to his left and the solid no-pass line was on his right. His left foot struck each dash, his right foot never seeming to stray from the line. His eyes were forward, the road lit by a full moon that was close to the earth, and shining silver like a voodoo woman's crystal ball.

He moved with no destination in mind. He walked with no purpose. He felt like a Phone Crazy from Stephen King's, *Cell*. Just a marching zombie, guided by some sensation or feeling that he had to keep moving. The way that many dreams are; you either cannot move at all, or you must move. Sometimes, choice is a fickle thing in the world of dreams and nightmares, just like in real life.

He walked until he saw something in the road. The light from the moon was obscured by streaks of clouds that had begun to pass overhead. Not too much for it to be difficult to see in the dark, but difficult enough to not see clearly what the thing was. It was a mass in the very center, with many little bits laying around it. Feeling a sense of dread the closer he got to the dark object laying in the road, Clay tried to turn his body and force it to go back. To divert course and go another direction at least, even if it meant going into the woods and dealing with whoever owned those piercing red eyes that looked like burning coals held up in pairs by unseen torches. He tried to cry out, trying to call for help. For someone to help him. His voice was muffled, almost non-existent, as most nightmares rendered the voice of the subconscious.

If I see it, I will scream. I will scream, and will probably die, right here in the road...

Little by little, the fingers of the clouds began to part, spreading to make way for the moon like a magician showing a magic trick. Light trickled through the sky in sharp rays. The lumps in the road were still difficult to comprehend, even from what was now twenty feet away and closing. But it was not impossible to see the crimson stains between Clay and them. Streaks of red appearing almost bright in the moonlight closed the gap, and as Clay walked he realized he was in his hospital onesie, and his bare feet was squishing in the blood. Because that was what it was. Blood.

(So much blood...)

The first lump soon came to pass. Clay passed it, his right foot almost *touching* it, it was so close. He refused to look at it though. The look would mean to succumb to the nightmare; to relive what he had seen. But he knew what it was without having to look. It was a sneaker. A woman's dirty black sneaker purchased from a Wal-Mart probably a year ago. The laces were frayed, and the sole was worn down to practically nothing. This time, it was full of blood. Was the foot still in there? Clay didn't want to think. The tremor he felt in his body did most the thinking for him at this point.

More lumps in the road, more *pieces*. He stepped on one actually, feeling it squish between his toes. Upon touching it, his foot began to itch. He reached down, and found he was able to scratch it, his fingernails scraping streaks of blood from the top of his foot. He approached the largest lump in the road, the moonlight now baring down on the destroyed body, whose face was somehow untouched.

The face, that turned to him paler than the moon itself, and with a sick grin spreading across it, fresh blood trickling out of the corners of her mouth and staining it like clown makeup. She reached out with a hand that was no longer there, the bones of her forearm sticking out shiny in the moonlight like the points of blades.

This time, Clay *did* turn. This time, he was almost able to run, to flee. But something had him by the ankle, and tripped him. He knew it was the hand that was missing. The hand that was now using it's fingers to crawl up his leg, causing his calf and thigh to tickle as it made it's way up to his neck, where it closed around the back. Clay tried to scream, tried to thrash the hand he knew was on him off. But it wouldn't budge. He was slowly waking up, which felt like sludging through maple syrup. He screamed, and thrashed, and screamed some more.

Screamed...

Thrashed...

And finally broke through the veil.

He sat up fast in his hospital bed. His body was *soaked* in sweat like a second layer and turning in the bed, he reached over and turned on the lamp by his bedside. Able to see the jug of water on the nightstand, he took it and filled the plastic cup. He drank as he tried to calm down, that vicious smile still burned in his memory.

As he went to put the cup back on the nightstand, he was able to see where he had been laying. The white sheets were damp, and were stained a hideous yellow color. Touching his back, he felt the hot moisture and brought his fingers back greasy and smelling foul.

Holy shit, that's *what it smells like?* It was the first time Clay was able to actually smell himself, and the scent made him gag.

Disgusted, he called for a nurse to come and change his sheets. He apologized on the intercom, and planned to apologize again when she finished. He got out of bed, and sat on the chair. His back was itchy, now that he had begun to dry off from his sweat-inducing nightmare. Per McFinnigan's direction, he was to shower vigorously after picking up some prescribed body wash and shampoo from the local Walgreens, and then lather himself with a moisturizing lotion that was to help with the glands. But that was still hours away, that was still a *lifetime* away.

His arms and legs were covered in gooseflesh, and now he was just staring at his pillow, which he realized had something else on it other than that yellow smear. There was blood, and a bandage.

He reached around to the back of his head, and touched the tender spot where he had found the wound earlier. It was larger, and more fresh. It felt slimy beneath his fingers and bringing it back, saw that the blood was so dark that it was nearly black.

While the nurse cleaned up, he applied a fresh bandage onto it after washing in the sink. The nurse asked if he wanted help, but he told her she was helping enough. By the time she was finished with fresh sheets on his bed, Clay thanked her and after changing into a new smock that she also provided, returned to it. They were warm, fresh out of the dryer. The wound on the back of his head was covered this time by gauze and tape because the size was now down to the nape of his neck. He didn't dare tell the nurse about how serious it was, and hoped she didn't ask questions when she saw how small the bandage was compared to the wound itself. But then again, perhaps she didn't think too much of it, when she saw the blood on his pillow.

Yeah, of course she didn't. She looked eager to get out of that room that probably reeked of death as soon as she possibly could. She thanked him for thanking her, and then left without another word.

Meanwhile, Clay just laid there in his bed. Unable to sleep. *Unwilling* to, actually. His foot began to itch, and he reached down and began to scratch. He felt a stinging sensation, and wondering what could possibly be wrong now, pulled back the sheets and looked at in in the yellow lamplight.

His big toe was red and emblazoned. The toenail was gone, and in the fleshy pink skin that had been hidden for so long, was yellow and in some areas was squirting in green pus. He found the nail under the sheets, that were now slightly stained. He tossed the nail into the nearby trashcan and applied another fresh bandage around his toe. As he worked he could smell it. He could smell the pus, and the sweat of his feet. He kept his feet outside the sheets to let them get some air, and he turned off the lamp so that he wouldn't see them. Too much was happening in order to sleep tonight, but eventually sleep *did* come back. For only an hour, but at least it came.

When he woke up, he thought he saw a face looking in through his window. He first thought that it should be impossible, given that he was on the third floor. When he went to turn on the lamp, he looked back to see that nothing was there. Just a pale moon, peeking in and probably asking why he was still up.

Nightmare... nightmare...

Ten

After some final X-rays and one last test, Dr. McFinnigan was satisfied with what he saw. "No buildup, and no dots. You are clear of mucus, and for the moment at least, cancer."

"Whoop-ee," Clay said. He didn't mean to sound sarcastic. He was tired. His night in the hospital was less than comforting. He had woken up again around eleven when McFinnigan walked in, craving a cigarette and his own bed, and not necessarily in that order. He just had to agree to the doctor's orders right now and he'd be long gone and hopefully this skin-thing would be a forgotten memory.

Around three o'clock, José came and picked Clay up. With his clothes, Clay received a prescription for some medication to help with his sebaceous glands in order to prevent more buildup of the oil and hopefully, the smell. He was also advised to wash every day and especially his face twice a day with as oil-free of a wash as he could find. Frederick also said to shower at night before bed, so that he would go to bed clean.

"And I would wash your sheets too," he added. "Just to make sure. The best way to tackle this is by good hygiene and less oil. Same goes for your diet, I would suggest less fries and more salads."

Clay said he would, but cigarettes were one thing, fries were another. There were just some things that were nonnegotiable.

"When will I get the bill?" he asked the doctor.

"In about a week or two. Be sure to consult with your boss, you should have some insurance provided by your work center that can make it easier."

Clay and José both thanked the doctor, and together they left to head to Clay's house. At the last minute, José suggested lunch if he was hungry and Clay was happy to take him up on the offer. They stopped at an IHOP and got pancakes and waffles, and then from there they arrived at the apartment where José dropped him off. Then getting into his own car, Clay drove down to the nearest CVS and got his prescription as well as a case of beer for the night. He felt like he deserved it. Tomorrow he would go into work, and shove Dr. McFinnigan's note into Mr. Maisel's pudgy little face.

When he got to his apartment, he was surprised to find it unlocked. Cautious, expecting to catch a robber, he stepped inside and saw Rachel taking a Swiffer Mop to his floor. Seeing her startled him, and he swore in surprise.

"Scared the shit out of me, Rachel," he scolded her.

Rachel Abbas, who had been there for the past hour cleaning his kitchen and scrubbing his shower, toilet, and doing his laundry, stood there almost propped against her Swiffer with a look that clearly said, 'You are welcome.' She was wearing a white tank-top today with a pair of camo shorts that made her dark skin appear to glow. Her hair was in a scrunchie, and her jade necklace hung around her neck. It had been a gift from her father before he passed away about a year ago. She still wore it to this day, apparently.

He also saw that she was still wearing the sandals he had purchased for her birthday, last October when everything seemed to be going good. When everything made sense and didn't make Clay feel like absolute shit about his life.

"Heard you were in the hospital. Decided to stop by and clean up a bit so you could come home to a clean one. I didn't mean to surprise you." She sniffed the air and frowned. "Is that you?"

That got him over his surprise in a hurry and Clay said, "I didn't ask you to come clean up."

"Neither did José. Besides, I needed to return your spare key anyway. My god, Clay... you smell-"

"Like shit? I know." Clay stomped over to the kitchen and poured himself a glass of water. He took some pills out of the bottle he had gotten from CVS and swallowed it with a chug of water. He took deep breaths and held them in before letting them out slowly. He shouldn't be mad at Rachel, and he knew it.

"Well… thanks for coming and… y'know, cleaning. I can actually see the bottom of the sink now."

That got a small smile out of Rachel. She had a pretty smile. An *infectious* smile, Clay once told her. Her teeth were as white as piano keys and looked absolutely perfect. The picture of good orthodontal care. "I'm almost done, then I'll be out of your hair."

"I'll be back," he told her passing by. "Don't go anywhere." As he passed her, he saw her twitch. On his way to the bathroom, he heard her cough.

He showered, and wrapped himself in a towel. Realizing he didn't bring in clean clothes, he had opened the door and asked Rachel to bring him some shorts. She did so without looking, and he thanked her before retreating to the bathroom to dry and change.

When he came back out, she was sitting on one of the barstools by the counter sipping some water. He came around and asked if she wanted a beer. She said no. He took one anyway and went to sit by her. When she sniffed the air, he thought better of it and retreated back to the kitchen to give her space.

"That bad still?" he asked her.

"I'm sorry, it's…" Rachel sighed, unable to come up with something and came clean. "It's pretty bad."

"Yeah, doctor said it was just my skin producing semen or whatever it's called."

"Semen?"

"Uh… something oily that comes on skin… I don't remember the exact name, he said a lot of words I don't know."

Rachel nodded. "What else did he say? José said you also had to have your lungs drained?"

Clay told her everything Dr. McFinnigan had told him. He told her about his skin, and how there had been black mucus in his lungs. "I'm healthy now, just... well, I stink. Plain and simple."

Rachel nodded as if to say, 'Understatement of the year.'

"You know," Clay said. "You could have called me."

"José said you would be home soon. He didn't tell me until today. Besides, I wanted to surprise you."

"Even so, I could have talked you out of it. Now your nose is getting beaten up."

Rachel shrugged. "I'm just glad you are okay."

Clay thought about his toe and the sore on his neck, and pushed the thought into a cluttered corner in his brain. He didn't want to talk about it. The worst was over now, it had to be.

Rachel sighed and said, "Well, I'm glad you're okay, Clay. Really." She then reached into her pocket and placed a single key onto the countertop. She and Clay both stared at it for a long time before Clay finally broke the silence.

"Final nail in the coffin, huh?" he asked. "Truly done and over with."

"Don't think of it that way," Rachel told him. The way she talked reminded him of a mother scolding a child. It made Clay angry with her. But he knew it wasn't right. He could hate this woman and think of every reason to do so. But in the end, this had been a mess the past year or two. He was mostly to blame, and he could admit that. This was what she considered to be the best thing to do, and he knew he loved her enough to do what was right.

Rachel then said, "Just... don't take it too hard, okay? I mean, it's for the best."

The way she said it sounded eerily similar to, 'We both knew it was never going to work, so why fight it?'

"It's just during the last few months," he said to Rachel. He thought about it, wondering if it was even worth bringing up. He decided it was. "I only got through it because of you. I want you to know that at least."

Rachel nodded, a small smile on her lips and tears threatening to spill from her eyes. God, she was trying so hard. "But the worst is over now. We got it figured out. The guy hasn't bothered you since last week, right?"

"Two or three weeks ago. But that's because he's in jail." Clay then thought about the man on the motorcycle and the face he saw last night. The man in question *should* be in jail, but what about his buddies? What about the rest of them.

Rachel said something but Clay didn't catch it. "Sorry, what?"

"I said, don't worry about them, and don't worry about me. You... you just try to get to feeling better."

Clay nodded, now feeling more sad than angry. Regardless of how she worded it, Rachel was driving the final nail into the coffin. Now the coffin known as the relationship between Clayton Couch and Rachel Abbas was going to be pushed into the sea, where it would drift forever until it finally soaked up enough water to sink to the bottom of the ocean. He knew it wasn't him in the coffin, but he felt like he was holding onto it now, allowing himself to be pushed in as well.

"Okay," he eventually said to Rachel. "And... thanks again, for the apartment."

Rachel nodded. She stood up and had raised her arms barely an inch away from her hips as if she was considering hugging him. But either because of the smell or because it would just simply be awkward, she dropped them.

"Well, take care, okay?"

Clay nodded. She gathered her purse and was about to walk out when he called her. He knew the answer already, but he wanted to hear it.

"Did we ever have a chance?"

Rachel pursed her lips. The question had her anchored where she stood, but she could have easily still walked out without answering, the answer was so obvious. In the end, she surprised Clay by saying, "I thought there was a chance. Once."

That answer was almost more painful than what Clay had expected.

"Take care," he told her.

She nodded, and then left. The door closed shut behind her, and Clay was all alone. His pack of beer on the counter, his apartment clean, and his medication in a little white CVS bag nearby.

He became aware that his canvas was stood up again in the back corner. The cotton sheet itself was gone, having been replaced with a new one. His paints were set up along the bar on the bottom, and a cup for water in the leg compartment. She had taken the time to set it back up for him, as if to say, 'You can still paint, even when I'm not around.'

"Not likely…"

Clay wanted to believe it. But he found it difficult. Like a priest questioning his faith in Jesus or a Muslim kid wondering if it was all true as his crazy elder strapped a bomb to his chest while saying 'Praise be to Allah.' To paint would mean to move on. To paint would mean to take up the brush all by himself, and try to move on with his life.

He just didn't feel ready yet. He wasn't ready when the conversation of separation first came up, and he wasn't ready now.

Remembering that he hadn't brushed his teeth yet, Clay drained his one beer and then made his way towards the bathroom to brush. As he passed by the Lady of Thorns, he noticed something and stopped to look at his painting.

Everything was more or less the same, but he noticed that the points on each thorn were red, and on the woman's body were many cuts and nicks as if she had tried to hug it. In fact, it looked like she was trying to now, the way her face was now grimaced, not smiling beautifully like before. Also, there was an intense look in her eyes, as if she was staring directly into Clay's own.

That wasn't right. Clay rubbed his eyes and looked again. The painting was unchanged. Thinking it was just a mistake (or he had just been completely drunk this whole time and never truly noticed), he went to the bathroom and brushed his teeth.

It was while he was brushing his teeth when he felt something hard bouncing around on his tongue. It happened so suddenly he almost swallowed whatever it was. Holding his hand out over the sink, Clay spat into it, letting the foamy toothpaste splatter on his palm and seep between his fingers. The white foam was pink, and as he washed his hand in the running water, Clay saw what he was holding.

It was a molar, glossy eggshell with a silver filling in the center. It had popped right out of his right rear gumline, which he found upon inspecting his teeth with his tongue.

Setting the tooth on the countertop, he stared at it for a long time. How the hell had *that* happen?

He decided he would go into a dentist to take a look at it later when he had time. In the meantime, the molar would remain in a small Ziploc bag which he grabbed from the kitchen before returning to the bathroom. It was strange, feeling the hole in his gums where the tooth had fallen. He felt like a kid again, losing his baby teeth or when he had his wisdom teeth pulled. There was no pain however, and that was at least a little something.

When he returned to the main room of his apartment, he passed by the Lady of Thorns again. This time, the painting looked normal. No stains on the thorns, no blood, no intense glare from the redheaded woman.

Clay needed another beer, but he decided he would wait until the taste of toothpaste left his mouth.

God, I need a cigarette...

Eleven

The next day after a restless night of sleep (made easy enough only because of the shower he took before bed and the gallon of beer he had drank while sitting in his apartment watching television), Clay went to work in the best mood he had been in a long time. He couldn't remember ever being so happy to go to the store. He smiled the whole way to the Team Member Center, as if he had the funniest joke in the world to tell.

Mr. Maisel was there talking to another employee about planograms needing to be set by the end of the week and what she would suggest for the front end, and he covered his face immediately upon Clay's arrival. The girl (poor thing) gagged and practically dry-heaved looking like a bird about to vomit into her chick's mouths to feed them. When he saw the source of the smell, Maisel's eyes burned bright and agitated.

"Couch," he said which told Clay he was in trouble. Last names without 'Mr.' or just 'Clay' *always* meant trouble. Seeing the fat fuck so mad made Clay have to bite his cheek to keep from laughing. He didn't notice that he had in fact bitten a chunk out of his cheek about the size of a dime and barely as thick, the flab of skin now floating in his mouth like an unwanted piece of gum. With a swallow just before meeting his boss, the skin of his cheek was down Clay's gullet and out of mind.

"Morning, Mr. Maisel," Clay said with a gleam in his eye. "How are you today?"

"Don't give me that. What the hell are you doing here?"

"Believe it or not," Clay said flashing Mr. Maisel a big PR smile that would make Jack Torrance proud. "I work here."

"I told you: You are *not* working until you handle that stench. It's worse than ever! Get out of my store!"

Clay pulled out his doctor's note like it was his ace in the hole in a badly losing poker game. He handed it to Mr. Maisel who looked disgusted to touch it since Clay had it in his pocket, but he took it and read it right there. By the look of dismay on his face, Clay knew he was in. He would be back to work, stink or no stink, and Mr. Maisel was looking at him now probably wondering why doctors were even allowed to give notes.

"So," Clay said smiling with good humor. He felt good. Better than he had yesterday anyway. The itching sensation was gone, and he didn't feel greasy nor did he feel sick. He was back at work, and seeing Maisel's face felt invigorating like a rush from a shot of heroine.

"I'm here now. If you haven't given up any shifts, where should I start?"

Shortly after figuring some stuff out, Clay replaced Jourdane Russel in the backroom for the afternoon. Mr. Maisel said he would be working there for the time being until the stink wears out. That was fine with Clay. He would be able to listen to music or an audiobook back here while he backstocked or loaded up flats for the morning's push the next day. Or he could hang out in the cooler or freezer and check dates; the skies were the limit and there would be no one to bother him. Speaking of which, he wouldn't be around anyone customer or employee who would bitch about the smell which apparently according to everyone, was worse. There were times when Clay noticed flies were buzzing around him and he began to carry Fly Spray with him. Still, the little fuckers kept buzzing around as if he smelled like a dead carcass in the road.

Like that one time-

Clay pushed that thought out of his mind. He didn't want to think about that. That was nothing more than a panicked rat inside his skull. As long as it was calm, as long as that rat was *asleep,* it wouldn't freak out and try to gnaw it's way out of his head and causing him to come completely undone. As long as he kept his composure and kept his mind busy, he would be all right.

The isolation in the back room really seemed to help him cope with what had happened, and gave him time to think freely without getting caught with his pants down on the salesfloor when someone wanted to know where the shampoo was despite coming to the grocery department. He could think about Rachel, what he was going to do with his life (work in a fucking retail store for the rest of his life or try to breathe life into his possibly dead hobby), what had happened with the gypsies, everything really.

But he couldn't, because his thoughts would be drowned by his rare 'illness' for lack of a better term, and the goddamn itching which once the high of Maisel's anger died down yesterday, became practically unbearable as the day went on. It had been *tolerable* earlier in the day he returned to work; An annoyance but nothing some ointment and a good long shower after work couldn't help the next. But today, it was practically unbearable.

His whole body felt like it was *covered* in goatheads as if he had been rolling around the desert. His back would itch, and as he scratched, it would not feel satisfied until he was applying enough pressure to break skin. At one point, he went to scratch, found it too slippery, and brought his hand back to see that dead, oily, yellow skin was stuck underneath his fingernails. It got so gross at one point that Clay had to rush to the bathroom to vomit. What had come out was a mixture of green and the McDonalds he had eaten. But still the itching wouldn't stop. Not on his arms, legs, back, *anywhere*. But the worst was by far his head. He would scratch it, careful not to tear off his third bandage this week on the festering wound that didn't seem to be healing any time soon. At some point he was on a ladder down one of the shelf hallways of the backroom scanning some merchandise when he started scratching his head. When he felt the itching cease, he pulled his hand back where he saw something sticking to his oily fingers.

What was stuck was a clump of his brown hair. He reached up to where the itch had occurred and grabbed a small lock of more hair and gently pulled. It gave without too much force and now Clay was staring at an even bigger clump of hair that when mixed with the oil from his scalp and fingers, looked like something you would pull out of a clogged drain. A 'Shower Possum' as his old man used to say. He rushed to the bathroom to look at the top of his head. There wasn't too much hair loss to be noticeable, but he figured it might be best to resist scratching his head for the time being until he got someone to look at it. As if he didn't have enough problems as is. It proved difficult to quit scratching entirely, but he managed.

At some point during the day, what would make him decide to go to Urgent Care the next day, would be when he was scratching his knee through his pantleg, and the fingernail on his middle finger *bending* and coming right off as if he was applying enough force to do so, and without the pain that usually accompanied such a feat. Blood and puss were visible where the nail had been, the tender flesh that was meant to be hidden by concentrated keratin, and the stench was nothing short of noxious. Calling Austin who was in charge for that particular evening, Clay left work and made for Kadlec. They were booked for the rest of the night and wouldn't get to him until possibly midnight, so Clay just went home, his middle finger bandaged heavily, and he went to bed. He had an appointment at seven AM sharp when the receptionist was able to get him in.

Sleep came rare and in-between cycles, with him waking up feeling like insects were crawling all over him he was so itchy. At some point around three AM, he got up and showered really quick to apply some more ointment and get rid of the nasty oil that was now soaking through to his mattress. As he scrubbed using his loofah, he heard something smack the bottom of the tub and when he looked down, he screamed.

A chunk of bloody flesh with black ooze on it sat there, the water causing the blood to stain the tub almost pink. Clay looked to where he had been scrubbing, and saw a chunk of skin missing from his right bicep. Not *huge*, but enough to show the deepest layer of skin. There was blood, and something that looked like black moss underneath his skin. Freaking out, he washed the wound, careful not to use the loofah, but that only seemed to make the wound more raw. The odor was pungent even in the midst of soap and water, and looking closer, Clay screamed at the sight of something *wriggling* in the meat.

There were *maggots* in the muscle of his bicep. Tiny, white, alien-like worms, wriggling, digging.

Feeding.

He got out of the shower and applied a towel to it. Blood and something green soaked through. He applied another bandage to it, and this time went straight to St. Luke's.

On his way to the hospital, he soon came to realize he was being followed. A pair of headlights had stuck behind him since he had left his apartment, and had taken every turn Clay had made, and always kept up at the same exact speed. At first, Clay didn't notice, until he began to realize that the headlights never once changed or went away. Concerned, he had purposely made a wrong turn, taking the long way to the Boise River where the hospital was. The car followed. He switched lanes on the highway, the car behind him did the same. It was mimicking his driving, down to a T. At some point, Clay thought the car would follow him to the hospital and catch him on his way inside. Then he would be beaten up or killed like in the movies.

Stop it, you moron! he chastised himself. *Your nerves are shot and you're being paranoid. You just saw maggots-*

(were they maggots though?)

and you lost a chunk of skin in the shower. Just relax. Just drive, they'll change direction eventually. They just need to go the same way you are going and-

But before he turned on West Jefferson Street coming from North 9th, the car kept moving forward, crossing the intersection and disappearing from view. Clay forced himself to calm down as he continued his route to the hospital.

"What the fuck?" he asked himself out loud. "What the *fuck* is wrong with you? Stupid!

He then realized he had been clenching his teeth the entire time he had been followed, and that his front bottom teeth had *bent* like weathered tombstones by the force and were now rattling in his mouth like a pair of Tic-Tacs.

"Holy-"

Bright lights, a sudden jerk of the car and whiplash. The sound of metal crunching and tires squealing. The Saturn spun around with it's left rear completely crushed. The Chevy pickup truck that had come off on 5th Street to catch up and knock him off course grinded to a halt in front of his car. Clay found himself dazed and his vision blurry. He heard his door open and a pair of rough hands grabbing him, unbuckling him and throwing him into the passenger seat. He then felt his car rolling, slowly, and chugging along like nothing happened. Somewhere, a car honked its horn and in the blurriness, Clay saw the person driving his car as a haze of colors and shapes. He tried to say something, and got slapped. He then felt something hit him square in the forehead hard enough to render his vision black, and Clay knew nothing of what had happened next. Only one distinct thought was there, and it lingered like a festering stink.

Kimberly...

The maggots... they are eating *me...*

(Oh god)

Ooho god...

Twelve

Clay woke up in a hospital bed. An IV tube was stuck into his right forearm, and his bicep and head were heavily bandaged with one of his eyes covered so that he was only able to see through the right. His lazy eye, of course, but at least he was able to see that he was in a hospital.

His neck was in a brace, so it was hard to turn his head, forcing him to use his lazy eye to look around. The effort it took felt excruciating, as if his eye was fighting against something holding it still. A pair of invisible fingers, perhaps. There were windows to his left, letting in some sweet sunshine with the sun itself at midpoint in the sky. Outside, cars were honking their horns and birds were chirping. Still unsure what was going on, Clay felt around with his left hand until he found the intercom, and called for someone to come to his room.

A cute nurse with pasty, white skin and hair as dark as coal came in asking how he was feeling. She had thin cheekbones and pretty blue eyes. She had a surgical mask around her neck, and she pulled it up as she walked in. The stench was probably horrendous at this point, although it might very well just be protocol as far as Clay was concern. Nonetheless, he did not take any offence and went straight to the point.

"What happened?" he asked her.

"You got into a car crash. Those who hit you brought you here. Said you were missing a good chunk of meat from your arm from it. We had to remove shards of glass from your cheeks, and the car looked like it caved in. I saw the aftermath on the news this morning."

"But it wasn't… wait, *who* brought me here?"

"Some teenager, said the crash was his fault. His buddy took his car and he drove you here. Said he's sorry for hitting you and is understanding if you wanna file a report. I have the information with the rest of your stuff. You got hit really hard though, Mr…" She read the sign at the foot of his bed with squinted eyes that gave her a cute expression. "Couch. Interesting name."

"Is the guy still here?" Clay asked her, not caring much for the compliment. He had never liked the fact that his last name was a legit piece of furniture, but that wasn't what was on his mind at the moment. When Nurse Baxter said the guy who hit him was in fact on hospital grounds, he asked her to bring him.

"Are you sure? Baxter inquired. "You should rest."

"I want to see him," Clay insisted. "Bring him in."

About ten minutes later, the kid known as Johnny Burrow, came walking in with the swagger of a rockstar, and the smugness of a cat who ate the canary. Clay felt his body grow rigid and ripple in gooseflesh, and a hot flash of newfound anger brought a redness to his vision.

It was the son of that goddamn gypsy.

The kid was tall, lanky, almost six foot with about a hundred and twenty pounds at most soaking wet. He was wearing dirty sneakers and a jean jacket over an AC/DC shirt that was full of holes and the logo in the front had faded away to practically nothing. He was missing some teeth, and wore a ponytail in his long, brown hair. He smiled sympathetically at Clay, and asked how he was doing. His accent was thick, not quite Hispanic but not quite white. Native American, maybe, but his skin tone was definitely tan because of the genes of his mother and father. Also, it was the eyes, the slight squint, and the raging green of seaweed or rich wheat before the harvest. Full of glee, and enjoyment.

"You hit me," Clay seethed. He felt his rage rising, restricted by his bandages but there, nonetheless. He felt his head begin to itch, but he refused to scratch it. He didn't even want to *blink* with this guy near him.

"I did, yeah," the kid said earnestly. "It was an accident though, I swear. It was my fault though, I'll make it right. My name is Johnny. Johnny Burrow. And you are?"

"You know who I am, you fucking *shit*."

Nurse Baxter looked uncomfortable. "Um, sir?"

"Call the cops," Clay told her. "This fuck hit me on purpose."

"No, I didn't," Johnny said appearing in surprise, his hands up as if Clay were holding a gun at him. Come to think of it, Clay wished he *did* have one right then and there. "It was an accident, I swear. Look, my mother is on her way here. You can talk to her and-"

"I'm not talking to any of you tree-hugging fucks anymore. Lady, this kid and his family had been *stalking* me. He hit me on purpose, and his father actually attacked me not too long ago!"

"I don't understand," Johnny said, the lying little bastard. "Ma'am, what's going on with him?" The nurse was speaking into a radio, calling for someone to come up to room 20B.

"You better go run to mommy, you little prick," Clay said, his voice rising to a scream at a point where spittle was flying past his lips, arcing and slightly discolored pink with blood. "Because when I'm through with you, you'll join your dad in the cell he's in! You are supposed to leave me alone! Look at me, you goddamn pup! DON'T ACT LIKE THAT! *LOOK AT ME* GODDAMMIT!"

At this point, a doctor in a lab coat came in holding a syringe in his hand. Clay was trying to tell the doctor to call the police, that the kid had it out for him, but the doctor and his two assistants held Clay down as he applied the syringe into the IV tube. Clay screamed and kicked, trying to tell the doctors to let him go, but none of them listened. They might as well have been giving medication to an asylum patient. They just watched as he wore himself out, and faded away.

When he next woke up, there were no doctors, and no nurses here. No cops, no one he trusted. He laid there, slowly waking up from his sedated sleep, seeing Johnny Burrow sitting in one of the chairs in the corner of his room, next to his mother. Clay had seen her before during the trial. She had been a woman of few words, her husband doing most of the talking. She was old, Asian-American, her black hair tied in braids and she was wearing many bracelets on her tiny wrists and necklaces on her neck. Necklaces that were consisting of beads, gemstones, and animal bones. She was wearing a poncho of some sort, something an actual Mexican would wear, and she was wearing sandals.

She was grinning at Clay, with a mouth that had no teeth, her gray gums looking like the raw hide of a baby seal or a rhinoceros after taking a bath.

"Hello, Mr. Couch," she said her voice quiet but thick with that accent and lack of teeth. "I am Astrid Burrow, but my friends call me Astrid the Chink. Clayton, right?"

"I know who you are," Clay said. Any haziness from his vision was gone now. His senses sharpened the moment he saw her, and smelled that rank *old* smell she had. The smell of age and cough drops. She didn't seem bothered by his own smell, and that made her distrust her more.

"Good," she said to Clay. "Then we won't waste time."

"Your son-"

"Hit you, by *accident*," Astrid said in an insistent tone that a lawyer might use if his/her client was flapping his gums too much and giving the other party too much unnecessary information.

"It was an accident," she repeated softly. "Just like *you* had an 'accident.'"

Clay motioned his lips. He was thirsty, he craved a cigarette. He felt his heartbeat in his throat; He was scared, and wanted out. He was about to reach for the intercom but Johnny stood and sprinted across the room. He slapped Clay's hand away, and stood by the intercom with his arms crossed. He was not going to be calling the doctors any time soon. Clay stared at him malevolently.

"No one will come until we are done," Astrid the Chink said in a malicious slur. Some spittle had accumulated on her lips, and she licked it away with a bloated tongue. "We paid the nurse outside to make sure no one comes in. That way, we can have a little... talk."

"There is nothing to talk about," Clay said hatefully, frustratedly. "I did everything I could. You guys took a lot already, what more do you people want from me?"

"Justice," Astrid said simply. "Which you didn't get. What my *daughter*, didn't get."

"The court found me not guilty," Clay said desperately. "I had no control, and both cases found that to be true! I could have hit anything at that speed and couldn't have done anything given the time and place."

"Maybe, maybe," Astrid agreed. "But, you didn't make *any* attempt to turn. You didn't even try."

"How would you know?" Clay demanded. "All you wanted to do was sue me for something that was your own daughter's fault."

"Really?" Astrid said with a raised eyebrow.

"Yes. Anyone could have seen that!" Clay snapped. "If your daughter was smart, she wouldn't have run out into the-"

Johnny's fist lashed out like a viper and struck Clay in the left jaw. It hurt like hell and rocked his brain in his skull. He glared angrily at Johnny, who took a pocket knife out of his pants and flicked it open. Clay bared his teeth at him angrily. "Fucking little *shit*," he snarled before the knife poked him in the throat, silencing him.

"Say another word," Johnny dared him.

"Fuck. You." Clay dared with an unblinking eye.

"Johnny," Astrid said without any concern whatsoever. "Calm."

Johnny stood straight up, 'calming,' but he did not put the knife away. He stared at Clay with hateful green eyes. Green, like something out of the Black Lagoon. Or something *in* Clay's own body, which the very thought of made his stomach do a somersault.

"It matters not who did it or not," Astrid said. "In the end, it was you. It was you, and the system calls it 'not guilty.' Out of your control, or so they say. But we know better. You didn't care."

"I did and I *do*," Clay insisted. To him he sounded like he was pleading, which, in a way, he was. He had cared. There wasn't a day it seemed when he couldn't think about the girl. Her red hair... her blood...

"You're lying," Astrid said. "You cannot hide things from me any more than you could hide it from my husband. We can feel the guilt on your heart. We know the truth, just like you do. Even when we tried to show that to everyone, they saw no fault. Blind, all of them! Not even enough to call it 'vehicular manslaughter.' They scoffed and laughed at us, saying you couldn't have done anything and so to sue would be pointless and spitting on our daughter's grave. No. *They* are the ones doing that. Because we are nomads, our daughter did not get the justice she deserved."

"It isn't justice you fucking people want. You want *blood*! Your husband only wanted blood for blood! He wanted someone to pay for Kimberly's *stupidity*."

Again, Johnny placed the knife at Clay's throat. He froze, feeling the blade gently bite into his Adam's apple. He stared up at him defiantly.

"Call my sister that again," Johnny said past clenched teeth. "I *dare* you, motherfucker."

"Your sister," Clay dared a second time, feeling exhilarated as well as angry and scared. Adrenaline was pumping through his veins, his heart slamming against his ribcage like a caged beast. "Was, *stupid*."

Johnny's clenched hand began to tremble, the knuckles going white as he clenched the knife all the tighter. But he didn't stick it into Clay, nor did he say anything. His face only scrunched up and twisted in an attempt to control his bloodlust.

Astrid said nothing this time. Only watched as her son held Clay hostage. After a long pause which felt like hours instead of merely two minutes, she finally spoke up.

"You look really bad, Mr. Couch," she said smiling. She reached into her pocket and picked out a pinch of chewing tobacco from a circular can. She plopped it into her mouth, and proceeded to suck on it with gums alone. "Look like you're… falling apart, so to speak."

Clay stared at her for the longest time. "What are you talking about?"

"Losing hair, losing teeth and nails, and now, your skin is falling apart. Surly you have noticed. Surely, you have gone to this hospital once before for treatment."

Clay felt his stomach curdle inside him. He glanced weakly at his arms, saw the tinge of gray in his pigment. The moisture that clung to where they had laid. "That night-"

Astrid held up a hand. "The doctors all think it's something *natural*. Why wouldn't they? Your wounds here, the result of a bad accident. A bad accident, involving a vehicle that will never be found. You can press charges against my son if you would like, we have prepared for that. But anything else… no one will believe you."

Clay thought of the itching. The sores on the back of his neck. The missing nails on his finger. The teeth falling out. The awful-smelling chunk of flesh that fell off of him last night.

The maggots…

He glared at Johnny, and then stared at Astrid. "What did you do?" he demanded. "What the fuck did you guys do to me?"

"*We,*" Johnny said. Clay could feel his breath pass through the bandages on the left side of his face. "Didn't do anything. We plead our case, and accepted defeat. That is all."

"Can't you see you people are *nuts*?" Clay said. "I didn't do anything! Your fucking sister got in the road!"

"And you ran her over like a *dog,*" Astrid said in a low, dry voice. The hatred in her tone was immeasurable. "Like my boy said, we didn't do anything. We only tried to find justice in our daughter's death."

"So what did you-"

"My husband," Astrid said cutting Clay off with a wave of her hand that was bony, and knotted with arthritis. "Did this to you. You, my *friend*, are not well at all. You, are *rotting* as we speak.

"You, are a *dead man*, and time is slowly catching up to you at last."

Thirteen

Clay couldn't believe his ears. He stared at Astrid for a long time, chewing on what the old woman had said. At some point, Johnny had removed the knife from his throat, and was now picking at his fingernails with the tip. Clay looked at his hands, which were heavily bandaged, and yet were already almost soaked through by yellow oil, and something green and rotten.

She's bullshitting. She's bullshitting, that's all they do.

"I don't under-"

Johnny then reached for Clay's head and grabbed something on the left side. He then pulled hard, and Clay only felt pressure and strain, but no pain. He cried out in horror, as Johnny held in front of his face, his left ear that was mushy and gray, with green goop and congealed blood dripping from the lobe. He dropped it into Clay's lap, and Clay screamed and tried to buck it away with his knee before Johnny slapped him.

"Scream again," Johnny said. "And I'll cut your throat."

"Fuck you!" Clay snapped. He tried to call for help but Johnny covered his mouth. Astrid only stood calmly.

"Johnny, put it away. It's time to go."

Johnny removed his hand before Clay could bite him, shoved his now-closed knife into his pocket and winked at Clay. "See ya." He flipped Clay the bird and went to join his mother's side. By then, the nurse came in, demanding what was going on, and then Clay began to scream.

"They tore my ear off! Help! Please!"

"It fell off," Astrid said now appearing distraught. "We don't know what happened, we were talking and-"

"They're fucking lying!" Clay cried out. "They're trying to kill me! They did this to me!" He pointed at his face, which was now so itchy that he couldn't stand it. He grabbed his bandages and pulled them down and off his face. He felt something slide down his right side, and down his front. When he looked down, he saw blood, and chunks of skin as well as a single lump of cartilage which he realized was his nose. Blood congealed to the point of blackness was now dripping down his face, and now the nurse's screams joined Clay's. Johnny, who was behind the nurse, stuck his fingers into his mouth and forced himself to vomit while Astrid made for the door. The two actors showing off their best past fox smiles.

On her way out, she shot Clay one last look of victory. Her smile clearly saying, "Nice knowing you, Mr. Couch," in that thick, and alien accent.

Doctors came in, held the screaming man down while applying more sedatives to the IV. Clay thrashed and screamed, watching Johnny Burrows step out to catch up with his mother. He saw feathers of hair fluttering around his head, and wherever his head shifted, a moldy brown smear covered the bed. Blood, pus, and whatever horrible things were in him now. Wriggling, hungry.

"You fuckers!" Clay screamed. "I'll kill you! I"LL KILL YOU!"

He screamed this again and again, until his strength gave out, and he was put under again. In a nightmare that just didn't seem to end, he returned to the road, and this time it was day, the time he had run over Kimberly Burrows on Route 199.

He and Rachel were arguing about her father. In the end, it was always about her father. How Clay always hated him, and never really supported her in her time of need. How she had needed him, and he wasn't comforting in the slightest. That he wasn't doing anything right, and making her father worry about his daughter. Clay was furious, his vision red with anger, and he was looking more at her than the road. The road that stretched on forever, and was one of the most dangerous highways in the United States.

Where Kimberly Burrows, age nineteen, tried to cross the road to apparently get her cat that had run out into it. She didn't see the car coming, or at least didn't think to look, and the next thing she knew, Clay's Saturn *pulverized* her at full-speed. No brakes, no turning of the wheel, just there one moment and the next, gone.

The first thing that struck Clay was the force. The Saturn struck Kimberly so hard that she flipped and crashed against the windshield and spun in the air like she was doing a cartwheel. By then her legs had been shattered by the Saturn's bumper and her body had *ruptured* from the force of the impact. When she struck the ground, her body was split with every bone broken and her guts squirming to escape her belly. Her dirty white sneakers had gone sailing across the highway, splattering the asphalt with blood. Her head had cracked open too like a watermelon, spilling brains and blood all over the division line. By the time Clay realized he had hit something, he stopped the car about a hundred feet away from where Kimberly had landed, both he and Rachel being thrown forward by the momentum.

They would both suffer aching backs and Rachel in particular would deal with a knot on her forehead from when she smacked the dashboard on impact. Clay then got out, seeing the front of his Saturn crumpled and the windshield cracked with some blood spatter. He turned and hurried to the woman he hit, screaming at Rachel to quit screaming and to call 911. Some cars slowed and the one coming down the highway towards them stopped, turning so that he blocked the way so that no one would hit them, emergency lights flashing in the process. By the time the driver of the SUV, a 98-year old man with white hair and an Indiana Jones fedora got out to see what had happened, Clay had reached Kimberly-

-who died quickly of her injuries, her body a deflating mass and her limbs mangled and sticking in unnatural angles with some having bones sticking out. Clean and white, with very little blood. Her skull an opened jar, her memories leaking all over the asphalt. He was screaming at her, telling her to look at him, but those almond-shaped green eyes only stared up at the blue sky above. Not seeing anything, not anymore. Her red hair, which had been loose and flowing, collected the blood and the brains, turning them a darker shade of crimson, which would stick with Clay for a long, long time.

When the ambulance came and took her away, Clay had already met Mr. Gaston Burrows, an older man with gray hair in a braid and wearing thick hoop earrings on each ear. Distraught and horrified by the mangled remains of his daughter, he *howled* hoarsely into the sky while his wife and son hung back crying in each other's arms. The whole community of gypsies who had been camping out within the tree line on this particular day, stared somberly at the horror before them. They all got onto their bikes and old trucks, and followed Clay and Rachel to the nearest hospital while the ambulance took the dead body away.

Cops asked many questions. Did Clay see her? Did she walk out? They also talked to Kimberly's family, who had forgotten all about the black cat Sebastian who ran out to join the creatures of the wood. At first, Mr. Burrows was silent, already grieving the loss of his daughter even three days spending at the Asante Medical Center, where Kimberly's body was being processed. Preparations for the funeral were made, and Clay, apologizing again to the Burrows, left with Rachel back to Boise. Neither of them had talked since the accident. There seemed nothing to talk about.

Until, Mr. Burrows and his gypsy group, the Flosvita Family, came to Boise, and demanded retribution.

The threats came first. Telling Clay and his whore of a girlfriend to kill themselves. Then the harassment at work or in public. When Clay finally confronted the Burrows, they said they wanted him to pay for what he had done to their daughter, and demanded to take it to court. The State of Idaho had already made their decision, after checking all the evidence including the speed he had been going when Kimberly stepped out, they found him not guilty of murder, but of manslaughter. Just a fine, no jailtime. So, then Mr. Burrows took him to Civil Court for one last effort for retribution. In the end, the evidence presented showed Clay had no control over what had happened, and he was not pressed with anything and the Burrows didn't receive a single penny.

This made them *furious*. Because of this, Clay found it necessary to request a restraining order against Mr. Burrows in particular. He was the one who would follow Clay and Rachel the most, and would make threatening gestures.

The last straw, was when Rachel and Clay had come out of the Barbacoa Grill. They had gone out on one last date, to finally decide that they were done. Too much had happened between them, and the accident only made them stretch further apart. Clay was devastated with the accident, and took no comfort from Rachel. He had gone numb. Even when he knew it wasn't his fault, he felt responsible since he had been behind the wheel. That only pushed Rachel further back, and when she finally said she wanted this to be over, he didn't even put up a fight. Only watched her get up to wash up while he paid the bill.

The night before, he had finished his painting of Lady of Thorns. He had started it long ago, working on the flower and then the person herself. He wanted it to be a girl, a girl in a beautiful crimson dress. In the end, he painted the face he remembered the most. Kimberly Burrows, so that she would remain a part of him forever. It felt right to him, to paint her in a way that made her feel like her spirit really was around. It had brought Clay comfort. Ever since then, he couldn't pick up a brush again. It had been his last painting, and Rachel, who already saw his paintings as a fickle hobby anyway, pitied him.

It was all he could think about anymore. That was why he drank so much now, why at the grill, he had drank a *lot* during dinner. Rachel just couldn't take it anymore, and it had been placed the second-to-last nail into the coffin. He had hammered it in, with bottles of whiskey and beer. And he relished every moment of hammering that nail in, and he knew it from the bottom of his heart.

Mr. Burrows had met them outside the grill on their way out. Clay was drunk, and needed help from Rachel to get to the car that she would be driving. His Saturn was still getting fixed up by José. Coming up from behind, Burrows had punched Clay in the back of the head, sending the man sprawling to the ground. Mr. Burrows then got on top of him, and began to choke Clay while Rachel tried to pull him off. There was rum on his breath as he screamed into Clay's face, his fingers coiling tighter around his jugular and causing Clay to see stars as he choked.

"Die, damn you!" he croaked/slurred at his prey. His eyes reminded Clay of a pig going berserk on the farm. Mom screaming at him to get out of the pen, but it was those muddy red eyes that made Clay break for the fence line and get free of the squealing berserker. "I want you to die! I want you to *rot*! Rot in Hell! *Putredine*! *Putredine*!"

Clay had managed to knee the old man in the groin and shove him off, Rachel and a few bystanders had already called the police. Burrows was not done, and actually lunged for Clay's legs as he was getting up, pulling him back down. All the while cursing his name, hitting him, and receiving blows from Clay who in the end, managed to keep the old man down. His nose had been bloodied and he would suffer a concussion. Still, the old man fought even as Clay held him down by the shoulders, still reaching for him, still cursing him, still telling him to die.

The police came, picked Burrows up, and locked him away for assault and battery against a restraining order. The man didn't look to upset being taken away, even as Clay felt the old man's green eyes glaring at him. They had appeared to be glowing that night, Clay would have sworn on his grave he thought he saw that, sobering from his drink or not.

    Those last two words were the only thing he heard from Mr. Burrows since. A shine from Burrows' forehead as if he wore a diamond headpiece from some pagan land far, far away. *Putredine, putredine, putredine...*

Fourteen

Clay awoke strapped to a gurney in a padded room. He was covered in more bandages, and he felt moist and sticky with oil and puss. He felt like an explorer who had been sitting in his own sweat in a tropic jungle for weeks, maybe even months. Streaks of white and green slithered down his legs, and in his left arm the itching was horrible. He called out for someone to come and scratch him, but no one did. He was alone in the dark, probably in some other nightmarish dream caused by the sedatives. His stomach hurt, and-

A throbbing pain seemed to grab it like an iron fist. It rumbled in his gut, and he passed gas that felt moist and *chunky*. He cried out again, feeling his bowels let go and he felt something *wriggling* beneath him. He felt his belly rumbling more, and he came to realize that it was thrashing as well. In fact, looking down at his stomach, he could see it moving as if something was pushing out from within like an alien from one of those Sigourney Weaver films. He cried out. He *screamed*. The biting sensation wouldn't stop, the itching, and the spewing of pus tricking down his arms and shit settling in his pants as something wriggled in it.

Finally, he felt something poke *through* his belly, and coming out of his stomach through a slit that had been chewed through, was a rat. He screamed at the sight of it as it burrowed out. He felt the movement beneath him shift, and he felt the slimy wet body of another rat sliding out and dropping to the floor, it's loathsome body slithering as it padded away. He cried out for someone to come and save him, but no one come. His only company were the rats, covered in blood and grime and squeaking in glutenous greed like the maggots under his skin.

Another time he woke up, he saw Kimberly in the road again, this time alive despite having fallen apart and was now crawling towards him. He was still strapped to a gurney on the

road and was unable to wriggle free or escape as she climbed up using her crooked arms and pulled herself onto the gurney with him. A female Crooked Man, who walked a crooked mile. Her face was a mask of crimson, what little paleness could be seen making her appear ghostly. She had seized him by the throat, and he woke up again screaming that he couldn't breathe. He was in some sort of metal machine, and someone pulled him out and the glare of overhead lights blinded him. A prick in his left arm, and he had gone under again. Under the depths of darkness, as if he were in an ocean with unseen creatures swimming around him, circling him, trying to determine whether he was no threat, or even food just as the maggots in his arm had decided.

Had there been maggots at all though? He asked himself this while he was in Rachel's apartment, back when they had first started dating. The walls were covering with pictures of her family, including some souvenirs from their time in Haiti on many decorative shelves. She was on the couch, naked after they had made love. The couch had been their agreed place after one morning when she had come out to find him making breakfast. He had gotten up early to make her favorite; French Toast with maple bacon. He had surprised her, and she had returned the favor. Whenever this sort of thing happened, it played out in Clay's mind like that of a Clive Barker novel. In fact, along with this whole nightmare of the past week or so,

(*Was* it a week? He couldn't tell anymore)

Clay's current predicament was almost *exactly* like that of a Clive Barker novel. Not just the sex part, but the horror that went along with it.

Rachel was lying gracefully on the couch naked as the goddess Venus, her dark skin healthy and well-cared for. Her long legs, her dark hair let loose to fall around her shoulders, that infectious smile of hers as Clay got up to grab the burning French Toast off the stove. She watched him, her dark eyes lingering on his pale and (in his opinion) nonexistent ass.

He had saved what was left of the French Toast, and turned to tell Rachel something. In the real world, in the past so to speak, he would be telling her about this gig he had received from Fiverr. Some new author in Washington was asking for a cover for a new novel he was working on; a Craig Miller from Pasco who was writing one under the pen name Joe Gaiden. Clay had never been a *huge* reader since he had graduated, but when the client pitched the idea for the book cover he wanted, Clay was ecstatic. It sounded like a really good one, a field of corn with a red sky like that of a sunset with something hidden within the rows. He said it was to be a horror novel, and he would like the eyes that would be the only thing seen of the creature as a pair of huge, yellow, cat-like eyes. Clay had responded to it the night before, and he wanted to talk to Rachel about it. He always told her about what painting he had in mind both as recreational and as business.

But this was of course another dream, another nightmare, and in this one, that didn't play out like it had in the past. When he looked at Rachel, she was no longer laying gracefully with that smile on her big and luscious lips. In fact, her lips were practically nonexistent. She was now standing before him, having gotten up and crept up behind him as silently as a wraith. Her hair was gone, her skin (what was left of it) pulled taunt over her bones. Her eyes were dark and hollow, as if birds had come to pick them clean, leaving only the worm that was now wriggling in her left socket. Her fingers, long and boney reached out and seized him by his cock. He gasped out as her other hand (this one having no skin at all, only bones covered in green slime) curled around his throat. He gasped out as her touch stole the breath out of him, and his dick was being crushed by fingers that shouldn't have any strength in them at all.

Behind Rachel, a disfigured Kimberly was holding her from behind, her broken arms around Rachel's naked waist and her bloodied face grinning at Clay. She placed a finger up to her lips, as if telling Clay not to discuss a dark secret held between them and with the same hand, reached up and caressed Rachel's left breast. The Rachel-thing sighed, and then Clay felt something wet on his groin and he happened to look down. His penis had *liquified*, bursting and spilling blood and congealed green jelly all over Rachel's fingers. He had cried out this time, because Rachel had let him go, let him fall to the floor and watch in horror as a crusty yellow tongue came out of Rachel's skeletal mouth and began to lick her fingers as if she was licking maple syrup.

In the living room, behind the two women, stood Gaston and Astrid, both standing side by side like that of an American Gothic painting Clay had referenced in what few college courses he had taken. All that was missing was the pitchfork, and the two were staring at Clay with gleeful delight as his ex-girlfriend descended upon him again with boney teeth and a thirst for his blood.

The last thing he would remember before waking up for real, was when he was in the hospital bed. Maggots and worms were burrowing into his skin, wriggling all over his body with crows perched on each of his shoulders. He cried out as they dug their beaks into his ears, digging out something that was wriggling within as if his head was really a nest full of wasps. He thought of meth-heads and their belief that their own heads were full of bugs and he cried out as his body tickled and itched all over as the worms and maggots bit into him and the crows dug into his ears making all sound seem muffled or scraped by their harrowing cries.

Standing before him at the foot of the bed, was Johnny Burrows and another man, this one being the biker guy from when Clay had gotten kicked out of his work the first day. Between them, holding him up by under the armpits, was Kimberly as if they were supporting the dead girl as she tried to relearn how to walk again. She was smiling again, holding something in her bloody hands. When Clay looked at them, he saw two things. One, Kimberly didn't have her lower half, and strands of intestines were dangling out of her like tube eels. The second, was what was in her actual hands, which was the head of Rachel's father, Jeremy Abbas. The black man's face was crusty and cracked as if he were made of leather instead of human skin, and his eyes were missing. His mouth missing his teeth since he wasn't wearing his dentures (no need to wear them now, Clay's mind supposed), had been stuffed with cotton like what morticians do before a burial. This bitch had gotten her family to dig up Rachel's grave and disturbed her father's body. *Desecrated* his burial site like it was a garden full of a weeds!

"Just doing what you did," Kimberly explained as if she was a kid rationalizing kicking a cat to death just because she saw her father doing it. "Spitting on his grave. Just like you are doing to mine."

"But I didn't!" Clay cried out. "Not a day goes by when I don't think about you! For godssakes I even painted a memorial for you because in the end I feel guilty! I feel guilty! I admit it!"

"Guilty enough to forget the other dead," she muttered. Her eyes, green and almost on fire by the looks of it, gave the head a toss and it landed in Clay's lap among the bugs. They began to work on him just as they were working on Clay. A worm slithered into Jeremy's mouth, writhing contentedly against the cotton ball the mortician had placed there before the old man's burial.

"Guilty enough to leave the living empty. You killed me. And you will pay. I look forward to having you near so I can thank you *personally.*"

This time, Kimberly was the one decomposing. Her skin seemed to liquify, first growing moss on the side of her face like Gage from Pet Semetary. (*You fucked me once, did you not think I would come back and fuck with you?*) Another book Clay had forgotten about until now. Then Kimberly's cheeks seemed to fall away, and her clothes fella way as her body shrank and turned to bones. Then to ash, until she was nothing more than a pile between Johnny and his buddy. The two of them smiled like ancient gods watching the demise of a pagan pastor who had defied them. Clay screamed and jerked and twisted to try to break free but iron-hands kept him down. Gaston and Astrid Burrows, Maisel, Rachel, everyone held him down, letting the insects feed. They only laughed as he begged. Only watched as he was feasted upon by the dead. His cries ignored, and they too watched as the crows finally pierced through the side of his skull, and began to pick at his rotting brain.

"Let me out!" he screamed to someone beyond the veil, someone who could hear him within the depths of his nightmare. "Let me out! Someone! Save me! Please!"

The gods only laughed, the puny mortal entertaining their savagery.

"Please…"

Save me…

Fifteen

Clay had woken a couple of times since those specific trips, but they were all hazy as if he was underwater the entire time, his nose barely breaking the surface and so allowing himself to breathe. He sometimes saw bright lights, sometimes he saw men in white coats. Sometimes he thought he heard Rachel's voice somewhere in the void. It was the fifth or sixth time he woke up, when he realized he was *truly* awake, and Clay grasped onto the life preserver known as that wakefulness and pulled himself out of the dark sea.

He was in a hospital bed again, but this time the room was very different. It was sealed without any window and the door had no interior handle. The walls were pleasant and clean, and there was a television with a cage around it except for a hole around the screen. The bed itself was a Stryker FL28C though Clay only knew that it was comfy and not what the name was. He was in a smock again, and the sheets were unfortunately soiled by the oil and clumps of rotted and rotting skin residue.

His rotting skin, that he began to notice was very different. His arm was no longer in a cast, but it didn't look dry or fragile. On his bicep, where the chunk of meat had presumably been lost, it appeared to have been filled with new skin that had solidified with stitches around the edges. It was a lot pinker than his actual skin, more *fresh* so to speak. They had given him a skin graft.

Looking at his hand, the fingernail was still gone but it looked to have healed over completely with new scar tissue, looking more like a finger condom some chefs use when they have a cut on their finger so they could still cook. He felt on the back of his head and felt new skin where the sore had been. Even the new skin itself felt brand new, not oily or dry like the rest of him. Instead, it was smooth, cool to the touch, almost like the scar tissue one would see under a disposed scab. He touched his head that had been injured in the crash. There were some stitches in his forehead and bottom lip, and his head had been shaven (or at least he *hoped* it had been shaved) and another set of stiches made a 'c' on the side of the parietal cap.

Other than that, he felt healthy. His mouth was dry and his head felt like they had taken his brain out and filled it with lead weights, but other than that he felt fine. He was hungry, but there was no intercom button for him to summon someone. He at the very least would have liked a mirror to see how he looked. He thought of touching his nose, his ear or lack thereof, but didn't have the guts to do it. In truth, he was afraid to see if both were truly gone. He wanted to hold onto the hope that both incidents had been his many nightmarish hallucinations. As terrible as they were, they would bring more comfort than the truth, should the truth be valid. Ignorance was bliss, and Clay was willing to be as ignorant as possible until he absolutely *had* to face it.

There was something else too... something else Clay was bothered by, but his head was so muddled he couldn't think of it. Best to let it go. After all, ignorance was bliss, right?

On the nightstand next to him were flowers in a plastic vase, a bunch which was bought at some Walmart or cheap shop, but still pretty, nonetheless. Beside the vase were a bunch of cards stood next to it. Clay reached over and grabbing the nearest one that had a picture of a cat in bed with a thermometer in its mouth, he read it.

"Get well soon!" the card itself read, with a space between it and "You are in our prayers!" that was at the bottom. Between the two lines, written in José's handwriting, Clay read out loud what his friend had to say to him. His own voice sounded hoarse and unlike him.

"Clay, heard you were hospitalized again, get well soon! – Josie." How long had it been since he had called José that just to tease him? Felt like an eternity ago.

The next card, this one with Batman in a hospital room in a full body cast while Superman stood next to his bed with an armful of flowers and a look of serene apology all over his face. This one said, "Sorry you aren't well." on the front. Inside was completely blank except for a Batman symbol on the left.

On the right, Clay recognized Rachel's handwriting. A hitch came up in his chest and he felt a sharp pain in his heart. Still, he read aloud, "Can't believe you are in the hospital again. Please call me when you get a chance. Love, Rachel."

That last part made him smile. She still cared for him. He supposed at one point she had every reason not to worry about him anymore, but the fact that she had dropped this off meant she cared a little. The fact that she wanted him to call meant the world to him, and Clay felt a million times better. At least she wasn't a hallucination. As bad as their relationship had turned out, she was still *real*. She was still very much real, and very much important to him.

"Love you too," he murmured.

About a half hour later, someone came into his room. It was none other than Dr. Frederick McFinnigan, wearing his usual doctor's coat and carrying with him a tray of food. A bowl of oatmeal, a side of toast, a glass of what looked like cranberry juice, and an orange. He smiled at Clay and took a seat in a chair that he pulled to the bedside with his foot.

"How are you today?" he asked Clay. "Long time no see."

"No kidding. What happened?" Clay asked. His head still felt heavy, and whenever he tried to think about what had happened before the numerous nightmares and horrors, it came out as muffled as if his brain was taking the day off. He didn't necessarily think that was a bad thing however.

"You had an accident," Henson said now peeling the orange that in his hand looked like a miniature sun held in the hands of some pagan and ancient god. He peeled it, and set aside pieces of the fruit so that Clay could just eat. "Car crash. You were brought here and we took you in. It was a good thing too. You proved to have more problems than just the accident, including your skin issue."

Clay thought about his nose and ear, but didn't want to ask about it, in case that hadn't been real at all. "But, everything is okay?"

"Mostly." McFinnigan offered Clay a spoon, and while he ate said, "You had an accident about four weeks ago. We thought you got away with minor bruising and some broken ribs, but you also suffered a major concussion. Hungry?"

Clay nodded, a mouthful of creamy oatmeal and chunks of fruit. He had drunk the juice first, asked if there was water, and like a magician Dr. McFinnigan took out a bottle of Desani water. Clay accepted, and drank it all in three long gulps.

As he continued to eat, Frederick took out a file he had on a clipboard that had been hidden beneath the tray. He opened it and pulled out a picture of what looked like a brain. Clay thought it reminded him of a cover from a band he used to like but he couldn't remember what. The brain was smaller than the picture next to it, and there was something thick on the left hemisphere.

"We had to take an MRI because of some symptoms you had been showing. See these spots here?"

He pointed at some circles drawn on spots where it looked like the brain had gone red. There was a big spot on the left hemisphere as mentioned before, but there were two smaller ones on the right. There was also some red color-coding on the frontal lobes.

"You smacked the side of your head and mashed it pretty good. This is the worst I've ever seen from a car crash victim, but if you look at the smaller spots it looks like it heavily damaged some other parts including in the center of the temporal lobe. In fact, see the holes here?" He pulled out a picture of a frontal picture of the brain. "It is similar in looks of an Alzheimer patient."

"What does that mean?" Clay asked.

"Means your brain is hurt, but it is healing. If you look at this one," Frederick pulled up another photo of an otherwise similar brain but with less spots on the main photo. "It is healing. The damage to the temporal lobe is still there, but that should heal as well. Temporary loss of some memories are prominent, but like time, it will all come back."

"That's a relief."

"As for the damage on your body from the crash, as you can see, you have received skin grafts. It'll look like that for a while until it heals to your skin. Which, by the way, is still producing a helluva lot of sebum."

"The oil?" Clay asked around a mouthful of oranges. They tasted sweet on his tongue, and he felt energized upon eating them. It was a good thing too, since he was still missing some teeth. Probably from the crash though. He was looking at his bed, which was almost soaked with oil. The memory of his first visit here was coming back. It made him think of his night in the shower, and then of his nose and ear again. Had it all been real though? Four weeks... it felt like only two days.

Frederick McFinnigan answered, "Yeah. It's causing a lot of tissue damage, which was no doubt more agitated by the car crash. We took some samples, but only came up with dead skin cells. Nothing *terrible*, mind you, but definitely something to look out for."

Remembering something, Clay asked Dr. Henson what he thought at the last moment to be a silly question. "Was there... anything inside of me?" Clay asked touching his belly. He remembered pain, something moving...

"Like what?" the doctor asked.

"I dunno... *something*."

"Nope," Frederick said smiling and putting the file away. "Nothing major anyway."

"Nothing... alive?"

The smile went away. "What do you mean?"

"Nothing, I just... I remembered having dreams... bugs on me..."

Frederick nodded sympathetically. "That happens when we use sedatives and Remifentanil during surgery. Causes bad dreams at times."

Clay nodded, understanding, but still felt as if something was crawling beneath his skin. Small, white, wriggling alien-like creatures. He suppressed a shudder. He remembered the face of a woman with red hair... and a man and woman... A boy too now that he thought of it. But their faces were blurry, their voices muffled.

Dr. McFinnigan checked his watch. "We are gonna have you stay here for two more days and do a final check on the last. If your brain shows no worse activity, you'll be good to head home. There are some pills on that tray there I want you to take."

"Pills?"

"It's to help with your skin and your surgery. One of them is Omega-3 vitamins. For your brain."

Clay said he understood, and downed them with another bottle of water. He felt so thirsty it almost drove him insane when he felt no relief from the beverage. Then he got to work on his toast just as Frederick said he would check in on him later. He did so later, checked his heart rate and helped Clay clean off some buildup oil on his body, and then left him to rest.

And so, Clay stayed for another two days. He had no nightmares, and no knowledge that anything was still terribly wrong. In fact, like most dreams, the nightmares he had before coming out of sleep like a baby being born, had all been forgotten. There was no panic in Clay's mind, no reason to be. He had the nagging feeling that he *should* be, but that made him feel like a dog that had been beaten his whole life and is afraid to fall asleep under the watchful eyes of the hospital staff.

He also avoided looking at any mirror, just for good measure. He didn't want to face anything yet, and besides, if no mirror was offered in the first place, then there was no reason for concern, right? Even the hospital bathroom had no mirror, and than in of itself brought a sort of comfort to him.

Maybe so those in the loony house wouldn't laugh at their own reflection.

Clay laughed bitterly, unconsciously, at such a thought.

Whenever he tried to think what he might be forgetting, the answer felt so close; right on the tip of his tongue like a word one knows and had said numerous times but in the heat of the moment their brain fails them. In the end, there seemed nothing left to do but to accept. Accept, and rest. If McFinnigan said all was well, or *should* be well, then he had to be right. He was a doctor, after all. There was nothing wrong with him. Some tissue and brain damage, but nothing else.

No chunks of flesh falling away.

No maggots...

No dead women haunting him.

He had called Rachel to come pick him up when he was told he could go. When he had all of his things, his medication and everything, he was rolled out to see Rachel waiting for him in her 1999 Honda Civic. He was about to say something when she came up and hugged him. His arm had been rebandaged for the skin grafts but other than that, he was unhurt. He hugged her back, feeling relieved that she was there. He needed this. He needed her.

"You okay?" she asked him after letting go.

"Hungry more than anything," he told her.

"Then let's grab something and get you home." Rachel opened the passenger side door for him, and Clay got in. This was the familiar scent that brought back some memories. He and her on dates, going out to see a movie, having sex on the bank of some river with only the moon shining overhead. The whole fighting/arguing stage that led to them splitting. He felt both joy and sadness at the same time as he buckled up. Glad to just be somewhere familiar, somewhere that felt *safe*.

"I don't remember much because of the crash," Clay said. "But... Rachel? I'm sorry, for how I was in the relationship."

Rachel looked stunned. Had he never apologized for his behavior before? She smiled and playfully (and *thankfully* not so hard), patted him on the shoulder. "Let's go feed you. Then we need to make some phone calls. The hospital gave me the numbers of the people who got you in the hospital, said they could pay for your car and your bills."

Upon saying this, Rachel didn't look too happy. In fact, she had turned her car on almost aggressively enough to convince Clay that she might break her key in the ignition.

He asked her who it was.

"The Burrows," she told him. "In fact, they left something for me when I came to see you. You were asleep and no one could come in. José had come too, left you a card."

"I saw them all," Clay said smiling. They were all in a small plastic bag with some of his other belongings. His keys, his wallet, and his medication just to name a few. The Burrows though...

Rachel smiled. "Good. The Burrows left me information in a card of their own. I'll show you when we get to your apartment. I left it there."

"How did you get in?" Clay asked as they started to pull out of their parking spot. "You don't have a key, do you?"

"You remember," Rachel said smiling. She was happy he was remembering some things. "I borrowed one from José. You never told me he had one."

"Did he have one?"

Rachel chuckled. "Don't worry. Food first, details later."

As they pulled out, something caught Clay's eye on their way out of the hospital parking lot. There were two Harley Davidsons parked near the exit where there was a sign that declared it. There was a man and a boy standing between them, staring at the passing Honda. The man, Clay recognized immediately. Cowboy boots, leather jacket, dark and long hair. The boy had a jean jacket on and was wearing a baseball cap. When they passed by, Clay saw that both of them were smiling, and the boy was tapping his wrist with his index finger as if he was asking for the time.

Immediately, Clay felt sick. He didn't understand why, but he knew in his heart that those men, were bad news. When Rachel asked if he was okay, that he looked pale (-er), he could only answer one way.

"I... I don't know..."

Sixteen

When they had finally reached the apartment, Rachel was in tears because of the smell. Apparently, it had gotten worse since they left the hospital. That would explain why they had gone through the drive-thru of the nearby McDonalds where Clay gorged himself with the cheeseburger meal and a chocolate shake, on top of a ten-piece Spicy McNuggets. Rachel only had a Coke and small fry, no doubt having lost her appetite. They had discarded their trash in the bin outside the apartments and went inside.

Rachel then 'instructed' Clay to shower and she would be waiting for him in the living room. Her instruction sounded more like a demand, but Clay wasn't going to argue. He had been unable to shower for over a month now, and felt as gross as he smelled. The shower felt nice and refreshing, but the new skin grafts on his arm and the back of his neck felt cold and clammy, as if they were things that didn't belong; Or simply didn't like touching his own putrid skin.

After he was done, he finally looked at himself in the mirror. A look of dismay was on the haggard and almost droopy face that was ashen and almost gray in color, save for a few dark spots where yellow sebum had saturated on his brow and cheeks. He was in fact missing his nose and his ear, just as Dr. McFinnigan had finally told him the day he was leaving. The guy thought Clay had known since he never asked for a mirror, and Clay was understanding. It still shook him that his nose, a prominent part of a person's face was *gone*. That had not been a hallucination, and the understanding of this didn't fill Clay with dread or disgust. Just a general acceptance that was far easier than he had expected.

Just need the other ear gone and I'll look like a victim of a bad fire, he thought bemusedly. He touched his cheeks, felt them flabby and almost spongey. They seemed to hang on his skull like moss, the bags under his eyes from lack of sleep making him look like some ancient Draugr from a Nordic tomb, or what maybe a mummy looked like under the bandages after only a few weeks in an Egyptian tomb.

He tried to smile, saw that he was missing some teeth still. McFinnigan had also said that ears and noses couldn't be replaced, and for some reason the *original* nose and ear were unable to be sewn back on.

"They lost a lot of mass, which was strange. Plus it looked terribly infected and so to put it on you would have caused more harm than good. It isn't nearly as bad as you think. I'm sorry I didn't tell you earlier, I swear to god I thought you knew."

Clay still didn't blame the guy, even as he looked at the way his nose appeared skeletal and his face ghostly. Even his sunken, yellow cheeks looked *spongey*, and poking at one with his finger, it *still* felt wet and mushy, as if he hadn't dried off at all despite having just dried and had been standing at this mirror for a good ten maybe fifteen minutes.

How long is this going to last? he asked himself.

When he came back out Rachel had some insurance documents laid out on the counter. She had already called the Burrows it seemed, because she hung up when he came in and said, "You look better."

"Do I smell better?" he asked with a slight smile which he regretted given the grimace Rachel expressed. He wondered if he looked frightening to her. If that was the case, she was a trooper for sticking with him.

"Well," she managed. "You still stink."

"Thanks," he said sarcastically.

"Not terribly though, not as bad as earlier, I promise."

"Well, that's good."

"The Burrows asked for you to call soon, but I said that we would just meet with them later."

"Okay... so what did they have to say?"

"That they were sorry again and that they would make up for it. Too late to make up giving the hell they put you through."

"Hell?"

"Don't you remember?"

"I remember *something*..." He was now looking towards the hallway, and he saw his Lady of Thorns painting. "... a highway... some girl..."

Rachel nodded. "Do you remember the trial? Mr. Burrows when he attacked you?"

Clay began to remember an old man attacking him outside some restaurant. There were cops. And that word... what had the man said?

Rachel reached over some paperwork and brought out a card. "I took this out of your room when I saw it, thought it would upset you. But maybe you should..."

Clay took it, and read it over once. This card had filled him with dread the moment he grabbed it, as if just touching it made him sick. Reading it had been far, far worse.

It was a card with a bushel of roses on the front, and on the inside the roses were in the hand of that of an old man with a bandage over his head. He was smiling and the caption above it read "Thinking of you always. Get well soon!"

On the bottom, written in way too good of cursive, was the following.

Hello, Mr. Couch,

We hope you are on the road to recovery faster than ever. We pray every day for God to heal you, and we have received word that you should be leaving soon. We wish you the best of luck, and hope you send word to us soon.

As for your car, do not worry. We will compensate for the accident. We have no insurance so there is no need to

bother whoever you use. We will also pay for your recent
hospital visit since in the end the accident was our son's fault.
     Warm regards,

     Astrid.

     P.S. It would be wise to get plenty of rest as you can.
For as soon as you step out of the hospital, it is up to you to <u>stay</u>
out. Keep in good health, eat healthy, and take your medicine.

     The familiar name brought it all back. The name brought
up the symptoms. The last line of the note, made Clay rush to
the kitchen sink to throw up. With his McDonalds collected in
half-digested chunks in the sink, he was staring at the card with
newfound horror. Like a flood everything came back, starting
with the disaster on Route 199.Rachelwas saying something,
probably asking Clay if he was okay. But he wasn't. He was far
from okay, and she was far, far away.
     Everything, fell right into place like a puzzle that hadn't
been completed in so long until now. All the pieces just clicked
right in, and the picture was clear as mud.
     The note, while appearing sweet and nonthreatening,
filled Clay with absolute dread. In fact, he hadn't even thought
about the Burrows and who they were until Rachel brought
them up. The letter was more than a 'get well soon' card. It was
a warning. They weren't done with him yet. Standing in his
kitchen, puke on his lips and in his sink with Rachel worrying on
him and filling a glass of water, Clay began to think. It was hard
to think, because somewhere in his mind a lot of what had
happened had been lost. He didn't know if it was because of the
drugs or the time he spent asleep-
     *(or perhaps something else is rotting. You thought of
that, old boy?)*
     -but he figured they both had something to do with it.
But he had to think. He had to study the picture, and think what

to do or say next as Rachel sat him down on his bed and he drank his water. Zombie-like, unaware of where he was sitting and what he was drinking. It could have been piss for all he cared, and the bed could have been a tombstone for all he knew.

A tomb just for me! Wheeeeeeeee!

"Jesus, Clay," Rachel said. "You're white as a sheet… like a ghost."

I'm going to be one soon, That thought, alien and unforgiving, made his stomach churn. "Rachel… I'm in trouble."

"What do you mean?"

The itching sensation appeared on Clay's arm again, around the skin graft. He began to unwrap the bandage, ignoring Rachel's telling him not to mess with it. He stared at the stitched graft that he realized had begun to turn gray almost instantaneously. The stiches, strained on his real skin had pus forming around it. Rachel began to say that the doctors didn't do their job correctly. That they would go back and have it fixed immediately.

"No," Clay said. His voice sounded shaky, terrified.

He *was* terrified. There was no denying that. The reality of what was happening was slowly sinking in, and Clay's brain was finally grasping ahold of the true horror he was experiencing. He thought he would go mad, go stark-raving mad like a character from a Lovecraft story. Doesn't that always happen? As soon as something beyond a man's comprehension came into play, the end result was always madness, because no one was capable of going through such experiences or witnessing such sights before they lost their marbles completely. That somehow made Clay desire it more, as he would be freed of all responsibility of such knowledge he now owned.

But madness didn't come, no matter how desperately Clay wanted it to. He was still here, he was still coherent, aware that Rachel was asking him why they shouldn't go to the hospital, why he was trembling so bad, and looking at his hands, he saw how bad they were shaking. His own fingers began to twitch he was so scared.

Clay looked at Rachel, tears forming in his eyes. Like a kid seeing a horror movie for the first time, he cried out of pure terror and dread. The kind of tears that were a mere pinprick of what the taste of madness really was. Tears of pure terror. There was no other way to describe it; No word that could possibly hold the weight of the burden now on Clay's shoulders and heart which was beating fast, causing him to break out in sebum-rancid sweat. He had never been so scared in his entire life.

"Rachel," he told her. "Something happened, after the accident."

Rachel, her beautiful face crumpled with sympathy asked, "In Oregon? What do you-"

"No. The one that put me in the hospital just now, but... I don't think that is what is happening to me."

"What do you mean?"

"What MdFinnigan and they all say, I don't think what they say is wrong with me is the actual problem."

"What are you-"

"Just listen! Please... ThIs Is going to sound crazy... but I need you to hear this."

The itching became almost unbearable, but he wanted to wait. He wanted to wait to show her, as well as himself. If it was what he thought it was, he was in big trouble still. If not, then this was all part of some hyperactive dream set upon him by maniacs that wanted to sabotage him.

He almost wished it was just that. So he could go back to the hospital bed, and just succumb to the madness and never have to worry about anything ever again. Ignorance was bliss, even if it was inflicted by the maddening thought of what was truly happening to him.

Seventeen

When he was done telling Rachel about how Astrid and Johnny Burrows had visited him after the crash and what they had told him, Clay told her what he had been feeling these past few weeks-

Months now, holy shit...

What he had dealt with, and what he believed was happening now. The itching persisted, but he fought the urge to scratch or shift in his position or anything. At this point, he felt more of a wet and warm itch on his bald scalp and even on his groin and knee-pits, accompanied by an occasional sharp pain that made him think of teeth. Needling, biting, scissoring...

Rachel listened, but she appeared skeptical, as he expected. Clay supposed he sounded like a lunatic, but he had never been more sure of something in his life. Though what was factual or what he actually saw or noticed was still slightly blurry, but the dreams he had in the hospital were coming back too, and they helped fill the holes and cracks in his story, and made way for more memories. Little by little, the neurons were connecting on the synapse bridges again. Part of him truly wished he was insane still, but he knew otherwise. His fear was real, and that fear brought the terrible truth with it.

"Clay," Rachel said after a moment's silence when Clay had finished. She was speaking slowly, carefully, and as judiciously as a parent about to explain to a child why their decision to say 'fuck' was vulgar and inappropriate. Or that the idea of a monster hiding in their closet or under their bed was nonsense and merely a ploy of their imagination. Clay hated that. It sounded condescending to him, but he knew she meant well. Still, he also knew that if this was how the start of the conversation was going to go, then he knew how it would end.

Rachel opened her mouth, closed it, opened it again, then clamped it shut for a second. After gathering her thoughts, said, "Do you know how crazy that sounds?"

"Look, I know it *sounds* crazy but-"

"Then... why say it?" This was Rachel's go-to when it came to something she didn't understand or didn't want to hear. 'So why say it?' 'So why do it?' 'So why think/say/do, blah, blah blah.' That also irritated Clay. How Rachel would use that rather than try to be sympathetic and talk to him and try to understand. She would just put him on the spot like a lawyer cross-examining a potential witness and/or suspect in order to make them uncomfortable and have nothing more to say because now they doubt themselves.

"I mean, c'mon," she finally said. "Really? You think *they* had something to do with this? You're just-"

"Rachel," Clay said as calmly as he could despite his frustration rising, a slight tinge of anger mixed in with it. "Hear me out, please. None of this happened until Burrows attacked me at that restaurant a month ago. Then about a few weeks, I start showing these symptoms. Smelling like death and more since then."

"The doctors said-"

"Lemme finish, please," Clay said past clenched teeth. He wanted to slap her, tell her to shut up and listen, but resisted such an abominable and barbaric urge.

"During that time, like I said, more happened. I started to itch horribly like something was under my skin. I began losing fingernails." He showed his left hand to prove his point. "I lost my teeth before the accident, even my hair."

"Clay, you lost your hair-"

"It was falling out *before* they shaved it all off!" Clay snapped. He was close to screaming at Rachel to shut up and let him finish but that would only cause more complications. So, he continued. "I was on my way to the hospital because the meat on my arm here literally *fell* off. It was mushy, mushier than my skin is now."

"Clay-"

"Will you let me finish!?" he snapped. "For fuck's sake lemme *finish*!"

Rachel's mouth was tightly shut. She was angry, but allowed him to speak. Her eyes however made him feel childish, the way they stared at him condescendingly. Like always.

"It fell off. It wasn't because of the goddamn crash, but those fucks wanted it to *look* like that. They crashed into me, took me to the hospital, and posed it to look like the accident caused this to happen. The doctors, seeing how hurt I was, went along with it. When I started screaming in the hospital, they put me under and checked for brain trauma, which I conveniently seem to have." Something else crossed Clay's mind at last. When his skin fell off, he hadn't felt anything. And then...

"And then in the crash," he said speaking his thoughts allowed. "I didn't feel hurt. I felt pressure, I felt *something*, but it wasn't pain."

Clay looked at Rachel again. Her face had relaxed but her eyes were vacant, undeterred. She was too logical for the madness that was spouting from her ex's lips. "Plus, did it ever occur to you how strange it was for the Burrows family to come and see me and wish me the best of health?"

This time, Rachel looked slightly perplexed. Something in her eyes had changed. Something passed behind them, a message from one side of the brain to the next. Telegram: auditory cortex to frontal lobe! $.50 collect please.

"I *did* think it was strange," she admitted. "Given all that they had put us through... what they put *you* through specifically..."

"Exactly! One moment they are lamenting, then they wanna make it a civil case, and even that backfired on them. And yet now they wanna see if I'm okay and 'help' me with insurance?"

"Okay, that *is* strange," Rachel agreed. "But maybe it is a change of heart. I dunno, it isn't like they should still have some ploy against you, Clay."

"They do, and I'm sure of it. After their dad cursed me-"

"It is *not* a curse!" Rachel's patience was running low now, but that still irritated Clay that she had interrupted him again. "Clay... *listen* to yourself!"

"Are *you* listening?" Clay demanded.

"Yes, and what you are saying is *bonkers*. Insanity! I mean, a *curse*? Are you serious?"

"If I wasn't serious, I wouldn't be telling you this," Clay said holding up his hands. "Look at me! Would I be this scared if it was nothing? Have you *ever* known me to not mean what I say?"

"You once said you loved me."

Clay paused, stunned. He felt like he had been punched in the sternum. It was an emotional jab, and Rachel seemed to notice immediately.

"Sorry, that wasn't fair. And not true, I know. But Clay, you gotta understand. You've been through a lot. Your body is going through a lot. But the doctors say-"

"The doctors don't know *shit*!" More venom in his voice because of the jab Rachel took at him. They were going into that spiral again.

"There is no need to yell."

"Apparently I have to so it can get through your fucking head!"

Rachel looked hurt but she kept her composure. This was nothing she hadn't dealt with before.

"Rachel, I *know* it sounds crazy, believe me, I can hardly believe it myself. But I am very convinced of this. What Astrid said in the hospital room-"

"The doctor said you were hallucinating-"

"JESUS FUCKING CHRIST!" Clay bellowed. He heard stomping in the room above his head, but he ignored it. "For fuck's sake, Rachel, please, for the love of God, shut the *FUCK* up! Quit interrupting me, quit butting in, JUST SHUT THE FUCK UP!!!"

Now it was Rachel's turn to look stunned. He had lost his temper on her before, but not to this degree. She was rendered speechless, and angry. But that made her quiet, and so Clay continued in a more calm voice (or as calm as he could muster). Although he had to clench his fists to keep his anger in check.

"I'm sorry I yelled," he told her. "But I need you to listen. When I am done talking, then can you speak and tell me how crazy I am. Bring logic into it and convince me I am nuts. I hope you can, honestly, but I know I'm not. But please, for now, just... don't talk."

"Fine," Rachel said softly. There was defiance and obstinance in those condescending eyes of hers, but Clay let it slide. If he gave in, he would lose it again. The next time might not be as reeled in as the last.

"Astrid and her son, said her husband did this to me and that I am *rotting* as she had spoken. They made my nose fall off, they cut my ear, and now I look like a fucking *ghoul*. They did this to me, and they used the crash to cover their tracks." Clay then told Rachel to wait, and he rushed to the bathroom. He came back out holding the molar he had lost before and said, "This fell out the day before. Does it look like it was broken out to you?"

Rachel inspected it, and admitted that it didn't.

"Exactly! They did this so that it made more sense when the doctors took me in. When I started screaming, they determined I had suffered brain trauma and maybe I did, but I think that's rotting too. Rachel, take my hand."

Without waiting for her, Clay had grabbed her right hand. He had to touch her. He had to somehow let her feel him as much as he needed to feel her. Her face expressed repulsion and she ripped her hand away. Clay would compare this to what she had done before once upon a time when their relationship started to crumble. But she was staring at her hand now, looking at the oily substance on her fingers. The smell had to be horrible too.

"This is *not* normal," Clay told her without apologizing for the mess on her hand. "Burrows said her husband did this to me. During the trial, they wanted me to pay. You said it yourself that they wanted blood for blood for what I did. They didn't plan on what is happening, but they are making it work to their advantage while their father is still in jail. They won't get a penny out of me, but they'll take my life if they have to. And even if the doctors or someone *does* believe me, would they even be able to help me? I would just be in some lab somewhere for them to study until I rot into nothing. Look at *this*, and tell me if this is normal."

He prayed to God that Rachel would see reason in this. He had never been a praying man, not since he was a kid. But he needed prayer now. He had to make her see. The itching was unbearable. If she could see what he could see...

He reached down, and grabbed a pinch of his new skin on his bicep. He had started to tug on it carefully, feeling no strain or pain, just pressure. Pressure from the tugging. He would take it off, and they would see the meat underneath. A normal skin graft was meant to secure and protect the tender flesh beneath, give it a chance to heal. But if he was right, then the meat beneath would not have healed at all. It would be stinking, rotting, and worse, possibly *full* of something.

By then however, Rachel had stood up. Clay stared at her as she grabbed her purse, not looking at him.

"Everything you need is here," she told him pointing at the stack of papers on the counter. "I should go."

"Rachel, wait," Clay reached out for her and she pulled her hand back like a kid who realized the dog in the cage might bite.

"Don't touch me. I know you have been through a lot, Clay, but this is madness. You are making this crazier than it already is even when I am trying to help you."

"Rachel, please, I-"

"You wanna believe in curses rather than what is actual possible? Then you can deal with this yourself. I'm done."

She started past him, but that last sentence had finally lit the match. The matchbox was up in flames and Clay stood and turned on her as she walked towards the door. "Like you made me deal with Kimberly by myself!?"

Rachel whirled around. Amazement and anger broiling in her dark eyes. "Are you kidding me? I was always there for you!"

"You like making yourself see yourself that way, dontcha?"

Rachel shook her head in disbelief. "Clay, I was *always* there for you. But after the accident you went cold. Even before, all you would do is get angry with me. I tried to be there for you, but you pushed me away."

Clay couldn't help but laugh. This was too hysterical not to laugh at. "I 'pushed you away' huh? Like when I broke down crying and you said you couldn't come to see me?"

"You were drunk!"

"Did I push you away? Or do you make yourself believe that?"

"Clay, this is stupid." Rachel turned and started for the door again, but this time Clay had just the thing to make her stop.

"Or have you been high the entire relationship just like your dad?"

Rachel stopped. She slowly turned, and stared at Clay slack-jawed and hurt. What was said had come out with furious spite. She couldn't believe he had said it. He couldn't believe it either, but it was out. The cold hard truth as to why her father passed away, higher than a kite and overdosed on coke. The dirty bastard died a dirty death, and Clay had to help this unhelpful brat get through it. She had jabbed him with something, why not jab her back? Give her a taste of her own medicine, especially since she was hellbent on just leaving him again.

"Did you ever care about me?" Clay demanded. "Or was I not scratching whatever itch you had? Were you numbed like your dad was when the coke finally did him in?"

"Clay-"

"No. Before Kimberly, all you wanted to do was argue and fight. I never did anything right, I was never enough. Then when I needed you the most, maybe I was quiet. Maybe I didn't want to talk about it. Maybe I drank some more, I admit it. But *where* were you? Where were you when I needed you those nights when I broke down and cried? Where were you when I couldn't go to work for a week because the image of her splitting apart was still fresh on my mind? Where are you now? Leaving me again, because I'm not worth it, right?"

"Fuck you," Rachel said. "You said that only to make it about yourself. It's always about *you*, Clayton. It was never about me. Because where were you when my father died? You didn't comfort me. You didn't deserve comfort and I tried to give it. But you didn't accept it. You can't give, and you can't take, it seems. You prefer to deal with everything by yourself. Even when it comes to us. You only got angry, drunk, or both. That is why this never worked. This is why *we* never worked. Because you can never hold in that goddamn temper of yours and you're an alcoholic asshole."

Rachel turned, opened the door, and stood in the frame for a long time. Clay was stunned speechless just as she had been before. She was now about to walk out, and he might as well have opened the door himself.

Without looking back at him, she said, "I never said anything before. But could anything be done about Kimberly?

Did you *really* have no control? Because maybe you would have, if you weren't screaming at me."

Her final gut-punch delivered, Rachel stepped out and slammed the door shut, leaving Clay alone, and baffled.

When he finally *did* have a reaction (he had been standing there staring at the door dumbfounded for a solid ten minutes unbeknownst to him), Clay went berserk. His head flared and he swung his arm out and struck the pillar at the end of his countertop holding up his ceiling. He sputtered nonsense twisted with anger, and he kicked at one of the barstools, sending it sprawling across the hardwood floor and causing it to smack against the side of his bed. He stomped over to the bed with his face in his hands. His fingers dug into his oily skin, and the sensation of it made him fly into a worse rage. He punched down into his mattress, knowing that if he punched at anything else, he would punch a hole through it if he didn't split his knuckles.

When he looked up, he saw that all his paintings were the same. All of them were Lady of Thorns, the face of Kimberly now staring down at him. *Mocking* him almost. Her dark eyebrows were raised, as if she were surprised at this outrage. But her smile said otherwise. It looked like she was smirking.

Blinded by his rage in thinking that now even his own paintings were laughing at his misfortune, he stood and stalking around the room like a dangerous dictator, took each painting down one by one and threw them to the floor, creating a scattered pile. When he got to the painting that he knew for certain was the actual Lady of Thorns, he punched his fist right through it. He needed to hit something, and other than himself this was the next best thing. He even laughed as the picture frame hung around his forearm, the canvas broken in like a torn sail.

His paintings in a pile with the actual Lady of Thorns on top with a gaping hole in it's center, Clay kicked at it and sent them scattering. Now the itching was horrendous, not just in his arm, but his legs, back, and head as well. Not caring anymore, he went and scratched. He felt his fingernails dig in, he felt stuff collect underneath them.

Fuck them, he thought. All care seemed to drain out of him and he made his way back to the counter to look at the paperwork Rachel had left out for him. For a brief moment, he thought of just swiping his arm across and saying 'fuck it.' But instead, he looked at the insurance papers, information regarding the Flosvita Family, and even hospital and medication information. Among these, he saw a letter from St. Luke's and he picked up the envelope and ripped it open.

It was his bill from the first visit when he thought all he had was some skin deficiency or whatever. Examination, sampling, the draining procedure (the thoracentesis Clay found himself surprisingly remembering). All of it, totaling to $3,434. Not terrible, but not comforting. His rent wasn't even a quarter of that.

"I'll go in tomorrow," Clay said, his voice sounding alien even to his own ears

(ear?). He decided he would go into work to figure out the insurance just as Dr. McFinnigan had suggested. In the meantime, he didn't want to think about the hospital, or the goddamn gypsies. He had been through so much shit and his own brain couldn't even seem to comprehend it. And the one person he trusted in this, had left him.

Because I lost my temper...
(alcoholic asshole)
"Did you really *have no control? Because maybe you would have, if you weren't screaming at me."*

That had been the worst thing Rachel had ever said to Clay, at least for the time being.

Fuck her. He didn't need her, he decided. He didn't want to think about the hospital, the gypsies, or Rachel. He didn't even want to think about the curse that he may or may not be under. If it was still around, it wasn't killing him right now. He just wanted to take his mind off of it all, and the best way to render a brain stupid was three things. One, was hours of television (the safest of his choices he supposed). The second, was get into another car wreck, but he would be damned before he set foot in a car again. Hell, his own car was in the junkyard right now so that wouldn't do him any good. Which lead to option number three: get drunk. He went to the refrigerator and found only food. No beer.

He decided he was going to the Incubus. He needed a drink. He needed to forget. He needed to be *numb*, just like he needed to be when this whole nightmare first began, back when Kimberly Burrows first bit the dust

(*or to be more precise, his now nonexistent bumper*).

That was cruel to think, but he didn't care. He just wanted to be numbed. He didn't want to think. He needed to drink.

Drink, or think?

It was no contest.

Eighteen

Two things became clear to Clay on his binging spree at the Incubus about an hour later after gathering some courage to go out again.

One, people seemed to care less the more they are surrounded by the stench. When he had first entered the Incubus some of the patrons had already been overserved and were putting in their two cents about the smelly man coming in. Either that, or rushing to the bathroom or outside to spill their guts. Some were so drunk one couldn't tell the difference what the cause was. Even the bartender who was a different one compared to the night he and José had gone out, made a comment that he smelled like the dead.

"Do I look better than I smell?" Clay had asked in turn. The woman said no, and then inquired if he had been in an accident, and then apologized for her rude comment. Ignoring her apology, Clay responded by asking for a shot of whiskey and a Martian Sunrise.

"What do you do for a living?" the gal asked as she poured him a shot and got to work on his drink. She was trying to make small talk. She was a short and pasty girl with brunette hair tied in a ponytail and she was wearing a Rolling Stones T-shirt. She was busty, and Clay thought that might pose to be a problem (maybe not) if he got a few more drinks in him. Which, of course, was his plan.

He had finished his shot and answered, mostly just going with the flow here, "I'm a garbage man. Dumpster fire got me." It was complete bullshit and the woman looked like she didn't quite believe him, but of course she couldn't tell for certain.

"Were you *rolling* in the garbage?" the bartender asked in good nature and with a pretty smile to go with, and Clay had grunted in response.

"Maybe," he admitted as he accepted his cocktail. He thanked her and placed a twenty on the table. "Keep 'em coming, I'm paying as I go until I have no more."

She took it and went to count up some change, asked if he wanted to start a tab instead, the usual bartender talk. Clay, thinking it might just be easier, especially if he planned on getting plastered, agreed and gave the woman his credit card.

After a while, the comments ceased. Whether it was because Clay's scent had coagulated with the stench of cigarette smoke, booze, and vomit, or he was already too far gone to give a shit. The newest patrons would scrunch up their noses if they passed him by, but nothing was said. All was lost in a haze of loud jukebox music, and drunken gossip. By then Clay was four drinks in not including the shot and didn't really care anymore

The second thing he that had become clear to him, was how *adjustable* his fingernails had become.

It started off as nothing, him playing around and tapping his fingernail to the music playing on the overhead speakers. Some rockabilly horseshit that he normally couldn't stand, but any music was better than none at this point. He was also scratching at the leather part of the bar table as he watched a Broncos game. Then he began to notice how much his middle finger on his right hand was rising every time he scratched the surface. He applied more pressure, saw it move more. He applied a little more, and this time it came off, trailing strands of white and green pus in the process. Now that it was hanging on only by the cuticle and the proximal, Clay raised it to his eyes and looked into the tender flesh underneath. Without so much as remorse in his system (having been replaced with his cocktails), he pinched the nail with his thumb and forefinger and pulled it right off, watching in awe of the sticky strand that stretched between them only to snap like a spider's web in the wind. Didn't even hurt.

The rational side of him, the side of Clay which was holding onto a thread as the man continued to drink, supposed that a normal person wouldn't be doing this given the predicament he was in. After all, he was *rotting*, wasn't he? He believed he was. No one else did, but he believed that the Burrows had cursed him. Shouldn't that had been enough?

No, sometimes self-belief isn't enough. Sure, maybe he was rotting, but perhaps not. Hell, weren't all human beings technically rotting away as they got older; every single one of us slowly dying? The doctors weren't concerned, so why should he be? Maybe he had some disease or ailment that was causing his flesh to become sickly mushy and oily, leaving streaks of it on the barstool whenever he got up to take a leak. Maybe those gypsies still had it in for him, and wanted to make him fear for his life. After all, they wrecked his piece-of-shit car and basically got him hospitalized for a couple of weeks. But no one believed him that he was cursed. Many great people who believed in themself died in vain. Look at John Yudkin. He knew sugar was what caused heart disease, but everyone and their mother believed fat was the culprit and he died not knowing how much his research would affect the world today. Clay knew he was no Yudkin, he would die alone and in vain without anyone believing in him.

Rachel...

Maybe Rachel had a point. Maybe he wasn't being rational. Curses don't exist. They aren't supposed to any more than monsters under one's bed or Santa Claus on his sleigh with eight tiny reindeer. Those things just didn't happen in the real world. Maybe Astrid the Chink and her punk of a son were only trying to scare him. After all, they were gypsies. They lived on the road, playing fake magic tricks and telling fortunes with tarot cards that did absolutely nothing to benefit someone. But people went to them anyway because they either think it is fun to do it like most 'rational' people, or they really do believe that they will die in three years or that their life will really mean something. Those are the irrational members of society; the ones Darwin would have said should die out so that the stronger members of the human race can live on, therefore proving that evolution exists.

Was Clay one of those members? Maybe all he had really was just a rare disease and his falling teeth and nails were only another symptom of it. Or maybe he did lose a chunk of his arm and teeth in the car crash because the gypsies wanted to hurt him. That what he remembered the night before had been nothing more than a bad dream, something caused by the gypsies attempt to hospitalize him.

Or kill me, that persistent and stubborn sober part of his mind pointed out. Clay ordered another drink when he registered those three words. The Martians were landing, and he was welcoming them with open borders. He chuckled and thought of that Led Zeppelin song about immigration. He did not only think of it, but actually sang to himself as he downed another drink.

"We come from the land of the ice and snow
From the midnight sun where the hot springs flow
The hammer of the gods
Will drive our ships to new lands
To fight the horde, sing and cry
Valhalla, I am coming!"

That was another thing too. Maybe the gypsies really *did* mean to kill him. They couldn't get a penny out of him because of what their daughter did. Mr. Burrows in his rage, attacked Clay and Rachel at the grill and was now serving time without bail. Giving how much money these people had, they probably would have gotten him out if the bail wasn't postponed. That of course made the rest of the family mad. The Flosvita had an agenda against him, and *that* could at least be rationalized.

Then did that made his argument with Rachel pointless? Invalid?

He supposed it did. It didn't make him feel any better thought.

Rationalization after all was what debunked legends and superstitions. The rise of scientific hypothesis' were what brought forth the answers so many believe they already had. The monsters that mankind had created were merely just to cope with the horrors of everyday life. Sure, there had been witches in the past, but *were* they actually witches? For some like Clay, he didn't believe in any superstitions before his unplanned meeting with the Flosvita Family. He had drifted away from his Catholic God and his eternal enemies. He did not believe in devils, nor did he believe in curses, or ancient monsters regardless of heritage or culture. The modern man had no such enemies, and he believed that regardless of how scared he was, there had to be a *rational* explanation for it all. He had been to St. Luke's twice after all, if anything truly was wrong, wouldn't the doctors, especially Dr. McFinnigan, notice something?

Or, would they 'rationalize' based on their years of study and knowledge? Everything that they determine in coming up with the diagnosis for him, was based off of years and years of medical history and research. On top of that, there was their own personal experience. If he really had something bad, even something close to an ancient plague, they would notice it immediately. So why should Clay worry? Why should he be fearful when in all actuality, maybe Rachel was right?

For some strange reason, a thought had wormed it's way

(*maggoted maybe?*)

into Clay's mind. Maybe that was the key after all. That was why he was afraid. The Flosvita Family's greatest advantage was the unwillingness of rational people to believe. The greatest advantage this curse or whatever it was had, was the same reason. People were too rational for their own good, to believe in curses and monsters, and maybe that's why such things if they existed won in stories. Because no one would believe they existed, even if they were standing right in front of them.

That may be true, but *are* there actually modern monsters in the world?

Yes, there were. And they hardly ever looked like monsters, do they?

Why was he still thinking about this? This was stupid. He had come here to *drink* not think. Drink and think don't go good together, especially when your agenda was to get drunk. Clay had ordered another, barely feeling the effects necessary for this agenda. He was definitely drunk though, his motor skills at this point were flimsy to put it lightly. His trips to the bathroom while numerous were a feat of their own. By the time he got back the last time, it was already one thirty. Last call. Clay hated last call, it always took too long to get one last drink and by then the shop would be closing soon. Deciding to just cut his losses (about $120 worth), Clay tipped the bartender and got up to walk home. Maybe he could hit up a gas station for some beer to continue his agenda at home. He had enough of this rationalization and de-rationalization bullshit. His attempt to drink only made him stupid enough to not see the current reality around him, and kept his mind locked in the reality that had been placed upon him.

But then again, was one's reality another's imagination? Wasn't reality a think sheet of ice everyone was skating on? A blank sheet of paper with everyone holding a pen? Could reality and fantasy be different between two people? Clay and Rachel for example? The Boise city and the Flosvita Family?

Clay was considering this as he crossed through the Incubus parking lot. A few bikes were parked as well as some Uber drivers waiting for their riders to come out. Some asked if he was a 'John' or a 'Charlie.' He was saying no to the last one, when he was violently turned around by rough hands and was brought face to face with a familiar and yet unfamiliar face.

"Well, well," hot boozy breath breathed into his face. An ugly face staring into his own, heavy jowls and a thick mustache, pig-like eyes, and gray tombstones for teeth. "The greaseball lover."

"Uhh…" was all Clay could say. The intensity in the man's eyes were familiar. Dangerous even. He felt scared but didn't dare show it, not when the man had him by the scruff of his shirt and making him stand on his tiptoes.

"You and your boyfriend picked a fight with us coupl'a weeks ago," the man said. He had two buddies behind him. All wearing the same leather jackets with sleeves cut off, and wearing heavy chains on the loops of their filthy jeans. Clay noticed that the man who had him was also wearing a bullnose ring on his apex cartilage. Clay had seen these men before, but… where…?

Realization sunk into Clay like water in a bottle of oil. *Oh, fuck me.*

He smiled bashfully. "Oh, hey, guys." He was looking at the side of the man's head, which had probably been bandaged after the fight. It was hard to tell in the dark if it had left a mark or not. The guy to his left had a broken nose, while the guy on the right looked unscathed, definitely unfamiliar. "How's it been?"

"Where's yer boyfriend?" Handlebar asked. He had rings on his fingers that sparkled brilliantly in the neon lights flashing on the Incubus' sign.

"Hey, guys," Clay said trying to give a huge smile and hold his hands out as if to say, 'Can't we all just get along?' "That was a bad night for us all, obviously."

"Yer fuckin' A right," the man said. His accent, it sounded backwashed like someone from Eastern Washington. A bit of hillbilly and a tweak of cityfolk. Neither of which made Clay like the guy any more. "Smacked me good."

"Um… sorry?" Clay really didn't know what else to say.

Handlebar chuckled and gently settled Clay back down. He let go of Clay with one hand and pulled his fist back, his rings gleaming wickedly. "Not yet, you ain't."

The fist came sharp and hard, colliding with Clay's cheek like a bowling ball. The sound a punch is supposed to make is hard, flesh against flesh with the force coming from speed and strength of the attacker. Like a combination of a 'smack' and a 'thud,' sometimes the occasional crack of a jaw dislocating. It was to sound like hitting a rubber ball and the wooden or cork insides cracking.

The crack was there, but the thud was muffled, and Clay heard while getting punched a squishy sound as if the man had punched a jellyfish rather than his face. He crashed to the ground, having felt the force of the punch but not so much the pain, not in his cheek. The pain was deeper, right in his jawline. He was on his side in the parking lot, groaning and moving his jaw, when he heard Handlebar above him.

"Wha- What the *fuck*!?"

"Holy shit, Jerrod, what'd you do?"

"I don't know! I mean... what the...."

"Jesus, his *face*!"

Dazed because of the hit, Clay didn't understand their terror until he saw something just a foot away from his right hand. Resting there in a miniature splat was a piece of yellowed flesh oozing white and green mucus-like pus. Feeling a sort of dread come over him, Clay reached with his hands up his jawline, his fingers feeling for anything out of the ordinary. He passed his lower jaw, and then his fingertips slid across something slimy and hard contained in a cage of tendons and bone.

It was his teeth, his molars to be precise, and the realization of that sobered Clay up instantly and his body felt like it was about to reject the alcohol he had inhaled back inside the bar. He pulled his hand back, expecting to see something on the fingertips. They were clean. Yellow, but clean.

"Holy shit, dude," Handlebar who was called 'Jerrod' said above Clay. He looked at the biker and saw that Jerrod was staring at his hand, particularly his knuckles, that were splattered with blood and a slimy *yellowish* substance. On his rings looking like tattered pieces of defiled leather, were more bits of yellowed flesh. He looked like he was about to puke as well as he shook his hand to try and be rid of the vile pieces.

"Holy fuck," he breathed again looking at Clay. "Are you all right?" All ill towards Clay was gone in an instant, replaced by a mixture of fear, concern, and repulsion. His buddies said nothing, both of them just staring down at Clay who was probably looking like Two Face from a Batman comic book.

"I…" Clay looked at the chunk of flesh in the asphalt that was his cheek, and he turned and vomited. When he had finished, with a lot of puke on the left side of his face where he had lost his cheek, Clay stood and began to mutter that he had to go.

"Wait," Jerrod said. "Shit, dude, you gotta go to…"

But Clay wasn't listening. He had already started running away. Let the bikers have his cheek. Let the bar take it. Let some coyote or rat haul it away and munch on it. If he went back to look at that, he was going to freak. He already was freaking. He was fucking terrified. Any attempt to forget everything and rationalize what had been happening to him these past few weeks were demolished in that one instant. This was no illness he had, no rational explanation or some miraculous human deficient.

This was *real*.

He knew it was.

Nineteen

When he had gotten home Clay immediately tried to call Rachel. He could have done it on the way there, but he wanted to be safe in order to do it. Being outside like the way he was, he didn't feel safe enough. It didn't feel right.

The illusion of being safe was gone, made worse given the fact he had no car anymore and had to walk. He felt like he was always being watched, probably by the gypsies who were now watching him rot away. Beady eyes always watching like cops tailing a criminal, waiting for him to fuck up and catch him in the act of doing so. When he had tried to call Rachel in his apartment which felt all too quiet, he got no answer.

No, he *did* receive an answer. It was way the call was dropped. He would hear the phone ring on the receiving end once maybe twice in the four times he tried to call, and then it would immediately go to voicemail. If her phone had been off, it wouldn't have bothered with the ringing. That meant she saw it, but rather than answer or let it ring, she just denied the call. He was simply denied. She didn't want to talk to him. That was understandable, but given the circumstances, it was gut-wrenching to say the least.

Frustrated, Clay had left a voicemail on his final attempt to call, asking her to call back immediately. Then he called José. This time the call went straight to 'leave a voicemail' and so Clay left him one, telling him to come as well. He was scared, and the thought of being alone all night was enough to send him into hysterics almost. But touching the side of his face was what did the trick, and Clay had to rush into the bathroom to vomit again. Without his mouth to funnel the vomit in a single direction, some of it spilled out the side of his face only to splatter on the bathroom floor or over his side. Clay didn't care though. He was beyond caring at this point, even as the side of his face was dripping.

After he had flushed once, he sat there dry-heaving and eventually *something* came out. There were clinking sounds inside the toilet bowl, but Clay didn't register it. He only flushed, and sat there trying to catch his breath. Without ever realizing it, he had flushed down some more of his teeth which had fallen free of his rotted gums which were now mushy and reeked of vomit. He turned on the faucet and splashed his face with some cold water, relishing it's cool touch. He stared at his dripping face which looked decrepit and scary. The cheek he was missing made him look like something out of a Halloween shop, and his eyes looked baggy and tired. Pocked across his sagging cheeks were broken blood vessels, and his eyes had turned red from the vomiting.

Well, one of them anyway. His left eye had turned milky in color, the pupil a single dark pinprick in the hazy marble. Mixing with the water droplets on his face, was a thin stream of a semen-like pus that looked like a milky teardrop. He wiped his face dry, trying to control the terrible shaking that had come over him like an illness.

Then he came back to his living room and after getting a glass of water from the kitchen, he sat down with his laptop and decided to do some research. If he thought he was going to get any sleep tonight, he was only fooling himself. He got on good 'ol Google, and looked up the Flosvita Family.

There was an old song called *Flos Vita*, two words instead of converged into one, and there was Flosvita business-launching company founded in Europe. There was also a Flosvita zoo, and there was a hashtag of the word going around Instagram and other social media outlets, with one bring pronounced #flosvitae and another called #flousvita. Clay had to scroll down to almost the bottom of the first page to see a news article on CNN about the Flosvita Family as well as an article on the second page.

He decided to read the article first. It had been published in the Los Angeles Times back in 1998, when crime rates had dropped supposedly 10% during the first half of that year. There had been four slayings within three months in La Habra only to be followed by more burglaries and vandalizing's, but none of which had specific ties to Flosvita. They were all random acts of violence that Los Angeles was known for. However, this particular article, written by a Damon J. Harker, had an interesting intake on the gypsy community who had come into Los Angeles back in December 1984 until October 1990 before they left Hidden Springs in Antelope Valley.

Clay skimmed the first part, about how crime in Los Angeles was not getting less and less but more and more, how the government wasn't doing anything, blah, blah, blah, until he came across the actual name Flosvita, which was enlarged in bold black letters above a picture of five elders all looking like dirty pilgrims with the one in the middle holding up a wreath of flowers while the others had rifles on their shoulders. This one and the men on his right, looked the same as him. Black men with large foreheads and scowling faces from age and experience. The two on the flower-man's left, Clay recognized as a younger version of the Burrows. Gaston Burrows was wearing a dress shirt under a jean jacket, and his wife was wearing a hand-stitched dress with colorful circles sewn in. The smile on her face was almost predatorial, like something Pennywise the Dancing Clown would have before he ate your arm and dragged you into the sewers.

Gathered in 1956, Jeffery and his three brothers, Cithus and Roger Flosvita migrated from the Colorado State and ventured West to seek a place to call their own. Originally just a group of African Americans who wanted to build their own community, they had gone through Utah to Las Vegas where they had been street performers and told one's fortune if they were willing to pay a small fee. When they made enough, they went to Tuscon Arizona where they became good friends with the Hispanic Community. They would assist in those seeking to heal themselves from demons and other

ailments as well as give their spiritual wisdom in regard to their gods whom they call, 'He who shines during the day and She who shines in the night.' Those who speak with these wisemen and women learn that the sun and moon are their gods, and they receive their power from them. Although many have sought this group out, there are very few examples where miraculous actions have *actually* been performed.

From Tuscon, the group moved further west into San Diego, where their numbers would grow into almost a rival compared to Charles Manson. In 1985 they found themselves in Los Angeles, where they said they were now looking for a potential threat in the area: Richard Ramierez who had left for Tuscon in August of the same year. During their time in Los Angeles, the community that had grown to nearly 300 members were well-known in the city, both as street performers and magicians who could bring forth fortunes to those willing to pay the price.

During their time in Los Angeles, specifically in Hidden Springs so that they would not trouble others, a significant rise in specific crimes had risen. Drive-by shootings usually by motorcycle, a heavy passing of drug trafficking, attacks against dangerous gang members, rape, and kidnaping just to name a few. While many speculate that this is just another one of the hills of crime that Los Angeles deals with on the regular, I for one as well as my colleagues find many similarities between the crimes themselves and Flosvita, which are shrouded in mystery as well as clever deceit.

In June, 1988, 11-year old, Livia Orozco Hernández was found dead in the Clear Creek in The Pines. She had been brutally raped, and sodomized with a branch to the point of death. There were countless bruising on the arms and legs, and there were bite marks on the victim's neck. The parents said to have been occasional visitors of the Flosvita Family, pressed charges against Gabriel Pérez and Daniel Beaumont, both of which were taken in for questioning and instructed to bite into molding putty for their marks. The bite on the victim's jugular matched that of Daniel (also known as Danny the Devil in the Family), and the duo was put on a waiting list to be put on trial for the murder. However, out of nowhere, Mr. and Mrs. Lope Hernández begged the judge to be merciful to the men, and not hurt them much to the surprise of the jury. However, the city of Los Angeles was prepared to take these two in for their crimes. That is, until Judge Todd Gaffery (shown on page 2) was forced to try the men not guilty by reason of lack of evidence provided to a 12-man jury. The jury itself seemed apathetic to the young girl's death, and none of the evidence shown by police or detectives were enough to convince them, especially when it was shown that Daniel Beaumont's teeth were broken upon his arrest.

    Some claim the Family did it to not draw attention. Others say Beaumont did it himself to save his own skin. But an eyewitness and the one who actually did the punching, was that of Richard Costello, a man sharing the same jail cell as Daniel and Gabriel before they were taken in for more questions.

    According to Richard who was in on a drug charge, he was talking to the two men who were talking about their family and what they could do. Richard reported feeling cold in the same cell as them, and whenever the men touched him via handshakes or a pat on the back, he felt sick as if he had a fever. At some point however, Richard had fallen asleep, only to be woken up as the jailers hauled him off to another cell after he 'allegedly attacked' Daniel Beaumont. The gypsy was treated with minor bruising in the cheeks and a few broken teeth, all of this not informed in the trial of the People Vs. Flosvita in 1985. Richard had no recollection of attacking the men, and said even if he had wanted to he wouldn't.

    "The men gave me bad vibes, like that you would see when some guys at a bar sizes you up. I looked into their eyes, and I felt small. Very small. They didn't feel like actual people

even though they talked like them. The whole time spent in the same cell as them, didn't feel real at all."

Those who witnessed the trial, were outraged by what had happen. Other reporters and journalists had tried to talk to the Hernández family in order to gather more information about the Family, but was reported dead by suicide. Lope Hernández shot his wife in the head as she slept, and turned the gun on himself in their own bathroom, with the word 'perdóname' ('forgive me' in Spanish) written in lipstick on the mirror.

Without much to go off of, I had my top informant whose name will remain anonymous, visit the Flosvita Family posing as a man who wanted to understand their teachings and their ways of life. In the three weeks he spent in Hidden Springs, my informant came across some disturbing and somewhat glorifying news.

This is some of his reports.

"The group acts like that of a street gang. All of the gangsters following the big cats (shown on the top right). The one in the middle, a Jeffery Flosvita, founded the group back in the early 60's and had his brothers (right of Flosvita), Roger and Cithus join in on leading the group as it grown to greater size. The two with the group, Gaston and Astrid Burrows (left of Flosvita), were known as money launderers, always making sure everything the Family brought in was distributed fairly in order to clothe and feed the entire community. Many of these gypsies carried jobs, but only part time because they intended to move north into Oregon, or so they say. Many of the children are self-taught, had never been in public school it seems and I doubt they are in the system of Social Security... They have a vast collection of guns. Almost every man and woman carries one with those who usually stand watch around their campsite carrying rifles. During my time here, police had come many times due to disturbances with the gypsies and their weaponry, but they always left empty-handed, as if they didn't care... There

is a presence here, and I can see where a lot of the superstitions seem to come. This community, this 'family' has ties with dangerous cults such as Jim Jones and the People's Temple. They also deal with growing marijuana, and whenever the police come to investigate this, they always leave, and I soon found out due to bribes offered by the Family. There are books on spiritualism, demonology, and astrology. All of which the children are encouraged to read and learn... Something is here too. The older members, they all are very persuasive with the police. They also conduct magic tricks that I at first thought were simply tricks of the mind and nothing more. The more I watch however, the more difficult it becomes to understand the tricks from the actual thing. For one thing, a Family Member spoke against Cithus Flosvita, and his brother, Roger, had said something in a language I've never heard of, and the man vomited a <u>rattlesnake</u> that had bitten his tongue and the man died the next day. There was no taking him to the hospital, and he was buried. I reported the murder, but once again the police were sent away. They seemed to be in a trance walking away, something I only just now began to notice... The Family grows suspicious of me. I will return to Los Angeles tomorrow, but you must call the police one more time. A lot of the children here, don't belong here. They had been kidnapped throughout Utah and Arizona. These guys are human traffickers and they must be caught!"

My informant was never seen again after this phone call. With this information in mind, the FBI was brought in and Flosvita was searched and detained. The group was founded guilty and many of the leaders were taken away. To this day, Jeffery Flosvita and his living brother, Cithus, is serving time in Los Angeles State Prison, with Roger committing suicide by swallowing bleach. The children who were founded to be reported missing, were returned to their families and the rest of the Family were disbanded. 196 children who had been kidnapped or encouraged to go with the community, most of

them young girls and strong boys. However, this would not be the last we would hear from them.

In 1990, the Flosvita Family, now lead by the Burrows Family, moved the community to Klamath Falls Oregon, where they lived for a year before migrating to Bend, then Salem, then Portland. There they moved along the Columbia River through the Dallas, up to Washington State where they stayed in Tri-Cities, to Yakima, Spokane, then into Idaho where they passed through Coeur d'Alene and stayed in the Flathead Reservation for five years before coming back down to Boise and then returned to Oregon where they had remained ever since.

During the years 1990-2010, wherever they would go people would go missing without so much as a trace. No murder trials were necessary but not questioned due to the Family's shady history. Since they had stayed in the Flathead's region from 2001-2006, they had received diplomatic immunity because of their favor with the Indian Tribes in the area. There, their numbers only grew, and with their Family's size so did the rumors of demons walking with them through their camps and the missing children and people being the souls they collect for their mysterious 'power.'

Upon the writing of this article, the Flosvita Family had remained in the Oregon State for the past decade, growing and migrating all around the western states with the changing seasons. In the past decade, while their criminal acts seem to have dropped, the true story has yet to be told. I of course have my speculation on the Family, but only time and more research will tell. As for the leading family members, the Burrows and now the Barkers (page 2 Fig. 5), are living in the outskirts of Grants Pass. They still keep mostly to themselves unless they come into town to buy supplies for their camp or perform miraculous fortune telling. Many State Policemen and Park Rangers meet with them from time to time, to keep an eye on the Family and make sure they are not causing trouble.

No reports have been made since 2007, but I wonder as well as many in Los Angeles, is this *really* the case? These people, shrouded in mystery and deceit covered by the Los Angeles government, are still out there. While their original leaders have been split apart, they are still thriving as a massive community. If history has taught us anything, is that it will repeat itself if we are not careful. I now know how much of the reports and stories are true my informant as given me and the Times, but we can only hope that the group has moved on from their criminal ways, and have finally found the peace that Jeffery Flosvita was looking to give to his big Family. He is currently off of Death Row, since Proposition 66 in 2017.

As a reporter and a human being, it is often hard to tell the truth because of...

Clay had stopped reading as the author was giving his closing speech. The article was posted in 2019, *years* after the Hernández case. Clay looked up other news articles and stories about the Family, seeing more reports of missing children and sudden suicides or deaths in the areas the Family was before moving. It seemed that everywhere the Family went, bad luck struck. Dying crops, lost animals and people, strange illnesses such as strains of E. Coli forced upon restaurants and other establishments, Flosvita certainly had a reputation, but where did it all end? Where was the boundary line drawn and why was it so hard to make sure to stomp the weed out rather that just cutting it and watching it regrow? Also, why do they get let off pretty easily given the case in Los Angeles?

In fact, if they had as much influence as the articles say they do, then how did he and Rachel get away after accidently running over the Burrows' daughter? Maybe Idaho State had enough, or maybe the entire West had enough. In any case, there was a report made on what happened on Route 199. It was a Fox News report, and he watched the video about how the gypsy community were in the woods when one of their own had been run down after running onto the dangerous highway. The defendant, Clayton Couch, was found guilty of no crimes and was let go. A Civil Court case was brought up between Couch and the Burrows, but once again the Family was thwarted. There were comments from many saying that the gypsy girl got what she deserved going out in the road, and others who had some interaction with Flosvita both good and bad stating their own opinions. The most interesting were those who believed in the gypsies, telling their stories about how they wished to find a wife or get rich and had because of these men and women, and that the man (Clay) who ran one of them over should get the needle. Clay thought it was charming the way people could state their opinion so much when they had no clue what was going on.

During this time, Clay was chewing on a pen he was using to take notes on a sheet of paper next to his laptop. At some point he felt something give and felt something hard bouncing on his tongue. He held out his hand and spat, and among a splatter of blood and pus, was another tooth. Clay sniffed it, and the tooth reeked of rot and decay. Like candy sitting in the garbage for too long. He sat it aside and felt more teeth loose in his mouth, all of which dropped out of it as he spat in the garbage can like that one scene from *The Fly*. Disgusted, Clay sat the pen down and only picked it up when he got some more information he wanted to write down.

Among everything he was looking for, nothing showed any legitimate proof that there were curses being placed upon people. There were speculations and rumors, devils walking among Flosvita, etcetera, but nothing that was *solid* and Clay felt very frustrated at this. By the time he had decided to call it quits, it was five AM. He wouldn't be getting much sleep but he needed it. He wasn't going to go into work today either. He would just call as originally planned.

He went to pee before he went to bed. He went into the bathroom, regarded the gangly yellow *thing* looking back in the mirror, and wincing at the missing chunk of cheek that exposed his cheek and part of the tendons in his jaw. He looked like Hell. Looking at his face, made him feel like that one girl from *The Exorcist*. And he was just as fucking terrified as the little girl, what was her name? Rachel? Regan?

Clay stood before the bowl, unzipped his fly, and began to pee.

Where he was immediately drenched on the front of his shirt almost to his chin. Piss was spraying upward and he looked down in horror to see something that was almost the most disgusting thing he's seen since this whole thing began.

There were two extra holes in his dick, one on top where the piss hitting the front of his shirt was coming from, and the other on the side closer to the base. Cursing with fright and disgust, Clay covered the holes with his fingers, allowing the stream to only come out of the one pisshole as God intended. Covered them like a flute master blowing into his/her instrument. Worrying and thinking what to do, Clay felt an icky sensation in his penis, especially on his pinky fingers that were covering his cold balls. They felt slimy, and pulling the pinky back he saw green slime.

Oh god, I'm gonna throw up. Oh holy shit, I'm gonna barf, I'm-

Another hole sprouted. It sprouted like a gangly flower, spilling more pee and some black mucus. Clay panicked, and squeezed his dick just as he was about to finish peeing just to cover the holes. But that only made it worse, for in that instance, Clay's dick *erupted* in his hands like a water balloon in a toddler's pudgy and curious hands. Lumps of flesh and black slime covered his hands, and with his penis practically disintegrated in his palms, Clay screamed and cried out in horror. In the process, he had dropped what was left into the bowl and fell back, his ass smacking the cold tile beneath him. The space between his legs now only had his groin hair, his rapidly sagging ballsack, and a stump that used to be his actual dick looking like something had torn it off and it was spewing more green and black slime. In the midst of the slime, wriggling in the mess was the worst thing that could ever be in there, and the worst part was that Clay was not at all surprised. A worm was thrashing in the mess, wondering what had happened to it's recent residency.

This time, Clay *did* vomit again. He sat there, mortified, and crying to the point where his now irrational mind couldn't take it anymore, and he fainted, unloading in his pants in the process and he remained there on the bathroom floor until eleven until he next awoke. Laying in a pool of vomit and slime, pants full of shit with his penis gone and liquifying in the toilet water, Clay escaped reality into the dark matter of his brain. Unaware of the shit in his pants, the vomit drying against his right cheek, and his manhood lost forever.

He went mad, and embraced the darkness like an old friend.

Twenty

When he awoke Clay looked into the toilet bowl and saw that the water was as black as oil, curdled like moldy cream. Thinking dreadfully that there was no use anymore, he flushed it and began to clean up the mess in the bathroom. He watched as what had become of his manhood swirl and disappear down the gullet of the drain. The very idea made him sick, but he had nothing left to vomit.

As he cleaned the vomit and shit off the floor, he moved in a sort of robotic daze. He felt possessed, as if he wasn't really alive. He didn't *feel* alive. He was crawling around naked on his bathroom floor with his filthy clothes in the corner to be washed, and his manhood that would have normally be dangling between his legs wasn't there anymore. He had placed some gauze on the wound and wrapped it with some tape. Probably a bad idea, given he would have to pee again or even wash, but he didn't care. If he looked at the space between his legs again, he would scream and vomit and scream again.

As he was washing, he noticed a considerable amount of change had happened overnight compared to the last few weeks. He determined it was because he was under constant watch of the hospital and any damage he had endured was patched up and healed. But then again, if the gypsies could place a curse on someone, could they *control* that curse? Clay didn't want to think that was possible. But what he saw all over his body, left enough room for debate.

There were sores all over his body. Sores similar to that on the back of his neck which had sunk deep enough to make it appear black almost like a hole. He had found this out when he removed the bandage on his neck, and touched the soft and slimy skin that he could easily pull over his head like a hoodie if he dared try. The sores on his body were fresh, brand-new almost. Folds of flesh pinched one another; their stability waned. Some of which looked more like holes burrowed into his thighs and arms like many miniature stomas from a heavy smoker patient. One of which was about a centimeter in diameter on his left thigh right above the knee.

Curious, Clay had stuck a finger into it (all of his fingers now had no fingernails at all, they had all fallen away during the course of the night). Just his pinky, but the skin stretched and a pungent odor escaped from it like it was a vent. At this point too, the yellow substance had stained his body, making it impossible to tell if he was clean when he finally went to take a shower. Without his hair, there was no need for shampoo, only the loofah, which he used only gingerly on his body but even that seemed to be a stretch. On his chest and back specifically, grains of skin would roll away, peeling back and landing in miniature clumps on the bottom of the tub, bloodless and only full of pus and congealed blackness that *could* have been blood, but Clay doubted it. He stared at these clumps rolling to the drain, past his feet which were covered in more sores and was only holding onto two or three nails per foot at this point. A worm came squirming out from under one nail as if it were a trap door, and Clay dazed and unfazed, bent over and plucked out the parasite before tossing it into the trash on his way out of the shower.

Standing before the mirror letting the water simply drip off his body for he was scared to use a towel, Clay studied his eyes. He had noticed it while staring at his ghoulish face in the bathroom, his left cheek missing and now his right ear looking like a mushroom about to mold and fall away. His left eye looked worse than before. Lazier, milkier, and he decided to try an experiment, something he hadn't done since he was in Elementary school. *Elementary my dear, Watson.*

He held up both hands and folded them together, creating a small hole between the thenar webspaces. He then brought his hands slowly to his face. This was to see if you were left-eye dominant or right. He remembered being told his left eye was his strongest and he often would turn his head at the nearby DOL to cheat on his eyesight test for his new licenses.

But when he brought his hands to his face, they had enclosed on his *right* eye. He then closed his right eye, and saw that his vision in his left had grown hazy. His right, not being is strongest, was more or less the same. But his eyesight was fading away. This alone made him feel despair, a childlike fear of ending up in the dark, and Clay held his head in his hands and cried.

Had this been what happened to those who crossed the gypsies? Those who hadn't joined them or disappeared off the face of the earth? Were they *driven* to suicide? Dealing with this right now, Clay wouldn't put it past the group or anyone who dealt with this. Anyone who could witness themselves falling apart into some unrecognizable monster had some balls, and a heart of stone. Clay had neither. His heart felt frail, weak. His balls had deflated like balloons whose air had been let out, sagging between his legs now. He didn't want to deal with this anymore. He just wanted to be done. He wanted this nightmare to be over.

He considered his options. He had a tub. He had sleeping pills and he could purchase a bottle of whiskey. One last drink. But that wouldn't mean anything. It would change nothing, and thinking about it only made Clay think of himself as a coward. That would mean the gypsies had won. He would be playing right into their hands. Playing along with their little games of life and death.

He should go to the hospital, if they helped him once they could do it again. But would that really matter? Would they really be able to do anything in the end? Also, even if they believed him that something was wrong, worse than they had diagnosed, they would keep him there until the figured out the problem, indefinitely if that was the case. They wouldn't though. Deep in his heart, Clay knew they wouldn't. He might as well go to the nearest mortician and pick out a coffin because if he went to the hospital, that was where he would die. Trapped, and the result would be the same; Him dead, and the gypsies winning.

So what could he do? He was now looking at the skin graft on his arm. He had meant to use it as an example to Rachel, but now it was more of an example to himself. The outline of the new skin had a darker tinge of yellow on it and some of the stiches were frayed. It was going to fall off soon, or join in with his own flesh and rot away with it. Even if he went to the hospital, they could reapply skin all they wanted, they wouldn't stop what was going on. What about his guts? What about everything else? They could patch him up all they wanted, but in the end he wouldn't survive. Plus, he would be trapped.

He couldn't commit suicide, he didn't have the balls to do it in the end. He laughed at the very thought of it, and was scared by how insane he sounded. But through his maniacal laughter, he also knew it would solve nothing. It would take the problem off his hands, but in the end, he didn't want to die. He didn't want to die, but he couldn't go to the hospital to get better. There was no way to get better. Those gypsies cursed him, and they would see him go to the grave. The thought made him cry now, and he found himself wiping the snot that was trickling out of his nose. If he were Jesus, he suspected he would be sweating drops of blood that was how stressed he was. He was caught between a rock and a hard place. Wanting this whole thing to just end, but not having the ability to carry through the method he had in mind not too long ago. He was turning into nothing but a bag of bones, and soon the bag would be gone. The thought of stopping it before that happened was too much, too scary to consider.

His only other option, the hospital, would only prove to be his final resting place and he knew it in his heart. Deep inside, he knew that whatever he chose, he would suffer the same fate and Lope Hernández and many others had suffered.

So what else could he do?

At some point he had come out of the bathroom as clean as one could be, wearing only a pair of shorts to cover his nonexistent groin. He scooped his phone up from the bed and saw that José had called him, his voicemail saying he was off work and was available if Clay needed him still. Which, he did. He needed someone. Anyone, but especially a friend, because to do this on his own… he just couldn't do it. He was scared about what José would see or say, but he didn't care. He needed to try. He needed someone to believe in him. To make *him* believe that he was thinking as rationally as one can in such a situation. Rachel couldn't do it. And there was no one else to really turn to except José. So that left him. He called José, told him to come to the apartment as soon as he could, and after exchanging goodbyes, he hung up.

In the meantime, Clay thought of looking up more stuff about Flosvita, but decided not to. He was already depressed enough as is, and to go through the history of the Flosvita Family to the point where they became a bunch of 'peace-loving' nomads would drive him up the wall.

What was so special about Jeffery Flosvita and his brothers anyway? Clay knew that back in post 60's, African Americans were having it pretty rough still. MLK Junior would be just about to start his march to end segregation and would be shot in less than a decade after Jeffery and his brothers decide to move to Utah and start a new life. Were they run out of Colorado because of their skin? Back then they would probably be harassed just for being what the locals back then would call negros, and when they started their own journey, what changes had become of them?

How did they learn the stuff they did? Did they see something like Muhammad in the desert? Did they meet numerous people who offered them a deal too sweet to refuse; power, something the whites couldn't have, until they became more welcoming into their growing family as more people of different races, cultures, and sex joined in. Hell, the Burrows were practically Irish by the mere looks of it, aside from Astrid who was borderline Asian.

Whatever history they had no matter how sympathetic in the beginning, couldn't excuse the power they hold and what they were willing to do to get what they wanted. Quite frankly, Clay didn't give a rat's ass about Jeffery Flosvita, his family both biological and extended, nor did he care what the family went through to get where they needed to go. Today, they had wrong him, and since they couldn't have what they wanted, like a little kid, they wanted him to suffer.

Clay suddenly remembered something he saw a long time ago. He didn't remember where he was or what he was doing let alone where he was going, but he had been on the road one day right behind a red PT Cruiser. On the back windshield was some sticker lettering that Clay couldn't read until they had come to a stoplight. The cynical message, all along the bottom of the rear windshield, said in big block letters, 'IF YOU CANNOT PAINT YOUR OWN PICTURE, STAIN SOMEONE ELSE'S.'

Rachel, who had been in the car with him, expressed how dirty the message was. How 'disgusting' it was, actually.

"Can't do something yourself so you drag someone else down? Why would that be something anyone would want on their car?" she had asked.

Clay didn't know either. He thought it was just stupid but at the same time unfortunately very real. A lot of people dragged others down when they couldn't do something or get what they wanted. Hell, a lot of the problems between he and Rachel's father was because of that very reason. It was something Clay would never tell Rachel, and he would take it to the grave if he could help it.

He remembered when he had first dated Rachel. About four months into the relationship, she had invited him to dinner at her father's house. When the old man saw that Clay was a white man, he started off nice at first. But the next time the two men were alone, Mr. Jeremy Abbas had taken Clay into the family room where pictures of family members hung on the wall. There was also a china cabinet that Clay felt drawn too, for it had those cute little angel dolls inside. Mr. Abbas had asked Clay if he liked them, and they discussed it for a moment but then the point of the invite came up.

Mr. Abbas, being a member of the Senate Committee for Idaho, was a very wealthy man. In fact, their home was actually in the outskirts of North Rock Garden where most luxury homes sat. Clay remembered coming up the driveway and just gawking at the house. He loved looking at houses, almost as much as women liked to window shop. But the man had made his impression of Clay clear, how he didn't like Clay because as far as he was concerned, no good would come out of Clay for his daughter. That him being white, was a disgrace to everything his family had stood for, and he would 'be damned if he had mutts for grandchildren.' Calling his future grandchildren 'mutts' had enraged Clay, and he almost called Abbas something nasty out of anger.

He then offered Clay a deal. Break up with Rachel, and he would give him $15,000 cash. The man had his checkbook out of his coat pocket and ready to be written with a ballpoint pen the man kept in his coat. He had expected Clay to immediately say 'yes' he was so fast in bringing out that fucking checkbook. Disgusted, Clay had refused. So, Mr. Abbas stretched the deal out. He offered Clay $25,000.

"My father and his father worked hard to get me where I am at," he had told Clay. "I worked twice as hard to reach the senate and I hope to make history in my family one day. You have more of a chance than I ever did as a child, boy."

"Because I'm white? Are you serious?"

"Yes." Without missing a beat, Abbas continued saying, "With this, your chances increase tenfold. You can go to a better college, become a better painter if you truly want to make a mere hobby something else. Even without my help, you could do it. I believe it. But I am offering this to you, if you leave my daughter alone. Think about the differences you two will have. Think of the children you might have. They will belong to no one. No one would accept them for the blood they share. I've seen it far too many times, and how it destroys them. Think of that, Clay. Think of how much trouble you would be saving my Rachel."

Clay, infuriated, told Mr. Abbas to shove his checkbook up his ass and use whatever cash he had left to use for the cocaine he often purchased. He knew Mr. Abbas used the stuff. The constant bloody noses and hints of powder throughout the house was proof enough. That and the man was constantly constipated, as was revealed by the countless fiber supplements throughout the kitchen cabinets. He then asked if Rachel knew about this blackmail he was offering, and Mr. Abbas told Clay he could go to Hell. Clay said that was just fine. He loved Rachel, and had no intention of leaving her.

But in the end, it seemed the old man got his wish. He was six feet in the dirt now, but his daughter was through with the 'white-trash brat' known as Clayton Couch. In the end though, Clay had lost his respect long ago with the old man. Since he couldn't have a respectable black son-in-law, he was going to have someone who was white. Ever since that day, Clay was never welcome in the house and whenever Rachel insisted that everyone got together for dinner, the rest of her family would be friendly to Clay and accept him, but not her old man, who made so many comments he could make every dinner an uncomfortable nightmare He couldn't get what he wanted, so he tried to make it worse.

He couldn't paint his own picture, and so he tried to stain another.

That was what these gypsies were. They were Mr. Abbas and then some. The Burrows wanted Clay to suffer for what had happened to their daughter, regardless of who was really at fault. And maybe what happened at the grill was a fluke. The ravings of a drunk man. But those who commit murder always have that on their mind, alcohol only gives them the confidence they need to do it. Maybe that was what Gaston Burrows had in mind. Maybe this was his last resort to get Clay to suffer, and if he had to serve time in jail for breaking his restraining order, so be it. Clay didn't know this for certain, but he was willing to bet whatever teeth were left in his mouth that he was right.

With this in mind, Clay sat at the counter and made a call to Mr. Maisel. José would be here soon, and he would need to talk to his friend about what was going on. But first, he had some business to take care of. If what he had in mind would work, then he would be able to return to work and his life without the gypsies around.

What if your plan doesn't work? his mind asked him. *What if the damage is already done?*

"I'll figure it out," Clay said defiantly after hitting the 'send call' button on his iPhone. That thought had crossed his mind after he thought about the possible things to do after he talked to José. He couldn't go to the hospital, and suicide was just out of the question. So, he needed to go straight to the source. These gypsies who were trying hard to stain his own picture, surely they would have some reason to listen to him. Maybe he could bribe them, or give them something to get them to remove the curse. Hell, he would drop all charges against Gaston if that was what it took. He needed to try *something*.

But first, his boss.

Twenty-One

Carol Dawson had taken the phone call after going through the operator at the fitting room, and asked Clay to hold while she got Mr. Maisel. She had first asked how Clay was doing, if he was doing good and if everything was all right. He lied of course, saying he was peachy, but he might be on a leave of absence for a little longer until things simmer down. She said she missed him (which he thought was a bullshit lie) and he responded in kind albeit more automatic than actually true. Clay hardly ever saw Carol and quite frankly didn't care about her. But she took his response well and asked him to wait.

He waited no more than two minutes before Mr. Maisel's voice spoke up in his earhole. He dared not touch the one looking like it was about to fall off.

"Clay!" the pleasant/bullshit high voice said. "How are you? We have been thinking about you here."

I bet. "I'm fine, not doing so hot still."

"Oh?"

"Yeah." Clay was holding the medical bills in his other hand. It occurred to him that he hadn't thought about how to approach this. He wasn't going to the store, that was out of the question. He could at least get some answers here and hopefully he could do whatever he had to on Workday on the computer.

"I'm gonna need some more time away still so I can heal. Doctors aren't so sure what is going on, and if you could smell me, you wouldn't want me there."

"That bad?" Sympathetic sounding. Why Mr. Maisel, I never knew you cared.

"Very."

"I see..." Mr. Maisel sounded nervous. Clay didn't register it until after the phone call, and continued on.

"Another thing I wanted to call about, and I'm sorry if you are busy, I just thought it was better to do this in a call rather than face to face because of... well, y'know. But I have these medical bills from the first time I had gone, where I got the note to work. They said I could talk to you and HR about what to do from here so... yeah. Is there something I need to log in for on Workday to get it figured out, do I come in to fill a questionnaire... how do I proceed with this?"

"Clay, did Hanna not call you?"

Hanna Crockett was who he was referring to. She was the store's HR Team Lead. The last time Clay had heard from her was a month ago, because she had been on vacation before he had been put in the hospital the first time. She was a nice enough gal, but she definitely wasn't around enough it felt like.

"No..." Clay answered. He felt a sick turning in his stomach. An image of a rat came to mind and he violently shoved it aside. He dreaded to ask, "Why?"

"Oh boy," Mr. Maisel breathed. "This is awkward..."

"Awkward?"

"Clay, I'm sorry, but, you don't work here anymore."

He might as well have said, 'You have cancer.' In fact, Clay would have preferred cancer over what he heard here. Hell, he would have taken cancer over this curse he had placed on him.

"Since when?" Clay demanded. His anger sparked as violently as a firecracker, and he was holding he phone so tight in his hand that his hand was beginning to hurt. If he applied any more strength to it, he would probably break the iPhone.

"You were supposed to be let go on the fifth, right after you had your car accident. She was to call you and say that you are let go, effective immediately. Last check would be sent by letter, all that stuff."

"What the hell for?" Clay demanded.

"No need to curse," Mr. Maisel said a little more sternly. It was the tone he used when customers were not taking 'no' for an answer. Or employees who decided to speak their minds. "On your first day back from your first visit to the hospital, it had come to my attention that you were not honest to the company."

"What do you mean?"

"Our security cameras caught you stealing while working in the backroom."

"Bullshit!"

"Don't curse at me, Mr. Couch." Gone were the first-name pleasantries with Mr. Maisel.

"I didn't steal anything! With all due respect, Mr. Maisel, that is *bullshit*! Did AP report that?"

"I saw it with my own eyes, Couch. You were seen taking a towel from the backroom, wiping your face with it, and tucking it into your pocket. You didn't purchase it afterward, and you didn't even scan it out. You stole merchandise, Mr. Couch. And unfortunately, *that* was strike three."

Clay couldn't believe what he was hearing. "I didn't steal anything, Mr. Maisel."

"You did. And you have the gall to lie to me about it too."

"I didn't-"

"No. I'm sorry, Mr. Couch, but your termination was effective *immediately*. That was the last straw. You no longer work for my store."

"You're full of shit!" Clay shouted into the phone. His voice cracked as he screamed, "You are full of *shit*, Maisel! *You're* the fucking liar here!"

"Calm down."

"No, FUCK YOU! You're lying, you piece of shit!"

"Mr. Couch, you swear or call me names again, and I *will* hang up. You will then be trespassed as well for your hostility. You won't even be able to purchase anything from us again, if you would even buy it and not *steal* it."

First let go, then terminated, then fired. The holy trinity of 'you're shit out of luck but good luck.' 'Hostility' didn't even hold a candle to what Clay was feeling but he still snarled, "'Hostility?'"

"Yes. Hostility. Also, the risk of you stealing again. We gotta make a living too you know."

"Fuck. You. I didn't steal *anything*, Maisel. I swear to god."

"You did, and we have proof. You're lucky it wasn't anything expensive or we would have you arrested. As for your future with this company, I'm sorry to say, you are not a part of this team anymore. If you need help looking for another job you can use me as a reference if you wish."

"So you can fuck me over that as well? Fuck, you, Maisel," he said deliberately pausing between each word. "What am I supposed to do about these bills? And my rent?"

"Since you have sworn at me again, Mr. Couch," Mr. Maisel said in a tone that sounded like that of a lawyer who got the defendant to say something self-incriminating. It was the tone of someone who had won a victory. Even though Clay had cussed at him after his threat. "That is neither my problem nor my concern. Goodbye."

"Wait! Maisel? Maisel!"

The call had ended. Clay was listening to nothingness in his hand. He stared at his phone, which was now slightly cracked and he angrily chucked it across the room, watching it punch through the canvas and topple the stand over only to burst into fragments of glass and plastic everywhere.

"FUCK YOU!" he bellowed.

Stomping overhead. Someone upset he was yelling. He shouted at them to fuck themselves as well and then he sat back down with his head in his hands. His head that felt heavy and buzzing with adrenaline like a swarm of angry hornets.

He was jobless now. Right when things couldn't possibly get any worse. He was left hanging out to dry. He was approximately nine miles up shit creek without a paddle. His boss fired him on something he didn't even do! Took the fucking life preserver along with the paddles and the boat.

I didn't steal anything.

As if to prove it, Clay went to his dryer and pulled out his work khakis. They were dry from sitting in there for weeks, and he felt around in the pockets. His old name badge was there and what was left of a tissue now all balled up and flaking.

His heart sank into his ass when he reached into the left front pocket and felt something else. Grabbing onto it, he pulled it out. Sure enough, it was a washcloth. Not a towel, but definitely not his. Green, and most likely had once been covered in that yellow gunk. Clay didn't even realize he had done it. He must have been in the zone so deep nothing really seemed real. Autopilot didn't even save him this time. So Mr. Maisel wasn't *quite* bullshitting. It was bullshit still, but it gave Mr. Maisel just the opportunity to get rid of Clay, and not deal with the stench ever again that would probably never go away.

That depressing thought left him feeling sick, and Clay didn't even hear the knocking on his door until the second time. Thinking it was José, Clay scrambled to the door and threw it open.

"José, tha-"

It wasn't José. It was Mr. Landlord.

Kevin Sparks, owner of the apartments, and a recently-transgendered woman. He had that feminine feature to him, wore makeup, and had breasts. But the jawline, brow, and hair, was unmistakably still male. He wasn't quite all the way changed yet, wasn't finished with whatever operations he was going through. It was all way above Clay's paygrade.

"Hey, Karen," Clay said almost in defeat, being polite enough to use Kevin's preferred female name not necessarily out of respect but in order to get this shit over with.

"Christ," Kevin said in a high voice covering his/her face. He/she looked mortified by what he/she saw. Clay couldn't necessarily blame Kevin, but the reaction still irritated him. "What *is* that smell?"

"I have a condition," Clay said. "Doctor's got me on medicine."

"Jeez, it *stinks*! And... my god, what *happened* to you?"

"Car crash."

"Jesus..."

"What can I do for you, ma'am?" Clay asked respectfully. Regardless of his thoughts on Sparks' transgendering, it was best to keep his opinion to himself. Especially if Kevin (or Karen he reminded himself) had bad news.

Which, he, or technically *she* did. "Well, before I kept getting complaints that something smells up here. Now we know. I came up here cause your upstairs neighbors said you were yelling. Everything okay?" With her holding her nose, the words came out nasally. It was almost comical. Almost as comical as her fake breasts.

"Yes, everything is fine," Clay answered. He was eager to get Mr. or Ms. Landlord out of here as soon as possible. "Sorry, I'll be more quiet."

"Can you at least do something about the smell?" Karen asked.

Clay gave the transvestite a huge PR smile that said 'go fuck yourself.' He almost said it too. "Nothing I can do. Doctors are working on it. Apologize to your tenants for me." Without waiting for Kevin, he shut the door. The soon-to-be-woman knocked, but Clay ignored him. Eventually, he went away, leaving Clay alone.

He almost wanted to be left completely alone, when José called saying he was coming upstairs. Clay told him to just come in, that the door was unlocked. Now it was time for the real test. He had just gotten so much shit in the past five minutes, and he needed some support. He needed a friend. He didn't want to be alone, he realized.

If he doesn't help me, Clay thought morbidly. *Then I really am on my own on this one.*

Twenty-Two

José thankfully didn't show too much of a reaction as Kevin Sparks had, but he still looked shocked and disturbed. He had sniffed and almost gagged, but he kept his composure, eyes watering and everything.

"Clay? Is that really you?"

Clay tried to smile, but even that felt fake to him. "Hi, José."

"My god… how bad did those guys hit you? The hospital said-"

"This isn't because of the crash," Clay said. "José, this is a helluva lot worse than that. Come in, please."

José looked reluctant but he allowed himself to be brought in. Clay offered him a drink, José said he would take anything cold.

"Got off work not too long ago… hotter than Hell outside." He sounded distracted as he spoke, as if just trying to make conversation without focusing too much on Clay.

"I bet," Clay said. "I only got water."

"That's fine." Was that disappointment in José's voice or was it only Clay who was disappointed by the lack of beer; something that would distract *him* from himself?

The two stood at the counter with glasses of water in hand. José was staring at his glass now, which had faint residue of Clay's oil on it. Clay offered him a napkin, and José accepted it graciously before picking it up again to drink, albeit hesitantly.

"Bro," Clay said almost chuckling. For some reason, this felt all too funny. His life had officially become a fucking comedy. Hurry, hurry, hurry! Step right up to witness the next living marvel; the man who looks like a zombie!

"I don't know how to tell you this man…"

"Tell me what exactly?"

"It's gonna sound crazy."

José took another sip of his water and gestured with the glass. "Fire away. Can't be any crazier than those gypsies taking you to court."

"Actually, it is."

And so, Clay told him. With the time he had to think the past evening, he had more to add to the tale and his suspicions than he had when he talked to Rachel. It also came more clearly, more sure. He had told José about what happened with Rachel as well, sparing no details if he could help it. While the first time talking about this sounded insane, Clay felt like he was more sure of himself this time than he was before. As for José, he sat quietly, absorbing everything in like a sponge. His expression remained unchanged, neither horrified nor skeptical. Seeing this strengthened Clay's confidence and resolve. He showed José the notes he took throughout the night, the stories and rumors about Flosvita, and what he had discovered that strengthen his assurance that he was right. José never interrupted him, except for only the occasional question. At some point in the story, he had in fact reached into his shirt and pulled out a small golden crucifix hanging on a silver chain around his neck. He caressed the figure of Jesus on the front, more vigorously as Clay explained the dark rumors surrounding the gypsy community.

Clay laughed inwardly. 'Community.' It was nothing but a *cult*. Maybe at one point it was meant to be a family, and maybe a whole community with different ideals and value. But many things change. Sometimes, those changes are not for the better.

When he had nothing more to add, Clay stared at José expectedly. His friend, asked for another glass of water as he read through the articles Clay had bookmarked on his laptop. For almost ten minutes he didn't say anything, and it left Clay alone to pace around the studio impatiently. At some point, Clay looked over to his toppled canvas, and approached it to stand it up. There sat the hole in the center of the fabric. His paints were scattered on the floor once more, and he picked them up and settled them back into their rightful place. The bucket that would be used as a strainer for his brushes, hung empty on one of the legs.

Clay looked back at José, who had been watching him. His friend's expression now carried something between disturbed worry, and proper skepticism.

"Clay," he said to his friend. "This is… this is crazy."

"Crazy enough to make sense?" Clay asked hopefully.

"None of this makes sense…"

"Why would I lie about the times I kept running into those gypsies even after that crazy fuck got thrown in jail? What benefit would I gain from that? Look at the fucking article, that's the *same* group we ran into."

"Literally… I don't know, but still, this is… this is not meant to be. I mean… my god, this is not supposed to be a *thing*!"

"C'mon," Clay said. No, he *begged*. He needed José to believe him. "Look, I know it sounds crazy, completely bonkers, I agree. But everything that has happened, everything that is happening right now, this is not something we can understand. And the hospital cannot help me. I could go in there and it is inevitable what will happen."

"And what *will* happen?"

"I will do what any corpse in a coffin will do," Clay said. "I will *rot* away." This time, he *did* laugh. It was genuine, and that alone scared him. By the looks of it, it frightened José as well.

"Quite the *grave* matter, isn't it?" he joked shaking his head. "It's funny, actually. Most of my life, I never felt truly alive. After the accident, I felt like a robot. Walking around- No, actually, I felt like the Walking Dead. Just… never feeling any purpose or reason to be alive. But ever since this happened… God, José…"

He was crying now. Tears and mucus were now spilling from underneath his eyes. They felt sticky upon touching his cheeks, stretching out as if someone had blown their nose on him. This made him cry harder, and José just stared, scared, not knowing what to do or say.

"I'm so scared," he told José. "My god, I am so fucking scared, José. I feel like a fucking fly trapped in a web, as the spider's saliva eats me away! Look at me! I'm... I'm scared and I don't know what to do..."

That wasn't necessarily true. He *did* know what to do. He doubted it would matter in the end, but he knew that to sit and do nothing, to go to the hospital, or to end it all himself, would be playing right into the gypsy's hands. He would be casting himself out like a pawn on a chessboard, with Astrid the Chink and her goddamn son making the moves. He felt like he had no control of his life anymore, and so the only thing to do was to disrupt the game if he could. Stain someone else's morbid and sadistic painting, so to speak. If there was even a one percent chance of it working, as crazy as it may sound, he knew he had to take a risk. He just didn't want to go in this alone, and since Rachel wasn't going to be there, who else better than his best friend?

If, his friend was willing to go to such a distance.

Clay then pointed to his bicep, where his skin graft sat in his flesh. "This is the new skin they gave me in the hospital. Look at it. It's not healing in, like it is supposed to."

"It's only been what, a day, Clay?"

"Longer," Clay told him. "They applied it when I first went in. It didn't heal all the way, so they stitched it up. Look at it now. The skin around it is green. It's *not* healing. It's just hanging onto me like a tag on a shirt."

"So, what are you saying, exactly?" José wanted him to get to the point. Clay was glad he said so.

Clay pinched the new skin, and said, "Look." If he was right, then this would be the turning point whether or not his friend thought him mad, would be so scared he ran away never to be seen again by Clay, or, he would stay, and watch.

He pulled on the skin as hard as he could, imagining it like a large Band-Aid rather than a piece of skin that was sewn into him like a patch on a pair of jeans. The stitches tore through his skin, not the graft he noticed, and he pulled it right off. The flab of skin hung between his fingers like a bloody leech that had been wrenched off, and both Clay and José were now staring at the chunk of flesh missing from his bicep once again.

Wriggling in the muscle that was now slick with pus and slime, were many little maggots. José was stammering, asking what it was, and dropping the piece of flesh to the counter, Clay, calmly to his own surprise, picked at the wound and pulled a wriggling maggot out of his arm. It squirmed like a worm until he let go, letting it drop to the counter. It inch-wormed around, wondering where it's warm and tasty home had been. All though this, Clay had felt no pain. The only sensation he felt was disgust and horror, and the smell coming out of his wound only added to the effect. It affected José more than Clay, because his friend had turned in his seat, and vomited onto the floor.

"Holy *shit*," José said wiping at his mouth. He stared with eyes as big as dinner plates, his mouth opened wide enough to let a swarm of flies fly in.

"That's not all. You've seen my fingernails. I'm missing teeth. This." He flicked at the mushroom-shaped ear on the side of his head. "Is about to fall off. This doesn't happen in some car accident. They did this to me. That fucker and his cultist family."

"Holy shit," José said again. He was looking at Clay like what many probably would have if they ever saw a zombie; a walking corpse or a bag of bones. This time he looked at Clay directly, his eyes locked with his friend's. "Clay... Can't the hospital see something is wrong? Surely someone can-"

"No one can help me with this," Clay said. "The hospital would have kept me there if they truly believed something was wrong. But they didn't even quarantine me as if I had some flesh-eating disease. They had a rational explanation for everything, and somehow for some reason, that works with the gypsy's plan. I don't know if this is really even their rational explanation or not. For all we know, they are under a spell as well. You've read the articles. Cops showing up, only to walk away empty-handed until the murder of that little girl. Everything it seems works in their greedy little hands. Somehow when Rachel and I ran that girl over, it didn't work in their favor. There were plenty of people still to resist them."

"You don't really think they are that powerful, do you? If they are powerful at all?"

"I don't know," Clay admitted. "But I do know that everything that I try to do since, only ends up with me getting worse and worse. Look at me, I look worse and smell worse since the first time this shit started."

"So what are you going to do?" José finally asked. "I mean... what *can* you do?"

This came across as a harder question for Clay to answer than he had originally thought. Now his idea seemed foolish, almost childish actually. He knew it was the best out of the few options he really had, but now that he had to answer, he felt silly.

Still, with effort, he managed to get it out. "I need to go see him. I need to speak to Gaston Burrows. See what it will take for this to stop."

"You really think he would do anything?" José asked. "Those bastards tried to fucking screw you in the courthouse *twice*, Clay. Also, you were attacked and harassed by them afterward. These aren't guys who can be reasoned with, we all knew that when you and Rachel were dealing with them in the first place."

"I agree," Clay said. "But maybe there is something else they want. Something other than me to suffer. Besides, they are after me and not Rachel. They are after the driver, not who was with him. They have an agenda and they are going to do whatever it takes to get it. Thing is, an agenda can change, should opportunity arise."

"You really believe that?"

"It's the best option I have under the circumstances compared to what else I have." Clay hoped he wouldn't have to explain those options at all, and thankfully José didn't ask.

"All right then, so, we go speak to Gaston?"

Clay nodded, hope spreading through his chest like a warmth. "You'll come with?"

"I said 'we' didn't I?" José tried for a smile. It was terrified, but encouraging, nonetheless.

Clay smiled back. "Thanks, man. Seriously."

"Besides," José added. "You don't have a car right now. Unless you plan on taxi-ing it to the jailhouse?"

"I doubt any driver would let me in…"

"Then let's go do it. Right now."

"You sure?"

"If you're on a timeclock do you really wanna wait any longer? Besides, I got nothing going on right now. No party, no meeting with Izabal, not even watching a Broncos game."

Clay had to smile again. "Thanks, man, seriously."

"Hey," José raising a hand to pat Clay on the shoulder, thought better of it, and put his hand down. "What are friends for? Besides, maybe you'll actually prove me wrong."

"Meaning you don't believe me. Not entirely."

José shook his head. At least he was honest. "Nope. But, I trust you. I trust you know what you are talking about. I just hope you are wrong. I hope there really is nothing wrong with you at all."

"I hope so too," Clay said honestly. But he didn't believe it. Not even a little bit.

Twenty-Three

The Ada County Jail was located near the Nordstrom Rack Boise Towne Square (which is a mouthful to say Clay always thought), on the same block as American Airline's Book-a-Flight. The government building was a ten minute drive from the Ada Courthouse next to St. Luke's where both the trial for the vehicular manslaughter and civil court case took place. José drove the two of them there with the windows rolled down so that the smell coming from his friend didn't make him faint. Clay did his best to cover himself up with a long-sleeved jacket and pants as to avoid staining José's seats. The entire way there he sat upright watching the roads like a bodyguard, on the lookout for any strange or following vehicles. He had his hood up when they pulled up to the building and went through the security check.

The security guards stared at Clay as they went through the metal detectors and went through their pockets. The man with the Garret Super Scanner had to cover his nose to scan Clay since no one wanted to approach him. Then they went to the front desk, and asked to have a sit-down with Gaston Burrows. When the receptionist who was as armed as any well-trained Boise Police officer asked for ID, Clay gave it to her, and she stared at both it and him for a long time before asking him to fill out a form.

"I need your SS number too, please," she said at last.

Clay said that was no problem and gave it to her. José was going through the same process as well, but he didn't have to give his social security. He decided he would be okay waiting in the waiting room with all the deadbeat mom's who was waiting to talk to their deadbeat husbands with their kids. A lot of them looked like crackheads the way their eyes darted around like they were expecting to get robbed of whatever cash they had, or arrested for the homemade cigarettes in their pockets. All the while Clay received a lot of stares, both in fascination and disgust at his appearance.

The wait was about an hour in order to do a security check. Usually, to visit in the jailhouse you had to fill it out online, and Clay had already done that and the request was for tonight. Since it was so soon, they had to make sure everything was in line. At the very least, Clay felt dressed for it. He felt very naked nonetheless, given how many cops were staring at him like he was not a human being but an undead ghoul. Clay tried not to let it bother him, although all the glancing eyes made his skin crawl almost as bad as the parasites infesting his body.

It suddenly occurred to Clay that he actually had no idea what he was going to do once he came face to face with Gaston Burrows. What was he going to say? 'Remove the curse pretty-please?' Would he threaten the old man? With what? He was already in jail. Bargain with him? What could Gaston want other than his blood? The dawning that he had absolutely nothing on the old man made Clay feel helpless. Burrows might very well just laugh in his face and send him away, and he would be no better off than he already was. He would just rot away, until the corpse that he was could walk no more and he turned into nothing.

The thought made him sick to his stomach.

Eventually, an officer came up to them and asked Clay to follow him. They walked down a concrete hallway and the man went through his check-ins using his keys and his radio. Alarms buzzed and metal doors slid open, and Clay found himself in a conference room with video-monitoring calls on the left and a glass face-to-face visitation seats on the right. Clay walked over to it, sat in the chair in the middle, and waited for the metal door on the other side of the glass to open. When it did, Gaston Burrows walked in and after getting checked in by the officer on the other side, the man sat down and regarded Clay with cold eyes that were both amused and disgusted.

His dark red hair was still long and in a ponytail held by a rubber band. He was wearing a yellow jumpsuit with a large G-2 on his left breast in bold black letters. His face, leathery and white, were clean from the time he spent in the jail. He still had about a year in the jail because of his crime, but with good behavior he would probably be out of here in a few months. If his friends on the other side had their way, he probably would have been bailed out long ago. His dark green eyes studied Clay as if he were some new species of bug that he would like to squash. Then he picked up the black phone on his end and held it to his ear, his finger curling around the thick steel cabling connecting the phone to the wall.

Clay, after some self-motivation, picked up his own phone and cleared his throat.

"The whoremaster," Gaston Burrows said in a raspy smoker's voice. "Hello, whoremaster. Where's your whore?"

During the trial the gypsies had taken to calling Clay 'whoremaster' with Rachel being the whore. It was something Gaston himself had started, and he seemed to have not forgotten. In fact, he seemed to relish now in the opportunity to use such a word again.

"I know what you did to me," Clay said in a low voice. He didn't expect to sound so angry, but he was. Seeing this man again, made his blood boil. Or whatever blood that was probably not curdled in his system in some way shape or form.

"Oh?" Gaston asked with a raised eyebrow. "That business in the grill parking lot? I was drunk, you understand. Not that these fools can. How can they? They weren't there. Given the circumstances-"

"You know what I'm talking about, you sonofabitch."

Silence. That cold stare right into Clay's own eyes. Then Burrows nodded, a smile creeping on the corner of his mouth as his eyes glanced upwards towards the ceiling, as if conversing with his pagan god.

Finally, he said without looking back down, "Do you now?"

"Look at me," Clay said.

"Hard not to."

Trying to let it slide, Clay said past almost grounded teeth (whatever teeth he had left), "Your wife told me everything."

"So I heard."

How?

Instead, Clay got straight to the point. "I want you to remove it."

Gaston met Clay's eyes at last. His expression impassive. "Not a chance."

"Please? Look, I'm sorry."

"So you said."

"But I've suffered enough. I'm... well, look at me!"

"I can see just fine."

"So please, have pity on me." He then added, "Sir."

"Not a chance in Hell, whoremaster. I'll never 'remove it' as you put it. I cannot. How can I? I'm in here."

"Don't lie to me."

"I'm not. How can I if I am in here? You and I can't even share a handshake."

"You know how to remove it even without being near me!" Clay insisted. He hoped he sounded more sure than he felt.

"Actually, I don't," Burrows said seriously. "Neither on this side of the glass or the other."

"Bullshit."

"None whatsoever," Burrows said calmly. He was leaning in his chair now, acting like a man who had all the time in the world. They only had thirty minutes, but he was willing to waste time.

If that was true though, Clay thought. *Why come in the first place?*

(To rub it in your face?)

Maybe.

"Look, I get it. You were mad. But there was nothing I can do. And the law saw it too. So please, just let it go. Take whatever you gave me back."

Burrows laughed. "You say it like it is simple."

"It has to be!" Clay implored. "Look, I'm falling *apart,* man. You want me to suffer? I suffered plenty with this. Please, you gotta remove it before it's too late! I'll do anything!"

"Even if I wanted to," Burrows said. "I couldn't. Not that I *would* even if I knew *how*."

"What is that supposed to mean?"

"It means how I just said it. I don't know how. I know how to... let's call it, 'giving.' But I'm not good at *taking*. Unlike *you*, whoremaster."

Clay had to bite his lip from saying something he might regret. Despite his frustration, he felt tears threatening behind his eyes. He didn't want those mucus drops rolling down his sagging cheeks.

"I don't believe you."

"Doesn't matter if you do or not. By the looks of it... you're worse for wear, so to speak."

Clay clapped a hand on the glass. Burrows looked at the hand with his eyes and brought them back to Clay's face. His head didn't move once.

"You *have* to remove the curse, you bastard," Clay said. Then with effort, he pleaded. "Please. I'm *begging* you here. I learned my lesson."

"I thought you did nothing wrong?"

"I *didn't* though!" Clay hissed. "Look... I don't deserve *this*." He gestured towards himself, which might have been comical to Burrows under the circumstances.

"Then what 'lesson' did you learn? Kimberly didn't deserve it either," Burrows said mildly despite his eyes saying so much more. "You took her away from me. You have no idea how much grief you caused me and my Family."

"It *wasn't* my fault," Clay insisted.

"Either way, she's gone. By your hand."

"It was an *accident*!"

"There are no 'accidents,'" Burrows said now sounding furious, his temper no longer in check. His voice was low, but it was dangerous. "You took her away from me. I was serious when I said I wanted you to pay. Drunk or not, that night, I regret *nothing* I said or did."

He's not admitting he cursed me, Clay realized suddenly. *He's being careful despite being angry with me.* "Please," he said again, in a husky voice just above a whisper it was so difficult to say it. "Please…"

"No."

"Mr. Burrows-"

"Don't bother with pleasantries you *swine*," Burrows said. "As I said before, even if I knew how to get rid of it, I wouldn't do it. I take pleasure hearing from my wife and Family, that you are *struggling*. I hear about the progression of your little… misfortune, and how it is plaguing your very way of life. Think of it as karma. What comes around, goes around. If that ain't 'justice' then I don't know what it is."

"I'm *begging* you here," Clay said again. "There has to be a way! There must be something *I* can do."

"I'm sure," Burrows agreed. "Not that I would share it with you."

"What will it take?"

"You know what it takes."

Growing even more frustrated, Clay managed, "There has to be something else! I'll do anything else! I swear!"

"Will you now?" Burrows asked, one dark eyebrow raised. It was so finely shaped, it could have been *written* on the man's brow for all Clay knew. This time, his voice sounded more curious than gleeful or angry.

"Yes," Clay said and then laughed uncontrollably again. Burrows didn't react like this was anything strange, but like he expected it. "*Look* at me!"

"Gonna lose your other ear by the looks of it," Burrows said with a smile. Within his thin and leathery lips, one could see the few stubs of teeth that were still in his pale gums. "Might end up with less teeth than me too. Your lower lip looks a little worn as well. And look at that, you left a smudge on the window."

Sure enough, a yellow handprint where Clay had smacked the glass was there. It reminded him of a crime scene after forensics in Law & Order dusted glass for fingerprints and handprints. The swirls in his fingertips looked muddled, as if they too were becoming mushy like the rest of his body that was now at the point of feeling damp inside his jacket. He felt movement in his gut, but he ignored it. If he focused on himself, he would never get what he needed out of Gaston.

"Please," Clay said again. "Do you want an apology?"

"You already gave one when we first met, and plenty after," Burrows said. "And your apologies mean nothing to me. Meaningless words said too often by those who believe saying it makes things better."

"Then what do you want?"

"Well, you can't bail me out of here any earlier. Boise State has decided they will not tolerate anything of my kind ever again. They will not tolerate us or our meddling. We get jailed, we get no bail, so to speak. The same happened to us in Washington, a few of us are in the Benton County Jail in Kennewick as we speak. This isn't new for us, and unfortunately, it happened to me. Thankfully, my sentence isn't as strict as some of the poor bastards who are incarcerated."

For some reason, the fact that the man said 'incarcerated' made it sound funny to Clay and he had to bite his tongue to keep from laughing again. He felt something give in his tongue and he released it. He had to remain focused. He was looking up at the clock above the door where Gaston had come in. He had fifteen minutes left at most.

"Name your price," Clay said. "There has to be something I can do to convince you to try *something*. There has to be something you can do. I can't believe that I'm doomed to die… like *this*."

"And what if you are?"

"I can't accept that."

Burrows chuckled. He looked genuinely amused now. "Well, there isn't much that *I* want. Only three things. You already know two of them."

Clay nodded. "Bail, or me dead. What's the third?"

"You can't get me it."

"Try me."

Burrows stared at him. "My daughter back."

Clay pressed his lips tightly together. Any hope he had slowly fading away like a candle. Melting away like wax on a stick, or decaying flesh on a skeleton.

(like you!)

"So, what then? I'm fucked?"

Gaston Burrows was quiet for a moment. He appeared to be thinking, debating. His expression softened somewhat, his eyes coming alight. A mental lightbulb had flickered behind those dark eyes.

"You can speak to my wife, and the Family," Burrows answered softly. "They won't know how to take it away either. We of Flosvita, we learn to give, not take. Only one person would know how."

"Who?"

"Nigger Jeff."

Clay's eyes narrowed in thought. Unfazed by the derogatory terminology. Jeff though… "Who?"

"Our founder, and my brother."

"You mean Jeffery Flosvita?"

Gaston Burrows shrugged. "Whatever you wanna call him. That was his Family name. He insisted upon it, said it kept him humble and not expect too much out of people, especially the white's who mined those mountains from which he came."

"And yet he took people like you in," Clay noted.

"Nigger Jeff took anyone in who looked worthy. I, who came off the boat when my daddy had enough of Ireland and her weakness, saw Jeffery as a brother as I did for everyone in the Family. If anyone can help you with your little... *condition*, it is he."

"Jeffery Flosvita is in *prison* though."

"Nah," Burrows said shaking his head. "He's free."

"Since when?" Clay knew the article was written back in 2019, not that long ago. Surely Jeffery Flosvita hadn't been released just yet, had he?

"Ahh, he ain't free like you are, friend," Burrows said. "Nigger Jeff is among the stars now."

"He... died?"

"Oh yeah. Died in his sleep. Poor sot died at the ripe 'ol age of ninety-five. Died in prison. Never got to see his Family again, how strong we have become despite our... troubles in the past."

"I know all about your 'troubled past,'" Clay told the man in a loathsome voice.

"Do you? Not everyone knows the whole story. Only those in the Family know."

"Anyways," Clay said wanting to move on before he got angry again. He could already hear the phone creaking beneath his iron-grip. "If Ni- I mean, Jeffery is dead, then how can he help me?"

"We have ways. My wife has ways. You really want this to end, whoremaster?"

"The name is *Clay*," Clay said past clenched teeth.

"A rose by any other name would smell as sweet," Burrows said in that irritating mild tone. "Just as any whoremaster would still smell like the *shit* he sticks his prick into.”

“Just cut to the chase,” Clay said now growing impatient with the insults. “How can your wife help me when your leader is dead?”

“Leader?” This time, Burrows sounded upset. No, he sounded *offended*. “Nigger Jeff was *not* my leader. He was my *brother*. We are all brothers and sisters in Flosvita, boy. We have a bond unlike anything the world can comprehend. I respected the man like an older brother. Hell, there was a time I looked up to him as my *father*. But no. He was not a leader. If he were in my place right now, why he-”

“Would curse me?” Clay challenged.

This time, Burrows kept silent. But that unnerving smile crept up on his face again.

“Fine, I need to talk to Astrid then,” Clay said more to himself than to Burrows. He didn’t need to ask to be sure. Burrows seemed to understand that as well. “But how do I know you are telling the truth?”

“Do you have any other options?”

“No... Well... then where are they now?”

Gaston Burrows chuckled slightly. He cleared his throat, mumbled something about needing a cigar, and then said to Clay, “Where we were last time we were here. Hidden Springs. Our camp is down the Dry Creek south of North Cartwright Road. You do well to remember that, Mr. Couch. You can’t miss it.”

Gone was ‘whoremaster’ and ‘boy.’ Now he was using the respective last name basis. It somehow assured Clay that Burrows wasn’t quite bullshitting him, but he was still cautious, for the cunning old man might be leading him into a trap.

Clay would remember it. He would remember it, and if he can convince José, he will be there by tonight. He had to. “What should I expect from there?”

"Nothing at first, I wouldn't think," Burrows said. "They know not to mess with you."

"They already did," Clay said angrily. "Or did they not tell you about their visit with me at the hospital."

"Not in the way *you* perceive," Burrows said amusedly. "Mess with you, in terms of *harming* you."

Clay pointed at his face. "This doesn't look like harm?"

"No. It looks like *justice* to me. But if it all works out, it might benefit us both in one way or another. The more I think about it even, the more it might be best if the... *condition* is removed. But no one at camp should bother you at first. They are merely to make sure that nature takes it's course, so to speak."

This time, Clay did smile for real. "You're a funny man, Mr. Burrows."

"And you, Mr. Couch, are interesting."

"Well, considering the shit you put me through, maybe I'll surprise you."

"Maybe, maybe," Burrows agreed. "Hopefully, you are willing to pay the price for the blood of my daughter."

"Even when there was nothing I could do?"

"*Was* there nothing you could do?" Condescending, a question worthy of Rachel.

"Absolutely nothing." Even as he said it, what Rachel had said earlier pricked the back of his mind like a stray nail. *Could anything be done about Kimberly? Did you* really *have no control?*

Clay was still staring at Gaston Burrows, who was staring right back. By the gleam in his eyes, Clay wondered if the man had picked that bit of information out of his head and would say something.

He didn't. He only stretched his arm out and asked, "Are we done then?"

"I have one more question for you," Clay said, wanting to give one last moment of spite before departing.

"I'll answer if I can. And if I want."

"What was your daughter doing out in the road?"

This time, Burrows looked angry. His fine eyebrows curled into his brow, making his scowl look as vicious as an angry Pitbull. "Are you trying to anger me, boy?"

"I'm just wondering what sort of smart person would go out into the road," Clay said grinning back. This was pointless, but he wanted to get under Burrows' skin, like they had his. "If she never went out there, on the most dangerous highway in the state by the way, none of this would have happened. We wouldn't be having this conversation now."

His goal was to ruffle Burrows' feathers, and Clay saw that he had succeeded. The man stared hatefully at Clay. If the glass wasn't between them, the man probably would have seized him by the throat and started speaking Latin again. Instead, the man smiled, the way a judge would should a man seal his own fate. It reminded Clay of the Godfather, the cynical smile of hatred that meant 'you'll get what's coming to you.'

"I think this conversation is over," Burrows said. "*Vale*, Whoremaster Couch." With that said, the man hung up his phone and stood up from his chair. He said something inaudible to Clay, and then turned and probably told the officer behind him that he was done. He was walked back to the door, where the same procedure would be performed to place him back in his cell. Wait at this door, say 'United States of America' and follow the white line.

Clay hung up his own phone, delivering an unseen salute to the old man with a wave of his hand. With Burrows' back to him, Clay promptly said, "And goodbye to you as well, you carrot-top sonofabitch."

Just as the man had said, this conversation was over. Nothing more could have been said anyway, and Clay couldn't have thought of a more proper way to end the conversation. Yes, he was willing to do anything to lift this curse. But that didn't mean he would have to be nice about it. And there was no way in hell he was going to fake it with the gypsies.

Question was, what would he really expect going there? Salvation, an early grave, or a prison until he rotted?

Twenty-Four

Hidden Springs was an unincorporated community about a half hour from the State Capital center. About thirty minutes through dusty terrain along the base of the mountain ranges, with most of the spruces and honey locusts along the Dry Creek that passed through the town and continued both east and west. The place Gaston Burrows was referring to was off of Cartwright where you followed the river past some private property where there were a few fishing spots and campsites. This was officially bear country, outside the city limits where the wild things roam.

During the drive, Clay talked about his visit with Gaston Burrows and what he had found out. José looked just as surprised as Clay thought about the old man's former partner, both in his name and his death.

"So, we are to converse with a *dead* guy?" his friend asked, emphasizing the word 'dead.'

"I dunno," Clay said honestly. "The whole thing... I dunno. Feels like we wound up in some fairytale. But like I said, there's nothing he can do, or so he said. Only his wife can help me find... Jeffery or whatever, and only that can help me."

"He could be lying, y'know. Making you waste your time."

"Most likely," Clay admitted. "But it isn't like we have any other options. Like I said too, it isn't like hurting me is gonna help these guys' case. They already did enough damage as is."

"Clay, I have a bad feeling about this," José said in a timorous tone. "The guy might be setting us up. Might want you at the camp so everyone can see what happens to you."

"How? Not like he's in touch with his little 'family.'"

"They *do* allow you to call from jail, Clay. It ain't like prison or some shit, the phone calls are open if you aren't in your cell."

Clay hadn't thought of that. "Even so, what is he gonna say?"

"Uh, hold 'em hostage? Wait until you quote-unquote turn to dust? Maybe just don't let them get anywhere near my wife and kid?"

"José, the guy had a… I don't know, a *hungry* look in his eyes. There is something else he wants. Something he thinks is beneficial to whatever it is these guys do. I could see it in his eyes."

"No offence, Clay, but you're not the best judge of character," José said honestly.

"I don't have to be. He was ready to just tell me to go on my merry way. Besides, like I said, what exactly do I have to lose at this point? If they really do mean to 'take me hostage' like you said, then I'll be in no worse position than I would be in a hospital or on my own."

"And there I am," José said. "In the same cage with probably a shrunken head to keep you company."

Now Clay felt discouraged. His friend was here with him. Maybe whatever terrible thing the gypsies could do when they reached them would be no different for Clay. He was a man who had nothing left to lose at this point.

José on the other hand had no beef with these guys. He also still had a life. He still had a job working his way through construction, a girlfriend, and family still. Clay had none of that left. Was it really fair to have José deal with this too?

"You're right," Clay told his friend. "Look, we're almost at O'Michaels, we could drop you off there if you want."

"Oh, so you'll take my car then?"

"I'll walk."

José started laughing. The laughter irritated Clay, and he demanded what was so fucking funny.

"Nothing, jeez, bro, you really think I'm gonna let you go by yourself? Out here at night?"

"If it is as dangerous as you say it might be-"

There was a central storage compartment in José's car. He smacked the top of the plastic lid and it popped open with ease. It was a two-section compartment with a shallow one on top for cards, insurance, registration, or a second set of keys with the larger storage space underneath it. The force of José's hand popped both latches open to get to the larger compartment. Clay could see inside, there were a few packets of receipts from Les Schwab, a pack of those car freshener trees, and a pink slip for the car. There was something else in there too. At first Clay couldn't tell what it was because it was sheathed in a kydex sleeve.

It was a gun.

Clay stared at José. "What are you-"

"I always have that with me in my car. Take it with me when I go camping with my brothers. We might need it. There is another gun in my trunk that you can have too."

"Jesus, José!"

"What?" José asked with a smile that clearly said he wasn't going to be sorry for this. "We are just going to exercise our second amendment rights. Not like we are gonna go in guns a'blazing. We are gonna carry it the same way we men carry condoms."

"Condoms?"

"Have 'em and not need them, rather than need them and not have 'em."

"I've never shot a gun before," Clay said staring down at the holstered weapon. He couldn't tell what kind of pistol it was. He only knew what Call of Duty had told him back when he was in high school. He was afraid to touch the weapon.

"Hopefully we won't have to use them," José admitted. "But we'll make sure they are ready before we go in."

"They might think it's suspicious if we get it out of the trunk when we get there," Clay noted. He didn't even know where exactly they would be stopping.

José nodded, appearing to consider that now. "You're right... one will have to do. I'll carry since you don't know how to do it. Call me your personal bodyguard."

"José, I didn't think of it before. You really don't have to do this."

"You want me to though."

"Doesn't mean you *have* to."

José rolled his eyes and shook his head at Clay.

"What?"

"I love you, bro," José said. "But you're a dumbass."

"*What*?"

"I'm just bitchin'. I'm not leaving you out to dry like this. I said I was gonna stick with you, so here I stay. If it does go wrong like I think it might, hopefully they just take you."

"Gee, thanks."

"Gives me a chance to get you out of trouble," José added with a wink. "We'll figure it out. I just hope you're right and this doesn't go south."

"Same... José-"

"Don't get sappy with me, Clay."

"I'm not! Just... thank you."

José smiled. "What are friends for?"

Clay smiled back. The first time he *really* smiled since they left the jailhouse. "Yeah, true."

It was sort of funny, borderline ironic now that Clay could think about it. It was just like he had told José back in his apartment. Most of his life, especially since the accident, he felt like he was walking around like a zombie. Alive and running, but not really living. He hadn't felt alive in almost a year or so. Rachel had brought back some of the old excitement, something he had described once as being on the Aftershock as a little kid in Silverwood. Scary, but thrilling without understanding where the ride was going to take him. It was the most fun he had out of the entire theme park, even before his father took him and his two sisters. That thrill was what the relationship felt like, a rollercoaster with some scary moments but at the same time thrilling. A reason to keep going and fighting for. After the accident, that excitement died out.

A similar excitement had taken over Clay right now as he sat in José's car stinking like the dead and sweating/ oiling with anticipation. It was in nothing like the Aftershock in Silverwood or his relationship with Rachel. It was a different kind of thrill. It was a fight for his *life*.

He was scared, oh yes. He was fucking terrified beyond belief. Panic was like a rat in his skull, the cage slowly rotting away and eventually that rat was going to come out if he wasn't careful. But this whole thing, good or bad, has made him realize how much he truly wanted to live and that he was willing to do whatever it took to save his life.

It was as if this whole thing was not him slowly decomposing into the grave, but a resurrection that can only be explained through the supernatural plane of reality that no human can look into and come back normal. As the car bounced it's way along the dark road, Clay began to hope and pray that all would be well. He would need all the help he could get, even from the Almighty, if He were willing for a decomposing wretch such as him.

Twenty-Five

When they crossed the Dry Creek with Hidden Springs to the east, they turned on a dirt road following the creek to the west. To their right the Russian Olives that lined Dry Creek stood like sentinels in the ever-growing dark. At this point, the sun had already set, and the moon was taking her rightful place in the sky among Venus and the other stars. They drove slowly, the car kicking up dust behind them like a trail of ghosts in the night. Coyotes were no doubt on the prowl tonight, and the car's brights were on to illuminate their way.

They continued on until the road took an immediate right and cut right through the Dry Creek, leading to another open area where they saw the dim specks of bonfires in the distance. Smoke was rising to the cloudless sky like many fingers reaching up to the heavens. As they drew closer to the lights themselves, they saw the dark shapes of many campers, Winnebago's, and tents that made up the huge camp of Flosvita. As they drew more near, they came across a stray camper with a man sitting in a lawn chair on the roof. The man had a rifle and was smoking a cigar. He looked about thirty or forty, with a full beard and wearing a tweed jacket and overalls. He waved at the approaching car and José pulled up alongside it. The man jumped off his camper, and approached the passenger side of the car, rifle gripped tightly in his hands. José rolled down his window, allowing the man to shing a flashlight that was attached to the weapon into the interior, and immediately stopped short when he saw Clay's face.

"Stars above," the man said in a raspy voice around his cigar. A trail of blue smoke was trailing from the end of the still fresh cancer-stick, and his big brown eyes were wise.

"Christ on a stick… What the hell happened to you?" He then covered his nose with a free hand, all for the better for him.

"I'm Clayton Couch," Clay answered. "I'm here to see Astrid."

The man studied him for a long time. "You the whoremaster Gaston the Gimp had trouble with back?"

"Yes, I... I was the guy who accidently ran over his daughter." Even saying the word 'accident' sounded to Clay like a blatant lie.

"Ahh," the man said nodding his head. "Rumor 'round the campfire was *something* happened to you. Didn't think it was so drastic. Goddamn..."

"Can we go in?" José asked.

"Sure, gimme a sec. The Chink though..." The man took out a radio and spoke into it. About a moment later, a beam of headlights came up the dirt path and slowed next to the camper. It was a four-wheeler, and the woman riding it gestured for José to follow.

"Go ahead," the man said to José. "Follow her."

"Thank you, mister...?" José let the question hang. The man didn't answer. He only told them to follow the four-wheeler again.

They started moving forward at a pace easy enough for the car. Thankfully the gal was in no hurry to get back to camp. Behind her, her white blouse and blonde hair sailed in the wind like sails on a pirate ship, her hair like strands of wheat. They got closer to the campsite where two larger campers were parked on either side of the path which stood Clay guessed as the 'entrance' to the camp since all the vehicles seemed to be parked around the tents like sheep dogs around sheep.

José's comment on the place was, "Looks like a carnies camp at a fair."

Clay couldn't agree more.

While most of the larger vehicles were parked in a somewhat scattered circle around the camp that was clear of sagebrush, the motorcycles and trucks were parked to the immediate left of the entrance campers. There were some campers opened up with laundry lines stretched out with string lights between each large vehicle. Just as José said, it looked like what a carny camp would look like; white trash trailer park but with more Hispanics and blacks than anyone else. Though those were the main demographic, there were still quite a few whites and Native Americans walking about the camp wearing heavy boots or nothing at all on their feet. Bonfires were scattered around the area dug into the dirt and filled with stones, and there were card tables set up with Colman lanterns sitting on them while men and women and children played cards, drank, or chatted absent-mildly. The girl escorting José told him to park where he was and the two got out and after she got off her ATV, she instructed them to follow still. Clay could see the bulge at her hip, and knew the woman was packing.

On foot, the gypsy world of Flosvita continued to be revealed. There were teens playing hacky sack near a black Winnebago and kids kicking a soccer ball close by. Mothers with children were sitting together under the awning of another camper, sipping wine or coffee while they bounced their toddlers in their laps, all wearing either just diapers or shorts. There was music playing nearby and as they walked closer and closer to the growing sound, they saw a group of men playing the violin, a guitar (Clay recognized the style as chicken scratch) and a front plate cajon box drum. Some girls Clay and José's age were dancing in the dirt, kicking up dust with their bare feet and laughing like witches in Salem; all of them dressed in handsewn dresses. Among them was a naked man who wore only a headdress of silver lace. His face was painted in a similar silver paint, making him look ghostly. The women had a chain around his neck as if he were a dog, and he danced with them drunkenly with a raging erection. It was a gross and also unsettling sight to behold.

All the kids around too... Clay marveled.

Some of the gypsies in the camp had turned to look at the new arrivals but the looks weren't necessarily out of fear or mistrust. It was fascination. It wasn't every day they got to see a Mexican walking alongside a ghoul in their camp.

The girl leading them to the far back of the camp introduced herself as Merrian the Mouse. She said she had been with Flosvita for almost five years.

"What brings you here to see The Chink?" she asked them.

"That's a secret," José said and when Merrian looked back at him, he gave her a flirtatious wink. She smiled back. The guy could be charming even when he looked as scared as he did. Clay only saw that look on his friend's face once when they were in middle school, when he almost got hit by a semi on their way home.

These guys weren't semi's, but they might as well be just as unpredictable when it comes to being out here in the middle of nowhere. There would be no civilized help if they got into trouble. Outside of Boise, out here in the desert, they were on their own. Because out here was where the wild things roamed.

Eventually they came across a 2016 Airsteam of golden tan. It was parked in the very back and had two tents pitched up underneath tarps stretched out from the roof of the vehicle from the front and back. The steps leading inside were out and sitting on it was Johnny Burrows talking to a man standing in front of him, passing a bottle of whiskey between one another. Clay recognized the other man as the guy outside the store when he had first gotten kicked out. Johnny stood when he saw who was coming and his friend stood alongside him. Both didn't look happy to see Clay, their expressions ghostly under the string lights dangling overhead.

"Merrian," Johnny said putting his hand on the butt of the revolver he had at his hip. He looked like a kid playing cowboy the way he did that. "Did Mother–"

"She knows," Merrian said. "She called for me to come get 'em. They're supposed to meet with her."

Johnny stared at Clay for a long time.

"Long time no see, cowboy," Clay said, unable to help but be snotty, displaying a toothless grin in the process that must have looked mortifying by the way the kid's eye twitched. "Chased off the Injuns yet?"

Johnny's friend stepped forward, but the kid placed a hand on his chest and said something. He then turned back to Clay and demanded, "Why are you here?"

"They are here to speak with me," said a voice whose owner was stepping out of the RV and onto the dirt.

Astrid the Chink look like she had just showered, her hair appearing damp and attracting mosquitos though none landed on her, as if she were some unclean demoness that they couldn't touch for fear of insulting their bloodsucking god.

She smiled in greeting at Clay and said, "Hello, Mr. Couch."

"Mrs. Burrows," Clay said. His voice sounded ridiculously high as he said it, and he had to clear his throat which made Merrian chuckle.

"Go on, Merrian," Astrid told the gal and when she left, the old woman sized José up. "And who is this?"

"A friend of his," José said. He had his crucifix out of his shirt and out in the open, Clay realized. He really was scared. Clay couldn't blame him. It wasn't just the gypsies that scared him.

This place… it just didn't feel right.

The stories in the articles had mentioned religious groups and churches claiming that the gypsies were notorious for occult teachings including being abusers of black magic. All of which were only speculations of those interviewed by Damon Harker. Clay, having not been a religious person since he was a kid, had no reason to believe in devils or angels. But this place just didn't feel *right*. It wasn't just the many eyes that were watching them. It was the eyes that he and José *couldn't* see. It was the unknown danger, like what a child might feel when an all too-friendly uncle invites them to help them with something in the basement. You couldn't see the threat, but it was there. The atmosphere in the campground, if Clay had to put it into words, had a tense feeling to it like an area where ozone was the strongest right before the Greek god Zeus threw a thunderbolt at the foolish mortal.

This was not a place where man was meant to go. This was a place where the wild things roamed. Where men walked with devils, and the feeling of constantly being under the watchful eyes of such things only scratched the surface of the paranormal that very few who experience it can walk the earth normally again.

Even Astrid the Chink, who was appearing innocuous, hid an unseen danger in those sharp snake-like eyes. Behind this woman's smile, lied inequity at it's absolute finest.

"All *friends* are welcome here," said Astrid. "Although, we have exceptions, to those who wrong us, Mr. Couch. However, my husband says you might be of use to us yet, *without* being dead."

"You've spoken with him?" Clay asked.

Mrs. Burrows nodded mildly. "Those who tie the knot within the Flosvita Family, have a bond incomprehensible to the average human being. It is a gift, of which many of us here carries. You say you are willing to do anything, to save your precious body." It was not a question. Not in the slightest.

Clay nodded. "What exactly is it that needs to be done?"

José added, "And what exactly should be expected in full? We need you to be straight with us."

Us. Not Clay. Clay felt a million times better knowing that his friend was by his side now, his fear not entirely gone, but abated.

Astrid regarded José with a cold stare. "You suspect me of wicked deals?"

"Look what you did to my friend," José said blatantly. Did he really believe they did this to Clay? It warmed Clay's tremulous heart to hear his friend say such a thing. "With all due respect, Burrows, I do not trust you or your buddies there." He nodded in the direction of Johnny and his friend.

His friend, grinned at José. A challenge in his eyes. "Feeling's mutual, greaseball."

"Myke, please," Astrid said calmly but not without the sound of amusement in her frail and yet witty voice. "Well, boys, you have come to the right place. As the most trusted member of the Family, I know how we can find a way to lift what has been placed upon you."

"So you can get rid of this?" Clay said gesturing to himself. "This curse?"

"Not I," Astrid said smiling. The smile this time was like that of a child with a dirty secret; one that would blow their friend's mind upon revealing what they have learned. "Only one person has the knowledge beyond me or my husband's understanding. Nigger Jeff is the one we must consult."

José looked just as uncomfortable as Clay felt when he had first heard that name. It wasn't just the word in general associated with Jeffery Flosvita. There was a chill in the air that Clay hadn't noticed back at the jail. Out here, the name alone seemed to have dropped the temperature by twenty degrees as if a wraith were breathing down his neck, causing gooseflesh to erupt on his skin. The name here, had a reprobational affect to it. That was the only thing Clay could really think of it as. Because this was not the real world where the name Nigger Jeff might be as meaningless as your average Joe. Here, in this campsite of Flosvita, there was power in the name. Power that both Clay and José could sense.

"I thought that-"

"He was dead?" Johnny Burrows said interrupting Clay. "Yeah, he is, at least dead in the eyes of you, whoremaster."

"What do you mean?" José asked. But Clay already had a dark suspicion as to where exactly this was going.

Astrid seemed to notice the expression or body language on Clay, because that smile spread all the wider. It was a smile that said, 'There is no secrets between us. Here, there are no secrets at all.'

"Let us talk," Astrid the Chink said. "In my home."

It was the last thing Clay wanted to do, but he felt *pulled* by Astrid's words. Both because he knew he didn't have much of a choice in the matter, but also because of that same reason but taken in a different way. He moved forward, with José following close behind. Astrid told her son and his friend to wait outside and when they climbed the steps and entered the home of the Burrows, that nasty feeling of the supernatural and disgust, reached a peak level that almost made him turn and run away like a werewolf on holy ground.

The interior of the RV was more spacious than Clay would have suspected under the circumstances.

The front two seats had a table in-between them with a dreamcatcher hanging above it, the eagle feathers beneath it swaying in the breeze coming in from the open windows. The main interior had a couch that had a removable center to lift up a table which was already extended with a paper plate of what looked like baked beans and a glass of wine. Above it on the back wall was a flatscreen which was off and reflecting the two men and woman within the RV. Next to the couch/table was another set of seats on either side, with the one on the left right in front of the little kitchen/sink area. There was a stove/oven right next to the sink, and by the stove was a refrigerator with a chrome vent attached to collect any oily fumes from the stovetop. Above the sink was a microwave, and between it and alongside it right behind the seat next to it, was the cabinets containing glasses or some creepy voodoo shit.

In the back hall was a bathroom with a toilet to the left and a makeshift walk-in shower on the right. Next to this was another cabinet where extra blankets and even a cot could be stored. In the very back was the sleeping quarters, which consisted of two regular beds with a storage space in the back, and two extendable cots with support beams capable of turning them into bunkbeds. From the back, a smell of marijuana and essential oils lingered, the steam/smoke from both lingering inside the RV like a faint fog. The rear window was open as well, letting the cool night breeze pass through the RV like a fumigation process, but Clay doubted it would have much effect. Finally, right beneath the window, Clay could see an alter built from scratch holding up a picture of Kimberly Burrows.

The picture was blown up, showing Kimberly as a young girl, probably twelve rather than nineteen when she had died. She was wearing a white dress and brown beads around her neck and wrists. Her red hair was in a braid decorated with wildflowers, and her bare feet had brass rings or bangles around her ankles. She was in a dancing pose in what looked like a barn with a stage with lights in the background, and small tufts of hay along the floorboards. She had a huge and infectious smile on her freckled face, her almond eyes bright and gray rather than green. Seeing the picture sitting between two black candles and among bundles of flowers, shells, and beads, Clay felt sick. It was if those eyes were watching him, judging him as he supposed God would if he were in His domain, if that domain happened to be an Airstream RV with weird knick-knacks and smells in it.

Astrid instructed the men to take a seat as she cleared the table. She placed the plate in a garbage hatch beneath the sink, and the glass of wine into the sink itself. She then reached over the microwave where the cabinets were, and removed three small glass mason jars from it and then from another cabinet, a large gallon jug of amber liquid.

"Might I interest either of you in some moonshine? My son made it himself while we were in Oregon. Made it with apples and cinnamon. Tastes just like an apple pie."

"I'll pass," Clay said. José said the same.

Astrid shrugged but placed all three glasses on the table anyway as if she hadn't heard them. Then she poured herself a drink after pulling the cork off the jug. The smell was strong, the alcoholic fumes reaching Clay's nonexistent nose and tempting him tenderly. He wanted a drink. Badly. He wanted to get drunk the night before. He wanted some way to numb the terror in his heart. But he knew that if he gave in, he wouldn't stop. Still, he had to lick his lips to keep them from salivating at the possible taste of apple pie moonshine.

Astrid drank, didn't even clear her throat, and sat the glass down. "So," she said. "Gaston says we are to consult with Nigger Jeff."

"I guess so," Clay said, surprised at the sound of acceptance in his voice.

Astrid nodded. Now she looked a little disconcerted. The hungry, greedy gleam in her eyes that was scarily identical to that of her husband's, was replaced by what looked to Clay like doubt. Not enough for her to deny them outright, but it was still there, nonetheless.

"The last we spoke to him, was about a month ago, when we were first dealing with the loss of our daughter," Astrid finally said.

"You talk to a dead man?" José inquired. Clay was glad it was his friend who said it and not him.

Astrid looked at the man. "You are surprised. I am not surprised." Hearing the word 'surprise' twice *almost* made Clay chuckle. "However, it is not at all something to be taken lightly. If I had my way, Mr. Couch, I would not be willing to do this. I would have sent you away. Or chain you up for entertainment. But my husband and his wisdom says that you might be of use to us yet."

"And because of that, we talk to Jeffery," Clay said.

Astrid nodded, finished her glass of moonshine, and poured herself another. This time the cup wasn't as filled as it was last. "I will do this. But in order to do this, we need you to see as well. I will need you to open your third eye."

"How do we do that?" José asked.

Astrid regarded José with surprise. "You wish to see as well?"

"I was wondering that myself," Clay said to José.

"Color me curious," José with a shrug. "Besides, I want to make sure what Clay is seeing is real, and not some hocus pocus bullshit."

Astrid smiled, the expression revealing her offence. "As you wish. Then to begin, I need some hair from the two of you." She downed her glass, and then stood to retrieve something from the pantry.

"I don't have hair," Clay said touching his bald head.

"I may be old but I'm not ignorant, Mr. Couch," Astrid said. "You have hair somewhere else."

If Clay still had his balls, they would probably had shrunken into his gut and out of sight like a turtle's head.

"You're kidding, right?" He had no hair anywhere else other than his legs. He was after all not a very hairy man in general.

"No, I am very much serious." From the top cabinet, Astrid removed a stone urn about the size of a gallon pitcher. She returned to the table with it and then went to retrieve a clay plate from the sink.

"Just do it," José said having already plucked a single black hair from his scalp. "What's the harm?"

Sounds disrespectful to me, Clay thought. He also shuddered at the thought of reaching down his pants with his hand being in close proximity to his dick that practically *liquified*. When he had covered it with a bandage he almost threw up again. If he had to peel back the bandage whose adhesive would no doubt peel away skin and God knows what else, he would lose it. He looked at the sink, knowing that as soon as he felt *it*, he would rush to the plastic hole. He supposed he could throw up on the floor of this bitch's RV, but he didn't want to cause any more trouble. In the end, his need to get this figured out and finished trumped his comfort.

So in the end, he stood and turned so that Astrid couldn't see him reaching into his pants. He then stuck his hand inside the waistband of his underwear. He felt the rough surface of his bandage and finding the edge he began to peel it back. Once he got the bandage partially pulled away, he stuck his other hand in using his wrist to hold open his pants. His fingers became moist, and he knew at once it was that slimy pus that was spilling out of him.

As he pinched one of his pubic hairs with his thumb and forefinger, he could have sworn he felt something brush his finger and he almost screamed before realizing that was what was left of his penis. The thought of what he had seen this morning made him sick to his stomach and he swallowed bile that had accumulated in his otherwise arid mouth. Then he plucked his prize, grateful that it was over. Once he had a strand of one of his pubic hairs out of his pants, he turned and Astrid instructed he and José both to place the hair onto the plate.

Then, she began to sprinkle ashes from the urn into the cup, forming an almost-perfect circle. She then took a candle from one of the drawers underneath the seats and lit it. Once it melted enough, she dripped wax inside the circle, covering the two hairs and forming an 'x' inside. Then she took four beads from her wrists and paced them in the acute angles of the 'x.' She then got up, disappeared into the back room, and returned with a handful of coarse salt.

Astrid kissed the salt, some of the grains sticking to her pale lips. She then began to sprinkle it onto the plate with her eyes closed. Clay and José both looked at each other skeptically. They didn't know what to expect.

Then, Astrid the Chink's eyes opened. Clay and José were both surprised to see that they had turned completely silver like ball bearings. Gone were the iris' and gone were the pupils. It was if her eyes were replaced with marbles like a taxidermy animal.

"Flosvita, Et ego invocabo te. Venit ad terram viventium, praeterita domum. Audite vocem meam, et responsum meum placitum. Nos tres volo loqui te, et audire sapientia tua de terra ultra. Per voluntatem Luna et Sol, venire ad me, Jeffery Flosvita. Lorem praesentia nostra in hora necessitatis."

Understanding none of what the old woman was saying, Clay was about to say something and then Astrid's mouth opened up to reveal black smoke belching out of her gullet.

"What the fuck..." José said just above a whisper.

Clay almost said something, but the words whatever they were, seemed trapped in his throat. The RV had suddenly turned into a cooler, the temperature dropping unsteadily and without warning. Vapor passed his lips as he breathed, and he felt his body erupt in gooseflesh. For a brief moment, the sensation of maggots in his flesh had ceased, and Clay could have sword he felt fingers caressing the side of his one and only cheek. He almost screamed, but the sound was trapped in his throat as well. This was not natural. This was not supposed to be.

The smoke coming from Astrid's mouth 'slithered' down onto the plate, breaking apart and reforming as it swirled softly like a lonely dust devil. The smoke turned a pale gray, and then as white as snow as it began to rise again, forming a moon-shaped sphere in the air above the plate. It swirled and churned, and Clay began to wonder if he was seeing what he thought he was seeing.

Within the churning smoke/vapor, he thought he saw dark specks that looked like eyes and a mouth, something ghostly or possibly alien. The 'eyes' disappeared momentarily, and then reappeared just as the last of the smoke escaped Astrid's mouth and the old woman gasped for breath. Immediately her eyes returned to their original green color, but Clay and José didn't notice. They were staring into the spectral sphere, and both knew that they were looking at the spirit of Jeffery Flosvita, left behind when his soul left this forsaken world.

I'm going to scream. I'm going to scream, and then I'm going to go insane. I'll be sent to St. Luke's where I will be in a padded cell for the rest of my life eating crayons and- Oh god, that face! That horrible face!

Clay felt his bowels shift in his belly, and without even realizing, his bladder had let go, gushing out of what was left of his deformed penis and soaking the bandage almost completely. At the same time, he shat his pants and felt the warm load smear in his seat. José was just as mortified as well; what the two were seeing what not something a mortal human was meant to see without going insane. With both men reduced to mute toddlers unable to hold in their bowels, they stared in pale-faced terror into the 'face' of the spirit before them.

The black streak Clay saw as a mouth seemed to stretch and open, as if the ghostly being was yawning after waking up from a long hibernation.

Twenty-Six

Astrid, who looked exhausted and bewildered from her unholy act of conjuring, regarded the sphere with a familiar bow of greeting.

"Nigger Jeff…"

The sphere of mist didn't move. In fact, it didn't appear to turn around to face her. It only appeared confused at first, as if stepping out of a cave somewhere and entering the light for the first time in forever. Then it released a breath of air, and the temperature of the RV plummeted even further.

"Ahh, Astrid the Chink," the spectral said in half a moan and half a whisper, as if the spirit was afraid of who might hear it in the world of the living. Tired even, as if the journey here had been exhausting. Clay could not help but stare glassy-eyed and chilled to the very bone. The very floor beneath his feet seemed to shift under the heavy and yet simple words of Jeffery Flosvita.

"You have summoned me again. To what do I owe the pleasure of seeing your face again? Who are these two? I don't recognize them, especially the one that reeks of death."

Clay felt his stomach turn to lead as the words settled into his brain. He was so frozen in terror that he couldn't even blink. He couldn't avert his eyes at all, just to save what little sanity he had left. José next to him, was in no better condition, muttering prayers in Spanish and rubbing his crucifix with a trembling thumb.

Astrid answered, "My brother, allow me to introduce Clayton Couch, and José Rodriguez." She had spoken José's last name without ever hearing it, which chilled the poor man and curdled his blood.

"Dios mío," José said in a whimper. He was rubbing his crucifix more vigorously now. Despite wondering how Astrid knew his friend's name, Clay also wondered if he would start praying again for a blessing for protection from the spirit of Flosvita.

"Ahh," Jeffery Flosvita said as if he were clearing his throat after a long drink of cold beer or iced tea. "Clayton Couch, I have heard much about you. My brothers and sisters pray to me with your name, but never in good faith. With the exception of one, who had been smitten with you. You are the one who sent Kimberly Burrows to me."

"Y... you can't be real..." Clay finally managed to say. His voice had cracked, the moisture in his mouth having evaporated long ago. Sweat was on his brow, despite the terrible cold that settled into his rotting flesh down to the bone.

Jeffery Flosvita's expression was impossible to decipher, but his chuckle revealed his amusement. "I'm as real as the slavers back when the north and south couldn't agree to disagree. Astrid, has Gaston become all gun-ho again?"

"He has," Astrid said in a controlled tone of voice. "But for a cause."

"Revenge is no greater a cause than murder. However, I sympathize as I always will. So, to what do I owe the pleasure?"

"We wish to remove the curse of *Putredine* from this poor unfortunate," Astrid said, and Clay's spine felt like it had been seized by many cold hands at the sound of that word that Gaston Burrows had bellowed into his face in what felt like an eternity ago. The hands squeezed, making him tense and hunch like a hunchback.

"You ask to remove it," Jeffery acknowledged. "And yet your heart says not."

Astrid looked like she had swallowed before nodding. "Yes."

"Then why should we?"

"Gaston said he would be useful to you. He said... he said that you would want to test his *hand*."

"Hmmm…" Clay felt Jeffery's 'eyes' on him, and he felt very uncomfortable. Knowing his voice would probably fail him, he moistened his lips and looked into the face of Flosvita.

"I told your friends I would do anything," he said in a pathetically tremored voice. "Please… I… I do not wish to die."

"No living being wishes to die," Jeffery Flosvita told them. "Those who *fear* death, anyway. I see potential in you, Clayton Couch. However, why should I bother with someone who had spilt blood from a member of my precious Family?"

"He didn't spill it on purpose," José said startling Clay and ensnaring the attention of both Astrid the Chink and the spirit of Jeffery Flosvita. "The girl wandered into the road like a deer, and was run over like one."

"How *dare* you compare my daughter to a *deer*?" Astrid said, her rage now visible, reminding Clay of how she had been during the whole civil trial between him and her husband. *There* was the woman he remembered.

José stared defiantly at Astrid, averting his gaze from Jeffery who was now studying him with what looked to be keen eyes. "It's the truth. Clayton couldn't have done anything. It was an accident, and everyone can see that except you and your no-good husband."

Astrid opened her mouth to say something, but her eyes suddenly widened, as if she were seeing, or rather *feeling* something the two men weren't. She was rendered speechless, and another sigh escaped Jeffery's ghost (if that was what he actually was, Clay had to remind himself).

"Although it was an accident," Jeffery Flosvita moaned. "Blood was still spilt. Just as maybe one from war may not wish to kill, he does still. I can see it in your eyes, Clayton Couch. You carry guilt, as one would. To take a life, it leaves even the most sane mad with the guilt he carries."

Clay remembered the articles, the random acts of violence, the rape and murder of a little girl, and possibly more kidnappings than what they had uncovered long ago. To speak out about this however, to contradict Jeffery Flosvita, would be a grave mistake, and he knew it as he looked into that ghostly face which little by little had begun to solidify into a clearer form. The large nose, the thick lips spread into a grin, the small eyes beneath the strong brow, if Jeffery Flosvita was still alive today and was made of flesh rather than smoke and ectoplasm.

"Maybe because anyone would feel how I feel, if they were just driving home and some girl walked out into the road," Clay answered steeling his resolve. "I just wanted to be home and out of the car, and then before I knew it, someone walks into the road. In a matter of two seconds, I watched as my car *annihilated* this person. I got out, saw the damage I had done to her, and every day since that image has not left my sight. I think of Kimberly Burrows every day. I see her face as clearly as I see you now. It is guilt I feel, yes. Guilt that I didn't see her. Guilt that I killed her. Guilt, because she is *dead*. But that guilt is something bestowed on me because of *her*. In the end, it was her own fault for stepping out into the road."

"Shut your whoring mouth," Astrid the Chink snarled. "You-"

"Silence, Sister," Jeffery Flosvita said. Although his voice was still more of a moan than actual expressive tones, the two words carried a weight that could be felt by everyone around the RV, even Johnny and his friend, Murder Myke, felt a chill pass through their beings despite the breeze barely feeling refreshing at this point in time. Astrid herself, looked like she was in pain, like an old woman suffering the beginning of a terrible heart attack. With her silenced, Flosvita returned his attention to the man before him.

"I understand your frustration. You see yourself innocent then?" he asked.

"He is," José spoke up. "Anyone reasonable can see that."

Flosvita turned to José, made the man develop a severe interest in the table he was sitting at, and then returned his gaze to Clay. For a long time, the spirit studied him, his eyes taking in everything seen and unseen. For a brief moment, Clay saw imagines in the 'cheeks' of the spirit. Memories of men and women dancing, joining together in peaceful worship of their gods. He saw men trying to destroy that peace, and saw bloodshed and the faces of those lost within the web of Flosvita. Moaning, ghostly faces, that Clay felt hypnotized by as if he too would be sucked in and forced to remain as a small piece of the embodiment of Jeffery Flosvita. A spirit, lost within one, never to be seen again.

"What would life be if we had no courage to attempt anything?" Flosvita asked humbly. "Do you know these words, Clayton Couch?"

Hearing his first and last name over and over again was staring to pierce through the terror and prick Clay's nerves but just a little. It was not enough to break the spell he was under.

"No... No, I don't know that."

"Pity. It is from the ancient painter, Vincent van Gogh. I assumed you knew his words, because I see that you are an artist yourself. A painter, yes?"

"I... well..."

"He used to," said José who Clay was surprised to hear and see the man looking up at the spirit again. "He... well..." He looked at Clay this time, either unsure of whether he should say what it was or not. Clay was touched by his tenderness, and as a result it melted some of the terror still freezing him in place. His heartbeat was still rapid in his otherwise curdled veins, and his pants full of shit and piss. But he felt his heart give way, just a little, in order to face Flosvita and not be so afraid to speak.

"After the accident, uh, sir, I couldn't pick up a brush again. Well, except for one last time."

"One last time?" Flosvita asked incredulously. It was as if the spirit knew what Clay was thinking, and was simply waiting as patiently as a ghost would for him to speak his mind.

"Well... this is gonna sound silly."

"I could use a laugh," Flosvita replied. It was humorous under the circumstances and changed the tone of the conversation so drastically, Clay almost started to laugh. It was not something he had expected to hear. No one by the looks of it.

"I painted Kimberly Burrows, as a way to cope. I painted her dancing on a rose. Thinking it would be... I guess meaningful to the family. But... The Burrows didn't like it. In the end I kept it, and with it... I could never paint again. Not without freezing or feeling like I was going to hurl uncontrollably."

"I fail to see what's funny in that," Flosvita said.

Astrid opened her mouth to say her part, but a chill fell over the RV again and she was rendered speechless again. She had no right to speak at the moment it seemed, not until the spirit was done with the man before him.

"However, I can understand the pain you feel. But I must confess, I've seen many painters in my family. Many of whom use their talents to share the beauty of the bright and wonderful world we live in. Why do you paint, Clayton Couch?"

Clay didn't know how to answer. He shrugged and explained as best as he could under the circumstances. Little by little, he was thawing, same as José.

"Well... it's something I just... like to do? I mean, I feel like I can create anything that I put my mind to. An image I never want to forget, even something that doesn't exist, but I can call it my own. People, places, they all come to life when I paint and when I do- I mean, when I *did* paint, my mind just... gets lost so to speak. I become invested in it, and I always wonder what I will bring out from my mind to bring to the canvas next."

Flosvita was silent for a while and then said, "You astound me, not knowing much of Van Gogh but still able to paraphrase like the painter- like a true artist in my opinion. You are an interesting man, Clayton Couch."

"Well... thanks?"

"You wish to be healed, yes?" Flosvita then inquired the rhetorical. "Healed as the paralyzed man at Capernaum, yes?"

"Yes." The answer came so easily, so fast, Clay's own voice startled him. That made him feel more confident in himself, and feel more hopeful for what was to come.

"Well then," Flosvita said. "Then there may be some use of you yet. But I suppose we shall see. Astrid?"

"Yes?" Astrid spoke, her voice coming easily, permitted actually.

"Fetch this man, Kimberly Burrows."

Both Clay and José were confused by Astrid looked paler than the ghost himself. She began to stammer, as if she hadn't heard him right. When Flosvita assured her that she had, Astrid stood and disappeared into the back room again.

When she came back, she had another urn in her hands, this one made of a similar clay but painted with flowers sticking out of grass with a blue sky painted on the lips that were holding up a lid with a cloud on it. Clay felt that freezing sensation seize his chest again, as he felt the dread of what he always saw in his dreams.

"First we will see what you are capable of," Flosvita told Clay. "Then we will have our price for your healing. Keep in mind though, until both are completed, you will not live to see the light of day. But, if you succeed, then I will personally heal your rotting body, and seal your soul within. You will not have to worry about your curse, or my Family again. What do you say, Clayton Couch?"

Clay swallowed with a throat that was as dry as a well in the desert. He looked at Astrid, wondering if he should ask for water (*or maybe moonshine*) and decided not to. He was too scared, too terrified to dare say anything other than his answer to Flosvita. With some effort, he looked at the spirit, and gave his answer in the form of a question.

"What do I have to do?"

The sprit gleamed, his face churning again as if the spirits in his being were becoming restless. "Then we have a bargain. Astrid, you will speak to him. I am weary. Goodbye, Clayton Couch. The next I see you, I hope you are ready, for what you must do next."

At that moment, the spirit of Jeffery Flosvita melted away, the smoke returning to the plate only to swirl and solidify into a form of a serpent. The serpent stared at Clay and José before turning towards Astrid and slithering towards her. Then climbing up her bosom, the snake went into her hanging mouth like a burrow and once it was out of sight, the old woman gasped and threw her head back as if she had been struck by an invisible hand. Her eyes flashed bright and silver like before, and then faded back to their original form.

She then bowed her head, exhausted with her face down onto the table. She took a long quaff of her moonshine, and returned to that position. She remained as such for a minute, and before either man could say anything, Astrid looked up at them. Her face looked haggard, as if she had aged ten years during the time she was on the table.

"No..." she whispered, and her eyes became brimming with tears. "Is it possible? No... yes... I see..."

She then returned her attention to José and said, "Bring in my son. Now."

Clay scooted out of the seat to let the concerned José out. He stuck his head outside, said something to Johnny, and the boy came in looking just as concerned for his mother as he approached her and asked if she was okay once he was by her side.

"Get Penelope and bring me all of her gear. This man is going to paint for us."

"Wait, what?" Clay asked. Before Johnny could ask his own questions, Astrid told him to just go. Reluctantly, he did so, hurrying out of the RV and leaving the three alone again.

"What's this about?" José inquired. "What is Clay supposed to do?"

Astrid shook her head, appearing to not believe what she had heard at all. "A miracle if I ever saw one within the confines of this Family…"

"What is it?" Clay asked now impatient. "What am I supposed to do? Tell me."

Astrid smiled. It wasn't a smile of spite or malice. It wasn't a smile that hid a dirty secret nor was it a smile of amusement because of something the man before he might've said. It looked to Clay like a smile one could express when they became *hopeful*. He and Rachel both had shared similar smiles when the court found favor in them, and not the Burrows and their hatred.

"My boy," she finally answered. "Jeffery has shown his humbled Oracle the way. You are going to paint my daughter again. *Properly* this time, mind you. You will paint her, and with my help, we are going to bring her back to life."

Twenty-Seven

Precious Penelope, as Johnny Burrows and another gypsy, Robert the Rotten introduced her as, was the human embodiment of the Flosvita Family's need to advance with the rest of the world both technologically, and medically.

While they were obviously living in their own time period, their power to thank for that, the nomadic group was not capable of living in the time period it had been born in. Regardless of their supernatural abilities or none, they were still caught up with the times if only a little bit. They still drove cars, invested in campers and probably dehydrated foods, carried guns, used flashlights, and other 21st Century marvels. Whether or not they had cell phones was another question; if there really was a 'bond' of some sort that Astrid was talking about. However, regardless of how much they had separated themselves from the modern world, away from things such as WIFI, health insurance, welfare, and other technological advances necessary for life in today's society, they still relied heavily on some necessities and Precious Penelope was the perfect example to show how the Family no matter how powerful they were, would still need to keep up with the times in order to survive.

Precious Penelope was *ancient*, as old as dirt as Clay would have described her once upon a time. Looking at the old woman, she reminded Clay of a movie mummy after their bandages/toilet paper had been unbound from their decrepit bodies. She was in a wheelchair, her feet and legs concealed by a thick plaid blanket with black and red patterns sewn across it. Her fingers were long and gnarly, almost eaten away by arthritis with bulging blue veins along the tops of her twisted hands. Her body itself, small and frail and shrouded by a blue shawl over a white sweatshirt. She was bald, save for a few wisping strands of hair that made her look like a cancer patient undergoing chemotherapy. Her eyes were glassy and pale, looking like the eyes of some fish in the darkest depths of the ocean.

In her lap was a wooden tote filled with painting supplies. She had a case of paint oils and a clay jar of different sizes of brushes inside, with a cup for water holding a few stencils and black chalk. Next to this carrier of supplies, was an oxygen mask connected to an accordion tube that wrapped around the woman's body and disappeared behind her chair. When she was lifted up by both Johnny and Robert into the RV, Clay could see that attached to the back of the chair was an oxygen tank about a yard in length and by the looks of the two men was just as heavy as the old woman if she were dripping wet.

When she was settled down into the space before the loading area right behind the front seats, Penelope greeted Astrid and the two men within without looking at them. She didn't even look at Johnny or Rob as she thanked them for their assistance. With those frail hands that groped rather than reach, she grasped the oxygen mask and held it to her face. The sound of a sharp click and a long, sharper hissing sound became audible, three long and uncomfortable breaths that sounded like many fingernails clawing at a chalkboard. When she was done, she placed the mask down onto her lap, and turned her motorized wheelchair to face the direction of Astrid's voice.

"Penelope, you look lovely today," Astrid had said kindly, familiarly.

"Do I?" Penelope asked still not making eye contact with the old Asian. "Had a rough morning, but Francis was nice enough to keep me company today. We listened to the radio and he was nice enough to turn on PBS. Bob Ross was on this afternoon."

"That's lovely," Astrid said sounding genuinely happy for the old gal. "Did you try to paint?"

"Not this time. Is that why you asked for me? Or are one of these young men going to try their hand?"

"This is Clayton Couch and his friend, José."

"Clayton Couch, the one who sent Kimberly to the Stars?"

"The same," Astrid said looking at Clay with that familiar look of disdain.

"Well, a pleasure I must say to meet you, Mr. Couch," Penelope said, her head having not moved once since her arrival. "You paint?"

"I uh… yes, yes I do." To tell the truth felt silly, felt *wrong* to be precise.

He had already tried to argue with Astrid after she had first told him of what he would be doing, saying he couldn't and even if he could he didn't understand how painting was going to help him. She said that he could and that he must if he had hopes of being healed again. He even excused himself to use the bathroom and to clean himself up, steeling himself for whatever argument came next.

In the end, it was José who talked him into keeping his trap shut. He was already busting his back for this group of gypsies, so what's one more thing? What's the harm in trying?

Clay tried to explain that if he tried this in particular, there would be *issues*. He tried to explain that he was too scared to even try painting again. He might freeze up, or choke, or vomit, or all three. It all happened after he had finished his first painting of Lady of Roses. In the end, Clayton had reluctantly agreed; that he would try, but he immediately broke out in sweat in the process. When he went to scratch an itch on the side of his mouth, he brought his hand back to see a little bit of skin underneath his fingernail. The sight of the yellow flesh alone was what drove him deeper into the corner he felt he was pushed into. He really didn't have a choice.

He didn't want to, but he had to try, if he really wanted to save himself.

Precious Penelope's mouth stretched out into a grin. With her skeletal face, she looked like a molding jack-o-lantern with tiny teeth that were surprisingly healthy despite being stuck in gums the color of iodine.

"What do you paint? Do tell."

"I think," Astrid said after clearing her throat. "It is best to let our friend get to work. This is business presented by Nigger Jeff himself."

"Oh, that old windbag used to be human, he understands interest in conversation. Tell me son, what do you paint?"

"Mostly whatever comes to mind," Clay asked.

"You good?"

"I... uh..."

"Good enough," José said with a smile. "Sells a lot of his work."

"An entrepreneur-artist, eh?" Penelope said now sounding uninterested. "Know what we call that back in Albany, boy?"

Clay said he didn't, but knew she would tell him anyway.

"Sellouts. No better than prostituting your work, I say. Astrid, is this guy really good enough to paint a picture?"

"Nigger Jeff says so."

Penelope sighed and said, "Well, I got my paints here. All you need is a canvas. Robby ran off to get some out of my RV. Such a nice boy. As for you, Clayton, I don't suppose you mind me staying to listen, do you?"

"Uh, no, not at all." *Listen?*

"Good. My eyesight might have finally failed me, but I can still tell things. I can see things you can't."

And I am willing to bet you can heal yourself like the paraplegic in biblical times, Clay thought to himself. He kept this thought to himself and instead said he believed her.

Astrid, after Robert (aka Robby apparently) returned with a piece of 3X6 canvas meant for long portraits that would go above a mantle or down a vast hall, placed the cloth board up against the kitchen sink facing the chairs. Penelope made herself comfortable next to the rear-facing seat and after Johnny and Robert folded up the table, the two seats were closed together to make a couch. They were then instructed to stand outside.

"Make sure our guest won't run off," Astrid said. "Penelope, you sure you don't want to join me outside?"

"I'll stay here," Penelope said. "These boys won't harm me. Will you?"

"Not at all," José assured her, but Clay had the sudden terrible thought that they *could* harm her. Say to hell with the painting and take the old cripple hostage and threaten them to just take the curse off right now rather than go through all of this.

But, he was afraid. Plain and simple.

Astrid said, "Suit yourself," to Penelope and went to filling the cup with water for the paint.

Penelope had a genuine wooden palette which Astrid, following her instructions, spilled thick spots of paint onto the wooden oval. However, she did something odd to the paint itself after spurting each drop. She had reached into Kimberly's urn and had taken a pinch of the dead girl's ashes as if she was pinching salt or pepper for a special dish. Clay thought this was incredible gross and disturbing, same as José, as Astrid sprinkled the ashes onto the droplets of paint before using a scraper tool to mix it in a little more and apply more paint.

I'm going to be painting with the dead girl in the paint, Clay realized.

The idea was asinine, insane, and incredibly revolting. Looking at the palette, Clay didn't even want to touch it. He looked at it like an archeologist might look at a cursed sarcophagus. Even when Astrid had finished sprinkling the ashes and placed Kimberly's urn back into the back room, the feeling did not pass like a breeze. He was now staring at the blank canvas with a horror both familiar and not.

If I spread her on that, he thought to himself. *I'm going to really see her. I will see her, and she will see me.*

But that was stupid. It was his painter's block making him scared not the superstition that the remains of the dead girl would be haunting him as he attempted to pain. But then again, he had just conversed with a dead man, and had seen stranger things still this past month. Nothing seemed to truly surprise him anymore despite the panic rat in his skull trying desperately to grasp onto the rational argument of what the real world was capable of.

'Creativity takes courage,' Henri Matisse once said.

But courage is also a leap of faith; borderline acceptance of insanity or something improbable. Especially in this situation. Sure, a picture of a painting can be looked at as a poem without words, but it can also tell a story no one can truly be prepared for. What story would Clay tell if he were to paint Kimberly Burrows again? The reincarnation of a beautiful and yet possibly stupid girl, or a resurrection of some evil entity like most horror stories are told? What if he painted her, she does come back, and bring something back from whatever Hell she returns from?

This all is of course *if* he is somehow able to paint at all. The thought of touching a brush, a *normal* brush and sticking it into *normal* paint to spread it on a piece of canvas, was enough to make him feel sick already. His painter's block was preventive enough for his creativity under the normal circumstances. Adding the possibility of a cursed set of paints with the soul of the poor girl lying in the balance, was enough to make him vomit right then and there.

Astrid stood by the door of her RV, giving Clay and José one final glare of warning. "Finish before sunrise. You are not to leave this RV until you do. Do not disappoint me." She pointed to the far room where the two men could see the picture of Kimberly on the makeshift alter. "Do not disappoint *her*."

Then without so much as waiting for Clay or José to answer, she stepped out and closed the door behind her. Outside the window, Clay could see her talking to Robert and her son before stalking away like a wraith. The two boys smiled up at Clay through the window, and Johnny in particular held up a middle finger towards him, and used the same finger to make a slashing gesture across his own throat. His own message to the one who would be bringing back his sister.

If, that was what Clay was actually going to do.

José sighed and sat down onto the combined couch. "So, you're going to paint now?" He was now staring at the moonshine Astrid had left behind for them. He was considering a drink.

Clay wanted one as well. That was how he used to do it anyway. Drink a gallon of beer or a bottle of whiskey and just let his mind out onto the canvas when he painted. It would make it a helluva lot easier. But, would the results be the same?

"Guess so," Clay answered now looking at the large canvas with discouragement. He imagined it being a door that he could walk through and step out of this nightmare and return to what he once considered reality. He always used to paint to escape the real world, and now he wanted to escape this 'world' and return to his old. Back when everything and yet nothing made sense the way it was supposed to. That ignorant plane of existence where nothing went wrong except for on the news or in movies.

"Well, sugar," Precious Penelope said picking up her oxygen mask and before placing it over her face. "You gonna get started or just gawk?" Onto her face the mask went. That grating hissing sound filled the RV and Clay felt his patience flare up with his temper.

"What do you need from me?" José asked. "Not like I can go anywhere by the looks of it, but what do can I do?"

"I dunno," Clay answered. He was now staring at the canvas with a new pair of eyes. A pair that he once thought of as his old friends. Like a writer brainstorming an idea for a book or poem, he was brainstorming an image for Kimberly Burrows.

Was it possible? Could he do it?

One way to find out.

There was paint thinner in the box of supplies and Clay poured some into the cup of water next to the canvas. He then picked up a brush, the largest one which was about four inches long, and after a moment's hesitation, he picked up the palette and held it across his right forearm. He never used one since his college days, never saw reason to, but this felt natural; like a real painter. Grasping the brush in his left hand, felt natural like someone who hasn't worn his wedding band in so long and finally found it near the bathroom sink and slipped it on, feeling the familiar weight in both his finger and his heart. All the while, Clay still stared at the canvas, seeing his shadow cast on it from the overhead light. For a brief moment, he imagined Kimberly's ghost being his shadow, looking back at him from whatever plane of reality she was currently standing in. His stomach folded in on itself at the thought of it, but still he stared. He stared at the canvas, and imagined Kimberly as if she were standing right before him, and not the remains that had been scraped off of Route 199 with those lifeless green eyes shaped like almonds.

Clay looked down at the palate and selected a green color and after mixing in a little black to get the pine color he wanted, he took the mop brush now covered in green and touched the tip of the brush tenderly against the canvas.

He didn't move for a long time, expecting his muscles to clench up and his stomach to roll around like a bowling ball. It was then when he became aware of a more foul stench. It wasn't the marijuana or the smoke coming from outside. It reeked of death, and Clay realized he was finally smelling himself with his hole of a nose. The smell made him gag but not in a way that he could mistaken it for an anxiety attack. With some effort, he removed the brush from the canvas and moved to the far left and began to make long and slow strokes towards the middle, as if he were creating a long-distance image of a sea of pine. His palms were sweaty, and he worried that he might spill his own oils onto the painting. Still, he worked, moving all the way down the canvas and going back up to get the upper half of the canvas, before moving the right side and mirroring his work until both sides met in the middle, creating the illusion that he was appearing at a ghostly figure in the center of the sea of green. With the more pale shades of green in the middle, Clay could easily fit his shadow into the space, even though Kimberly would be much smaller than he.

No clenching. No shortness of breath. No spontaneous stomach cramps that would insinuate a retching. He was working. He was painting, and selecting a thin brush after placing the big one into the cup of paint thinner/water, Clay began to fill in little black trunks within the sea, clarifying the vision he was trying to reach.

Behind him, José watched wordlessly. Precious Penelope, was 'looking' down at her gnarly hands, but she was smiling, appearing pleased almost. It was if she were seeing the world through Clay's eyes, and could see the forest he was creating like God who filled the land with trees and many plants.

Making as little noise as possible, knowing that any disturbance that brought Clay back to the real world would mess up his concentration that had for so long been gone, José poured himself a glass of moonshine. It smelled strongly of cinnamon and gasoline, and the first sip burned his tongue and throat but felt so righteous going down. Penelope held out her hand to José wordlessly, but he understood and filled up a glass for her as well. She took smaller sips than he, and didn't show any reaction to the burning as if she had been drinking the illegally-crafted drink since she had first learned how to walk.

Clay then took up a smaller brush, a two-inch flat fan and began to mix white and a little bit of brown, creating a tanner version of white but not too dark in order to begin creating the figure of Kimberly Burrows. He had decided he was going to paint her naked, since clothing would be too difficult at this point in time. He could do it, but he didn't know how realistic this would bring forth the real Kimberly if that was what was to happen. If she came into this world, would the clothing be stuck to her skin? Would it be a part of her? He supposed that was stupid to think about; he might even butcher her *actual* body. After all, he never really saw her naked, only his artistic and possibly perverted projection had imagined her as such; flawless, beautiful, and yet gone.

But he didn't know what else he could do to make sure he didn't screw this up. In the end though, he supposed that if Astrid the Chink found the painting revolting, he could easily paint over Kimberly with something dark, no matter how long it would take. After all, she had never done this either. It may not even be possible in the first place. However, as a newborn baby coming into the world would emerge as, Clay had decided Kimberly would emerge as such. It was the closest thing to natural as he could imagine it.

He had to apply a second coat after carefully creating the main image of Kimberly onto the canvas. The 'girl' in the painting was about five feet tall, as Clay guessed she had been before she died. He would use a small rigger and pinpoint brush for the nitty gritty details, but for now he had to only make an image, as if he were looking into a pool of water and she looking up at him. That made it easier to paint the otherwise hazy legs that were crossed to hide what would soon be her crotch as well as her arms that would cover up her bosom. It made no sense to paint her as if she were a corpse on a metal cooling board. It wouldn't be right. He wanted Kimberly to try to make herself decent, just as Eve had once did when she realized her nakedness in the Garden of Eden. He wanted to give her a sense of existing, of understanding and being an actual living human being with feelings.

Taking the mop brush again, Clay mixed some black and red to make a more rusty red, and then from the circular bit of flesh that would soon be Kimberly's head and face, he made long strokes to the right, using then an angled brush to create her long hair that would be 'flowing' within a current of wind. He thought of applying leaves to the painting as well, make it more realistic, but he could do that later if he chose to.

During the moments he became aware of himself and what he was doing, Clay felt happy for the first time in a long time. He was working. *Really* working, and painting a picture. Despite the horrors he had experienced thus far, despite all the pain and suffering he had been exposed to, he was actually doing it. He was escaping into his own little world, a world where Kimberly Burrows was alive and well, living among the animals and Father Pine in the mountains somewhere.

Where would she be? The Cascades? Somewhere in Colorado maybe? The possibilities were endless, the secrets the painting wouldn't tell being his alone. Clay soon realized that he didn't smell himself anymore. He was unaware of where he was and who he was with. All ill he felt towards Astrid the Chink, her husband and son, and all of Flosvita was a distant memory as of now. He was lost in his own world, and he would not break away unless he chose to, or he was violently ripped out of it like a boy having his first wet dream before the alarm for school woke him up. It was incredible, and Clay looked at the muddied 'face' of Kimberly that was still unfinished.

Where had the time gone? Why did you abandon me?

But he had never been abandoned. Not entirely. He had pushed many people away during this time of pain and suffering. He had tried to push the image of Kimberly away when Gaston and Astrid basically told him to go to Hell. He pushed Rachel away, his job away, becoming just a walking corpse; a bag of bones. He had never once felt alive until he and

José came to the Flosvita Camp, determined to save his life and now, he felt like he was actually *living*. He was creating something from a few oil paints and the biggest piece of canvas he had ever worked on. Consequences be damned, time on his dying body be damned. If he disappeared into this world and never came back, Clay would be just fine with that.

Now, selecting the pinpoint brush and applying some black paint, Clay got to work on the most difficult part of the painting: the face.

He tried to imagine someone realizing that they were not dead but alive. He tried to imagine a combat soldier surviving a bomb blast and despite having lost his legs or part of his face, was still breathing. He wondered how car crash victims who were still alive felt despite the impact that could have easily killed them. He thought of how he felt, after Gaston said there might be a way to save him. He centered it all around the sensation of receiving a second chance, and that made it easier to apply the expression he wanted Kimberly to have. Those almond eyes full of hope, those cheekbones stretching her pale lips into a smile, as if she were about to bust out laughing. Just as he had once laughed, but this would not be manic or the laughter of insanity or fear. This would be laughter of genuine happiness; the realization that life has found a way, and whatever god she worshiped had found favor in her.

Despite being naked in some unknown forest with the wind in her hair, Kimberly *did* appear happy. Despite the face not being close to being completed, she appeared happy within the veil that looked like looking down into a pool of water.

Taking a break from the face, Clay got to work on other parts of her body. The wrinkles on her hands and her fingernails, the freckles on her arms that were far apart compared to the freckles that he would apply on her face. Clay supposed he was making all of this up as he went, since he didn't see Kimberly in such a way. But the way he imagined her when she was alive, filled in the blanks for her. One of which he didn't quite understand, he imagined her having a kidney-shaped birthmark on her belly to the left of her bellybutton. He didn't know if she had it or not, but he had a feeling that this was what she looked like. She had a cut on her right ankle from when she had gone swimming in one of the Twin Sister lakes a month before her death.

Clay was thinking about something as he got to work on the formation of her knees. How he somehow knew what the rest of her looked like having only pictures of her face and the image of her body after the accident to go off of. How does he know about the birthmark, the few blemishes on her otherwise milky complexion? How did he know that her nose would be slightly crooked, and he would have to make it look like she was about to turn her head to create an illusion and hide such a blemish? How did he know she had s birthmark and what it looked like, what her fingernails looked like, how everything that he shouldn't know about her looked like? Even as he didn't paint it, how her breasts and everything that was covered looked like? In his mind, he knew he had a perfect idea of what Kimberly looked like, and who she really was.

Maybe it was the paint.

Or maybe...

Maybe Kimberly was somehow *here*, still sentient and was standing with him, guiding his hand that was stroking paint infused with her ashes. *A touch of white here, and a little less there...*

Regardless of how it worked, Clay was both disturbed that he knew so much and yet thankful at the same time. With this information he could create a splitting image of Kimberly now. He would not lock up, and he would not make mistakes.

Because artists didn't make mistakes. They made happy accidents, like with Kimberly's nose or the fact that she wasn't 'standing' but almost floating like a woodland spirit of ancient German folklore as her ancestors had no doubt spoken of, or maybe a story of her Asian heritage of the forests of ancient

China or wherever Astrid the Chink had come from. The beauty of a birth of different worlds being in the woods, made clear by unknown ways incomprehensible by the human mind. Because none of this was in reality. Not Flosvita, and not this painting; this world that Clay was creating with a being that would soon be sentient.

Kimberly would be sentient. She would be alive just as she would look alive and real in the painting. Clay knew this despite having not believed this before. It would happen, and underneath the faith he had, he had the hope of his salvation. He too would be made whole again. He too, would be resurrected, completely, fully, and unblemished.

Behind him, Precious Penelope spoke for the first time in the three hours applied to the painting. By then José was slowly dozing off, due to the time and the booze taking hold of him. Her voice had startled him almost as bad as the oxygen mask she would apply to her face between speaking with the man.

"He's gone," she had said before taking a good long breath of oxygen.

"Gone?" José asked drowsily, thinking he knew what the old woman was talking about but at the same time unsure.

"He is long gone, my friend." Another pause to take another gulp of air, and this time Penelope sat the mask back into her lap. "Can't you feel it? He isn't with us now. He is somewhere else. But he is happy, I can tell. Surely you can too?"

José could. He may not have the insight that those in Flosvita have, nor was he psychic, but he could feel it. He remembered Clay when he talked about painting. It always sounded boring to José and he honestly never thought he would have been able to sit and wait through the painting process to see what he was talking about. Clay was definitely lost in his own world, and he was bringing a part of that world out for everyone to see in the form of a woman in the woods. The image of Kimberly was really coming together, and even José began to wonder just what else he would experience before the night is out.

Still, in the underbelly of his gut, he couldn't help but feel uneasy. It was as if a great storm was on the horizon, the clouds gathering like a bad omen. All of this felt right because Clay was happy, but at the same time everything was off just like it felt off coming into this strange camp. They weren't out of the woods yet, not by a long shot, and José worried about what was to be expected of them after the painting was complete.

These thoughts alone were what kept him both awake and sober, and he watched his friend with the intensity of a fan of a football game before the touchdown that would tip the balance of the last quarter. He sat, and watched, and he no longer thought that painting was boring. How could it be? Clay's life was on the line.

And to make sure his friend was brought back, Clay would have to bring back Kimberly Burrows. And to make sure he *stayed* back, José would do whatever was necessary to protect his friend. He had made his decision before the jail and everything else, and he wasn't about to back out, no matter how scared he really was.

God help me, he prayed inwardly.

Precious Penelope however, said something that wilted that prayer like a parched flower in raging sunlight. "We'll see if he does or not," she said, smiling knowingly, and hauntingly into José's eyes.

Twenty-Eight

The last stoke of Clay's brush was given by 5:42 in the AM. Sunrise would not arrive until a half hour later at this point in time, and everyone in Flosvita had retired long ago. Everyone except for him, José, Penelope, and their guards outside Astrid's RV.

He was tired, the yellow bags under his eyes turning a slight shade of blue and purple. But Clay felt good. He had put in a whole night's work and the painting was almost completed. Every time he took a step back to look at the painting and make some minor alterations, he became more and more confident in his ability. The painting looked as if it was really a mirror and Kimberly was in his place jumping in the woods somewhere it looked so real. It was true that most paintings could not exceed what real life could look like, but it was damn near perfect. This was better than Lady of Roses, maybe better than any of his other paintings. It was definitely the biggest he had ever done.

He was willing to bet top dollar that someone somewhere would want this hanging on their mantle inside their big mansion in Beverly Hills where paintings worth millions could be admired by all visitors over champagne and lamb chops. Maybe it would be purchased a year later and placed in an art museum in New York where more people could drink and nibble on snacks while admiring it. They would ask questions like 'Who is this girl?' and 'Where is she now?' and 'What does this painting mean?' There would be some stupid college boys making sexual comments and they would get kicked out by some security guard wearing a tuxedo that hid all of his muscle.

Such dreams distracted him, and he began to put the finishing touches on Kimberly's long red hair. Making sure each strand of red locks stood out, and captured the attention of all who would look upon such beautiful hair.

As the sunlight began seeping through the RV's windows, Clay began to notice that the red hair looked almost like it was on fire in the sunlight, those piercing gray eyes that he once thought were wicked and unforgiving, were gleaming like silver bearings. The beauty in the painting, while unparalleled, was still hiding one more secret that only Clay knew. Some hidden danger within, and the unbalance of nature of the universe tied with how reality was meant to be. Still, knowing this, Clay placed the final stroke that finished the dark eyebrows of Kimberly Burrows, and stepped back to admire his work one last time.

"It is finished," he finally said.

José, despite his efforts, had been asleep for almost an hour. Only a few drinks in, and was snoring on the couch. Penelope, who hadn't slept the entire time, smiled knowingly. She could see it too. Clay didn't know or understand how but he knew she could see. It was written all over her face by some unknown force of insight.

"It is beautiful," she responded. Her eyes, having once looked like pale scales, were now bright and silver. The inhuman nature of those eyes made gooseflesh erupt on Clay's flesh again, but he knew she and whoever else was watching was pleased with his work.

As if on que, Astrid the Chink had unlocked her RV and stepped in. She looked as if she had just woken up. Her hair was an unruly mess, and she was wearing a light sweater against the morning air. She stood beside Penelope and stared amazed at the portrait of her lost daughter. She called for her son to come in, and Johnny Burrows came in alone, and he gaped at the portrait with just as much amazement, but with a particular sense of disgust in his eyes.

"Why is she *naked*?" he demanded glowering at Clay now, how, his admiration now gone, and Clay understood that it was rightfully given. How would *he* feel if someone drew his sister- his *dead* sister, naked as the day she was born looking so madly happy?

She was practically born. Reborn, I think.

"It's beautiful," Astrid said in a voice that was in awe and foreshadowed the tears coming in her eyes. "Sun and Moon, my daughter…"

"You like it?" Clay asked feeling slightly embarrassed now.

Astrid nodded. Her face became serious, and she brushed past him and went to the back room. She soon returned wearing a set of bead bracelets on her wrists and a bowl of red paste. She sat before the painting, and spread the paint-like substance on her cheeks, making her appear aboriginal and raising her hands up over her head, she began to speak in fluent Latin as before.

"Will you help me out of the RV?" Penelope said sounding afraid. "I think my time here is finished." Clay rushed to help Johnny Burrows and despite the weight of the chair and the woman, they got her out of the RV and back inside. The chanting awoke José, and he asked what was happening.

"I don't know," Johnny Burrows answered. He was tired too, with black rings under his eyes and looking as worn out as a dead person, almost like Clay.

The three men watched Astrid the Chink, as she continued to chant, and outside the RV the sunlight seemed to have been snuffed out as clouds rolled overhead. Dogs ceased to bark, and the morning birds stopped their singing. Those who were awake, sensed something happening and remained in their tents and mobile homes while the sleeping rested like the dead.

Clay then saw his painting beginning to shimmer as if it really were a mirror and not some fabric canvas with paint on it. The canvas shook more and more, the shimmering brighter and brighter as the eyes of Kimberly Burrows seemed to glow brighter and silver-

And look directly at Clayton Couch who felt his heart stop in his chest, and he gasped as if he were about to have a heart attack. This time, he *did* scream, as one of Kimberly's hands reached out and pierced the veil between the painting and the real world, and her hand stuck right out of a hole that appeared and was followed by another. Then her head came out, those eyes silver and burning bright, and then the rest of her tumbled out of the painting, leaving a smoldering hole in the canvas as if someone had stuck a burning poker in the middle and it somehow took shape of a human being. Her mother continued to chant as she laid on the RV's floor, and when she finally finished, Astrid looked down and fell upon her daughter, cradling her and calling her name while kissing her freckled cheeks. Johnny, who broke out of his trance, rushed forward to see if it was real.

Kimberly, whose almond eyes were now opening, were as green as the pine in the painting and completely normal. No silver. They were human eyes. She blinked a couple of times, breathing heavily as Johnny hurried away and returned with a blanket to cover his sister. She moved her mouth, testing her voice as a baby does when mimicking the noises her mother and father make. When she *did* speak, the first word almost any baby would speak escaped her pale lips.

"M... M... Mom...?"

"Kimmy!" Astrid cried out hugging her daughter close. The old woman was in tears, same as her brother who was exclaiming their disbelief that she was back. Clay and José stood back, their hearts warmed by the sight despite the scare they still felt.

This is not normal. This was not the way the world worked. This is... unnatural.

This wasn't right, and Clay's realization of what he had done began to sink in like the Titanic in the ocean, slow, but painfully so.

Is this... is this what it feels like to play God?

After a full ten minutes of crying and laughing, Astrid stood, and Johnny took his resurrected sister to the back room to put some clothes on her. Astrid's face, with tear streaks on her cheeks and her eyes puffy and red, were stone cold and serious. Clay knew he wasn't done yet. None of them were as of yet.

"You brought her back," she said to Clay. Was that gratitude in her voice? It sounded like it, but also something else no one could quite put their finger on.

Admiration maybe?

Fear?

Both?

"I only painted her, as I said I would," Clay answered. Now he wanted nothing more to move on from this.

"You have your daughter back. Will you remove this curse now?" He was amazed how bold he sounded, and with José now fully awake by his side, he felt unstoppable. Maybe it was the sensation of playing God, maybe it was simply the fact that he could paint again. In any case, he had done his part, and he was ready to receive what was coming to him.

Astrid the Chink answered, "You forget there is one more piece to your end of the bargain, and only then will you be healed."

Clay grounded his teeth, putting a hold on his impatience at least for the time being. "What now?"

"You have brought my daughter back. I have helped with the words provided to me by Nigger Jeff. Now we must do what he intends to do. You must bring *him* back as well."

That sinking feeling accelerated and applied more pressure on Clay's chest, and he stood speechless before the woman who from his point of view was covering the smoldering hole in the canvas.

It was José who said what was on his mind, "Are you fucking kidding? The guy painted all night! He can barely-"

"He may rest," Astrid assured them both. "It is better to finish this before sunrise, and we just barely finished anyway. You may rest, Clayton, and then you must complete your end of the bargain. Only then will the curse be lifted."

"Astrid," Clay said surprised to find his voice again. It was a miracle it wasn't cracked or sounded dismayed despite what he felt. "This isn't normal..."

"We aren't normal," Astrid answered simply. "No one in this Family is. You don't have a choice anymore. You *will* do this, Clayton. Now it isn't a matter of you getting your body back or not. Now you have no choice. You brought my daughter back, and for that I am eternally grateful to you. But now you must bring Jeffery back. You must bring the heart of Flosvita back, so that we can be at our full potential again."

"Full potential?" José asked bewildered. "What does that mean?"

"What it means doesn't concern you," Astrid said. "Either of you. Do this, and you will be healed. You may rest. You have the day, but that is it. Tonight, you will paint again. One way or another, Jeffery will return to this world again, and this time, he will *stay*. Afterward, you can both go on your merry way, and you will never hear from us again. This I can promise you, Clayton."

"So, what, we go home and come back?" José asked this of Clay, but it was Astrid who answered for them.

"No, you'll stay here. We don't want you running off, not when we have the chance of a lifetime. Johnny, escort these men to the livestock tents where they can rest."

"Woah, woah, woah," Clay said holding up his hands as if he meant to stop an incoming vehicle. "We aren't staying here, I painted all night and-"

"You're not going anywhere," Astrid said with her voice dropping ten degrees. "You are here to stay until you are done, Mr. Couch. Your friend can go, but you will stay."

José stepped up and stood beside his friend. "I ain't going anywhere without Clay."

"Then you can stay too," Astrid shrugged as if it made no difference to her.

"Come on, whoremaster," Johnny said brushing past them and opening the door for them. "Let's go."

That was when José reached into his pants as he charged for Astrid the Chink. He seized the woman by the neck with his arm and spinning her to place her in front of him he stuck his pistol into her temple. At the same moment, Johnny Burrows whipped out his own pistol, which was a Colt revolver, holding it in both hands and immediately yelling at José to let his mother go. Clay meanwhile backed away, getting out of the line of fire between the two men and appearing dazed.

"Drop it, dipshit," José hissed jamming the barrel deeper into Astrid's head. "We are going, so you better cooperate, or Mommy gets it."

"Fuck you!" Johnny bellowed. "Let her go, asshole!"

"We're leaving! C'mon, Clay!"

Clay started forward then Johnny took aim at him. "Don't move, fucker," he warned him.

Then José turned the gun on Johnny, seizing his attention and when the Colt was pointing back at him and Astrid, he turned his pistol back into the old woman with a sneer.

"I'm not kidding, kid. Drop the gun. I'll kill her, I swear it."

"You kill her and you *both* don't make it out of this alive!" Johnny screamed. "Let her go!"

It wouldn't occur to Clay until later that he wouldn't be hurt by the shot. He wouldn't die, he was already technically dead. But in his panic, he did not register such a thought or idea.

Astrid began to mutter something under her breath. It was too quiet for Clay to hear but he knew she was speaking

Latin. José told her to shut up and he smacked the back of her head with the butt of his gun. Johnny swore at him again and it became a screaming match as Clay tried to move towards the boy only to get corralled back by the revolver's gaping barrel. Then José turned his gun back to Johnny, and the boy whirled around and both men fired at the exact same time, the adrenaline and intensity in the air finally reaching their boiling point and unleashing terrible violence. What followed alongside it, was a string of terrible luck in an already unlucky place.

José's pistol was a Berreta 92X Compact he had purchased in 2011. He had bought it off of a friend from El Paso, Texas and had never had to use it for defense once in his life. He had taken it out into the hills to shoot beer cans and practice targets but other than that never really had to use it for self-defense. It was an old gun, and José never took the time to really clean it or keep it in satisfactory shape in order to operate safely and without trouble. All that time putting off the cleaning process or even taking it apart to ensure no grime or gunpowder dust was accumulating in the chamber, became the death of José and he would think about all this time in the split-second it took for him to die.

At the moment both men squeezed the trigger, two things happened. One, the magazine in José's gun pushed the bullet ready to fire with enough pressure to squeeze against the firing pin but rather than prick the primer, the bullet grounded against some buildup in the chamber and got stuck. In that moment, the gun jammed and nothing happened, just as the second thing happened, which was Johnny's Colt automatic hammer struck the primer on the .44 Teflon-coated bullet that once upon a time would have been referred to as a cop-killer bullet due to their ability to punch through ballistic armor. In the split-second for José to realize what was happening, his head was *ripped* apart by the polytetrafluoroethylene-coated bullet. The bullet went right through his right cheek under his eye, and removed the upper half of his skull in a flurry of splintered bone and brain.

The eruption of Johnny's gun was deafening, but Clay could practically hear the sound of bone splitting apart and flesh tearing with the brain of José Rodríguez turning to paste. José's headless body staggered back, letting go of Astrid whose face was painted completely crimson in the blood splatter, his skull completely destroyed and gushing gore what hadn't been blown against the back wall. Bits of gray matter slid down a sheet of red. Kimberly was screaming in the back and Astrid whirled around and sprinted past José who had crumpled to the ground like a sack of laundry. Clay who had received a little of the blood-spray, stared in mute horror at the remains of his friend's face. He had moved to fall upon José but was immediately grabbed by Johnny Burrows and shoved to the ground with the Colt jammed into the back of his head. His ears were ringing, the blue smell of gun smoke in his nostrils mixing with the metallic scent of blood, but Clay could hear a muffled echo of what was escaping his mouth as he stared at the body sitting in a pool of blood.

"José! José!" He screamed it many times, until the pressure of the Colt was removed only to be replaced by Johnny Burrows' boot.

Astrid returned, her face smeared with gore, her expression angered and yet relieved it had all gone according to her favor. She sneered at Clay with that gummy grin and approaching him, she kicked him upside the head, scraping a bit of skin off the right side of his skull.

"Lock him up with the pigs," she told her son. She crouched down with her hands on her knees so that she was closer to Clay who stared up at her dazed and borderline deaf. "Your friend made an idiot choice. And look where that got him."

"Fuck you!" Clay bellowed.

Astrid looked up and nodded, and another blow went to the back of Clay's head. He laid there with his face on the RV floor, his cheek almost touching the pool of blood accumulating underneath the broken remains of José. Another kick to the back of the head ensued.

Then all he knew was darkness, and pain.

Twenty-Nine

The first thing that struck Clay upon awakening was the smell. Hay and livestock, sludge and shit. The second was the pain in the back of his head, and touching it Clay felt a bloated bump that popped upon him prodding it and he felt pus coat his fingertips. The third and final thing was something by sight, which was in the far corner in a cage built for a zoo animal.

Flosvita had a goddamn *cougar* in their livestock tent.

The tent was located on the eastern side of the camp in-between two large trailers used to transport livestock. There were two cows and a calf tied to the central support beam of the large blue carnival tent. Everywhere else, there were makeshift pens like what one would see at a county fair where pigs, goats, and chickens were corralled. Clay was tied to a large metal tent stake with his hands tied to it behind his back. On his left was one of the goat pens where a black billygoat stood chewing on some hay. The ram had large horns on it's head as black as it's beady dual-pupiled eyes. It stared at Clay like he was the most fascinating animal in the world.

To his right was where the cougar was in a cage with hay covering the bottom for It to lounge in. The cat was small, probably a teenager and he too was looking at Clay with big green eyes like he was lunch. Next to the cougar was a shelf where glass boxes of rattlesnakes were contained, probably for whatever poisons were used by this insane cult of a family. The entrance to the tent was straight ahead from where Clay laid in the hay, and he saw that it was closed off and was trapping the sweltering heat coming in through the tent fabrics. It smelled horrible in here, and was unbearably sweltering.

What was the icing on the shitty cake were the *bugs*.

Drawn by the heat and stench of shit and animal sweat, the flies and wasps were having a feast. If they weren't hanging out on the animals or eating the piles of manure on the floor, they were on Clay enjoying themselves on his blistering skin and molding cheeks. A fly had even tried to go into his nose, and he had to exhale with as much force as one could muster to blow the insect out. Snot and pus came out which only drew more of the insects that were crawling all over him and he was constantly having to twist and thrash to annoy the insects and cause them to buzz away. This was not like one of the other animals in the tent who didn't care if they were having flies crawling all over them; this animal was a rabid wolf that wanted out. The ropes that tied his wrists together bit into them, cutting deep and almost to the bone. If Clay was to get any rest here, it wasn't going to happen with the goat and the cougar watching him as the goddamn bugs only doubled their efforts to get a taste of the rotting morsel in the tent.

Sorry, guys, I'm already taken. I got worms and maggots in me. Battle for it to the death for all I care!

This was worse than being in the drunk tank back home. Clay had only been arrested and thrown in the drunk tank once, and he remembered being in the concrete cell with two other sobering inmates wearing only a thin smock where it was colder than sin and the foam blanket provided to him was only four feet long. He remembered that being the longest twelve hours of his life, but this makeshift cell took the cake. The only similarity between the drunk tank and here was the time to think and reflect on what had happened and what to do from here (despite this time having livestock for company rather than drunks or druggies).

His friend was dead, and this was the primary thing that came to mind and Clay found himself crying tears of mucus at the memory of it. The image of what was left of José was burned into his mind like a boy's first visitation of porn. It was something that was never going to go away. In his gut, Clay felt responsible for what had happened. He had brought his friend out here. José had expressed how bad of an idea it was, and despite what Clay had said he chose to stay. But because of that, because of his sense of loyalty to Clay, he was now dead. Dead and probably getting a secret burial somewhere in the plains.

Or worse, the panic rat in Clay's mind said. *They are gonna chop him up and feed him to your buddy over there.*

(how's that for a bit of hope, dingleberry?)

Clay looked over at the cougar, and felt his stomach fold and he got sick. What a fate to have. Go with your friend to help him, end up getting killed and fed to a cougar or maybe even the pigs. Don't they eat humans too? 'Here lies José Rodríguez, great friend, and tasty morsel.'

"Fuck you," Clay said to the cougar. The feline's tail twitched as if it were saying, 'Not for all the meat in the world.'

What was he going to tell Isabel? Would he even get a chance to? Would he ever be able to leave Flosvita alive? Or was he going to be a prisoner; end up like one of the kids snatched by these guys back when they were at their strongest? As soon as they were through with him, just simply dispose of him?

There were still people in camp. There were cars and motorcycles heading out by the sound of it, but there were voices outside the tent. Someone was playing the guitar, and at some point during the day (Clay had no idea what time it was since he couldn't check his phone) he heard a firecracker go off. Flosvita was not as lively during the day as it was at night, but there were some still lingering.

It was because the wild things loved the night; they *thrive* in it, for they hate the light which revealed their dark hearts and desires.

Horseshit.

Another thing that came to Clay's mind, was what exactly happened with Kimberly Burrows. He replayed what had happened in his head (it was the only way to get José off his mind) over and over again, and he still couldn't quite believe it. The adrenaline rush of feeling like God was no longer in him.

Instead, he felt absolutely disgusted with himself. He had helped Astrid the Chink defy the laws of nature, and the girl he had destroyed on Route 199 was alive and *walking*. She had been reborn from his own painting, and Clay no longer saw beauty when he looked back at his work. He only saw an abomination. He felt like Frankenstein after realizing that he did not create a being of beauty from playing God. That he had instead created a monster, and even though Kimberly did not appear monstrous, she was not a thing of beauty either. She was not what God had created her to be while she was still in her mother's womb. She wasn't even the image that had in Clay's mind been perfectly sculpted on the canvas; his best work.

She was a creature reincarnated through unnatural methods and was no longer human but something else. Not quite zombie-like, but definitely not completely human. Maybe Stephen King was right. Maybe dead was better. Maybe *God* was right. Maybe the *universe* was right. Dead should remain dead. All things must come to an end. And by unknowingly playing the part of God with the members of Flosvita, Clay felt disgusted with himself. Himself, who appeared more like a zombie now, and would probably look much worse by the day's end, especially given his current location and status.

Another thing too, was what was expected of him. He had been taken prisoner, his friend killed for trying to defend him, and he was expected to do the same with Jeffery Flosvita; the founder of this cult. Regardless of what vision he had when he first chose to depart from civilization and create his own community, whether he had accepted such changes or encouraged them, it was no longer what he first had in mind. But did Jeffery Flosvita care? He obviously didn't, otherwise he wouldn't have given Astrid the capability to conjure her own daughter out of his painting. An experiment to see if whatever dark sorcery it was would actually work, and now that he had seen that it did, he was ready to force Clay to do it for himself.

(then probably leave you to rot in the end anyway)

Yet another thought occurred to him after considering such thoughts. Did Flosvita know such a spell when he was alive? Did he know how to resurrect the dead before he went to prison? During? Or did he learn it from wherever his soul had gone when he died?

Did he learn it from the ghosts he wandered the earth with? Or did he learn it from the demons of Hell? Such a man certainly didn't go to a place like Heaven. He couldn't have. No god mythical or considered real should ever accept someone who created a group such as Flosvita, at least that was Clay's thinking. But still, where had he learned to do that? How *could* he know? And why did it so perfectly work out, when he knew Clay used to paint? This had to be a dream, it had to be if it worked so perfectly to only *now* bring back his ability to paint. It felt like he never truly had control.

Did he ever have control?

After all, if what he used to believe as a child was true, they all lived in a world someone else imagined. Could it be that someone else had complete and utter control of all the inhabitants? Was it a fate set in stone? Was humankind's destiny controlled by the hand of an unforgiving god? Ever since he had first encountered Kimberly Burrows and the rest of Flosvita, it felt like every move Clay made was watched, and everything that has happened thus far was just to contradict what he was trying to do: heal.

However, the God he once believed in wouldn't have done this. After all, God didn't choose sides. He allowed the world to run as it did, because whether He agreed with the people or not, they all had free will. His gift was free will to choose how one will live. To deny what was happening to Clay, would mean to deny the free will of Flosvita.

Did that make it right? Clay didn't think so. It just wasn't fair. Because now he was decomposing between and goat and a hungry cougar, as flies buzzed all over him. His friend was dead, and the girl he had killed was now walking. What was there to believe in anymore?

What a concept, he thought.

At some point the tent flap opened a man came in and selected a chicken from the pen. Clay called out to him, saying he was thirsty, and the man only laughed and stepped out ignoring him. He was terribly parched and had to use the bathroom. But these guys were willing to let him sit in his own filth and be on the brink of death; not like he could get any worse at this point, right? As long as he was still breathing by tonight in order to attempt to paint their leader, they didn't care of his condition. They didn't care about the wasp that was now crawling across his face and tasting his bad eye, lapping up the mucus and finding it revolting, buzzed away.

"That's it then," Clay found himself telling the billygoat who was munching away absentmindedly, the hay now more interesting than it's neighbor. "I just won't do it. They *killed* José. They can all go fuck themselves. That's what I'll tell them. What do you think?"

The goat made no comment. Would it be funny if it had, or terrifying? Would it even surprise Clay? Probably not.

He was a dead man anyway, and at the end of his long thought process, Clay had finally accepted his fate. Would they really heal him? If they were going to, he didn't want to live knowing he brought back some people from the dead, and got his friend killed in the process. If they didn't heal them, they would just kill him afterward. Nothing would really change for Clay, and he would only be helping this fucked up family benefit from his efforts. So he just won't do it. He didn't care what they did, it wasn't like he could feel pain anyway. Even as he screamed as his flesh fell off his bones and animals pecked at the remains, he wouldn't do it. He couldn't do it. If he did what he did with Kimberly again, he would never be able to look at himself again, healed or not. Not with the knowledge of his friend lost forever.

Was José lost forever? Clay would wonder that very soon, when he finally had an actual visitor. It would be someone he had *least* expected to see.

Thirty

His visitor had come when the sun was just beginning its descent to the western side of the world, it's glow shining through the tent and creating an orange/pink globe effect.

By then the overall temperature of the state of Idaho had reached its peak; 104 degrees Fahrenheit which wasn't the hottest in recorded history but still unbearable; and the interior of the tent made it all the more terrible.

Clay was thirsty, and he had all but surrendered to the flies and wasps. He had accepted his role as Lord of the Flies, specifically, He Who Feeds His Swarm. When the tent flap had opened, he didn't even notice. He was like a comatose patient, unaware of the world, and unwilling to look it in the face as of now.

That is, until a bottle of water came into his view. Aquafina, the plastic wrapping said in bold lettering. Clay's tongue rolled in his mouth, feeling absolutely dry to the point where he felt a chunk of it fall away and roll down his just as arid throat. He began to cough, and delicate female hands unscrewed the cap and pulled his chin up as the mouth of the bottle approached his. It touched his chapped lips, and very slowly the water flowed into his mouth, wetting his tongue and throat and quenching his unbearable thirst. Clay then closed his lips around the bottle greedily, and chugged without his visitor's help. Some of it spilled through the hole in his cheek and dribbled down the side of his face but he didn't care. When the water was gone, the girl removed another bottle from behind and unscrewed the cap and helped him drink. He drank more slowly, as he felt his insides cool and become rejuvenated.

He looked up to his visitor, ready to thank her, whoever she was. The words remained stuck on his molding tongue, for crouched before him wearing a new white dress with brown boots and her crimson hair in a ponytail, was Kimberly Burrows.

Behind her, her brother stood with his arms crossed. He had a cocky look on his face as if he was studying a rare species among the goats and pigs.

(and the cougar of course, can't forget the cougar, Clay)

"Sleep well?" he had asked.

But Clay wasn't looking at him. His attention was solely centered on Kimberly who was studying him with those intense green eyes. They looked almost nothing like Lady of Thorns'. Since she was right here in front of him, he could clearly see every freckle and blemish on her face, the life in her eyes that hadn't been there during the aftermath of the accident, but had been there when he had painted every single one. He saw Gaston and Astrid in this person. He saw both beauty and an abomination sharing the same body. He stared at her for a long time, knowing full well that she *was* real, but still couldn't truly grasp the fact somewhere in the back of his rotting brain. It was like he was in limbo, unable to understand despite it being right in front of him like a secret hidden right under his very nose. He felt joy and disgust at the same time, understanding and yet none. He had never felt this way to a person living or dead in his entire life.

That's just it, the panic rat in his head claimed. *She is neither living nor dead. She is something more. And you made it possible.*

"Well?" Johnny demanded impatiently. He brushed past his sister, starting for Clay. He stomped on the man's leg and went to kick him, when Kimberly's voice, low but soft, reached Clay's ears.

"Leave him alone."

"Kimmy-"

"Let him sit up. Please."

Now Johnny backed off unhappily and Kimberly was sitting inside it with Clay. She sat cross-legged with the half-drank bottle of water in her lap. Pale legs peeking out from under the paler dress. She asked Johnny to give them some space and he protested, saying that he couldn't leave her with the whoremaster.

"He can't hurt me, not when he is tied up. Please go. I need to speak to him, *alone*."

For a girl just recently resurrected, she sounded very clear and coherent. She didn't make any guttural moaning sounds like Clay would associate with a zombie or a being like the Frankenstein monster.

Johnny grumbled something *in*coherent but then walked away and stood by the pigs. He was leaning against the pen watching them, but his expression was stern and unhappy. He was far enough away to give his sister and Clay the privacy Kimberly wanted, but close enough to step in should any immediate danger arise.

Now that they were alone, Kimberly expressed a small smile. She looked very pretty smiling, but the smile didn't sit right with Clay. It felt like a sight of depravity or ill will, as if she were about to say she was indefatigable; untouchable with the one who helped bring her back really a pawn in some twisted game. Therefore, Clay still didn't smile back. He only stared, in disbelief and yet in belief.

"So, you are Clayton Couch," Kimberly said. "Clay to your friends."

Clay said nothing.

After a short and somewhat awkward pause, Kimberly said, "You obviously know who I am. I'm sure it's scary, seeing me like this. I didn't expect to see you with earthly eyes. I wanted to... well, I wanted to thank you for bringing me back. I doubt it was what you had in mind coming here, but still. Thank you. I mean... I'm sorry, I'm still a little overwhelmed myself. I mean, to be brought back by someone who *painted* me? I tried to help you best I could, but you hardly needed it. I've known about you for so long, watched you for longer it seemed, since the accident. So, to see you now... it's really incredible. I guess I also want to say, I'm sorry for wandering out in the road. I know you didn't do it on purpose. I'm sorry for the trouble I caused you. I'm also sorry for... all of *this*."

With those petite hands, she gestured to Clay as if she were nervous about what to really say given Clay's current predicament. He definitely was a sight for sore eyes, he knew that much at least at this point. But the whole 'sorry, sorry, sorry,' only made Clay resent her more. In fact, it angered him, but he simply did not have the energy to lash out as he normally would have.

"This isn't right," he found himself saying to her, surprising himself. "I know that by some degree I should be happy, I brought back a life I took on that road. But... this is *wrong*. I'm sorry but... you shouldn't be here. I shouldn't be having this conversation with you."

"But you *are*," Kimberly said gently and without any offence. She spoke with an authority and yet a tenderness that made it seem possible to believe her. "You *are*. I know it is a lot to take in, but anything is possible in The Family. And thanks to you, you made it happen. I guided your hand while you painted. I have always been there, watching, listening. I will not say that what my father did was right, because it wasn't. Not to you and everything you have been put through since. I can still feel your pain now. It is still there. But now you have a chance to get your body back, and when you finish, it will happen."

"Yeah, and I lost a good friend in the making," Clay said coolly. He was wondering how Kimberly could see him, thinking back to how clear the image of her was while he was painting her. But his curiosity did not obscure the fact that his friend was dead now. "As far as I'm concerned, I have no reason to believe I will be leaving this camp alive. Not with the history your family has."

"You don't know us," Kimberly said just as coolly and defensively. "You know nothing about us or what we really do, Clayton. Or can I call you Clay?"

"I'd rather you not say my name." It gave him the creeps whenever this person, this *thing* said his name aloud. It felt like he might be cursed again at any moment.

"Fine. I understand your caution. But Nigger Jeff is not a liar. He will heal you. Also, there is something else you obviously haven't considered."

"What's that?" he asked sarcastically. "I'm just *dying* to hear." He was just all full of jokes, wasn't he?

Yes sir, it's a grave matter indeed. That was a good one.

Kimberly smiled, no good humor in it whatsoever. "What you did to me, what you will do for Jeff, you can do again."

A cold sinking feeling settled into Clay's stomach. He understood where she was getting at in an instant. "You're out of your mind."

"Am I? You say this is not natural. But it can be because we made it possible. I'm sure in your world, it is wrong. You were probably told and shown your whole life that bringing the dead back is wrong. Tell me, do I *really* look wrong? No, actually, tell me this. Does bringing your friend back *really* sound wrong to you?"

Clay opened his mouth to say, 'Of course it's wrong, you psychopath!' But the words got caught in his throat as the thought slowly took root and made him wonder.

Did José deserve to die? Does *anyone* really? Astrid the Chink, Clay believed for absolute certain. He didn't quite think anyone else had the right, but definitely not his friend whose only crime was sticking by his side to the bitter end. The bitter, skull-shattering end. The gruesome image bloomed into Clay's mind like a rosebud, and just as crimson.

She's here... could Juan be as well?

Kimberly smiled. The smile clearly expressed that she saw it in his face what he was thinking. Or maybe she plucked it out of his head as if she were merely picking a daisy, if she was *more* than human at this point.

"You think it is possible again. You are not wrong. Nigger Jeff will surely not stop you for doing so. He might even welcome it, and help you bring your friend back himself rather than have my mother do it. You see, *nothing* is truly impossible, Clay. Jeffery found a way to cheat the laws of nature that no man had any say of. By doing so, he created something bigger than this wonderful Family. He showed us a way to truly open our third eye. He did the same with you. You had a taste of it. Was it truly horrible or bad at all? I think not. You have greatness in store for you, Clay. I can see it. I've *been* seeing it since you ran me over. And I am glad you did what you did."

She pursed her lips, and then reached out and touched the side of his face that wasn't missing a chunk of his cheek. Clay felt cold at her touch. Her fingertips felt alien, not alive at all.

"I'm *really* glad," she then added. "I am eternally grateful for what you've done for me, and I promise we will make it right for you. We will lift the curse placed on you. This won't be the final chapter of your life, Clay. I won't let that happen. In this camp, even if the others don't see it quite yet, you have a friend. You have a friend in me."

"Why were you out there?" Clay found himself asking to both his and her surprise. Out of all the questions he could ask, he had only this. "Why did you wander out into the road? And why... why didn't you... why..."

He didn't know how to word it. Why hadn't she gotten out of the road when she realized where she was? Why didn't she sprint away when she saw the car coming? Even from around a corner, she would have at least a *few* seconds to process the danger she was in. but they were on a straight stretch. There should have been no reason to go out into the road. There should have been *no* reason that Kimberly had to become roadkill, by Clay who just so happened to have been screaming at Rachel to stop nagging him instead of paying attention for that split-second the girl was out on the highway.

Kimberly pursed her lips again. She seemed to consider her answer carefully, hedging away whatever was unnecessary or none of Clay's business in order to produce a reasonable answer if one was there. She must have come to the conclusion that she didn't have a good enough answer, so she opted for the truth.

"In truth, I don't know *why* I went out there. I remember my father chasing me, I remember a cat too, I think, but I don't know why. When the accident happened, only bits and pieces came back. A lot of who I was is muddled, and hard to distinguish. I only know what the spirits tell me, what I heard my mother and father speak of you to one another, and what I saw and heard while following you."

"Please, think," Clay said realizing he was begging a girl to remember the few moments she had before she was struck dead in the road. For some reason he couldn't quite comprehend, he *had* to know. "Think as hard as you can. Why did you go out into the road?"

Kimberly looked at him with a flustered appearance of curiosity. "Why is that so important to you?"

"Because... because..." Clay sighed, hedging his own thoughts and yet finding nothing to trim in his answer. "I know nothing of you. All I know, is that you were so important to your dad, like any parent should I suppose, that he was willing to place a curse on me in order to kill me. I always spoke badly of you, calling you stupid for going out onto the highway in the first place. I don't know, to think that now, seems incredibly wrong of me."

"Not something I can't understand," Kimberly replied softly. "I wish I knew what was going on through my head. I even wish I knew what it was like being a kid growing up. All I have are memories my Family has. They aren't the same as your own."

"You can see memories?"

Kimberly nodded. "It is a gift shared by many. A lot of the memories in this camp, however, is hurt and yet excitement. Hurt because of what had happened to my father, and that eases into hatred towards you. Excitement, because the word is out that Nigger Jeff will once again walk the earth as I am. I've spoken to him as well, on the other side, and although his memories and knowledge is helpful, I still strive to know myself for myself. I hope to figure that out soon. As soon as I can, though, maybe someday I will tell you."

Clay nodded, finding it surprisingly easy to understand despite not having any experience in what exactly Flosvita and their inhabitants are truly capable of.

"Can I ask you something else then?"

"I'll answer if I can."

Clay nodded. He realized he could very well get to like this girl. She had a decent personality, compared to the rest of her fucking family. "You say you know me. You said you followed me, have been watching over me. That includes what I think of? What I dream of, right?"

"More like conscious thoughts, but yes."

Not understanding but accepting the answer still, Clay nodded again. "Then... when you look back from like my perspective of what had happened... do you think I am guilty?"

"You *feel* guilty."

"But am I?"

Those lips pursed once again. "In the beginning, I *did* blame you. I was angry at you. You hurt me with your car. But the more I listened to you, your girlfriend, and my parents, the more I couldn't help but feel sorry for you too. It could have happened to anyone, and it happened to you. You didn't see me. You *tried* to stop though in that split second, but it was still too fast. There really was nothing you could do. No one else here may truly believe that, but I do. So please, rest assure I do not hold any grudge against you. Only gratitude for what you did in the end."

Clay nodded. He was glad that the person he killed didn't *hate* him for it. But still, there was something in Kimberly's voice that didn't sit right. The more he thought about it, the more it was clear that it was nothing she could really control. It was more of what she was what drove the feeling of anxiety into Clay.

"Well," he said after a moment's pause. "I'm glad you feel grateful. But I'm not doing it again. I *can't* do it again. Not for your leader, and not for my friend. I don't believe I'm making out of this alive, even if the curse is lifted. I got nothing to lose anymore. So, sorry, but I'm not doing it."

He wasn't *really* sorry, but he felt like he had to say it. To justify it.

He could try to justify it all he wanted though. A flare erupted in Kimberly's eyes, something that had never been there since her arrival even when she was cold towards him earlier. All good nature seemed to vanish for less than a second. For that moment, Clay saw Kimberly for what she really was. An angry demon with an ugly scowl and furious eyes.

When she smiled softly again, it would have easily passed for a figment of one's imagination if anyone else saw it. But Clay could still see the fire and lightning in those stormy gray eyes. What he saw hadn't been an illusion. Kimberly Burrows was not as kind as she was making herself out to be. What was hidden behind that pale and pretty face, was something more than human. No person who dies and comes back could possibly be the same upon their return. Her statement of her loss of memories proved that. Looking into those eyes, Clay could see it. There was something *else* working like clockwork behind those eyes. Something sinister, and disingenuous.

"Sometimes, dead is better," said Jud.

"Darling," it had said.

"What you bought, will eventually come to you."

"I think you'll change your mind," Kimberly said. "Forgive me for saying, but you look worse for wear. You really don't have a lot of time left. Look at you. You are already beginning to *liquify*. Soon your guts won't have any reason to stay inside you, and you will shit them out and still be able to walk around. You'll walk until you can't, and you will lie and rot, if the buzzards don't pick you clean when we send you out into the dessert. You *will* do this, Clay."

"I got nothing left to lose," Clay said again, undeterred. He wasn't going to be pushed around by something that wasn't entirely Kimberly Burrows. "Thanks for the water. Now you and your brother can go fuck yourselves. Heard you gypsies were into that."

Kimberly grinned again. This time there was no kindness in that smile at all. Those little teeth looked to Clay for a moment like teeth that belonged to a wild animal. That storm in her eyes, not letting up. "Well, I was going to say you've had a rough enough day. But, I can see I was wrong. Johnny-boy!"

Her brother came up and joined Kimberly by her side. He asked what was wrong, his eyes staring daggers into Clay's face.

"Clay can't sense pain, right?" she asked.

"It would seem so," Johnny said reeling his foot back and kicking Clay in the chest. He felt the pressure in his chest, and knew the sensation as a rib being cracked or broken, most likely an unchecked injury from the car wreck

(*vehicular assault*)

not too long ago. It didn't hurt, and Clay thought about saying ow, but he was too busy glaring at John and Kimberly.

"Go fuck yourselves," he said again.

The smile was now on Johnny's face and Clay could clearly see the resemblance between him and Kimberly. They were definitely brother and sister. Both mutts from biracial parents, both with some differences, but still having that same connection all siblings have. If it had to be anything that stood out the most, it was the grins on their faces like skeletons. The terrifying grins that said, 'You wanna fuck with us? Watch us fuck with *you*.'

"Show him," Kimberly said. "Not the head, though."

"You think I'm an idiot?" her older brother said but he was still grinning as he removed his Colt and pressed it against Clay's right knee and pulled the trigger.

The force jolted through Clay's being as the kneecap shattered and the joints pulled and tore. Muscle ripped, spewing blood and that slimy pus. Clay screamed, not out of pain, but of horror as he stared at the severed shin resting next to the stump just below his right thigh. The fragger bullet ripped through and tore it almost clean off, leaving strands of flesh and slime pouring out and soaking into the hay. Jagged points of shattered bone pointed at it almost accusingly. All around the three humans in the zoo the animals went ballistic. Chickens squawked and fluttered around their cage stupidly, the pigs squealed and cows bellowed and tried to get away but were stopped by the ropes that tethered them to the tent. The billygoat next to Clay screamed with those dual satanic eyes wide and terrified. The cougar, that had been watching them, was on it's feet and snarling and hissing fiercely at the unwelcome sound that probably reminded it of hunters in the hills.

Clay stared at the severed leg, and then looked up at the siblings. "You fucking psychopaths!"

"You'll be fine," Johnny said. "You aren't going to bleed out. Your blood is moving too slow in your veins at this point. You're already dead anyway. You weren't just made to rot, you stupid city-boy. You were made to *suffer*. You will suffer until there is absolutely nothing left of you. You don't wanna play by the rules? Here is a recap: You will do what our mother says. And for doing so, you will save your life; save your *soul*. You don't, and we will make sure you watch yourself rot away into nothingness."

"Fuck you!"

Johnny turned, flipped Clay the bird as he started to walk away. "Come on, sis."

"One moment," Kimberly said. She had squatted back down to her original spot, smiling at Clay tenderly again like a politician who inculcates a college student that he was right and everyone else was wrong. 'Trust me,' that smile said, which only made Clay feel repulsed by.

"You really don't have a choice, Clay," she said. "You think you do, and you're wrong. You don't have the right to make the *wrong* choice, not when it matters so much. You *will* change your mind. You will see how we see. You just need to let go of what you believe in, and trust in Flosvita. Trust in the Family."

"I'm sure that's what Jim Jones said to his followers, you fucking, undead, *bitch*."

The smile didn't fade, didn't falter. There wasn't even a twitch. Her stare was cold and wicked. Regardless of the persona she showed in the beginning, she was no different than the rest of these nomadic hillbilly fucks and Clay was not about to let her push him around. He felt his heart pounding with adrenaline surging through his veins like heroine. They blew off his fucking knee, just to show him that he would either be okay like they said, or he would bleed out.

There wasn't a lot of blood soaking into the hay though, not as much as there were of that nasty green pus. That fact alone wasn't enough to comfort Clay when he would be left alone to stare at it and contemplate. If anything, seeing his severed leg gushing that slime that smelled of death, only made the feeling of dread sink in deeper and cut even deeper to get to his core.

Kimberly's final words to Clay for the afternoon, were "You think we are insane. That we are *wrong*. We aren't. Soon, you'll see, once your third eye opens completely. It opened a bit, I can tell. It's a sleepy eye, hasn't fully awaken yet. But it will. They all say the same things you say- to a degree. But it all turned out the same in the end, Clay. I know it is scary. I am sure what we had to do to you in order for you to listen is jolting. But take comfort in the fact that you are now part of something greater. A greater purpose for the life you thought you were doomed to live. I look forward to seeing you again, Clay. I truly am."

And with that Kimberly and Johnny Burrows departed from Clay. They didn't look back and ignored him as he called out to them, cursing them and screaming for someone to save him. His words fell on deaf ears, only the livestock and cougar truly listening to the mad one-legged man that reeked of a corpse. Even as the two left and closed the tent flap, Clay screamed. He screamed until his throat became dry again, raw from the constant noise. At last, someone outside the tent told him to shut up. To quit his screaming and not disturb the peace.

Clay's last scream was, "Fuck you! All of you! You *FUCKS!!*"

At last, he gave up his screaming, and instead sat up to stare dead-eyed at the stump that used to be his entire right leg. The flies, having sensed a detachment from their host and the chunk of leg sitting in the hay, had all converged on Clay's leg and were crawling all over it. Ready to slowly devour it, lay their eggs, Clay knew, and he felt his stomach turn at the thought of it.

Soon, you'll see, once your third eye opens completely. It opened a bit, I can tell. It's a sleepy eye, hasn't fully awaken yet. But it will.

Out of everything Kimberly Burrows said to Clay, that was the part of her speech that still echoed in his mind like the ringing of a bell. Despite the disbelief in the loss of his leg, despite the raw terror he felt in his chest, Clay could not to save his life stop hearing those words. He felt like a man who had been undone like a roll of twine. Spread out and revealed to be

a cardboard center for someone to pick and prod at and
eventually throw away.

But Kimberly's words continued to resonate and made
him feel like an unwound spool of twine, but she wasn't picking
at the center. She was letting the center do the consideration
and thinking. That was all he could really do at this point. Think,
so that he wouldn't go insane.

I'm already *insane,* the panic rat in his skull claimed.
Wheeeeeeeeeeeeeeeee!

Clay felt he had gone insane. That would be the only
reason why he felt so calm now. Why he was no longer
laughing, no longer feeling anchored to the world. He just
wanted to slip away. He just wanted to disappear.

Fuck 'em, he thought. *They can make the rest of my life
a living hell all they want. I'm not putting myself through that
again. I will not look into the eyes of another resurrected person
again.*

Even if it was José? the panic rat inquired, trying to
plant another seed and force Clay to go into hysterics.

At this point, Clay didn't know anymore. He didn't want
to know. He didn't want to think. He just... wanted... to...
disappear.

The cougar looked at him with eyes that clearly said,
You cannot. No one can. Flosvita, is forever.

(Soon, you'll see, once your third eye opens completely)

What did that *mean* though? Would it open? Was that a
precise guarantee? Moreover, did Clay have any choice at all?
Or has fate decided already? Did he truly have any control at all,
as he had thought before?

(It opened a bit, I can tell)

Because of the painting? Because of what he had
witnessed and experienced firsthand? Clay didn't understand
that part for certain. He thought about what Kimberly had said
earlier, that if he helped to bring back Jeffery Flosvita, he could
very well just as easily bring his friend back. The rational part of

Clay's mind, the one that was present when he was speaking with the undead Burrows girl, said that was a stupid idea, and a dangerous thought in the first place. That he would be no better than a zombie. He'd be like Kimberly, something that was never meant to be. *Shouldn't* be at all.

But maybe this was where the third eye came into play. Because regardless of what that rational side of Clay's melting brain said, there was a small part of him that said he didn't know for certain. That José wasn't truly gone. That the panic rat was not trying to drive him any more insane than he already felt, but was giving reasonable thoughts to think.

Besides, didn't he owe José? Was it fair that he was dead because Clay brought him along? If anyone deserved a second chance it was *him*, not Kimberly.

He couldn't undo what he did for Kimberly, but maybe he could make it right for José at the very least.

(It's a sleepy eye, hasn't fully awaken yet. But it will)

What would happen once that became true? If it really was true at all?

What power did Flosvita *really* have? Where had it come from? Nothing biblical, maybe something much older. These nomads had not only departed from mankind as a community, but from any known gods in their hearts in pursuit of who they had found. But who had they found exactly? Who was the sun and moon god they spoke so often of? Where was the boundary line that defined man and gods and kept them separate as nature intended? Clay remembered his mother telling him this phrase when he had decided he no longer believed in God at the age of sixteen.

"If you dethrone God in your heart, guess who ascends the position? Satan."

At the time, Clay didn't think much of it. Whatever entity Flosvita had an accord with, it was definitely not the biblical God he had known as a child. It was something just as ancient if not much older if he had to put it into words. Knowing this, *believing* in this, and coming to grasps that there really was no boundary line or neutral ground for Flosvita. They were a group in of itself; a world unknown to what he once called 'reality.' A world full of obvious happiness and fellowship, but also a world of terrible power that made any natural disaster sound feeble. Just what has the family done over the years that no article or news coverage has said?

How many people disappeared, claimed by incurable diseases or just snatched like Krampus with his sack full of children? What else were they capable of? He was to share that power in order to do what they wanted.

The very idea was not something that Clay could comprehend. Because regardless of what he believed in, he was no god. He had no right to play with the forces of nature, and bring back something that had obviously expired from the real world he lived in. But even as he told himself that, he was afraid. It was a childish fear, influenced by obvious recent events, but also because of the unknown. Because even though he would never admit this to anyone, he was scared of what Flosvita would do to him. He was determined to not bring back Jeffery Flosvita or anyone else. It was a burden that was just far too heavy for him to carry alone. Even so, he was scared. Scared, because he truly had no idea what he was up against, despite all that he had experienced thus far.

Because if a fear cannot be understood to the point of being able to be expressed, then it cannot be conquered.

This thought stuck with Clay, up until it was time to see Astrid the Chink again, and her hideous brood.

Thirty-One

Two men, Robert the Rotten and another guy, a Native American named Injun Ion from Colville Washington (as he dutifully recited with great pride) before he joined Flosvita in 2006, came into the livestock tent and untied the tired and terrified Clay. They lifted him up by each arm, and he thrashed, saying they were leaving his leg behind in the pen. The stump on his right knee (or what was left of it, had solidified into a fatty substance, the slime reminding him of mucus he used to cough up on the regular every spring and summer when tumbleweeds bloomed and gathered pollen.

"Don't worry about it," Robert (Robbie) said. "We'll feed it to Ginger."

Ginger. The goat, or the cougar? Did it matter? The end result was the same either way: Clay being sick knowing that another part of him would be inside another animal.

(Animals are already inside of you. Remember the maggots? The worms? Soon you'll have flies flying out of your ass! How's that *for an image?)*

They took him out into the clearing away from the other tents and cars. Astrid's RV was still a walk away, but they were stopping here. A lot of people had stopped to gawk, their eyes brightened by the setting sunlight. Astrid the Chink was waiting beside a black pickup with another gal, and the old woman approached the men and smiled at Clay with a sense of familiarity that he despised. What made him uneasy, was her attire.

All she wore was a shawl of gold and silver, symmetrically split down the middle. She had paint on her face, beads dangling from her hair, and her eyes were burning bright with either liquor or marijuana.

"Did you rest well?" she asked, grinning like a demoness in the firelight which casted eerie shadows across her face.

"Fuck you," Clay answered.

"Still fighting it, I see. Kimberly said you were. You'll see our way soon enough."

"Fuck you," Clay said again. He was scared, but he was *not* backing down, even when Robert and Ion dropped him to the ground like a sack of dirty laundry and stepped back as Johnny Burrows got out of the passenger side of the car and opened the rear doors of the Silverado. The upper half of his body disappeared from view as Astrid spoke to Clay who was laying on his belly, propping himself up with his hands and glaring venomously at the current leader of Flosvita.

"Fuck you, you-"

"Watch your mouth," Robert said stepping on Clay and forcing his face into the dirt. Something cracked in his wrist as he tried to push himself up, and he remained prone. "She's talking."

"Goddammit, get off!" Clay barked defiantly. More pressure was applied to Clay's back, not that it hurt him in the first place. He wasn't going to give in. He couldn't. Because he knew that if he gave in again, if he allowed himself to follow those who lurk in the darkness casted by Flosvita's shadow, he too would be engulfed in it, and he would have no one to blame but himself.

Astrid folded her hands behind her back, pacing towards Clay only to change course and begin to circle the downed man. Injun Ion stepped away, joining the gathering crowd while Robert still stood on top of him as if he were a hunter with a prized boar.

"Kimberly tells me you have a strong will, that you refuse to open your third eye. That you will not help us in order to save yourself."

"You killed my friend," Clay said. "What I did is *not* worth it. So you can take our deal and shove it up your wrinkly ass."

"Oh, I am *quivering* with fear," Astrid said with a sarcastic chuckle. "You mean to defy us, because you claim you have 'nothing to lose.'"

"I don't."

"Really?" Astrid raised a hand, her thumb and middle finger pressed against one another by the tips. "Let's see then." She then snapped her fingers, and Johnny came out of the truck holding something in his arms.

Clay stared, couldn't believe it, blinked, and then started to laugh like a maniac. "No... No, no, no, no... Noooo, no, *no, NO, NO!* You gotta be FUCKING kidding me!"

His voice sounded so watery, so defeated, it began to crack. "No!" He kept saying that word over and over again, as if it would actually change what he was seeing. For what he saw was the most cliché and most bullshit move Flosvita has done since the death of José. Despite their confidence in their other-worldly influence on Clay and his 'third eye,' they were willing to do whatever it took to get what they wanted. They wanted Jeffery Flosvita back. And they were going to have him back.

Even if it meant kidnapping Rachel Abbas, tying her up, driving her all the way out here, and dropping her onto the ground with bound hands and feet with a stretch of duct tape across her mouth.

Her eyes were wide and wild, looking around and becoming wider when she saw Clay. She was a nightgown, her feet were bare, her hair was loose, and she wore no makeup. She must have been home asleep, and somehow Johnny and whoever else accompanied him managed to subdue her and take her with them to this nightmarish place where human monsters (*the wild things*) roamed. She was screaming muffled cries behind her gag, and when she tried to roll away, Johnny grabbed her by the arms and lifted her up, twisting her shoulders and forcing her to stay still. She stared at Clay, pleading for him to help her.

"Don't you hurt her, you fucking faggot!" Clay bellowed. He had never felt so angry in all his life. His shaky temper had never been so far pushed over the edge that he felt his veins popping out on his face, his slow and curdled blood boiling to the point where he could have thrown Robert off if he actually tried.

Johnny bared his teeth at Clay in a snarl/grin. "Make me, whoremaster. Missed your whore that badly, huh? My old man used to say you ain't a true lumberjack until you cut into some dark wood. You feel like a lumberjack, whoremaster? Maybe we should show your whore what a *real* man can do?"

He was goading him, trying to make Clay angry. Nothing could make him more angrier than he was now. Nothing could *scare* him more than he was right now. All around him was gone, all that was left in this nightmarish world was Rachel, and Rachel alone.

"Rachel," Clay said staring at his ex and not looking anyone else in the eye. "Are you hurt?"

She shook her head, looking so frightened that tears were now rolling down her cheeks. First José was being roped into this, now her. When, just *when* was this nightmare going to end?

He looked up at Astrid, who had ceased her pacing and was standing over him with that stupid fucking grin on her face. That Flosvita grin almost everyone seemed to share.

"You bitch, I'm gonna fucking kill you! She has nothing to do with this!"

"She does now," Johnny said dropping Rachel to the ground again. Dust puffed up from beneath her, the gesture reminding Clay of dropped flour back when he was at work.

"So, Mr. Couch," Astrid the Chink said in a pleasant voice that made Clay want to bellow and vomit at the same time. "Here is an *extension* to our deal. You paint, Jeffery Flosvita, you get your body back. And then, with your new body…"

She snapped her fingers again, and Johnny pulled out his Colt again. He shoved it into the back of Rachel's head and her eyes widened, tears spilling and seeming to absorb Clay who stared in mute horror in realization.

He had just enough time to scream one last time before the kid blew a hole into the back of Rachel's head without any warning. She had been there, and then there was only her shattered skull replacing the look of terror on her ruined face. *BLAM!* Destruction.

Clay stared in horror, watched her brains turn to goo and spill into the dirt. She slumped, one of her eyes dangling out of it's shattered socket like a dangling yo-yo. The murder was so sudden that it took him completely by surprise, worse than the case with José.

It wasn't enough to take his best friend, they took his girlfriend as well. They murdered her, and Clay watched mute with tears rolling down his face as Johnny Burrows picked up the body still dripping gore. He was laughing like the sick fuck that he was, grabbing ahold of one breast and then fondling the spot between her legs, defiling her corpse which made Clay only see red. He watched Johnny go behind a camper and stared at the spot where he had turned the corner as Astrid continued to speak.

"With your new body," Astrid said. "You can paint your friend and whore, and we will bring them back for you. The deal of a lifetime. Do it for us, and their deaths will no longer be on *your* conscious."

"I... You..."

Nothing. There was nothing Clay could say no matter how hard he'd try. They had taken everything away from him. Time, his body, and now the closest people he cared about. They killed them, to use them as leverage so that Clay *had* to do it. There was nothing he could do though, they were dead, probably about to be buried somewhere in the desert, or fed to the livestock.

Were they? the UFO panicked rat asked.

Now it felt like the right thing to do. It felt necessary, considering he was the one who got them killed in the first place.

Alone, he could rationally reason that what he had done was wrong. That no one should be brought back regardless of the reason behind their death. But now, it felt like the rat had more of a hold on him, feeding him everything he needed to make up every sweet excuse to believe that this wasn't the end; using his grief as a weapon to force that belief down his throat.

My fault… all my fault…

Maybe the Flosvita Family pulled the trigger, but he got them into this. He was to blame, he was the guilty one. Just as he had been when he had run over Kimberly. In his heart, he believed that still. Just like he believed, that the real world was far away and no longer applied to him anymore. Here in the Flosvita campground, their law was the *only* law. Their methods were the right ones. Their gift, was what could make the impossible possible. It was a gross and yet hopeful feeling, that Clay felt he couldn't ignore. He didn't want any of his friends to die. And now that they were, he felt like he *had* to make it right. He didn't care about himself. He just wanted to save Rachel, who was innocent and had no part in this. José, whose only crime was protecting his friend.

God… Rachel…

Clay was crying now. No longer angry, no longer even hopeful. Just broken. Broken, like the rest of his body.

Still, those thoughts came back, fueled by his grief.

Can I do this? he asked himself. *Can I* really *do this again? It's… it's…*

Wrong, and yet, so right. If he allowed himself to rot away, then he would carry that guilt with him until there was nothing left of him at all. Their death would remain on his conscious, and he would never be able to look them in their faces again, if he joined them wherever they were now. He felt defeated. He was defeated.

Astrid crouched down before Clay. She gently took his chin, and lifted his face up to look at her. "It's possible, my friend. We will make it right. If, you do this for us. You can bring back the one person who can save the lives you brought us. It will be like nothing, ever happened."

("Nothing." The memory of it all would remain, no fooling yourself on this one, Clay)

Maybe, but...

"Now, do we have a deal?"

'The lives you brought us.' That was a bigger kick in the head than anything this woman ever said to Clay. He was scared, terrified to pick up the brush again. Terrified of what horrors he would experience during and after. Afraid, for his immortal soul and the burden and sin he would be tainting it with. But in the end, all that came to mind, was the faces of the two people he loved more than anything and anyone in the world.

(have you changed your mind?)

He clenched his jaw, which denied him any pain to distract him. He wish he could feel physical pain now, for the pain in his heat was much too great. His tears stained his face, gooey and congealed. His grief, his only pain, was simply unbearable.

"Fine," he said, defeated. "Fine, you fucking bitch, I'll do it."

Astrid released him and stood, her hands in the air as she addressed the crowd that had completely encircled her and her new artist. "Nigger Jeff will return, thanks to Clayton Couch of Boise!"

Cheers and clapping resounded, but Clay wasn't hearing them. He didn't care. The only thing that mattered to him at this point in time, was the blood now saturating into the dirt before him. The lamb he had unwillingly led to slaughter among the wolves, just as José had been.

I'll make this right, he told both himself, as well as Rachel and his friend. *I'll make this right. I'm so sorry... I'll make this right. Oh, god, Rachel...*

Within the crowd, Kimbely Burrows was not celebrating. She was not joining in with the cheers and clapping. She was staring directly at Clay, a hideous frown on her face. Another death for this. This wasn't exactly how she had planned, but she was happy for the results. So why did she feel so uneasy?

Why did she feel, that Clayton Couch's will, had not been broken entirely?

Thirty-Two

Back in the RV, a prisoner within the very home of his enemies, Clay was shoved in, followed by Kimberly and Astrid. They waited with him, a pump-action shotgun in Kimberly's hands now pointing at him the entire time they waited for Precious Penelope and Johnny to return with more paints and a new canvas. When they did, Johnny set it all up as he had before, with the added folding chair for Clay to sit in, and told his mother and sister he could stand watch in here.

"Not yet," Astrid said. "I want to watch. I want to witness the process."

Clay, who had been sitting cross-half-legged in the hall leading to the back room this whole time, only stared at the large and blank canvas with a sense of anxiety. He felt his chest tightening, his stomach churning and his rotting body sweating. He knew this was wrong, but he had to do this, for Rachel and José. They deserved it, he knew that. He *had* to do it.

Johnny said that was fine and said he would sit outside. He shot one more warning glare at Clay, and then left the RV, leaving him alone with the two women. Kimberly was sitting on the couch, the gun and her eyes pointed directly at him. Astrid had turned one of the front seats of the RV so that she could sit comfortably and watch where she was.

"All right, Mr. Couch, the canvas is yours."

That's right. The canvas was his. His own black ball of darkness and all he would have to say is "Let there be light" and the process would begin. Quite an analogy.

For a long time though, Clay just sat there, feeling something bubbling in his lower tummy, and picking at the remaining fingernails on his left hand. His remaining eye remained sharp, he had a vision as to what the setting could be (although he briefly considered just painting the actual person). For some reason, it felt like a necessity. Something to bring forth the life of the person in the painting. Kimberly's had been the forest, and at first Clay didn't quite understand why he chose a forest background for the painting.

Could make him come out of some dark alley, a morbid thought came to mind. *Make Flosvita appear to be giving fellatio to some bum.*

As humorous and defiant as that would be, it would no doubt get Clay into trouble.

But then he realized it was what Kimberly *felt* during the aftermath of the accident. That moment when she was struck was how she was projected into the painting. She was floating out of her body, and escaping into the woods like a sprite from ancient folklore. What he had painted was her spirit in the very beginning of her second life. The same would probably become for Jeffery Flosvita. Realizing that made Clay even more reluctant to pick up the brush, but that wasn't just it.

He felt disembodied between inspiration and temptation, where the boundary line is unclear and hazy; where grief apparently had no place, he also realized. When he had been painting Kimberly, he had a *vision*, but the more he thought about it, the more he felt like his hand felt guided and not stroked by his own free will. He would start his work, but he somehow just *felt* what needed to be expressed in the portrait. Because of this, he was able to actually paint for the first time since Lady of Thorns.

Was it possible that the gypsies didn't only take away his body, but his ability to paint? Did they or Kimberly even, took away his artistic vision and his ability to paint, only until they wanted him to? Was that the only reason why he was able to paint again? Because they wanted him to, and they could easily take it away again? Thinking this made Clay think back to what he thought of earlier; that he had no control over his life at all. Not anymore anyway. Ever since he had run Kimberly over, everything was happening under accordance of the Flosvita Family's will, as well as Kimberly herself.

Even now, he knew that if he picked up the brush, he would be able to paint. Only because Jeffery Flosvita, and his family members sitting with him in Astrid's RV, wanted him to. What Clay began to question was, what else would his painting of the religious leader lead to? Would he only be able to paint when they wanted him to? *Come, Jeeves. Time to work!* Was Precious Penelope the same way, or anyone else here who had passion or ambition? The idea of having to be given *permission* to paint made Clay mad which mixed bitterly with the muddled grief.

Also, would they really allow him to bring his friends back to life in the same matter as Kimberly or their leader? Or would he have to jump through more hoops just to get there? Hell, the deal went from resurrect Kimberly to see if the same could be done with Jeffery Flosvita, and then do *him* in order to get his body back. Then José and Rachel were killed, with Rachel having been dragged here against her will. Kidnapped and *murdered*. They said they would help bring them back, but what would *he* have to do to get to that point? There was no such thing as a free lunch, and Flosvita seemed very fixated on that logic, and would squeeze whatever they could get out of someone before helping them like the leeches they were.

Leeches... yes, he supposed that was what Flosvita really were. Not that it mattered what he thought.

What still came to mind is what Kimberly seemed to have started talking about. This 'third' eye everyone seemed to be curious of. If there was such a thing, and his 'third eye' really did open completely, whatever that truly meant, what would happen then? Would he even want to? Would he even have a choice in whatever happened next? Would he end up as a member of the Family, and never leave Flosvita again? Become a part of the hive mind and travel the United States aimlessly, with no artistic passion or talent until it is *permitted*?

If there was ever a more detailed illustration of Hell for artists and story tellers and musicians, Clay thought Flosvita was the perfect illustration. A Hell full of leeches hungry for blood. Always, *always* hungry.

His thoughts went to a line from the poem Dante's Inferno. He thought of the first circle, Limbo, where the unbaptized and pagans roamed aimlessly in a lesser form of Heaven. Then he thought of the fifth, Anger, where the wrathful and sullen received punishment. But what came to mind the most was one of the Bolgias from the circle Fraud. Where sorcerers and those who use unearthly insight to 'usurp God's prerogative by prying into the future,' have their heads twisted so that they can only look backwards as they wander the ninth circle of Hell aimless as they are tortured by the demons that afflict their punishment without remorse. For always trying to look more and more forward, they would only be able to see where they had come from, and nothing more.

For some reason that image comes into Clay's mind, seeing Astrid the Chink, Gaston the Gimp, their biological family and the rest of the Flosvita Family, all wandering a black pit where the heat is unbearable with their heads twisted around as they are punished by winged creatures and maggots and worms eat at their flesh. Such a punishment seemed to fit them, but why was he thinking that now?

Why was he thinking this, when the picture of Jeffery Flosvita was so fresh in his mind he could almost describe it then and there?

(just do it and get it over with)

Yeah, it would be almost too easy.

Was it *Flosvita* showing him this? Some other spirit? Some other divine power, hoping to intervene so that such an abomination to God's law can never be attempted again? Just as those who falsely preached after the death of Jesus were beaten and stripped naked by the demons who say "I know of Peter and of Jesus, but who are you?"

What is going on? Clay wondered rubbing his chin, feeling the skin peel and squish beneath his fingertips. If he kept it up, he would surely strip all flesh from his chin, and he would be rubbing against bone, but he stopped of his own accord when something else came to mind. Something he did not recognize nor understand. He saw it in the canvas, as if some ghostly hand was painting the reel of an old movie, or as if the canvas itself was a television screen to show him whatever 'it' wanted him to see.

He was standing on what most Idahoans would call 'flatland' if you travel further south. He saw no hills, only miles and miles of flat land dotted with shrubs and Baby's Breath. Behind him, he saw a singular road with many little wooden shacks and old western billboard saloons and shops. There were black people everywhere Clay walked, and he didn't see a single white man or woman in the entire dusty and otherwise poverty-ridden town of what he knew without truly knowing was Dearfield Colorado back in 1920, when the Great Depression was in full swing and by the looks of the many carts and burros being loaded up, people were leaving to seek better opportunity while a well-dressed-

(*Negro,* Clay's mind immediately registered. *In this day and age, he would have been called a negro. Maybe even a nigger.* The thought made him sick to his stomach and thankfully was jarring enough for him to come back presently.)

-black man wearing dark pants and a white dress shirt. He was trying to convince some people near a closed down clothing shop to stay, but they would not hear any of it. The town was cut off enough as is, especially given the town was to be a 'safe haven' for the black community. There were some people from the nearby town of Wiggins, who welcomed the departure of Dearfield and their founder, Oliver Jackson who Clay knew at once was the well-dressed man. The town was going under, and there were now only 12 legal members of the population. Those who were from Wiggins, would often swing through and jeer at the town and any family leaving. Clay saw a family of nine, a man and woman and their seven kids packing up their wagon ready to head east to California or Oregon.

Clay knew that this family were the Flosvita's. That one of the boys was Jeffery with his brothers Roger and Cithus. They were watching their mother and father load everything up while some white men driving a motorcar say some obscenities. Those who no doubt came to gawk and oversee the desolation of the town.

"Finally leaving, nigger?"

"Never knew a nigger without an itchy foot."

"Hey, Darkie, yeah, you. Good luck getting married."

"Hey, Flosvita, you know they still hang yer kind way out west? Still legal there, I hear!"

The parents ignored these foolish men. They only gathered their things, and with their kids riding in the wagon, they snapped their reigns and ventured west into the unforgiving dessert of Utah, where Clay knew they would stay for a long time in Salt Lake City. There the parents would have Jeffery, his two closest brothers, and one sister, wait for them somewhere in West Valley City, where they would be abandoned, the parents having decided to take two of their favorite kids with them to wherever they had gone. Jeffery, being the oldest, would make the decision to return to Colorado with his three siblings, where his sister, Maryann, would die of typhoid on their crossing of the Utah and Colorado border.

The three brothers were in Avon along the Eagle River in 1942, when the United States retaliated against the Japanese and the Pacific Islands were all caught up in the ever-growing World War 2. Jeffery being now 27 with his brothers 23 and 24, were registered for the draft but by the time 1945 came along and almost 416,800 people died, Germany had surrendered, and Hiroshima had been annihilated in a nuclear blast. Jeffery, now 30, was working in a church as a Deacon for what was known back then as Avon Community Baptist Church before being renamed ten years later, when he had an experience that reminded Clay of the story of Joseph Smith Jr. who had experienced visions and appearances of God and Jesus and other angelic beings who shared with him the vision of the 'true Christian Church' which would create the Book of Mormon. Clay watched through the eyes of Jeffery Flosvita, what he had experienced while taking a walk among the Eagle River.

He was walking, when he looked up into the sun. He stopped, staring directly at it despite the burning sensation in his pupils. Clay himself felt the effects of solar keratitis slowly settling in, and yet still the young Jeffery continued to look up into the sun. He felt transfixed, hypnotized by something in the blazing sunlight. As the UV light burned holes into the retina tissues, Jeffery Flosvita started to go blind, only seeing the blinding white light of the sun boring into his brain. Even though he felt the pain, he did not look away. He only stared into the sun, as if it were the most beautiful thing in the world.

When he finally brought his eyes back down to Earth, it was pitch black. He could not see, but he could hear the river to his left, the forest to his right, and feel the sunlight soaking into his black hair. Clay himself couldn't see anything despite knowing where Flosvita was exactly, and that there was now someone else walking along the river with him.

The feeling Clay felt when the presence approached Jeffery, was nothing short of repulsion. The heat of the summer in 1946, was gone instantaneously and he felt gooseflesh erupt on every pore in his body. He felt sick to his stomach, and the fight or flight response became registered into his body like how Flosvita used to feel when white men or boys would assault him on his way home from work. The two responses became jumbled, and with the wires crossed Jeffery remained stationary, as if he were anchored to the ground by invisible hands clutching his dark ankles.

"Who's 'dere?" Jeffery demanded, his broken English taught only by his mother instead of school, barely coming together in adulthood and wouldn't for another year when he would be able to speak with the clarity of a politician in D.C. "Show yoself!"

"I am right in front of you," a voice that was both seductive and abhorrence. The voice was male, but it was as if the words had been drizzled in honey to mask the bitterness inside.

"I can't see... who are you?"

"I am Hama, husband of Yareakh. You dared to look into my face, and have lost your sight."

"The... the sun?"

"In your tongue, yes. You are a strange man, Jeffery Flosvita. You have dared to look at the face of god, and now you must do my bidding."

In a voice that sounded like that of a child without any choice in the matter, Flosvita spoke. Clay tried to speak out, tried to tell whoever it was to leave him be and go away, but Flosvita's voice carried forward.

"What would you have me do?" A willing slave to an otherwise merciful god, who only took away his sight.

"Arise, go into town, and you shall know what to do." The being said this as Lord Jesus once said to Saul of Tarsus.

Blind, unsure where to go, Flosvita moved forward. He followed the sound of the river, his hands outstretched before him. He walked for nearly an hour, for he was far from home. He knew not where he was, but his feet moved with a clarity that very few blind people had upon first losing their sight. At some point, Jeffery recognized a voice, and knew it was Cithus. His brother asked what happened, and then like Saul of Tarsus, scales fell from Flosvita's eyes and something else fell away as well. He could see clearly what the stranger in the woods wanted him to do, what he wanted him to say.

He told both of his brothers, it would be time to leave very soon. He told them of his encounter, and their *eyes* were opened as well. They knew they had a purpose, and they began to preach to the blacks in Avon, telling them to follow them and they would become a family strengthened by fellowship away from the pains of the world. He would make a speech at the same Baptist Church, saying "We must show others the beauty the world has hidden from us!"

This of course went against the community, and Flosvita and his family were chased out of town. However, they took many others who had decided to call the Flosvita Family their own, and they moved to Las Vegas in 1950, not 1956. They arrived, preaching wherever they went about the glories of the Sun and Moon and the power granted to their devout followers, and the community grew to a staggering 100 by the time they reached Sin City.

It was only then, their Family grew. The community grew. Flosvita met the Burrows, who he regarded them as close friends and the greatest white man and Chinese woman he had ever met personally. Then the crimes began, the kidnapping, the shootouts, and Flosvita would only care for his followers and love on them, and tell them the world knew not what they were privileged to. That their family has been cheated long enough, and that they had something no one else did. Despite all the hardships the family had both legal and not, they thrived, they grew, and as their 'third eye' opened up more and more, more could be seen and done. Flosvita could see spirits wandering the earth, their skeletal beings marching aimlessly in the realm unseen by human beings. Clay felt himself shaking as he looked into the faces of dead men.

Everything down here, is death, one spirit would tell Jeffery before the FBI would finally be involved enough to arrest the religious leader and his brothers and scatter the community known as Flosvita. There, Jeffery experienced more visions in prison, where he would project them through the bond shared by all members of the Family. He would share the passing of Roger who could not take being locked up any longer, and it would be Cithus who would pass Jeffery's spirit along to Gaston and Astrid Burrows, who would lead their family south to Los Angeles where they would await Cithus' release.

However, with the recent events, the Burrows were distracted, and Jeffery was furious with them. But then, he got to see Clay through the eyes of his latest member of his 'ghost family' and with his current knowledge presented to him from the Sun and Moon, he planted his idea into Kimberly Burrows, who in turn rendered Clay unable to paint. Despite the disastrous curse planted by Gaston Burrows, Flosvita allowed Kimberly to do what she felt was necessary and would go meet Clay, until he was summoned by Astrid just yesterday. Clay saw himself, ghoulish and decaying in Astrid's RV.

This was the spirit that wanted to return. Flosvita, who created his community not by his own free will, but by what vision he had by some unseen being who promised power, something he never had before that walk in the woods. With this information now implanted (that seemed the most appropriate word for it) in Clay's mind, Clay had a clear picture not just of what Jeffery Flosvita looked like, but who he was as a *person*.

If he even was a person at all.

Perhaps a pawn in some divine game maybe? Or was it something else? His vision corrupted by greed and sorcery which included conjuring the dead, placing curses on those who denied them, and even, Clay realized, using his Third Eye to control the entire gypsy camp.

Everything the Flosvita Family has done was clear to Clay now. The kidnapping, the poisoning of food in Dallas Oregon, the plague of rats and locusts in some farms in Washington, the sudden spread of measles throughout the states back in 1981 until Jeffery and his brothers' arrest in 1990. It had also been Jeffery who implanted the idea of another disease in California to Gaston Burrows in 2010. The deadly whooping cough that claimed the lives of ten infants and rendered many children weak, lasted for four years. Deadly animal attacks in zoos, random acts of violence by gangs especially from members of the cartel, sudden earthquakes and tornados, and many, many more.

What seemed to ground Flosvita for the family they really were, were the terrorist attacks in 2001. They had watched the World Trade Center and Twin Towers fall. They had watched with many others on the outskirts of New York, joining the silence of respect to the fallen both civilian and firemen and police. But Flosvita, who was seeing it all through the eyes of his Family, only felt glad.

The empire the United States had worked to build was now under attack, just as his old home back in Colorado had been attacked and plagued. His joy was expressed by all the members of Flosvita at the time. The smell of fresh spirits now wandering the world, the taste of their pain on their tongues and the absorption of despair those around them felt whenever they thought back to those days.

These were not human beings who only wanted to gain power and fellowship. These were all vampires who caused plagues, disasters, and sucked the very life out of others. They caused anarchy, and despair to those who either wronged them directly, or had nothing to do with it despite being only reminders to Jeffery Flosvita those who wronged him. Like the FBI, who would be scrambling for the rest of their days on the war on terrorism and other disasters and wars to come. He watched them scramble, trying to keep the peace contained in the United States and retain their hard-won empire. These were men and women who followed a man blinded by some entity, only to think himself as one and above mankind.

The image of Jeffery Flosvita was clearer now, clearer with his history offered to Clay. This image was clear in Clay's head and he could see the painting complete on the canvas despite not having started yet.

And yet, he still felt repulsion and despite his urgency, he did not want to do it. The temptation to paint was there, he felt something pulling on his hands to move forward now more than ever. But then again, something pulled him back. Something that made him think of Dante's Inferno, and helped him to see the real image of Jeffery Flosvita and not what the spirit was undoubtedly trying to make Clay see, just as Kimberly made him see who she was.

Who was it though? *What* was it? Clay didn't know. All he knew, was that he had a vision. He had a vision, he knew who Jeffery was and where he would like to come from, and so he took up the brush.

The brush fell from his hand. Surprised, Clay stooped over to pick it up. His left fingers refused to do his bidding. Studying them, he flexed his fingers. They would contort backwards or not move at all. All that could move was his left pinky. Realization fell upon him, and he realized that the muscles in his wrist or arm had snapped, rotted away and rendering his left hand useless.

His dominant hand.

His *good* painting hand.

All the time painting the day before had taken it's toll, and he flexed once more. This time, he heard something crack, and the pinky went slack. He tugged on it curiously, thinking to pop it. He was disgusted by the wet tearing sound as the pinky came *right* off his hand as if he had plucked a dandelion from the grass, a strain of pus trailing after.

"Oh, fuck," Clay managed before standing with his one foot and hobbling to the nearby sink and vomiting. The pinky fell from his grasp and sat in the sink among his vomit which was mostly water from earlier, as well as a few squirming insects. Unbeknownst to him, his stomach lining had torn due to it's rotted fragility, and a lot of his stomach acid was swimming around the rest of his guts. There was not much to conceal the severed finger in the RV's sink.

When he was done, Astrid came over and turned on the garbage disposal. Clay watched in horror as his finger was taken.

"Back to the canvas," she said once Clay's finger had been sliced and chopped up and sliding down the drain.

"I can't…" Clay said miserably. His good painting hand was useless, and he told her so.

"Paint right-handed then," Astrid said impatiently. "Or you'll lose *more* than a hand."

Crying strands of mucus now, Clay allowed himself to be led back to the canvas, and he picked up the brush with his right hand. With some effort, he managed to put the oval on his left arm, his useless hand supporting the tray of paints. His right hand, his weaker hand, Clay didn't think he had the capability to paint now.

But instead, he made a mixture of red and brown, and feeling the sensation which reminded him of a Kindergarten teacher assisting him with coloring inside the lines of his coloring book, allowed himself to be led. He took up the brush in his right hand, which felt awkward and unnatural like a kid trying to write with his right hand after receiving a beating for writing with his left, which was apparently 'wrong.' In the end, he felt the pull again, and so he relinquished all control.

His bad hand was guided as he began to paint for the second time.

Thirty-Three

"Do you really care about those rubes?"

It had been silent for so long, that Clay was startled by the sound of Kimberly's voice and then remembered that she and her mother were still in the RV. Astrid, who was smoking a joint and reading a book, Hell House by Richard Matheson, appeared also surprised by her daughter's sudden question. The girl's eyes were not stormy as before, they appeared more darker, more grim, and it made Clay's molding flesh crawl on it's bones.

"I'm sorry?" Clay asked taking his attention away from the rusty-colored canvas he had been working on. It was all coming together nicely, all things considered.

"I said," Kimberly said with the patience of a preschool teacher. "Do you really care about those rubes? Those who died?"

Clay's temper flared. "You mean my *friends*?" His one good eye began to see red, and now it was becoming hazy from the strain, as if his very skull were pushing the eye to the extent of trying to kick it out of its socket.

Seeming to understand the vagueness of her question, Kimberly rephrased, saying, "I mean the rubes you see now. Those who welcomed Flosvita with open arms, only to turn us away. When we had tried to spread out to the east, we were rejected. No one appreciated our views. In the end, someone else got to New York for us. A pity, really, especially given how many innocents were in that tragic attack. But they are no great loss."

"No great loss?" Clay said unbelievably. "How can you say something like that?"

"They do not carry the greatness that we carry. Neither did those in Jeffery's hometown when he and his brothers left to form their own community and more. A *family*. Yes, it was a shame they died. It was a shame when California decided to rebel against us as well. Because of this, because of Jeffery and his brother's trial, we made the rubes of this country pay with the measles. Thousands died, but they were of no great loss. They do not carry the greatness that we see, nor did they have the insight of what the world could be. Those who *did* survive, their eyes had opened. They could see their true potential, and the potential of this Family. Darwinism at it's finest."

Clay scowled, a pit forming in his stomach, just enough space for a possible host like a rat from a dream.

Kimberly continued, "When Jeffery died in prison, we did what was necessary in California, and thus the coughing disease was struck upon them. Nothing we do in this family is for nothing or out of cruelty. The only time that was done wrong, was by you for my father's rage. You didn't deny us like many others did. And look at you now. Your third eye is opening. Are you able to see the pointlessness of those who cannot see?"

Clay's brow furrowed, the lack of eyebrows making him appear ugly and borderline ghostly. "That is something I would expect a Nazi to say."

"Another unfortunate event," Kimberly admitted apathetically. "Maybe they saw something similar to what we see. Who knows? Not like we can ask them. We will never know for certain, and those who have returned from Europe and joined our cause do not have the answers either. But that is them. This is us. This Family, it is all we *truly* need. Just like you do, whether you believe it now or not. Oh, don't you worry. You will understand, sooner or later."

Astrid, who was staring at her daughter this whole time, appeared perplexed and a little disturbed. She was watching Kimberly as if she were not her own daughter, but a complete stranger.

"Who are you?" she asked.

Kimberly looked at her mother and smiled. "What do you mean?" Kimberly asked.

"Your voice… who are you?"

"You dare question?" Kimberly asked, this time Clay heard the significant difference in the girl's voice. It was cold, alien even. Though he only knew her for almost a day, Clay had a feeling that it wasn't *entirely* her. "I am simply putting Clay's mind at ease. Can't you feel it? He is in turmoil, and he doesn't understand why."

"I think you know damn well why I might be 'in turmoil,'" Clay glowered. "I've been through hell, my friends are dead, and I'm being *forced* to paint."

Kimberly looked at him. "Forced? No one has 'forced' you. How can it be forced when it is what you really want to do?"

That wasn't entirely true, although Clay had no argument. Despite him knowing it was wrong, despite the knowledge he had been exposed to, he wanted to paint. He felt the *need* to paint. It was like an itch when this curse and whole nightmare first began. He did not feel comfortable or happy until he scratched it. Clay felt himself disappear as he painted, and during the time he was painting the rusty backdrop for the painting, he did not once think about Flosvita and his history, the Burrows women behind him, or the death of his friends. He had Kimberly to thank for bringing him back to reality, but even so, he longed to escape again. To set his mind free like a bird in a fleshy cage that was slowly rotting away, and more importantly, get away from the girl's strange behavior and twisted philosophy.

(*Fuck philosophy; they are only* allowing *you to paint an* abomination, *and you wanna pass it as* art?)

Maybe, maybe not. Clay was beyond caring at this point.

His thoughts from before should have been enough to convince him not to do this. So *why* was he still doing it? Why did he feel like his mind and heart was the center ribbon on a rope for a tug-o-war?

More importantly, especially since he was essentially trapped in here, why did he feel like Kimberly *wasn't* Kimberly? He might as well be back at the livestock tent conversing with the billygoat and the cougar. Hell, just the cougar would be fine. After all, it and Kimberly practically shared the same predatory eyes, didn't they?

Clay supposed they did.

A thought broke through to him then. Was it Flosvita? Was he speaking through her? Or someone else? Maybe, *something* else?

Astrid closed her book, her placed marked by a playing card from a botched deck; the queen of clubs Clay knew without seeing, although he didn't think much of it. She stood, stretched, and said she was going outside. That the smell was getting worse.

"Smells like something *died* in here," she said with a sick grin of spite on her face. "Want me to bring Johnny in here to take over, hon?" Astrid asked her daughter, seeming to forget about the possibility that she had heard someone else talk other than Kimberly.

"I'm fine," Kimberly said. This time her voice sounded genuine; her original tone and it set Clay's mind at ease to hear it as he began to clean another brush to use.

Maybe it was my imagination...

Yeah, that had to be it.

"I shall stay. I'm enjoying watching the process."

"Suit yourself," Astrid said giving her daughter a look that clearly said, 'If you need something, scream.' Kimberly flashed a smile with a look that responded with, 'Don't worry, I will. Count on it.' For all Clay knew, their 'third eye' made them telepathic as well as magicians. Then Astrid was gone, leaving Kimberly alone with Clay the painting, and whoever

(*whatever*)

else was inside the RV.

"You can feel it too."

That cold voice said again after a momentary silence, as if to make sure Astrid was not coming back in anytime soon.

Clay froze in mid-stroke. He forced himself to pull the brush away before he left a splotch on the canvas that he may not be able to fix. It wouldn't be a 'happy accident' as Bob Ross would say. That voice... undeniably Kimberly's, and yet...

"Can you?" she asked again.

"I feel creeped out," Clay said not looking back at Kimberly. He was afraid that if he turned around it wouldn't just be her voice that would be different, but her appearance as well. He feared he would see Jeffery Flosvita sitting behind him, or whoever the Sun was who spoke to the man first in this whole thing decades in advance. "If that tells you anything. I'm sick to my stomach and freaked out."

"You are *scared*." It was not a question.

"Of course, I am," Clay said resisting the urge to turn. He felt like invisible hands had cupped each side of his face, and was just gently trying to turn his head to look back. It would only be a matter of time before they got impatient and turned more aggressively, with the possibility of breaking his neck. How's that for ironic and a strong taste of bad luck?

"Fear only blinds you," the voice said. "It keeps you from seeing your true potential, just like me."

Clay, now about to apply some yellow tint to the backdrop, dared to ask in a voice that sounded hoarse and dry. Arid like the skin of a rattler. "J... Jeffery?"

A sly, knowing smile creeped across her face like a shadow during sunset. A grim expression. "Maybe, maybe not."

"Kimberly, that isn't funny."

"I'm being serious," the voice said. "Don't talk like you are one of them, Couch. You're not. Even if you want to be, you have just had a *taste* of what a human being is truly capable of. Look! You are opening a portal for the head of the Family, and you will be on his right hand as you make history for Flosvita forever."

That's what I'm afraid of, Clay thought but couldn't express into words. The RV felt so cold, so dense in the air that he felt compressed like beans in a can. Except the can was the RV, and the beans were going bad and apparently smelling worse than ever. Sulfur, like rotten eggs.

Another thought came to mind though. *There is another way to open the portal.*

The backdrop, the dark skies whose clouds looked like smoke. The tall and crumbling buildings engulfed in flames with thin dark blotches within to eventually reveal the tortured souls owned by Flosvita. He could clearly see the little Hernández girl, the picture he saw in the article now blackened with skin flying off like burning paper. He saw José who could easily reach out and touch him he was so close. He saw Rachel, unaware of what had truly happened and questioning why she was there and not in her own bed, her eyes begging Clay to save her.

There were others too. Oh yes, there were many others. The fire was like Legion, for there were many. How many fell at the hands of Flosvita, be it through violence, or some other form of curses? How many souls did they breathe in on 9/11? How many brothers and sisters who saw through their crooked ways were crucified for being traitors? He could see that too. Burning trees with bodies hung in them like-

(Niggers in the west)

Oh god, what am I seeing? Clay had to grip his chair for balance, feeling as if the RV was really a ship rocking back and forth, to and fro.

We are all *niggers here, Clayton Couch. We are the unknown, we are the minority, and the uncared for. We* are *however, those who will tip the scales, and show the world true power. This is the purpose of Flosvita; this is the purpose of me, and my family.*

Clay stopped dead in his tracks, having started on the outline figure of Jeffery Flosvita coming out of the fire with outstretched hands like a prophet of fire that reminded Clay of that one Avenged Sevenfold's song which he had not listened to since he had left high school.

Don't you see I am your pride
Agent of wealth
Bearer of needs
And you know it's right
I am your war
Arming the strong
Aiding the weak
Know me by name
Shepherd of fire

Clay felt that Shepard's hand on his left shoulder. It was cold and hot at the same time. Burning and freezing, no middle-ground. The hand sent a tremor of ice through Clay's being, and at the same time scorched his skin. He knew it was Kimberly's hand, it had to be. No one else *physical* was here. But the hand didn't belong to her. It belonged to that of Jeffery Flosvita, and Clay could hear the undead man breathing down the back of his neck. The breath was hot and moist, and reeked of decay. Years of being in the dirt with worms chewing on those rancid black gums now filled Clay's nostrils, and would have made him gag if he breathed in any deeper. But he couldn't. He was frozen. The place on his neck where Flosvita was breathing on seeming to crawl, as if the maggots that were in his spinal fluid were having a reaction to the presence.

"White boy," Flosvita said in Clay's ear, the molted remains of cartilage seeming to age rapidly and Clay felt slime accumulating on the side of his face as he felt the flesh on the right side of his face about to join the left in it's similar state. What made it worse was that was what Jeremy Abbas used to call him, whenever he and Rachel would visit the family after the incident with the checkbook. It was one of many ways Mr. Abbas tried to put his future son-in-law down.

"When this is over, I can promise you that you will not look back on those tragedies as losses. I can promise you won't look at what you've been through as a tragedy. You won't even look back at your whore and Mexican buddy with dread. For it will all be a distant memory that we can repaint just as you can repaint what you are making right now. Finish what you have started, and I can promise you not only a new life, but peace, and *power*."

Through the ages of time
I've been known for my hate
But I'm a dealer of simple choices
For me it's never too late

"That's all you always wanted, isn't it?" Kimberly/Jeffery inquired of the otherwise comatose Clayton Couch. "Power. Control. That was all you really wanted, isn't it? You feel like you never had control? Well, you have control now. You are controlling your own destiny right now. Forget everything you have been taught. Surrender it all to really *see* what you have been missing your whole life."

Open your third eye, and see the world born anew.

Open your third eye, and succumb to the Family. Become a member of the Family. Join, and enforce the way of the Family.

(Thus sayeth, the Lord), he who blinds those who look into his face; the face of god.

The hand lifted from Clay's shoulder, but the heat remained. His elbows felt almost rubbery and he had begun to break out in yellow sweat that dripped into his eyes, seeming to soak into them rather than slide off the sclera. His hands were trembling, the one holding the brush causing some droplets of black paint to drip off and fall to the floor where it splashed like oil being dripped in some refinery. Or like a drop of blood from the latest victim who has been trapped by the monster.

There are no monsters here, Clay thought thinking about a bumper sticker he once read that said, 'there are no town drunks here, we all take turns.' *There are no monsters here, we all just take turns.*

(And they all look like people with good intentions)

"You okay?" Kimberly asked from behind.

Clay didn't even resist the urge to turn around and he was glad he did. Her voice had sounded the same as before, her expression no longer grim but smug, with only a little *hint* of concern. Maybe *there* was some kindness in this undead girl after all.

That's all she is, a girl now. Nothing more, at least not now.

"You look pale, actually."

"Do I?" Clay looked at himself feeling absurd. Ever since this whole thing began, he had gotten used to being described as 'yellow around the gills' so to speak.

"Do you need some water? You can use the sink."

"Uh, yeah, I think I should."

"Do you want something stronger too?"

Clay thought about it. The thought had come in so sharp and so fast that it felt like an arrow had been shot through his brain and implanted the thought by force.

"Yes, actually. I'd like that very much."

Kimberly stood as he placed the brush down and went to the sink. He opened the cabinet above him and rummaged for a cup. He had found a green Coca Cola cup they used to give out at McDonalds. *Jesus, I'm old.*

"I'll be back," he heard Kimberly say before she transferred to the back room.

When Clay saw that she was obscured behind the canvas between them, he looked down at the drawers between the sink and the cabinets below, and began to open them one by one as quickly and as silently as he could. Those that got caught on something he didn't bother trying to muscle it or pry it open. He would simply close it and try another. He didn't dare try the ones on the other side of the canvas near the microwave and stove in case Kimberly noticed. Hearing her return, he closed the last drawer softly, and went to drinking his glass of water.

It had been a waste of time and effort. What was he expecting to find? He knew he had to find *something*, but what? And what prompted him to do such a thing in the first place?

"Here," Kimberly said taking his cup when he was finished and filling it with her brother's apple pie moonshine. "You can use another glass if you get thirsty for water."

"Thank you," Clay said. He sniffed the cup, smelling the sweet and bitter aroma of apples and cinnamon, and then took a ginger sip. It burned his lips and throat as it passed down, but the warmth that spread from his stomach up to his head was amazing. He thanked Kimberly again, genuinely, who smiled and asked if he needed something else.

"My phone?" Clay found himself asking and then chuckled at the absurdity of that too. Of course she would say no. They confiscated his phone, his pocket knife, almost everything in his pockets when they locked him up with the livestock.

Not *quite* everything, he found himself thinking. He felt his loose change in his pocket, as well as a receipt, some Chapstick, and something else, something he felt gave him a little more weight in the right watchpocket of his jeans. He casually placed his hand on his hip as Kimberly laughed with him, apologizing and saying that she couldn't give him his phone back.

His hand touched the item he remembered as if to make sure it was still there, and electricity sparked up the length of his arm and into the back of his brain, burning the fumes of the alcohol that had already started to accumulate after that first sip. He asked Kimberly if it was possible that he could eat, and she said she could heat something up in here if he needed it. He expressed his gratitude for such hospitality, and said he would let her know if he needed something. He then went back to the canvas, appearing as if he was picking up where he left off on a mental state that most artists had to endure when returning to a project.

When in reality, he found himself thinking long and hard about the Zippo lighter in his pocket.

He didn't understand why he was thinking about the lighter in his pocket. He didn't have his cigarettes although at the thought of them he wished he had one and thought of asking Kimberly if he could. He doubt they would care if he smoked, but he passed the idea away. He never smoked while he painted. He never wanted the smell to end up on the canvas' he worked on.

Why would it matter this time? Flosvita is standing among burning ruins; the smoke might even be a nice touch.

True, but he decided against asking nonetheless. He wanted to keep as clear from fire

(cast it into the fire)

at the moment as possible. The idea had come in swift as an arrow, but the idea was muffled. Why did he first try to look for one in the first place, and why wasn't Kimberly or whoever was here picking up on such a thought? Because it was meaningless? Another painful reminder of how much control he actually *didn't* have here in the camp?

No, he said thinking. *It's for the painting. The painting...*

Was it to help reference the nature of flame? To get a clearer picture what he was seeing past Jeffery Flosvita as whatever it was behind him burned? Clay thought of taking it out to light it but thought better of it. All at once it felt like a bad idea. But was that his thoughts or someone else? He didn't know anymore.

Then another thought occurred to him. Another idea planted like a seed in order to grow an apple tree. Except the idea was to spur another thought, and that thought brought to Clay something he didn't realize before. Everyone here referenced the Sun. But what about the Moon? What was her name?

Yareakh... bride of Hama. Pronounced like the word 'eureka' with a *khi* sound at the end. Hebrew words, turned into names for two unknown entities that only one of which made themselves known as far as Clay was concerned. But also, he knew that Flosvita seemed to only follow Hama. They respectfully included the Moon, but it was the *Sun* whom they feared. As everyone should to some degree. You could look into the 'face' of the moon like the face of a mother who should love and nurture her child just as the Sun who should be strict should teach and raise the same child. The Sun, who you couldn't face, because of its blinding light as proven since the beginning of time, nearly. Unlike the Moon, who encourages you to look at her, and admire her beauty.

Why was he thinking this now? What did Yareakh have to do with all of this? Why was the thought of her/it and his lighter coinciding? Hell, how did he *know* such a thing?

An idea came to pass.

Could it be... you're here too?

(got a light for a smoke, Clay?)

Clay stared at the painting with now a perplexed look of dread. Now the picture in his mind didn't reveal Jeffery Flosvita rising from the flames like a prophet of the souls he had taken. He looked like a man trying to escape the depths of Hell. The dark figure inside the fire seemed to grin at this despite having no recognizable features to the human eye. Clay could almost see that toothy grin of Jeffery who stared back at him as if the canvas was not a canvas at all, but a window to the other world.

White boy, the grin seemed to say. *You know nothing of Hell. Do not stop now. I'm almost* back! *Open it up. Open it up, and you will be rewarded beyond anything your current mind can comprehend.*

Open the portal?

Open the third eye?

Clay had an idea then. He could see something else in the painting. Something that he hadn't before. Something about that seemed to stand out to him as something he didn't remember painting in the first place. Within one of the flames on top of what he realized was a building, was a brighter light at the base of the flame that made it look like a dark birthday candle. Within the luminous zone of the flame, it was not dark red or yellow, but a more pale white. He did not remember using the white paint at all yet for this painting. He had been using more dark more deeper colors in order to grasp the concept of burning and darkness. It was something he knew Jeffery wanted to be depicted, but as well as the

(moonshine)

Moon.

The question was, why?

Clay sighed, thinking how much he wished he had a cigarette. He took up his glass of moonshine, his own version of Moon, and tipped the glass back to drink. He swallowed, once, twice, and then something slid down his throat and he got caught.

He began to gag and choke, dropping the glass and trying hard to force himself to cough as he felt the airways in his throat and chest become clogged up. Kimberly stood at once, immediately registering something was wrong. She called his name out, and he responded to what he compared a goose choking on a piece of bread he used to give out as a kid sounded like.

Then she responded like a parent whose own kid is choking, and went behind him and hugged him from behind, making sure her clenched hands are in a ball in front of his stomach. She then started to perform the Heimlich maneuver, making Clay feel like his eyeballs would pop out of their sockets before whatever it was blocking his windpipe did.

It did though, and it shot out like a cannonball from a pirate ship. Clay didn't see it sail through the air only to land onto the floor a good five feet away, he was too busy trying to take deep breaths with his hands on the back of his head. Kimberly watched him concerningly, asking if there was something she could do.

"I hin I'm o'ay," came out of Clay's mouth and he was stunned at the infancy sound. He then tried to say 'think' again, realizing he couldn't feel his tongue brushing the tips of his upper teeth. With a gun-wrenching feeling now severe in his belly, Clay slowly turned to look at the object in question on the floor.

It was his tongue. Small, slightly gray in the red, black at the base where it had come loose and fallen away and nearly choked him. How bad had it been since this whole thing started? The natural bacteria on the human tongue now counterbalanced by bacteria meant to eat away and help decompose. It had been working on his tongue probably longer than his gums and his teeth of which only a few remained at this point.

Now with his tongue gone, he felt like a medieval slave or spy who had his tongue removed from talking too much. He stared at the tongue now oozing black goo out of the stump, and little white worms wriggling in the tender piece of meat. He thought of a piece of rotten lengua he once saw at a taco truck; discarded in the nearby trashcan and accumulating flies. He felt the drink come back up in his throat. He swallowed hard at the bile building up, and went to get another glass of water.

It was hard to swallow the water with what little tongue was left in his mouth. According to Kimberly who offered to look inside, there was hardly anything left. The lack of tongue made it hurt to swallow, and even as Clay managed to take some down, it did not leave him feeling quenched or otherwise relieved. He was losing his nails, had lost his hair, his ears and nose, one of his eyes, and now his tongue. He was becoming nothing more than a walking pile of flesh that could occasionally make Neanderthal noises incomprehensible by the English-speaking tongue.

You're running out of time, white boy, the spirit of Flosvita and whatever else was in the RV with them. *Better hurry.*

Yes, said the other alien UFO thought that immediately followed after. *Hurry.*

Like a puppet on strings, Clay felt himself turn away from the sink, ignore Kimberly asking if he was okay, and picked up the brush again. He was back in the zone, following the hand that guided him. This was not the time to quit yet. He was running out of time, most definitely. He may not have much longer after anyway, but he had to try.

Kimberly, watching him with intense concern, allowed him to work while she discarded the maggot-riddled tongue.

As he got to work on the actual being of Flosvita, Clay thought more and more about how much he wanted to smoke, which little by little made him think how much he wanted to just see fire; the symbol of power in ancient times as gifted by the Titan, Prometheus. Where man rose to almost godhood.

Fire...
(want to smoke?)
Rachel...
José...
Is that you, actually?
(is it really?)
Like a prayer unanswered, there was no response.

Thirty-Four

He began to work on the facial features of Flosvita, which considering his age the old man didn't look too bad nor was it too difficult. It all came together as smooth as silk, however untrue the very flesh of Jeffery Flosvita was.

Only a few wrinkles on his large forehead, those huge teeth that looked like stones still filled his mouth, those deep but sharp eyes as if he was not almost a hundred, but only twenty. He was missing a part of his left ear, Clay knew this because Flosvita remembered the imperfection of his structure and Clay felt the insecurity behind it. A dog had bitten it off, submitting not only a deformity on the man's otherwise handsome face, but also a terror of canines.

Clay found himself less imagining and more just following the path laid out before him. Still feeling like a child drawing in a coloring book, where the lines showed you where to stop using blue when the sky stopped and to begin using green where the grass began. That invisible hand keeping a firm grip on his own and guiding each and every stroke of the brushes at Clay's disposal; which he considered to be a good thing since he was absolute shit at painting with his less-dominant hand. This of course made him question whether or not he was the one actually painting but in the end he was satisfied enough with the fact that while he was the artist, he was not in charge of this rodeo. Jesus take the wheel or in this case, a brush.

As he allowed himself to continue to be led, something seemed to change in the RV as well as himself. The presence in the RV was no longer feeling as suffocating as it had before. The RV did not feel as compact, nor did it feel as stuffy. It felt like he had more room to breathe, as if an invisible elephant finally got off of his chest and allowed his poor lungs to take a deeper breath. It still didn't feel like he and Kimberly were alone in the RV, but it was still manageable.

With this, he was able to endure the feeling of being a child taught to draw in a coloring book. The lack of control he was having in order to gain control, according to the spirit inside the RV made all the more sense. But there was something else too. The Moon, Clay was once weary of the possibility, thinking her as an unnatural enemy along with Hama.

But now he wasn't sure. The presence felt familiar, comforting. It felt like his friends. It felt like Rachel, the way she used to make him feel as they were dating. It felt like José who was always there when he was down throughout their adolescent years and beyond unlike most friendships this day and age. He felt comfort, and assurance that what he was thinking was not at all crazy, but perfectly sane. That he was not a puppet in this camp like everyone else was who was roped into Flosvita's lies of prosperity and power. Because power can be given, and yet taken away at the same time. Or it can consume, just as fire can consume if handled improperly.

He began to feel aware that Kimberly was no longer with him in the RV. The sound of her heavy breathing made him wonder and when he paused to look back, she was leaning against her seat sleeping soundly. She had been fighting the urge to sleep (his mind suggested boredom) for almost ten minutes but had lost the fight. She was fast asleep, and with her gone he felt the presence of Flosvita faded but not *entirely* vacant, the guards including Astrid outside seeming to forget he was in there. It was this part of the atmosphere that still felt compressing and overwhelming, a sense of impatience and frustration that could be felt but not capable of being overcome by. Clay felt the little ribbon in the center of the tug-o-war rope wavering, moving away from such sensations and drawing closer to the feeling of comfort and support, making him feel more confident in the plan that he had put thought into.

I can take her hostage, he thought. *Take the gun, threaten to kill her again, escape.*

But then what? Where would he go? Since he had shown what he could do, would Flosvita even let him escape? He would just eb dragged back here, probably losing another leg and becoming a complete paraplegic who can only paint just like Precious Penelope. This realization also pointed out his handicap, which would be a problem even if he were to try and escape.

Then don't. Have a smoke, Clay. It's all you really need and-

Get off, you goddamn cunt, suddenly came to Clay's mind. The thought came not angrily but irritatingly by the sound of it. It wasn't Flosvita's voice either. His voice- his presence seemed to have been *muffled* somehow, as if his head had been put underwater while someone else was trying to take the reins. Trying to take control.

Another thought came to mind. Another thought plunged into his mind like a hypodermic needle containing morphine or some other medicine. The moonshine was sitting next to Kimberly on the table. He thought of adding it to the water, making it sort of like a primer over the painting that was still a while away from being done. But his concern was what if Kimberly woke up? What if whatever was in here with him presently alerted her to what was going on in his head? What if Astrid or whoever was standing outside got anxious and decided to step in and see?

Would they be able to tell the difference if he did it fast enough? Was it worth the risk?

What am I trying to do? he asked himself. *What* should *I do? I don't what to*

(do you?)

do this, do I?

Yes, he had to, one way or another. Not only that, but he *wanted* to. Whether it was influence or not, he wanted to in order for his plan to work. He felt like it was the only way to complete the circle and make him feel whole again. He had never felt this good in forever. He had never been able to paint with such clarity in forever.

(what if you lose it again? What if your passion dies along with Flosvita?)

Clay hesitated at that. Whether it left him feeling handicapped or not, wasn't it still a good thing? If Flosvita was indeed true to his word, wouldn't that benefit Clay in the future? What if the old man was right? What if there was more to life than just simply being human? Because that was what it came down to. Being human, having no control, working and paying taxes until you finally drop, was a disease while this Family possibly had the cure. As twisted as their methods and reasons were, as horrific as their deity's ideals were, didn't that make them the lesser of the two evils? Control and power, or being a drone for the rest of his life (depending how long he would live anyway)?

If you believe that, wake Kimberly up then. Ask if she is okay, be a good guy.

No, it really wasn't. Because in the end, Flosvita as good intentions as he may have had in the beginning, became something else in the end. Doing good made him and his Family evil men and women who had a sense of playing god. The devil was the same way, and the devil would tell a thousand truths and quote thousands of scriptures to tell a single lie. Deep in his heart, not in his mind, Clay knew this, and that was what made it easier to pass through the fog of uncertainty that kept on coming back over and over again. He almost questioned too if this was really his thinking, his moral judgement, or if it was placed upon him like the thoughts before from whoever else was in here?

The river is almost to the sea, another thought came to mind. *You cannot dam it. Speak with him.*

A memory suddenly came. Not Flosvita's, not Kimberly's, not whatever is in here with him. This was Clay's memory, and at the thought of it, his brush faltered on the bridge of his painting's nose. Rachel, standing beside him, watching him paint with her head on his shoulder, occasionally kissing him on the cheek.

"It looks beautiful, babe," she said both past and present. The RV and his studio were one in the same now. He looked to his right towards the back room, and saw his window looking out over the road beyond the apartment complex. To his left, where the driving cockpit of the RV was, he could see his kitchen. Here, he could feel Rachel. Comforting him, and loving him as he worked. Supporting him and giving her own personal opinion whether it was valid or not, even if she did not have an eye for art.

Clay felt a tear spill from his last good eye, and became blinded. His vision was more hazy with the salty and slimy tears, and he knew he didn't have much time. Someone would notice. Someone would break free. He was scared, yes, but what more could they possibly do to him at this point? If he lost his sight, it was over anyway.

(do it)

Turning around, Clay reached over and took the moonshine jug. Then very carefully, he poured the water cup out into the sink, watching the colors swirl down the drain as he then filled the cup with the moonshine. When that was finished, he replaced the jug in it's rightful spot, thought about it, and then left it there instead of taking a sip. He then set the washing cup down and after washing the brush he was using before, he applied more paint onto it and then finished Flosvita's nose. Once this was done, he could prime the painting with the moonshine.

Upon doing this, Clay felt strong hands clench around his throat, causing him to not breathe for a moment. His gasp came out in a cold vapor, as his vision faltered even more so.

"What are you playing at, you goddamn whitey?"

It was Flosvita's voice now. No doubt.

"What are you doing to my portrait? Damn you!"

Clay whirled around, hooking his elbow to a point as he did so, and it collided into the throat of Kimberly who had been awakened after all and was being *used* to get ahold of him. Possessed like Regan before Pazuzu.

Her windpipe crushed, and therefore she was unable to scream as she stumbled back into her seat. Then Clay, feeling his own body being seized by cold hands, hopped over on his one and only foot and landed on top of her. She held her head still as she began to thrash but before she could scream or knock something over or hit something hard enough to make a bigger noise, Clay took the brush he had in his hand and *plunged* the wooden handle into the girl's left eye. There was a soft and gross popping sound that reminded Clay of a grape getting squashed and Kimberly thrashed some more.

"My turn to fuck with *you* now, bitch." he snarled past clenched teeth, however without his tongue it came out guttural, sounding almost like the worst depiction of German without any 't's or anything requiring the tongue. "My 'ur oo fah wich *you* ow, bich,"

It was easy to commit to the act. This was entirely Clay working on his own, letting his anger and frustration finally out so that he didn't need any outside help unlike Kimberly

(Flosvita)

who thrashed as her one good eye bulged in pain and anger.

To make sure she didn't scream still, Clay clapped a hand over her mouth and drove the brush deeper into the depths of the undead girl's brain. She thrashed, kicked, bucked, slowed, and then stopped moving altogether. Her one good eye staring accusingly at Clay above as her skull filled with blood and the angle brush sticking out of her skull like a black flower dripping paint off it's bristles. Clay stood there panting, feeling tired and otherwise victorious at the same time.

The realization of what he had done had come slow and painfully. Having felt like he was in a dream, nothing what he had done felt real. He hadn't wanted to kill Kimberly, not at first, but whoever was with him now had. The feeling of guilt for what he had done remained for about two minutes as he sat there staring at the body. By then, something else swept over him. That victorious feeling again, telling him that he had done right after all. He had committed a heinous act bringing the woman back from the grave, and with his own hand he had placed her right back into it. He had restored the natural order of how life was meant to be.

However, he couldn't help but shake the feeling that he wasn't done yet. If everyone in Flosvita had a bond like Astrid said they did, wouldn't they be able to sense the spirit of their own having freshly escaped the cocoon of their body?

A sound, a feeling, swept through the RV like the moan of a ghost. Was this Kimberly? Or whoever it was taking over her and making her do what she had to in order to stop him. To give him a chance to reconsider what was on his mind, he realized. Or was it a sigh of relief by whoever was in here helping him? Whether it was Rachel, or the Moon. It was not José, he knew that much for absolute certain. But whoever it was who helped him, he felt truly grateful for it.

Whatever or whoever it was, it wasn't going to let Kimberly or Flosvita leave. He didn't know how he knew this, but Clay had a feeling what whatever was happening in this RV was going to *stay* in this RV, third eye or no third eye.

"Hanchk you," he said to the *physically* empty RV. He then turned back to the painting, and ignoring the dead body

(you killed her again)

went to work to complete it.

He *had* to finish it. It wasn't just what he wanted. It was what both of *them* wanted. By then however, Clay was growing completely blind, and he would be shrouded in darkness in no time at all.

Focusing his remaining attention and sight on the painting, he worked fast and vigorously. He painted Flosvita in a pair of jeans and work boots, wearing over his torso a red sweater with the straps of his pants going over his shoulders. He was wearing a straw hat, which Clay added at the last minute. By the time he finished the final details in the black man's dark eyes, Clay's final eye gave up the ghost and he was completely blind. He couldn't see the painting, but the last memory of it was still there, his willingness unaltered.

Now for the final straw. The final thing that would change the course of this whole thing. Flosvita was still here, he was trying hard to fight his way out like a rabid dog caught on a leash. Occasionally, within the darkness that blurred his vision, he could hear Flosvita's voice bellowing in his brain like a terrible migraine.

Lemme go, you traitorous bitch! Lemme go!

But now Clay was left with something else. He had to finish the job. Feeling around, he got to work finding the one brush he hadn't used yet since the beginning of the painting. The large fan brush. As a general rule, he always stuck his brushes handle-first so he could see what he was getting and not waste time searching for one. Now with time and sight against him, he felt around the tops looking for the fan brush. With most of the brushes either wet or still stained with paint, it was hard to tell for certainty, and he could have sworn he kept grabbing the same one despite moving down the line.

Then it dawned on him that someone or something was *shifting* the brushes around, making it impossible for him a blind man to catch on.

You could see, y'know, the UFO thought came to mind. *If you really want to. C'mon, white boy, open that eye. You'll see, both the brush and more!*

As fun as that sounds, Clay thought groping more vigorously. "I'll pach."

Don't talk down at me, boy. *I'll have you- Goddammit, you whore! Lemme go! Lemme go, goddammit!*

Clay ignored the screaming in his head as he continued to search for the brush that seemed to evade him at every turn. Despite the restless spirits holding each other off here, there was still power to ensure that Clay didn't find what he was looking for. He then felt his hand grow warm as if a hand was touching it and guiding him past the box of paints and brushes. He felt automatic relief through the air and realized something had been released and was now alerting everyone outside the RV.

To me! To me, my Family! TO ME!!!

(What you are looking for)

Clay reached at last with perfect clarity.

(is here)

He didn't need any invisible hand to guide him anymore, and he went to reach for the one thing he knew for certain *wouldn't* move. He seized the wash bucket and immediately outrage burned in his nerves. He took up the bucket and splashed the painting with the moonshine. Cinnamon and booze punished his nose and some droplets had bounced off the canvas and sprinkled him. He could feel his left eye burning as alcohol splashed it.

Had it struck the canvas? What if he had instead hit the wall and missed completely? What if he didn't end up hitting the painting at all and instead he doused something else in the RV entirely?

A smile curved across his lips.

(have a smoke, Clayton)

The deed was done, he had his fuel. He dropped the bucket to the floor and then dug into his pants pocket looking for his lighter. He peered through the darkness, hoping to catch a glimpse of whoever it was who saved him but knew it would be pointless. When he removed the lighter and attempted to flick it. His left hand didn't obey his commands. It was still useless. Frantically switching hands, Clay flicked the lighter with his right. But he was still worried; he couldn't tell if it was burning or not. He decided to flick it again, and then he heard the front door being kicked open.

At that very moment, a phenomenon came upon him, something under the influence of the Moon who won the unseen battle with the Sun which was no longer up in the sky as she took the reigns, and Clayton Couch's sight momentarily returned from an eye he didn't have before.

Thirty-Five

It wasn't necessarily that he had regained his sight. Instead, Clay had gained a sort of understanding of the world around him, and he could see it without sight with absolute perfect clarity that left his chest feeling cold and breathless.

For a moment, maybe five seconds, maybe ten, Clay just stood there. He could see everything, as clear as day. He saw Johnny Burrows standing in the doorway, his mother by his side. The Colt was out but he wasn't bringing it up. The two of them were staring back at Clay, who held the burning lighter in his hand right in front of the painting of Jeffery Flosvita, indeed dripping with cracked moonshine.

At the same time, Clay saw four more things. He saw Jeffery Flosvita himself, standing beside his former colleagues. Sure enough he was wearing the overall jeans and red sweater and straw hat that reminded Clay of a pre-civil war slave from a documentary. He was staring at Clay outraged, and behind him were two beings. One was a dark shape with a golden head with indistinguishable features. It was fading even when Clay realized it was there. The other who remained was black as well, with a silver head holding that glowed brighter. It was looking at him, but Clay could not tell their expression for even with his third eye, they were incomprehensible; like the true face of a superior being.

To his left, standing beside him, Clay didn't have to look to know who it was. He had felt her presence since he had begun this painting. She had been here the whole time, helping him to gain the upper hand and maintain his own sanity without the influence of the world beyond that he was now exposed to.

I'm sorry... she said.

Yeah, me too.

He watched as Astrid moved forward towards him, telling her son to stay put. Her beady black eyes darted between

Clay, her dead daughter, and the painting with her friend on it. With his Third Eye, Clay could see a sort of wavering tendrils reaching out from her head like tentacles or shifting seaweed. She was reaching for more of the cult to come to the RV, and Clay didn't need to hear the barking of approaching dogs to understand that he was running out of time.

Oh, but the look on Astrid the Chink's face, was blissful and heartwarming.

Gee, Astrid, you look a little worse for wear, he thought gleefully.

"Clayton," Astrid said holding her hands out like a cop trying to convince an overwhelmed man not to shoot himself. "What have you done?" She was looking at Kimberly as she said it, her nose wrinkling either by the scent of blood, or of pure outrage of the fact that her daughter was taken from her once again.

Clay couldn't help but smirk. *She got something in her eye by the looks of it.* Astrid winced as if she had been slapped. Had she somehow heard him think that?

Nah, she probably sensed it somehow, in some way Clay could both understand and not.

He extended his arm towards the canvas, the flame from the Zippo lighter flickering in the movement.

Astrid went pale when she saw Clay again. Fear emanated from her being like pheromones off an animal. "*No. Wait-*"

"Isn't it beautiful?" Clay asked everyone, his speech a blurb of nonsense but at the same time understood as if he had never lost his tongue in the first place. "I think I would call it 'Shepard of Fire.' Kinda like the song, isn't it? You know Avenged Sevenfold, John? Nah, you're probably a Tom Petty fan."

John Burrows said nothing, only stared in silence. A look that would have made Paul Sheldon proud.

"Clay," Astrid said not caring about whatever bands Clay could list off at the moment. Behind her, Johnny had pulled back on the hammer of his Colt, now taking aim but with a glimmer of fear in his eyes. Uncertainty *pulsated* off of him like a heartbeat's drum. He didn't know what to do. Good.

Jeffery Flosvita, merely stood there, an expression that was sad and depressing to Clay despite all that has happened in this RV. The man, the ghost, the spirit, looked defeated. Could Astrid and her son see him?

Did Clay even care?

He didn't.

"Go ahead, Astrid," he offered. "Say it. I'm all ears. Whatever I have left now."

"Think about this," she begged. She was scared. She didn't know why, Clay could see it in her eyes and sense it in her soul, but she was scared of *something*. He was able to feel that much now, and she was willing to listen to Flosvita's cries if it meant doing good for her family.

"I have," Clay said looking over at Kimberly, and finally Astrid looked over to the seats where she saw her daughter dead once again and sprawled out across the floor. "Thought about it for a while, actually. She helped me to decide."

Astrid's mouth hung open, tried to close, probably trying to scream but couldn't. She stared back at Clay, a look of dreadful horror and hatred in her eyes that could only come from someone who knew they were screwed. That they had lost.

"You're right, Flosvita," Clay said not breaking eye-contact. "I can see everything now. I can see why you wanted to share this. But someone here, has had enough of this. And I'm going to help her."

"Clay," Johnny said raising the gun and pointing it at him. "Drop the lighter."

Bizarrely, a quote from The Dark Knight came to mind and Clay almost laughed it was too perfect given the position he was in, and how the canvas had been set up. Just barely at a 70-degree angle so that it could be propped up against the counter. The perfect position to hold onto something, and provide the roughest slope which would catch and hold for at least a few seconds before dropping said-something to the floor.

"Very poor choice of words," he quoted.

And then, without any remorse or fear, Clay dropped the Zippo onto the canvas, and the flame merged with the fires of Shepard of Fire. The lighter dragged slowly down the makeshift slide, only to drop onto the floor as the entire painting went up in sweet-smelling flames.

The canvas went up in a plume of yellow flames that burned everywhere except the black figure that was supposed to be Flosvita. In that moment, Clay saw the spirit of the same man, seemed to *jump* into the painting like it was a long-lost friend. Clay would realize some time later that the spirit had been *sucked* in like sun in a black hole.

At the same time, the burning portrait seemed to open wider, creating a sort of mouth or vortex that deep within, Clay could see a tunnel going down to a lake of fire, the smell of burning flesh and brimstone assaulting his nostrils worse than the moonshine had before. During which a blinding light flashed through the RV and outside a powerful gust of wind began to pick up. The roof of the RV began to cave in and before it could crush anyone, was sucked into the wormhole as well, creating a sort of opening for a tornado-like swirl of black smoke to erupt and reach for the skies. Everyone both inside the RV and out stared at the wonder in horror as the wind began to pick up and Clay watched as Astrid and Johnny Burrows were the first victims of the portal he had opened to a reality man was not meant to see.

Astrid screamed out as her hair billowed around her face like she was on a boat in the high seas. Her son, having been forced to his knees and forgetting about his gun, was holding on desperately to the metal hinges the front seats were secured to as his mother's face was pulled slowly and painfully off her skull. Flesh and blood *peeled* from her bones after her clothes were stripped by the wind, and then when all but a standing and screaming skeleton remained, the eyeballs having been sucked into the hole last, the skeleton burst into flames and the ashes swirled into the painting, her soul being sucked down to whatever dimension Jeffery Flosvita thought he had control over. Her son was next, his legs being stripped of all flesh and his pelvis splitting and pulling away from his spine. Entrails were being dragged out and getting sucked in as well, until nothing was left of his lower body and he didn't even have to hold on to anything for he was already hollowed out like the juice from an Otter Pop, and was easily pulled into the eternal punishment worthy of Dante's Inferno.

All that was left was Clay and Kimberly, and Clay watched unmoved by the flow of wind as if he was pure, untouched by Death's grip which also pulled onto Kimberly, and without any resistance whatsoever, she too was pulled into the painting, her body dragging behind a streak of blood all the way to the canvas; it too beginning to flake and swirl off the floor and into the painting. It was if the hole would not be satisfied with just the flesh but the blood of it's victims as well. There were to be no trace of anyone, and Kimberly was completely gone at last from Clay's view who stared in awe at the phenomenon he had placed into action.

All around the camp, other members of Flosvita were being sucked into the portal. Their flesh pulled violently from their bones, their organs sailing through the air leaving empty husks that would crumble to dust. None were spared, like the wrath of God upon the Egyptians. Men, women, children, even the animals in the livestock tent were all ripped apart and shredded before being pulled into the realm of the Sun and Moon, wherever the spirits came from. Cows, pigs, and chickens howled and bellowed in both pain and terror as feathers and fur joined flesh and blood, then bones and guts. The cougar even snarled in defiance even as it's body was pressed through the bars of it's cage, it's own organs being sucked out of it's body like slugs from their shells.

The wind grew ever more powerful, pulling more and more people through, even pulling a young boy who had been sleeping in his camper bed only to be ripped apart by splintering metal as his body was forced through the very window of the camper. A dog that was on it's leash was lifted into the air and pulled taunt to the point where it's own collar decapitated it. A cat that had been sleeping peacefully on top of a nearby camper clung to the fabric of a nearby clothesline before it's claws were pulled right out and it too was sucked into the void yowling as it was churned and ripped apart like hamburger in a grinder.

Back in the city, Gaston Burrows who had been sleeping in his cell with another inmate, was pulled violently from the bed and against the steel door where his body was *forced* though the thin air vents leading to the rec room. He screamed as his skin split, and his blood and guts squeezed through the cracks, leaving nothing more than a shrink-wrapped skeleton that once turned to ash, followed the liquified bits of him. His mangled body parts that were nothing more than a paste sailed through the glass window and into the night, sailing like a flock of autumn leaves in the direction of his old campsite. The man who shared the cell with him had witnessed the gruesome fate of the old man, and went utterly mad at the sight. He would be first accused of doing something to Burrows, but the police would find no trace of him, for not even bloodstains were left behind. *None* were spared, nothing was left behind, and Clay saw everything and what was left of them going into the painting he had created, and had been instructed to use in order to destroy the gypsy family.

The tornado began to subside, the wind seeming to decrease and be contained within the remaining walls of the Burrow's RV. Then the tornado disappeared, leaving only a smoldering canvas with the fires still burning but the hole gone, filled in by the flames that were now beginning to spread throughout the RV.

Clay felt a sort of shove on his back, an urge to go with the fight or flight response telling him to go, now. He bolted for the door, lost his single footing on his way out and crashed into the dusty ground. He crawled on all fours

(threes?)

for a good fifty feet before stopping and turning to look up at the RV that was now completely engulfed in flames. Black smoke belched straight towards the sky, the wind being completely gone, along with the feeling that there were otherworldly figures walking around. There wasn't a soul in the entire camp other than Clay, who up until this point had been able to see everything, shut his eyes.

When he opened them again, pitch-black darkness surrounded him. As easily as he had opened his third eye in order to see his final hand against the gypsy family, he had closed it. He could see nothing anymore. He could *feel* nothing anymore. He could hear nothing but the crackling flame that ate away at the family RV.

He was alone. The Flosvita Family was no more.

It was over.

He coughed, thrusting his hand up to cover his mouth. His jaw had become unhinged, and his palm was warm and wet. The pain in his chest was apparent, and he realized what that meant now that he was truly able to *feel* again.

God, I feel like shit...

Clay fell back on his back. He breathed in the cool night air that would be breaking for dawn soon. He could smell the chemical smoke from the RV, but it was being blown away by a slight breeze that felt nice on his otherwise rotted skin. A breeze that came as unexpectedly, but it was pleasant.

"Thanks... Rachel..." he spoke/slurred in his deformed speech to the night as the moon overhead watched over him, shining over the camp with brilliant rays of silver light. "Thanks... I'm sorry..."

Clay sighed, collectively. Despite having finished nothing with himself, he had purged a plague unlike anything the world could possibly comprehend, or at least refused to all these years.

The Flosvita Family.

Flosvita himself.

Everything; It was gone.

Clay knew this, and didn't have to look around or worry about any Family Members outside the camp to know this. With his final painting, he had done what should have been the impossible. The only regrets he had, were the loss of Rachel and José, and that he couldn't paint one last time. What would it be? He thought about it.

He could picture what his last painting should have been. Three figures on a hill somewhere. Maybe in Washington, near one of the cherry or apple orchards. José would be at the bottom of the hill, waving up at the top as he stood next to a motorcycle maybe, something cool to match his personality. Maybe he would be wearing basketball shorts and a jacket despite the unforgiving sun shining on a hill in a sky that looked like God's nosebleed, with the moon in the distance reflected by the light and position of the sun. On top of the hill, hand in hand, was a couple shrouded in the shadow cast behind them. He and Rachel, waving back at José, staying to watch the sunset as they had on their very first date. After a day of going out to eat, walking at the park, and then going to the bar for a drink, they came back to a hill, where they sat and talked and watched the sunset. It was here where Clay would tell Rachel he wanted to be a painter. To create something out of paint and paper or canvas until the day he died. Maybe work as a contractor and paint for companies and freelance.

The memory brought a smile to his face. Despite knowing his fate, despite knowing what would happen to his body now without Flosvita to take away what they had given to him, Clay was at peace. He laid there in the sandy remains of the Flosvita campground, and breathed in the night air in peace.

"Wait for me, guys," he said to only the moon, who he knew was still watching. "I'll be there soon."

Epilogue

Sgt. Dennis Clemet
June 26th, 2025
08:56
Case #0056G02

At approximately 04:36pm on June 26th, my partner, Sgt. Matthews and I were dispatched to investigate a disturbance in Hidden Springs. Yesterday after the sudden dust devil, one of the locals, a Mr. Glenn Kelly, reported a bunch of abandoned RV's and Campers with license plates from the following states: Washington, Oregon, Nevada, Colorado, Kansas, Ohio, California, and Idaho. We arrived at the location south of the Dry Creek at approximately 04:59pm.

Just as the Mr. Kelly had said, the campground had been completely deserted, with everyone's cars and campers abandoned in the dessert. One of the RV's (license plate under document #2) had been completely burned to the ground, the embers still hot upon our arrival. Fire Response was dispatched shortly after to contain the possibility of a brushfire. Upon further investigation, we saw that no one had packed any clothing or food, and we called in for forensics under Detective Cara Robbins to come and join in on the investigation when we found a single human body. The body appears to have been dead for a couple of weeks although the boys at the lab will be able to give us an approximate time of death. The body was in a late state of decay and was missing large portions from local wildlife. It is now being sent to the Boise County Mortuary to be analyzed. As for the owners of the vehicles, we just sent the plates to the DOL for transmitting.

We returned at the station at 08:26 and have been here up until this report is finalized. As of now I have nothing else to add that those at the lab and the detectives won't be able to follow. We filed in our findings, and this ends this report.

-Sgt. Dennis Clemet
Badge #BD699

DClemet

What the sergeant didn't include in his report, was that while inspecting the corpse found at Dry Creek, he could have sworn he had heard a *sigh*. It sounded like that which a man would exhale after holding his breath for so long, or in Dennis' experience, the death sigh when someone finally gave up the ghost. The sound of a light breeze through a lonely tree. He had only heard it three times in his life, but he would never forget such a sound nor would he mistaken it for something else. A half-moan, half-sigh.

He could have sworn it had come from the decayed corpse which was practically all bone and very little meat due to scavengers and the weather. The missing pieces of tissue and bone and the lack of one leg had even made Matthews sick, and he had to step aside to compose himself. Neither of them had seen a body having been dead for so long, and it was nothing like how they describe it in books or display them in movies with dirty skeletons and barely any meat on it. The smell had been rancid, and pus and blood had seeped into the ground as if the man was a sponge.

That sigh...

He eventually dismissed it though as the wind, and had written his report and dropped it into his out box. He would go home and take a long hot shower, and drink a case of ice-cold beer, and it did not have to necessarily be in that order. With that corpse on his mind, he would be hard-pressed to get some decent sleep.

The case concerning Flosvita and who the corpse had been, was no longer his concern, but to someone else. He had heard of Flosvita, and was glad they had moved on if that had been the case. To completely disappear though...

No. That was no longer his concern. It was someone else's problem now, and he had just passed the baton when he dropped in his report. Matthews would be in the same boat as he, and unbeknownst to the two policemen, Boise and the rest of Idaho itself would not be concerned with the Flosvita Family ever again. Neither would the rest of the world who like a living human body unaware of a parasite or an illness in their body, wouldn't even notice once that illness passes or that parasite dies.

The only thing he would get from the body that was sent to the mortuary, would be the name. Clayton Couch. He remembered the name. He remembered being on duty during the trial Couch VS. Flosvita a while back. He remembered feeling sick the entire day, and he could easily picture the poor man who faced against the horde of plaintiffs. To think that such a young man had been dead for weeks, and to end up looking like he had back at the creek...

Clemet felt sick just thinking about it. It was one thing to see a dead body because of a recent crash or even an overdose or alcohol poisoning. It was another thing entirely to see how harsh time can be on that body. But he stepped out of the department building, and breathed in the cool evening air, which both refreshed his mind and flushed out all troubles of the day. The day was over, and the sun was setting at last. As for Clayton Couch, whatever had caused his demise (although he had some suspicion given Flosvita's history), he only hoped that it had been quick and painless.

He prayed that he had not suffered.

The End